By Leah Banicki

Book 4 of Wildflowers Series
Published by Leah Banicki

https://www.facebook.com/Leah.Banicki.Novelist

Dedicated to all of those that have been broken by the hands of someone they trusted. May the God of everlasting love and healing comfort you.

Chapter 1

Oregon City - May 1851

The cabin at Grant's Grove was large and spacious, with an open kitchen with plenty of counter space, a brick bread oven, a large cook stove, a dining room and parlor with an open feel that made many cabins in the West seem tiny. Before Lucas and Corinne Grant had married it had been built by another family, with hopes of grandchildren and a life in Oregon full of blessings. Life had not played out that way and the builders gave the home to Corinne and her bridegroom, Lucas. Tragedy had struck for the first family but a blessing had come anyway. The home was full of love and the dream of carving a place in the West was alive within that large cabin.

There was a large wing on the western side of the cabin, with a bedroom and a private sitting room, bookshelves and a warm fireplace. These rooms were for Violet Griffen, the housekeeper of Grant's Grove, still in her early twenties and sweet natured. She had been with them for a year or more and had become part of the family easily, with her sweet temperament and good cooking. Corinne Grant had not wanted to have a housekeeper, but her job on Grant's Grove proved to her, over time, that her husband was right. One cannot do everything.

In front of the cabin was several water barrels that were filled every day by Lucas and Corinne's younger stepbrother Cooper, who was learning the fine lesson of hard work and diligence from his stepdad.

Beyond the door was a path that led south to the closest neighbor, Corinne's father's home John Harpole and his new wife Marie, and north to Corinne's business. The greenhouse was a medium sized glass structure with heavy wooden window panels on the top that could be cranked open to let in fresh air when the weather was fine. Inside was a plethora of plants and trees, flowers and herbs, all tended by Corinne to help her make ointments and teas, oils and tinctures. Corinne's love of botany was bone deep, inspired by generations of woman who cherished anything green and growing from the earth.

Further north up that path led to a laboratory, where Corinne's dream was further realized. Along one of the walls were brick fire ovens, with large copper alembic pots to distill the medicinal oils from plants and natural materials. She made lavender oil from the fields of lavender that her husband tended to the east, past Spring Creek to the edge of a wooded forest. It was a beautiful piece of land abutting the horse ranch on one side and more farmland on the other.

Beyond the farmland to the east were the rocky mountain bluffs, with high peaks and rugged rocks that sheltered them there in that fertile valley.

Grant's Grove was a blessed place, where the days were full of work and toil, there was plenty to eat and plenty to do. At night the cabin would be full of music, sweet worship sung by the joyful Violet, and the harmonious sounds of the violin when Lucas was inspired. Corinne or Lucas would read the bible or other books aloud, their friends would share their table, and with family nearby they were never without company for long.

In the summer and fall their land would bloom into a heavenly vision with rows of purple lavender gracing the air with fragrance. Grant's Grove was heaven on earth.

Violet Griffen

Violet was alone and cooking when her boss Lucas Grant had stopped in the cabin to deliver mail. She loved this kitchen, it was home to her. Her hands were competent; the heavy pots and pans her tools. The smell of fresh baked bread was soothing and sweet. She worked the spoons like a skilled chef and people from miles around learned her secrets. She had many gifts to share.

Her blond hair was pulled back with simple braids pinned around her head. She was humming a song that she had sung at church a few weeks before. She nodded to Lucas as he came in and dropped the mail into the bowl on the table and then made his way back outdoors. Her hands were wet from peeling the potatoes but she kept looking to the pile of mail. Just knowing that something from her husband could be there spurred her into peeling faster. She had only received a few letters from her husband in California but the hope bloomed every time the mail came. She waited until the job was done to investigate the pile. She thought of her husband, Eddie, with his mischievous smile and booming laugh as she peeled.

She finished in short order and rinsed her hands at the washbasin that she had filled with water first thing in the morning. The fresh towel was there and she swiped her hands across the soft cloth. Within a minute she scooped up the pile of letters and found one addressed to herself. She squealed the tiniest little squeak, knowing she sounded like a young girl, but she would never apologize for being joyful. It was just her way.

'Mizzes Grifen' was printed on the front of a folded paper envelope in a sloppy scrawl. Her husband Eddie had poor penmanship but it looked different from his writing style.

Violet felt a rush of emotion and a stomach roll thinking about her husband, so far away in California territory. Their marriage of six months had long been overlapped by his year and a half absence in search of gold.

She gingerly ripped it open, careful not to damage the paper in any way. The light blue ribbon she had given her husband as a love token had fallen from the opened paper, the one that he declared had matched her eyes so perfectly. She watched the ribbon fall, it soundlessly landed on the tabletop as her heart crashed against her ribcage. Those cornflower blue eyes read along the first line and all rational thought left her. She may have gasped or cried out but she wasn't certain of it.

Deer Mizzes Grifen,

I found yer huzbond's boddy today. He looks to hav had a bad fever and periched. I am sorry to hav to give you sush bad news. There was a papr with this adrez in his pockit. He had been robbd of everthan cept this ribbin wen I find him.

Miy condolinses

Gerard Bankser

'I found yer huzbond's boddy today.' She read the line again. Letting the truth of it sink into her. The visual of a fever ridden corpse played through her mind, her sweet Eddie's face sunk in, or swollen in some grotesque way. Violet tried to shake off the thoughts but couldn't turn off the parade of images. Her pale hands reached up and touched her lips, knowing Eddie would never kiss them again.

She didn't want to breathe. She wished the letter would go, she could burn it and pretend it never existed. All it would take is a moment to toss it into the stove and it would disappear from her life. The irrational thought played through her, and she wanted to consider it. But she knew it was no good.

She settled the letter on the table after she had read through it several times. She felt cold and numb. She was now a widow.

She tripped over a throw rug in the kitchen and caught herself close to the cook stove. Her left hand grabbed for something to settle herself and her fingers grabbed the side of the hot boiling pot with potatoes. It was the briefest of contact but the searing heat made her yell out. Her forefinger was smarting fiercely but her heart hurt so much worse. A searing pain ripped through her middle and she found it hard to breathe again. She made a slow fall to the floor and settled into a hard sob.

Her sweet Eddie was gone.

Corinne Grant - Grant's Grove

Corinne Grant walked through the rows of plants in her greenhouse, the plants healthy and green around her, her babies. She touched and spoke to them as she worked, she coaxed and coddled, it was her passion. The plants were the children she had now, the hope within her heart to have a daughter or son, or both to teach and share her passion with in the future.

She was a young wife with a thriving business in a time when women weren't usually allowed that freedom or respect by men. Her husband, Lucas Grant, had been such a sweet blessing. Kind, wise, and affectionate, Lucas was the perfect husband for her. In many ways she felt she didn't deserve him still. Luckily, he calmed her insecurities by declaring that he felt the same way.

Their young marriage had a good start, even with the trials and struggles that it would always bring. Lucas had stayed by her side as she had lost a child through miscarriage, and been a loyal companion and supporter when she was criticized for being a businesswoman instead of staying home and cooking and cleaning.

Corinne loved living so near her father, whose large cabin abutted her own property. His new wife, her step-mother Marie, was a sweet woman and Corinne enjoyed the companionship she saw between her father and her. It was a sweet balm after his despair years before when Corinne's mother had passed away. Throwing their lives into upheaval. He had come west first, wanting a fresh start. Corinne had come out a few years later. She was thankful every day that she had braved the unknown and come to Oregon. The West had been good to her. She would be twenty years old in the fall and she loved her life. Her days full of work that she loved, nurturing plants in her greenhouse, and also the science behind using plants for medicines in the laboratory. It had always been a passion for the women in her family, and she was taking it further than she could have ever imagined.

Her medicinal oils were being sold along the western frontier. She had had offers from the East as well for her products, she knew as her fields were planted more and more people would be blessed by her work. It made her proud and, if she were honest, a little fearful too. There was so much work to do and she would soon be missing her co-worker, Dolly. The three years since the young half-Hopi girl had joined her wagon train had flown by. Dolly had known little English but had been sent to learn from Corinne how to harness the plants and make the medicine. The tribe that had sent her had come back for her.

Dolly Bouchard had been raised by the Shoshoni, her mother had been taken in by them years before, and after both her mother and French trapper father had passed on the Shoshoni had raised Dolly. Corinne had felt the relationship between them blossom when she realized that Dolly had her own vast knowledge of herbs and plants. The quiet half-Hopi girl was a fast learner, her quick grasp of English helped bridge the gap and they were fast friends as well as eager learners and always hungry to know everything that nature had to offer. Corinne was extra-ordinarily upset that her friend was leaving.

Dolly only had one day left of work and Corinne was broken hearted about losing her. It was about more than just the business. Her friend had been growing in her Christian faith and was open about wanting to stay in Oregon instead of returning to the Wind River Mountains. Corinne honestly could not imagine her world without Dolly in it. She felt selfish about her feelings, but she did not want to lose her. Corinne had spent every night that week hashing out her feelings with her husband Lucas. Sometimes her housekeeper Violet would join in.

"I don't understand why she feels she can't refuse them. She is half-Hopi, she is not Shoshoni by blood." Corinne had exclaimed again every night. "Those Indians just showed up here and expect her to hop to and leave with them. She is not beholding to them."

Her husband, Lucas, in his wisdom always spoke calmly. "We have to respect her decision."

Corinne had her closest friends that all lived on nearby farms and ranches. They had had several get-togethers to talk this through but 'respecting her decision' had been the consensus. They would have to abide by the young girl's wishes. Corinne wasn't sure she could watch her ride away. The two Indian men that had come for her were waiting, but Corinne worried whether or not they could be trusted with her friend's well being. One of them looked kind but the other seemed harsh, and was determined to get away from Willamette Valley as soon as he could.

Corinne had done some work half-heartedly in the greenhouse and visited with Dolly at the lab. The alembic pots sat along the brick fire pits on the western wall. The fires wouldn't be burning in them for a month or two. Small batches of summer plants, or even a shipment of limes or lemons from California could get her to fire them up early in the summer season for distilled oil from the plants. But the main use for her lab was for lavender oil distillation, pine oil, and a small batch of jasmine each year. Dolly had just made a suggestion after reading some European research about the use of mint leaves in its affects on the stomach and digestive problems.

They had made plans to forage the forest in the surrounding areas for peppermint or spearmint plants. If they could be easily transplanted to the greenhouse they could try for a small batch within a year. Corinne had been looking forward to that. Her heart broke again at realizing she would be doing it alone.

Dolly had been stoic when Corinne had talked to her. She was gathering her papers and drawings of plants. Her dark brown braids hung down her back, she had begun wearing them like that again since the tribesman came for her. They had been surprised by her appearance; her hair and clothing choices were not how they expected her to be. The braids may be her way to appease their glares.

"I do not know what to do." Dolly declared and her forehead showed distress. Her dark eyes were focused away from Corinne, not wanting to look her in the eyes.

"You do not have to go." Corinne broke her promise to say nothing. She could have slapped her own mouth as the words tripped out but her will to have a say in this matter won over.

"I feel that I do." Dolly said simply. "I don't think I can stay there, but I need to explain to the Chief, about the work we are doing and the book we are writing." Dolly sat on a nearby stool and rubbed at the side of her head.

Corinne was worried that Dolly was in pain.

She wanted to suggest that she could send a message through the messengers. They could live without her, that Corinne could not, but she felt that selfishness rise up and was so ashamed of it.

"It is just a small headache, too many thoughts." Dolly calmed her friend. She could read Corinne's mind as if her thoughts were displayed in Corinne's expressive brown eyes.

Corinne bit her tongue about her thoughts on the matter.

"Will you keep working on the book while you are gone?" Corinne asked, finally relieved to find something safe to say that wasn't interfering. They had been planning to release a book together about plants and their medical uses. Corinne knew she would never publish the book without her. It was a project they had been planning for too long.

"I think I will leave the bulk of my work and drawings behind, as a promise to myself that I will be coming back. I will take a blank notebook to continue to draw in and make notes." Dolly said and gave the briefest of smiles to Corinne. "I do not want to let you down." Dolly usually kept her emotions very guarded and not shown.

"Please don't say that, I could never..." Corinne felt foolish as she pushed back at the lump forming in her throat. She was going to sob and make this so much worse.

Dolly stood and hugged Corinne; they didn't need words right now.

Corinne sent Dolly home at lunchtime for good. She felt there was no need for more work today. She knew her own heart wasn't in it. She was emotionally drained and so tired from the last few sleepless nights.

The walk was short from the lab to her own cabin, the stone path had grown every year of her marriage as her industrious husband found suitable flat rocks. She was trying to focus on her plans of planting some sort of shrub or plants along the walkway but the joy of the planting ideas were deflated at the moment.

She walked into her home and was struck by terror when she saw her housekeeper, Violet, lying on the floor of the kitchen.

Her heels clicked across the hardwood floors as she ran, she knelt beside Violet to see if she was conscious. The girl had her eyes open, they were swollen and red-rimmed and she was breathing. Corinne placed a hand across Violet's forehead.

"Are you in any pain?" Corinne asked, her voice on the edge of frantic. Violet looked up to her, wordlessly for a minute, the pain and loss was there and Corinne didn't know what to do.

"I am a widow." Violet whispered.

It was a minute before Corinne spoke. Instead she took her hand and ran it gently over Violet's blond hair, the braids were coming undone. She brushed some wisps of hair away from Violet's face and even removed a wayward pin.

Corinne had been a widow for a short amount of time when she had been on the Oregon Trail, just three years ago. It had not been a good marriage. It had not even been a consummated marriage, but simply one of convenience to allow her to travel to Oregon to reunite with her father. Corinne's first husband had been... well, Corinne didn't want to express aloud her thoughts on the pompous, careless and mean-hearted man that she had married. She searched through anything in her mind to say from her own widowhood experience but came up with nothing comforting to say.

"Are you certain?" Corinne asked softly.

"He was found dead. He had the ribbon..." Violet held the ribbon close to her chest but moved it to show Corinne.

Corinne hadn't known about the ribbon or any story associated with it, but she could tell by Violet's soft cries that it had meant something special to her.

The pot of boiling potatoes stole away the moment of silence and a bit of water cleared the sides and hissed dramatically when it hit the hot stove.

Corinne jumped up to check that the pot wasn't boiling over. It was a false alarm and Corinne was satisfied that the water wasn't likely to do more than splash over a little if any more at all.

Violet was sitting up, looking dazed and emotional. She seemed ready to try and stand. Her cheeks were pink and her eyes red-rimmed.

"You stay put." Corinne bossed. "Those potatoes don't even have ten more minutes of boiling. I can handle it."

Violet cried more tears. "Please don't, I need something to think on." She attempted to stand.

"I must insist. You just stay there. Or go sit on the rocker. I have a fresh stack of hankies on the table there." Corinne made her point and Violet nodded dumbly.

Corinne helped her stand up and Violet turned to give her a much-needed hug. Corinne let Violet sob for a minute on her shoulder, realizing it must be a day for that. Her skills of friendship were being tested, she said a prayer while stroking the hair of her friend.

Lord Jesus, please comfort my friend in her grief. Corinne prayed silently.

After the sobbing slowed to soft sniffles Corinne helped her widowed friend to a comfortable chair. She left Violet to her thoughts while Corinne saw to the lunch details. The shaved beef and gravy was already done and cooling on the counter. The potatoes were ready to be drained and mashed.

Dolly Bouchard

The room was bright and cheerful, a patchwork quilt lay on the bed, and Dolly sat mutely on it. Wishing she could feel good about her decisions. She was leaving the valley, and she felt that strange fluttering in her stomach when she thought of it.

Dolly was packing up the last of her things from Chelsea Grant's house, trying to stop the myriad of thoughts that pervaded her. This and several other cabins throughout the Valley had been home to her. It was her nomadic way of being here in the White Man's world. Never settling too long in one place. But Chelsea's home with young children running about and the warm fire had been her home the longest. Leaving here felt the hardest. Her world was coming to an end, at least for a time. The two men who had come for her were waiting, and she didn't want to make them wait any longer. She wasn't sure her own heart could say goodbye any more. She hadn't said the words aloud many times, but her heart was saying farewell to all the things that she loved. The small church by the river, where she had found her new faith, to her many friends that felt like family. They all were lodged in her heart. The pain of staying when she knew she had to go was urging her forward, to get this journey over, and then she could come back and begin again.

The men that had come for her were impatient, and so was she.

Gray Feather was a warrior in the Shoshone tribe. She could not tell his age with any determination, but he seemed to be young enough to be strong and healthy. His black hair was long and smooth, with a chunk of hair in front swept aside and it was wrapped around eagle feathers that had seen rough wind. He bore the scars of many battles on his shoulders and arms. His ears on each side had three brass earrings with green glass shards hanging down from each. His frown was extreme when he was angry or impatient, but his eyes were dark and unreadable.

Dolly had not necessarily remembered him from her life before with the tribe, he seemed older than her eighteen years and he had probably been with the men since she was a young girl. It had been three years since she had had left the tribe. She had been fifteen and very absorbed in the life of a female in her tribe. Gray Feather was a warrior by appearance and actions, with the scars of battle on his chest.

Dolly had spent some time with Gray Feather and his companion Bright Son. Bright Son was a pleasant young man, he wore a smile nearly every second he was awake. His hair was long down his back and his high cheekbones made his smile show even brighter.

They both wore fringed leather pants, Bright Son had a black and brown flannel shirt that Dolly assumed had been a trade. Bright Son was the opposite of his companion in nearly every way. His eyes alert, his features expressive, and his smile was infectious. Everyone who had met Bright Son in the valley discussed how well his name fit him. His behavior was bright and joyous, like a beautiful sunny day.

Dolly was not surprised they had come for her, but she was disappointed that it had to be this moment in her life, when everything had been going so well for her. The expectation of the arrival of someone from her tribe had been in her thoughts for the last year, weighing heavy on her heart. Knowing she was trapped in two worlds. Her past within the tribe had taught her so much about nature and its many wonders. A part of her had always been curious of the whole world that she had never known, the world in which her father, Joseph Bouchard, had grown and also had never shared with her. She knew of him only from stories from her mother. This chance to join with the group traveling west seemed the perfect opportunity to know a taste of the 'White-man's' world. She had jumped upon it so very willingly three years ago. To have it taken away from her now seemed such a difficult transition.

When she had seen these men on horseback just the few weeks before had been a shock, as much as she thought she was prepared for it, she was not ready. But the sense of honor she held within herself she knew she could not say no. Promises had been made... she would go.

Gray Feather had explained the situation the first day he had arrived. Dolly felt a strange relief hearing her own language spoken after a few years of speaking English. It was a small comfort though, because Gray Feather's gruffness and unbending personality was going to be a problem.

"The Chief has sent me to fetch you back, he has agreed that we should be wed when we arrive." Gray Feather had said. His eyes were unreadable and dark.

Dolly wanted to choke on the word "wed" but she held her tongue. She waited for Gray Feather to continue.

"I am ashamed to see you dressing like a white woman. Where are your clothes?" He asked, his eyes narrowed and judgmental.

"I was several years younger, I have outgrown my old skirts." Dolly said with no nonsense or defensiveness in her voice. He could make any assumptions he wanted. She did not need to answer to him.

Gray Feather seemed satisfied with her answer.

It had been agreed that they would leave within two weeks. Her dear friend Clive Quackenbush had allowed the men to stay on his land, his easy way of communicating with the men made it a good choice. They waited for her answer there.

Dolly had not agreed at first that she was even going to leave with them. She definitely had not agreed to being married off to anyone, but she kept quiet. Knowing she would get more respect from Gray Feather with a quiet countenance than with a mouth full of demands.

Bright Son had been polite with everyone. He was a good communicator and used Chinook well enough to converse with a few people in town. Once she had ridden out to Clive's property and informed them that she needed a few weeks to prepare they consented, though Gray Feather was irritated to wait longer than a few days. Clive gave them freedom to hunt his property and that kept them busy while Dolly came to grips with her decision.

Dolly had had visitors every few hours throughout the first days as news spread through the small town. First had been Chelsea Grant, her bosses sister in-law who lived a mile down Spring Creek Road. Chelsea and her husband had taken her under their wing as soon as she joined the wagon train; her chief had sent her with the wagon train to learn from Corinne Grant about plants and medicines but also to learn English. Chelsea had been an excellent teacher and also a much needed mother figure.

Reggie Gardner, a friend who had recently shown interest in her, had come when he heard the news and that had been a difficult conversation. He had asked to court her a month or two before and she had regretfully denied him. Dolly had regretted it since. Reggie was a good man of God and she felt a pull of some kind toward him. But her sense of duty to Chief Washakie from the Shoshone was still strong. She felt that her return to the Shoshone was too soon though, and such a big part of her wanted to say no to the two Shoshone men who had made the long trip to fetch her.

Reggie had been noticeably upset, asking her so many questions, he had tried to hide the hurt he felt at being denied the right to court her. He now seemed even more hurt that she was leaving, taken out of his life forever. His protectiveness was endearing and confusing, causing more pain in her heart than she was perhaps willing to admit. He seemed certain that she would not be safe, alone with these two men who knew her so little.

"How long will you be gone?" He had asked, this was one she had received from all of her friends. The moment was still and quiet until Dolly answered.

Her answer of "I am not sure," was not very comforting. She could see that Reggie was struggling within himself. He had no official right to his protective feelings. It stung Dolly to know that she had done that to him. She caught the look of pain in his eyes and fought within herself over it. She had not wanted this.

He had a few questions that remained unasked but she could see his eyes asking her. 'Would she remember him?' was one that tore through her. She would take the image of his face with her wherever she went, she wanted to tell him so but she did not have the nerve to say it.

She had questions of her own. *Would Reggie wait for her... and did she truly want him too?* She seemed as unready for courtship as she was unready to return to the Shoshone. *Would her quiet ways and uncertainty drive him away?*

No one could answer these questions but she prayed so much over those two weeks. The journey would give her plenty of time to think. She had so many days of travel ahead.

Chapter 2

Clive Quackenbush

Clive liked to think of himself as a wise ol' coot. His black hair peppered with white, and his short beard showing his age of sixty-one years. He had a thin frame, tall and lanky, with strong shoulders and more energy than he knew what to do with usually. He had lived in the West for the most of his life, taking on the lifestyle of the trapper in Michigan when he was in his teens, then moving west to the unknown shortly after.

He enjoyed his life and pursuits, he was a self-made man and enjoyed it. His business ventures and political jobs throughout the years made him feel well rounded. He wrote in many journals throughout his life, documenting his many adventures and he enjoyed telling his stories over and over. It was a joy to have many friends from all walks of life, from the many native tribes that he had communicated with from the Potawatomi tribes in Michigan, the Shoshoni in the Wind River Mountains, the Duwamish and Puyallup tribes in the Washington Territory and the many tribes he came in contact in California with his business travels. He felt a part of the West and the people, including the new breed of frontiersmen and women who joined in the quest to make this land great. Seeing the log homes sprouting up across the Willamette Valley every year was a joy to behold, knowing the land would bless so many with its fertile harvests.

Oregon City had become a grand place to plant roots, his eldest son, Jedediah Quackenbush or JQ, had settled here, his granddaughter Chelsea was nearby with her beautiful children, his grandson Gabriel had settled in nearby in Portland. It was home to him, his nomadic ways seemed calmer than they had been in years past.

The last trip to and from Michigan just three years before had been a promise to himself to travel east one last time. Taking the Oregon Trail back west with his Granddaughter and family back had been a challenging road and his bones had felt every mile. Though he was not one to complain. He had been on that trail three times and each one had its own challenges. But he had to admit, this last one was a special trip. He felt a connection with this group of travelers most keenly.

The young people that braved the long road west had invigorated him in a new way, the start of the great migration West was alive and inside of him.

He realized that he was mentoring the new generation of pioneers and he relished the job. Sharing his insights and friendship was not only a job but also a calling in his heart. He thanked God everyday for the inspiration that these young folks gave him, he knew that his world had broadened by knowing these people. He was proud to call them his friends and neighbors.

Willamette Valley was his home, with its rugged peaks, wild rushing rivers and abundant wildlife was more home to him than ever before. He felt within him that his wandering days were done. He could live out the rest of his days here, and love every moment of it.

Angela Fahey

Angela Fahey lived in a large farmhouse, on Spring Creek road. It was the largest house in Oregon City and its grand wrap-around porch was the envy of many wives throughout Willamette Valley. It was yet unpainted but it was still a grand sight sitting on the hill overlooking the farm and nearby horse ranch. She felt a little silly for building such a huge home some days, realizing she was only just engaged. She had the money she had inherited from her parents, it had been long overdue and she wanted to spend that money on her future. She had grand hopes and these walls she built would house the treasured memories of her life, the best part of her life. The past and its troubles could be forgotten.

Angela had built the home with the dream of filling the rooms someday. She had the dream of marriage in her heart last fall when it was built, but she had only letters then, from her dearest Ted, who had been in upstate New York with his family. He had returned west with his family in tow. It had been a strange struggle within her as the courting was clouded by his mother's rejection of her. It was months of inner turmoil for Angela to come to terms with her feelings for him. She had a deep inner need for family and acceptance, but she hadn't been willing to set aside her love for him because of his mother's moods. She had healed the rift with his mother and had accepted the proposal a few weeks ago. Angela felt peaceful about her choice and looked forward to her future with him.

Her focus had been to make her huge house a home, but the many rooms were mostly empty and daunting to her. Only her bedroom and one room upstairs were fully furnished. The other bedrooms bare accept for a few wood stoves that stood in them, dusty and lonely looking. The kitchen and dining room were coming along nicely, she was pleased with her progress. The parlor had nice chairs and a soft loveseat that was welcoming. The lack of area rugs was a concern to her and she had some on order. But waiting for goods in the West was always a challenge. Orders could take months. She had time.

Angela Fahey stood staring at the drawing that was framed and hung on the wall of her bedroom. The new wallpaper had been hung just a few weeks before, pale green and beige stripes made the room bright and airy. It was beautiful to see the portrait hanging there, making the room even more hers. It was a drawing of her family when they were still all together, before they came to America. The glass reflected her own face back at her in a faded way that made her throat tight. She could see bits of herself in every face she saw, she had her mother's eyes and her father's smile, her brother Sean looked so much like her father and she could say from her own memory that he looked more like him as a grown man. She had come west for him, and herself, but the reunion had gone poorly. He was not willing to see her more than a little, his words of rejection lingered painfully since she left him behind in San Francisco the year before. She thought of him often, even if she tried not too. Having his young sweet face looking at her daily from this portrait was keeping them all fresh in her mind. She was thankful for every item in the trunk that her friend had retrieved for her. Corinne Grant and her lawyer in Boston had secured the inheritance and the trunk after a battle with Angela's stepfather. She never wanted to think of the despicable man who had placed her and her brother in the work orphanage, but knowing some justice was done made Angela ready to move forward and put those days behind.

She mourned her parents a little every day she saw that drawing but she refused to take it down. She knew it was good for her in little bits to remember them, this was the only portrait she had. The artist had been talented and she was grateful that she had this little piece of them.

Angela pulled herself from her bittersweet thoughts and tidied her hair, knowing her betrothed was coming by soon.

Ted Greaves was the handsome and kind young man who had won her heart. She felt in many ways that she didn't deserve him, but she fought off those feelings. He had been patient with her while he bided his time since arriving back in the west last November. She would thank the Lord everyday for showing her how to trust again. His gentle ways had won her over slowly, first in San Francisco and then again over this last winter. Ted was soft-spoken but somehow he had expressed his love for her in so many ways, his willingness to treat her as an equal partner had been the thing that had earned her trust and affection more than anything else.

She had only been engaged a few weeks now. He had proposed at her housewarming party and surprised her completely. She stared at the ruby and gold ring on her finger and knew she had done right in saying yes. He was a good man of God, supportive and funny... and handsome, she admitted, that was a part of the equation too. He had been handsome, his tan cheeks, and curly blond hair had captured her gaze quickly that first day when she had met him in San Francisco more than a year ago. But the time apart when he had gone back east to his family had allowed him to grow up just that little bit more. He had no more boyishness in his looks anymore. He had grown into a man, and Angela was pleased that he still held his affections for her. She glanced in the mirror and still saw the youngness in her face, and the stubborn few freckles across the bridge of her nose.

Her body had changed a lot in the last year and a half too, she had given many of her dresses to her young friend Galina, the 14 year old girl she befriended and hired to help her with odd jobs around the house. Angela felt the body change made up for the childish face a little but she still struggled with feeling inadequate.

She would definitely be praying about that. If she were brave she could talk about it with Ted sometime. If she wanted to marry the man she should be able to speak up about her feelings.

Angela heard the back door of her farmhouse open and close and wondered if Dolly was home early from her job at Grant's Grove. Dolly had moved into her farmhouse as soon as it was livable in the fall. Angela was devastated that Dolly would be leaving. She was at a loss of what to do to persuade her to stay.

"Hello." Dolly's voice called out.

Angela was happy to see her and immediately saw the distress on the girl's face.

"You upset?" Angela asked simply.

"Today was my last day working with Corinne." Dolly said and flopped into a dining room chair. She leaned back and let out a big sigh. "I also cleared out my things at Chelsea and Russell's home."

Angela could tell that Dolly had a lot on her mind but Angela knew if she waited that Dolly would share. Angela walked to her kitchen and boiled some water for tea.

She had spent an hour talking with Dolly, rehashing some of the same conversations they had had all week. Angela didn't mind though. She would never deny Dolly a chance to speak about her future. Dolly came up with no solutions but the time had been well spent, Dolly had reconfirmed her faith in God aloud, and her determination to go back to the Shoshone only to tell the Chief that she had chosen a different life.

Angela understood the soft-spoken nature of Dolly, being a quiet girl herself. They made good roommates and Angela felt a sense of loss knowing her home would be empty now until she was wed. Angela was only eighteen and the idea of living completely alone made her uneasy. She wouldn't share those thoughts with Dolly, though, for she had enough confusion over leaving without adding guilt atop of it.

Olivia Greaves

Olivia Greaves was facing facts that she was forty-one years old. She ran a bristle brush through her strawberry blond curls and fretted over her looks for a moment in front of the looking glass. She pinned her hair back with skilled hands that were used to delicate work.

She had first married when she was sixteen, her sister, Amelia, had been touted as the prettiest girl in town and Olivia second prettiest. It was a silly comparison back then and even sillier now when she was a grown woman. If she was feeling honest about her appearance she wasn't too incredibly worried. She had kept her trim figure, but she had never given birth, a fact that she would not allow herself to dwell on at all.

Mostly she didn't worry about her appearance because in the West it didn't matter much. She felt pretty enough at her age. Her hair, which she had always been a little proud of, was bright and behaved with only a little bit of fussing. She knew how to make the best with what she had to work with.

She was a divorced woman. She was no longer ashamed of that fact, she was honestly thankful for it in many ways. Her cheating, stealing husband had stolen away enough years of her life. She would not give him any more time or thought. She had her years of repentance for the sin of divorce and felt God had more than forgiven her, but also given her peace about it. She had understood early on that she was free of guilt, having never participated in any infidelity herself, but just the judgment of narrow-minded people, calling her a sinner and worse had taken its toll early on.

Her ex-husband was in California territory and she had chosen to join with her sister's family on a boat to Oregon territory, to start over. It had come at the right time for her, after her fortieth birthday. She had mourned that birthday the most. Not because of the signs of growing older, but she felt it was the end of the dream of having her own children. The dream of finding a husband again had withered within her after small town judgment had heaped its vengeance upon her head.

Olivia grabbed a hot iron from atop the wood stove in the kitchen and took a small tendril near her ear and created a small spiral curl, the oval mirror nearby showed that her work was done well.

Divorce did carry a stigma that she had expected. In upstate New York she had been dealt a harsh blow when she was ostracized from her small local church. He, the philanderer, had still been allowed to attend until he left town for California. After his many indiscretions and public humiliations he had dealt her she had been brought low by small town judgment. But Olivia felt she had risen above it.

Her new life with her sister's family in Oregon had been a fresh start for her. She had even told the pastor of the Spring Creek Fellowship Church how her divorce had transpired. She wanted no secrets about her past. She had been accepted with open arms and that had done wonders for her heart. Oregon City was good for her. It had that ruggedness that charmed her and the sweetness of good people that eased her mind.

What does one do with oneself at forty-one? She wondered.

She was a skilled lace maker, she wasn't sure how many generations that her family had been making lace. Her grandmother had spoken of learning at her own grandmother's knee. When her nephew, Ted, had made the offer for her to join his family on a trek west, she had been ready. Knowing they had a vendor to buy lace and a place set up made the decision easy. The boat trip had been mostly smooth, with only her own sister as the thorn in the side of everyone along the way.

Her sister had a valid excuse for her bad attitude, mourning the loss of her husband, but Amelia Greaves had taken it too far. Olivia spent many hours in prayer over her sister and her biting tongue. Her 14-year old niece Sophia had done a lot of confiding in Olivia and their relationship was stronger than ever. She loved her family very dearly, especially her grumpy sister. She would never give up on her.

Olivia was proud of their business, a small townhouse with a storefront, Amelia and Sophia were her partners and they spent their days with strings and bobbins making lace for the women of the West. They were told by their buyer, Clive Quackenbush, that their lace was being purchased all through Oregon, Washington and California territories. They were all proud of their craft. Knowing in their small way they were bringing civility to this new world.

She made a comfortable living and since arriving in November had earned the respect of this small town along with her sister and niece. They did good work and to Olivia it was almost enough.

She knew what she wanted, and knew she didn't have the courage to tell anyone but she did talk to God about it. Knowing He wouldn't think the desire in her heart was a silly one.

She wanted to be loved again before she died. It sounded melodramatic inside her head. If she had said it to anyone else it probably would have categorized her as a silly female, which she took pride in staying away from. But it was truth, she wanted to be loved by a real man, a good man.

She may be past the age for dreams of children and the white picket fence but she wanted to be cherished by someone that wasn't a cad. She had never known a love that was pure and unselfish. Her first husband had tried to crush her spirit so many times but now she wanted to try again. Her prayers in the quiet of night had been asking God to take away this desire if it was a futile thought, if her divorce had made her untouchable or sinning in a way if she was to seek out a new marriage. She felt a sense of peace after such prayers, like God was telling her that her life wasn't over, and she could be loved again.

She didn't know how she would accomplish this feat. An older woman was not usually put in this position to search out a potential mate, well it was not something anyone talked about in her circles. She had no plan of action or scheme she was hoping to use, she was too mature for that. But she did have a potential partner in her sights, and she was going to go after him.

Chapter 3

Oregon City

Oregon City had plenty to gossip about, with Dolly Bouchard leaving with Shoshone Indians, rumors of Violet Griffen's husband dying of fever in California, and the summer Independence Day Festival announced, the town was busy.

Spring was a time for renewal and new beginnings. The Willamette River ran thick with logs, the mills ran day and night. The town council discussed building a boardwalk down Main Street, and the newspaper ran every week supplying news and information to all the citizens far and wide.

Nearby Portland and Salem were growing as well. With trade routes opening up on rough roads hacked through the mountain passes. The West was coming alive.

Fields were being cleared and thoughts of sewing seeds and growing orchards were talked of often.

Violet Griffen

Violet was keeping her head together through the first few days since she had found out about her husband. She had too. Her life wouldn't actually change much she realized. Instead of mourning his absence on a daily basis she will instead mourn the loss of his company in a more permanent way. He wasn't returning to her, the hope of it could not be held any longer. She was coming to terms with it.

She felt numb. She went about her duties because she wanted to. Her employers, Corinne and Lucas Grant, had both told her to cease her housekeeping duties for a few days, with pay included. Violet refused.

"If I have to sit in my rocker and crochet and cry for days on end I will lose my sanity." Violet protested louder than she had intended.

Corinne and Lucas had looked at her in surprise. Violet was a soft-spoken gal on most occasions.

"Please let me do my work. If I am struggling I will take a rest." She promised.

Corinne and Lucas had agreed and Violet had been working hard to keep her mind at her work. She failed often and had stopped many times over her daily tasks to wipe away tears. It was a hard time but a healing one too. She felt God's promises within her.

Jeremiah 29:11
For I know the thoughts that I think toward you, saith the Lord, thoughts of peace, and not of evil, to give you an expected end.

This verse gave her hope for her future and she thought of it often. Violet was clearing off the breakfast table when she heard a scratch at the cabin door. Violet smiled weakly and went to see her visitor.

Pepper, Cooper's dog from next door, was waiting for Violet expectantly when she opened the cabin door. The dog's furry tale swished back and forth and was a welcome sight to Violet's bruised heart. He was a fluffy shepherd dog and his enthusiasm was infectious.

"Come in fella." She spoke sweetly and was rewarded with a heartier tail wag. Violet bent down and ran a hand through the dog's soft fur. She took only a second to decide to sit down next to the dog and give some proper attention.

The dog butted into her face with the top of his head and rubbed along her jaw. Violet was certain that that was the closest thing to a dog hug you could get. It was comforting and the sense of well-being rushed through her.

Pepper belonged to Cooper Harpole, from next door, his mother Marie, was the second wife of Corinne's father. Cooper was energetic and usually had Pepper by his side every moment throughout his day. But Violet knew that Pepper got tired of staying at the schoolyard all day waiting for Cooper, so he trotted back home, and had started a new habit of visiting with Violet. Violet didn't suppose the treats of table scraps had done anything to lessen the affection but she was glad for the company in the afternoons.

Violet gave the dog a healthy rub and scratch and let herself enjoy the quiet moment. The dog pranced around her kneeling body and gave her several more hugs before he turned to watch a man approach the cabin door. The tail wagging commenced again.

Violet looked up when she realized that a shadow had passed over the light from the open door.

"May I come in?" Reggie Gardner held his black hat in his hands. He was tall and broad shouldered; he had intelligent dark eyes that were showing trouble behind them.

"Oh certainly." Violet swung a leg around awkwardly to get up from her position on the floor.

Reggie offered a hand to let her up. Violet grabbed a hunk of a leftover piece of biscuit and gave it to the dancing dog at her feet. He licked her hand and escaped out the door, seeking another adventure.

Violet cleared away the breakfast dishes and settled them on the counter to wash later.

"Ya want some coffee?" Violet asked and pointed at the chair for Reggie to sit. Reggie obeyed and settled his hat on the table in front of him. His dark eyes were troubled. He ran a hand through his thick black hair.

"You don't have to trouble yourself." Reggie said finally. "You want me to shut the door?"

"Nah, the spring air is glorious." She sighed and smiled again. It was a stronger smile than before and she felt the smallest hint of herself returning. Her usual joyful being was smothered by the cloak of mourning. She had hope of shaking off the cloak soon. She wanted to feel light-hearted again. "No trouble for the coffee. It's made fresh a half hour ago, still hot." Violet poured two cups. She added milk and sugar to hers and kept Reggie's black.

She settled into a chair herself and examined her guest. He had recently been to the barber because his black hair was cropped shorter. He seemed upset, though, and Violet was praying a quick prayer that she could help.

"What's troubling you, Reggie?" Violet started and took a sip of her coffee to give him a chance to reply.

"I came to check in on you. I needn't trouble you with anything in my own head." Reggie said sincerely.

"I am a widow, not dead myself." Violet said flatly. Her sadness was wearing off to be replaced by new feelings. "Crying about it isn't going to change anything." It wasn't her usual joyful way of being, and she didn't like it. She felt harsh and tainted by her emotions. But she knew she wouldn't hide her feelings. To get through meant she had to feel them, and be honest about them.

"It's gonna be a while of feeling out of sorts." Reggie offered. "Bah..." He said under his breath. "I don't know what to say to help. I am sorry Vie... I feel like a lousy friend." Reggie admitted.

"You coming to check in on me does a world of good." Violet smiled, wanting everyone to stop feeling bad for her. She would get through this. "Tell me what's troubling you, I can see it in those sad eyes of yours."

"Dolly..." Reggie said and his voice tightened.

Violet sighed, every neighbor she had was sad in some way over Dolly's predicament.

"She leaves tomorrow." Violet said softly.

Reggie nodded, he dropped his head to hide the emotions in his eyes. He had not meant to fall for the quiet girl, she had made it known that her future was not free for courting, but his heart had traveled ahead of him. He seemed to have no control over it. Violet had been the first to notice his affection for Dolly.

"Dolly showed me the picture you drew for her." Violet said to make him feel better. She knew the affection that he carried for Dolly, she said a prayer for him. "I think she has shown everyone in the valley."

Reggie smiled and laughed in a strangled way. "What should I do? She feels that she must go. I met with the two Indians yesterday and the warrior that has claimed to be her betrothed is a harsh fellow. I don't trust him." Reggie chuckled again. "He didn't trust me either. I think he has a general disdain for our white faces."

Violet had heard a few things that had been translated from folks who had talked to them. Violet wouldn't participate in the talk, but she had her own fears for Dolly. The mountains were treacherous even for experienced travelers. Violet had said many prayers for Dolly already, and would say many more prayers for her friend. It was going to be a long wait to see that kind young lady again. Violet and everyone that knew her was going to fret until she returned.

"The only thing we can do is put this in God's hands." Violet finally said. "We cannot force her to do our bidding. She is now of age and can make her own choices."

Reggie nodded and took a swig of coffee; his face was awash with dread.

"I have to have faith." He said finally. "I have already made my feelings known to her," Reggie said huskily. "Not fully, because I didn't want to scare her away. But she did not accept my bid for courtship."

"I am sorry Reggie." Violet said then sighed, knowing how much that must have hurt. She could not imagine refusing the bid of courtship of such a fine young man. Violet wanted to laugh at her silly thought. She was not really interested in Reggie, but being sought after was pleasant, and it reminded her of her courtship with her departed Eddie.

"She only resisted because of the Shoshone tribe. She said she would have accepted my suit otherwise." Reggie admitted painfully.

"She has repeatedly shared that she will be returning, Reggie. I have hope that this is not fully played out. She is leaving most of her belongings behind, I am told." Violet had formed a good friendship with Reggie over the last few months, she hated to see him so heart broken.

Within a minute the subject changed, and they sipped the coffee and discussed lighter things.

Violet watched him go soon after the coffee cups were empty. Violet returned to work and tried to enjoy the fresh breeze through the cabin.

Clive Quackenbush

Clive held the attention of six young lads as he tramped through the woods, two Varushkin boys, Milo and Pavel, Brody Grant, Cooper Harpole, and the newly adopted Forester Whittlan. Clive had promised them a day of adventure in the wilderness, trapping and exploring. They had all been told to bring a pocketknife if they had one. Clive had brought enough with him in his wagon to give as a gift to any that didn't have one. Brody Grant and Cooper Harpole had been the only two that were already supplied.

The ground was moist and the air full of a morning mist as Clive began the journey through his own property north of Oregon City. The trees showing off their new coats of green leaves, the spring air smelled of rich soil and the promise of summer. It was a grand day to be in the woods.

Every boy had to be warned a few times to put the knife in their pocket while he had been talking but he smirked whenever he turned around, certain he too had long ago been an excited young boy with his first knife. He said his own prayers that not too much blood would spill from his gift as these young boys learned to handle the knives.

He pointed out different species of trees and some easy tricks for finding bait for fishing. He came across his first snare, and then settled them all in for a talk. He talked about the construction of primitive traps.

"The first thing I do when checking my traps and snares is perceive whether or not there is a captured animal." Clive said. "If there is what should I look for first?" Clive asked to determine the knowledge of the youngsters.

A few shrugged, the others just looked on, waiting for an answer.

"Well, if the critter is trapped and alive the first thing I want to do is make sure it isn't suffering." Clive said.

"My Pa says that we should never ever intentionally make an animal suffer." Cooper said with a grin, excited that he knew something. He was the picture of his Mama with blond curls and pink cheeks.

"That is right. Trapping and hunting are for many good reasons. But it should never be about enjoying the kill." Clive said seriously.

All the boys nodded at that.

"We use the meat of the animals to eat, and the skins to keep us warm. What else do we use?" Clive asked.

"My mama uses the bones to make soup." Milo shared.

"We sometimes eat the livers." Cooper said and made a face.

Clive joined in the laughter of the shared experience of some disliking liver.

"The Indians are the best at using every part of the animal. They use the bladders to hold water. I once saw a carved jawbone that was used as a hairbrush. They use the tendons and sinew for ropes and cords, even to make snares to catch more animals." Clive was rewarded with looks of awe from his young charges.

"I believe that God gave us authority over the creatures on earth, but we need to have a respect for the world we live in. Every life is valuable. Taking an animal's life should be done with humility and respect for the animal that feeds and clothes us." Clive pointed to the empty snare. "This one hasn't caught anything yet but I just set this one last night. Let's walk around it and move along the trail."

Clive continued tramping along, enjoying the chance to teach again.

A few hours later he returned the young men in the wagon, each one to his own home. The day had been fruitful, each with a full game bag to be shared with the boys' families, and young minds full of promise.

He returned the wagon to the barn at Russell Grant's farmstead and then saddled up his horse. His home was a few miles north and he wanted to make quick time. The spring rains had brought the green out in the grass and the buds on the trees were showing off. The air smelled like wet dirt, it was thick and heavy. Clive enjoyed the ride over rocks and tree branches as he took the most direct path to his home through the woods.

His cabin was a little bigger than the original cabin he had had on this land years ago. How he had raised his kids in that tiny cabin was a mystery to him. He had built a better one when he opened the trading post. His wife had been happy with the improvement. The old cabin still stood but was an eyesore, he kept promising himself to tear it down. He was certain that a few raccoons were making a lovely little dwelling place, along with the spiders.

Clive had a moment of heartbreak remembering his two wives. He had loved deeply twice. Both women had been strong in their own way. Christina had been his first wife and Martha his second. Christina had been all about her babies and caring for him. She was every bit of feminine and fluff. He laughed at how she had loved him, the rough and tumble skinny twig of a man. She had given birth five times, only three still alive today, Jedediah, then Thomas, and Greta. Jedediah was the only one who stayed west, Thomas had a big farm spread in Michigan, and Greta married a businessman in Indiana. When he married Martha she wanted so badly to have more children but instead raised the three children that needed a mama. Both women occupied a space in Clive's heart. He could still see glimpses of Christina's face in Chelsea Grant and her son Brody. With Martha he only had the memories. He had so wanted to give her that child she so desperately wanted.

Clive settled his horse in his small barn and gave him a good brush down.

When he got inside he checked the water in the pitcher on the washstand. It was clear and he took off his shirt and splashed a little water on his face and let it run down his frame. He gasped into the empty room at the chill of the water. He dried off quickly with a hand towel and went to his tall dresser in his room for a fresh shirt. He looked around his home with a critical eye. Seeing all the things that needed fixing up. Nothing was in terrible disrepair for he was always tinkering at things, but he remembered the days when the cabin had been full. The old bright cotton curtains with lace had long ago worn out. The children had stomped and raised a ruckus through these rooms. A spare room still held the notches in the wall that young Jed had put there when he would practice his knife throwing skills after bedtime.

Clive and Martha had taken turns yelling out, "Stop throwing knives in the house!"

Clive started a fire in the wood stove and puttered around in the pantry. He found some canned stew that his granddaughter Chelsea had put up for him. He wrenched on the jar with some force until it finally gave way with a knocking sound. Even in the jar it was a good smell. He dumped its contents into a copper-bottom pan.

A thought occurred to him as he stirred his supper. He felt a change was coming. He looked around the room almost if someone nearby had whispered the thought to him but his place was empty. Only the sound of the crackling wood in the wood stove beneath him was to be heard but he felt that familiar nudge.

He harrumphed and said a prayer. "Alrighty Lord, if change is coming I better get used to the idea." Clive knew better than to question the urgings of God. The Lord above spoke in whispers but

Clive felt the implications like it was a mighty large steam engine barreling his way.

Chapter 4

Dolly Bouchard

The pack mule held her leather satchel that contained everything she would need along the way, extra clothes and survival gear. Dolly had a small bag on her person that had a small knife, a few loaves of Violet's sour dough bread, a flint and a small bag that Clive had given her at the last moment before she left. She had been crying too hard to even open it then, Dolly tied her belongings to the back of her saddle, and the steel gray horse was gentle. All her resolve she had made to herself as she lay in the warm bed last night had gone away when she had seen everyone waiting outside that morning. All of her female friends had red-rimmed eyes and had looked as she felt.

Everyone had a haunted and sad look, the morning was early and the morning mist set the mood. Reggie perhaps looked the saddest but as she said goodbye and hugged the girls and Clive, Reggie stayed back. His eyes looked conflicted.

Gray Feather was talking quietly to Bright Son, they were ready to go, but Gray Feather was agitated already. His gestures were jerky and quick and he stared at Dolly often in encouragement to be on their way. The glass shards that hung from his ears clacked softly as he swung his face around in agitation.

With a farewell wave Dolly allowed Clive to boost her into the saddle. She gave the horse a rub on his neck and then wiped at the tears that were blurring her eyes. She felt all wrong. She knew she didn't want to leave but felt honor bound to go back with these men.

Dolly had dressed warm to start the journey but knew by noon she would be removing her wool coat. After an hour on her horse the coat felt bulky and unnecessary. They were starting at a slow and steady pace. Gray Feather naturally took the lead.

Bright Son made a few efforts to be kind to Dolly and she appreciated his attempts to see how she was faring. His eyes were kind and he meant well but there wasn't much for him to say that could alter the situation. She was leaving this world behind, and it was not settling well in her heart. She tried to watch the valley pass by with a distant acknowledgment. Not thinking of the many times she had galloped through these woods and fields. The many plants and herbs she had gathered in the woods would sit undisturbed and not help the people of this valley, the days that would pass here, without her. Would she see the lovely lavender fields again in full bloom? Smell the sweet jasmine? Would she hear the bubbling of the alembic pots in the lab again, knowing she was doing something so extraordinary with her life?

Dolly glanced at her pendant watch often. Every hour that went by was felt like daggers in her heart. The sad faces of those left behind were the tortured thoughts of the day. She prayed but her faith felt choked out. Perhaps her faith was like the ember of a fire, being pulled away from the burning hearth of the community that was left behind. Would her small faith survive the separation from those that held her up?

The day moved on as they always do. Dolly had made her choice. There was no turning back.

Chapter 5

Corinne Grant

Corinne had survived the morning. It had been emotional and painful but the world had not come apart. She had learned through several hard experiences that the world always does move forward, even when catastrophes come. It sometimes seemed like an insult... To see the sun shine after her miscarriage a year and a half before had seemed cruel. The sunrise through the grey clouds had seemed like a slap for a moment. Its beauty so breathtaking that she had been angry to see it, to have any kind of enjoyment in those first few days after. She had learned, over time, with prayer and staying close to her Lord that her suffering was not a punishment, but a part of life. Not all babies conceived could be born.

Corinne walked to the creek near her home, watched the water rush and stumble over the rocks and mud. The mountain snows were melting and all the creeks and rivers were chilly.

Corinne held a hand to her belly, wondering if the thought that came just a few hours before was true. Just a hint of the idea had made her start. Watching Dolly leave in the early morn had made her restless and anxious all day. She had puttered in her greenhouse but was wandering about her business with a detached air. She had decided to leave the lab closed for a few days. It was strange without Dolly there.

Corinne saw her husband, Lucas, through the trees on the opposite side of the creek, he waved and immediately she dropped the hand from her belly. She had only the smallest of inclinations, no certain proof.

She watched her handsome husband walk closer, his large frame moving with purpose, his face clean-shaven, and his smile bright. He seemed happy to see her and her heart warmed. She was so very lucky to have him. He was the perfect spouse for her. He was the calm reason to her headstrong ways, and she was the one to pull him away from his quiet thoughts to see the beauty.

He was only on the other side of the creek, preparing to jump across when she yelled out.

"I think I am pregnant!" Corinne felt the relief go through her. It may only be her imagination. But she knew it wasn't. Her fear had been pushing her symptoms aside. She was not tired, achy, and emotional because of Dolly, though she was very sad about it. Her body was creating another child.

Lucas stopped moving; he stood there, stock-still, knees partly bent. His eyes were bright and looking to her with anticipation. Corinne wanted to laugh at him. But instead she just grinned widely. It was all she could do.

Galina Varushkin

Galina had arrived home from her tasks for the day, doing laundry with Violet at Grant's Grove. She arrived at the small cabin a mile away with a large laundry sack of family clothes. They had been drying on the line at Grant's Grove for a few days and she set about putting them all away quickly so she could steal a few minutes away to read in the loft before her father returned from logging.

Her mother, Magdalena Varushkin, was humming near the stove, her youngest son strung around her mother's back with a wide piece of cloth tied around.

"You are home early." Her mother spoke with a thick accent, she was from Poland by birth but had married Slava, Galina's father, who was Russian. Galina got her looks from her mother, dark hair and intense brown eyes with long sooty lashes.

"Yes." Galina grinned as she settled the heavy bag of laundry on the dining table.

"Once you get that put away you may have some time to yourself. I have stew cooking and not much for you to do." Her mother gave her a warm look, knowing Galina's secret of reading in her spare time.

"That was my hope." Galina said and kissed her mother affectionately on the cheek, she ruffled the downy curls on her brother's head.

"This lad is getting a bit big for this." Magdalena grumbled.

"It could be time to have Papa build a pen for him." Galina looked to the parlor opposite the table. "You could let him play over there and he wouldn't be underfoot."

Magdalena looked to the empty space. "It would be inconvenient to walk around it but might help my aching back. He is growing so fast."

Galina nodded and headed to do her work. Her hands flew as she sorted the laundry into small piles for each person in her home. Within a few minutes each person had clean laundry. Galina climbed the ladder to the loft and sat near her window on her cot and read, she was reading through the New Testament that Violet had loaned her. She still struggled over many words but she understood them better than she used too. Her father would punish her for wasting time on an unnecessary frivolity. "Reading was not needed by a young woman!" He had declared many times. But Galina had her mother's support when she could find the time. Her mother had never learned to read and lamented it. Galina had offered many times to teach her, but Magdalena wouldn't budge. It was enough for her that her daughter was learning.

An hour flew by and Galina heard the door open and her brothers, Milo and Pavel, barreled in with heavy steps and loud voices. Her mother yelled out something about dirty boots.

Galina hid the testament under her mattress and went down the ladder reluctantly. She treasured every moment of her reading but it was not to be today. She had gotten a thorough beating from her father a few months before for attempting to ask to go back to school instead of doing her laundry work. She had gotten another a few weeks ago when he caught her with a book in her laundry bag.

He had burned the book of poetry, a gift from Angela. She had watched the book burn in the fireplace through the tears. The bruise on her cheek had healed faster than the pain she'd had over the burnt pages. She had promised herself that he would never see her reading again. Her mother helped her keep her secret.

The boys were put to work on chores, and Galina went out to the portion of the land that was not yet tilled. Her father wanted a larger garden and all hours not spent at work were breaking through the sod. It was back breaking and tedious but she knew if she wasn't working when her father returned she would be punished again.

She worked today with a lighter heart going over the things she had read. Having her secret gave her something that was hers. It was what she clung to.

Chapter 6

Ted Greaves

Ted Greaves watched Angela set dishes on the table as he wiped his hands on the towel. He had used the washbasin to wash up, moving slowly as a snail while he watched his fiancé. He saw the ruby ring he had placed on her finger and enjoyed the feeling it gave him inside his chest.

He didn't know when it would be but someday soon, weeks or months maybe, she would be his wife. He was proud of her, her spirit, and her compassion. She had a meekness about her that wasn't weak; instead she was strong when fighting for others. He knew in his heart she would make an excellent mother. She had handled his mother's moods and criticisms with strength and a Godly grace that had impressed him. His prayers over the winter months had been unending, feeling somehow that he was losing the love of his life. By the early spring he had resolved to try harder to communicate his affection. It had paid off and she now wore his ring, a promise of their future together.

"You are so beautiful to me." Ted said finally when Angela was just a few steps away.

Angela lifted her head slowly and her green eyes flashed appreciation, that hint of a smile would be his undoing. Her cheeks were pink, her green eyes so pretty he could happily drowned in them.

"Am I silly to say you are beautiful to me too?" She said after the look between them had grown more intense.

"Perhaps." Ted replied, keeping to the other side of the table, not sure if he trusted himself. "I should sit on the porch and wait for Clive." Ted said with a resigned sigh.

"Yes." Angela let out a breath herself. With Dolly a few days gone her house was empty, it made seeing Ted more difficult. Her reputation was probably already in danger from the gossips in town. A single woman keeping company with a man in her house alone was considered a harlot, no matter if she was innocent.

Ted left and Angela continued with her dinner preparations. She knew Clive was coming, she was glad of it. She needed to reconnect with her mentor. He seemed to be happy to play chaperone so her and Ted could talk. She had asked Earl who was usually up for dinner but he was visiting at Orchard House with the manager, Ms. Gemma Caplan.

Though Angela had taken over ownership of the boarding house Earl had taken it upon himself to do most of the visits. Angela found his praise of the optimistic Ms. Caplan to be ever on his lips. He was happily eating supper every weekend with the manager and boarders on Sundays after church service. Angela was glad to see him out and about. She secretly hoped that Earl would be married again. Knowing it would do him a world of good.

Angela pulled the hot buns from the oven and spread melted butter over the tops. She settled the buns on the table and brought over the beef roast that had just finished its slow roast in the brick oven over the fireplace in the other room. She was feeling confident in her cooking skills, so very grateful to Edith Sparks first and then to Violet Griffin. They had shared the love of cooking and passed it on to her.

Clive arrived, in a grand mood.

"You are shaping into a fine cook iffen that tastes as good as it smells." Clive praised.

Angela put him and Ted to washing up. Then supper was served.

Clive shared his adventures, talking about the young boys and the day he had had with his usual vim and vigor. Angela was pleased that there was no lack of joy at the table. The conversation flowed easily and laughter had been good for her. She needed the distraction from Dolly's departure.

After supper they all sat on the wide porch, talking and laughing together.

Dolly Bouchard

Dolly was glad the first mountain pass was behind her, the dark cliffs and rocky ledges had been hard to face. Her heart was in her throat as they walked along the dangerous passages that Gray Feather had chosen. The tall pines were tiny as she looked down, her stomach had clenched painfully as she let the horse have the lead. She feared for her life many times. Gray Feather had a course laugh that pricked at Dolly's temper whenever he noticed that she was afraid. She bit her tongue when she wanted to speak to him, she had nothing good to say, only words that she would regret.

The days were long and Dolly had so much time to think as she rode behind the two men on horseback. Gray Feather was always abrupt with her. Always assuming she knew nothing about traveling or making camp. His instructions were insulting. Dolly felt that inner urge to prove to him that she was a capable young woman. Not that she cared if he liked her or not.

She decided after a few days of travel to keep her thoughts and words to herself. Bright Son was the opposite of Gray Feather and Dolly had appreciated his attempts to make the situation bearable. The travel was slow and difficult. Mountain climbing on horseback was not easy and after the dangerous passes Bright Son would always find a way to lighten the mood.

The road they traversed the first few days had been the one Dolly was familiar with, having used that road with the wagon train coming west. But soon after Gray Feather abandoned the easy road and they went a more treacherous path, according to Gray Feather it was a faster trip and easier for horses. Bright Son had protested, but Gray Feather insisted that he was the most experienced. Dolly had no say in the direction and remained silent.

On day five of her journey she offered to go hunting with Bright Son.

"You are to stay at the fire, I do not trust you in the wilderness." Gray Feather laid down the law.

"I was not informed when I left with you that I would be treated like a prisoner." Dolly said before thinking. She instantly regretted the outburst when she saw the lines of disapproval on Gray Feather's face. He had an angry line creased across his forehead and his lips pursed. He looked about ready to go into battle. The dangling rings in his ears swung with every jerk of his head. The dangling beads and glass that hung from his ears clattered together softly. Sometimes his angry movements gave Dolly a ridiculous urge to giggle. She wrote down some of these thoughts in her journal as she traveled. She was determined to write only things that amused her, not her fears. Sometimes they snuck onto the page regardless.

"I will not allow for you to question my decisions." Gray Feather said flatly. It was a cold and unforgiving stare that followed.

Dolly wanted so badly to ignore him. She desired so strongly to rebel against his authority and prepare for a hunt with Bright Son, and leave the angry man behind. Dolly watched Gray Feather thoughtfully, trying to keep her face neutral as she considered her options.

She broke eye contact after she realized that she had better keep her rebellious thoughts in check. She was in the wilderness, with two near strangers. She decided that for today she would behave and stay near camp.

"Would you like me to make the fire?" She asked a minute later, she would try and make peace with Gray Feather.

"Yes." His voice was short and not at all grateful for her acquiescence.

Dolly gathered a few stones on the rocky terrain and settled them in her gathered skirts to hold. Gray Feather watched her for a long minute. Dolly could feel his eyes on her. She continued her perusal of the ground, the area was heavily wooded but rocks were plentiful. The sun was shining through the canopy of leaves above.

Eventually Gray Feather got busy with his own tasks. The nights still got cold so he was creating a shelter with long tree limbs shoved into the ground. He bent the branches toward the middle and bound them together.

As Dolly stacked her collected rocks to make a fire pit she watched him. She wanted to make sure the fire was protected from the wind that would whip through these hills at night. She brought a piece of charred cloth that Clive had given her, it made lighting fires a lot easier and she gathered everything else she needed nearby. Some dry tinder from Bright Son's satchel, he had gathered as they rode throughout the day.

Gray Feather watched Dolly as she struck the flint against her steel blade. The white-yellow sparks flew down over the bit of tinder and char cloth. Within a minute the cloth caught ablaze and with quick hands Dolly slid the tinder over the top. She bent low, careful to keep her braids away from the smoke. She blew softly and the tinder took the encouragement and yellow flames made their welcome appearance.

There were larger sticks stacked nearby and Gray Feather handed a few to Dolly. He seemed to be huffing over her fire-making methods. It was not their way.

Bright Son came back to camp within a few hours, the fire was healthy and crackling and the shelter was looking good.

Dolly would have enjoyed this scenario so much more with her new family. Clive would be telling stories, and Corinne would have asked Dolly to go hunting for plant treasures. She missed her life in Oregon City already.

She sat and ate her fire-roasted rabbit in silence.

Angela Fahey

The heavy warm rain was thudding on Angela's head as she closed the door to her chicken coop. She was glad her fiancé had built them a nice roof. Her 'Chickies' as she called them would stay dry in their coop.

She grumbled to herself for not bringing her umbrella as she picked up speed to get back to her house up on the hill.

She was excited to know that her fancy farmhouse she had built in the fall was soon to get a coat of paint. The wood siding still looked like the wood it had been built with. *It needed color to make the house come alive,* she thought.

The barely worn path up the hill to her back door was thick with mud and Angela had to work to get up it. The last two days the rain had been off an on but when it came down it was serious about it.

Angela was glad to get inside but lamented the appearance of her clothes, her white blouse was soaked, and her blue cotton skirt was coated in mud at least six inches from the hem. It would take a lot of scrubbing to make that decent to wear again.

She harrumphed and stripped out of every wet thing and ran quickly to her room nearby to grab the soft dressing robe.

Ted and his sister, Sophia, were coming to dinner later, Angela had invited Ted's mother and Aunt along but she wasn't sure they would. Ted's Aunt Olivia was extremely pleasant to be around, but

Ted's mother was a little harder to handle for Angela. At first it had been very hard for Ted's mother to approve of Angela and it had nearly cost them their relationship.

Now, since they were engaged, Angela wondered if his mother would continue with her seemingly better moods, or if she would revert back to disapproval when talk of a wedding was bound to surface. Angela did not like her thoughts sometimes, especially lately when she had a secret impossible wish that his Aunt Olivia was somehow really Ted's mother, and they could all live happily forever after.

It was not a very nice thought, she told herself whenever it crept in, but it was proof to Angela that she had a vivid imagination.

Angela dried herself and her hair by the fire as she read a book of poetry that Chelsea Grant had loaned her. By the time she was dry she was in a romantic mood and was floating through her motions. She started a roast chicken in her shiny black stove. She put on a simple blue dress with several layers of petticoats underneath to give it a nice elegant flow. Then she grabbed her largest apron to keep her dress pristine for dinner.

Angela heard the approaching wagon as she pulled the coffee cake out of the oven. The large roasted chicken, which she bought from the grocer in town, was displayed on a platter she had received as a house-warming gift the night of the party, when Ted proposed. Everything in her mind somehow weaved back to thinking about that night. The ruby ring on her finger as she worked, the gifts from her neighbors and friends, everything reminded her of her Ted.

Angela heard the sounds of feet walking up the stairs near the front door and quickly untied her apron and settled it on the counter top. She realized as she ran to the door that she had been cooking in her stockinged feet.

Argh, she thought. Knowing she had no time to put on her shoes before then would knock on the door.

The knock came a second later and she could see Ted's smile through the window, with his sister peaking around him in mirth. Two shapes were behind them and Angela knew in an instant that she would have extra guests.

"Welcome everyone." Angela said cheerily. Everyone was smiling as they came in. "Please forgive me, I do not have my shoes on. They got soaked earlier, and I never checked to see if they were dry enough."

"Oh, I am sure we don't mind that silly!" Olivia, Ted's Aunt, declared. "Certainly we should all remove our own shoes, the mud is dreadful. I wasn't sure we were going to make it through on the roads."

Ted winked at Angela and started untying his boots and he slipped them off and deposited them by the door. He then gave a look to everyone with him to follow suit. The look of horror on his mother's face was comical and Angela had to concentrate to not laugh, especially when Ted was grinning so widely.

"I don't think..." Amelia Greaves began to protest.

"Mother, we would not want to muddy up her clean floors now would we?" Ted said and Angela wanted to slug his shoulder. He was enjoying the flustered look on his mother's face too much.

"I don't mind in the slightest." Angela said to placate her.

Then it was an awkward moment of Amelia looking between Ted and Angela, deciding what to do next.

After the awkward moment, Olivia made the suggestion of using a towel on any muddy boots. Angela could feel the weight on her chest lift as Sophia ran to the kitchen counter and scooped up a clean towel. She cleaned her mother's boots and then plopped on the floor to wipe away any mud from the others that had been removed.

Angela wondered in dismay if things were ever going to be easier with Ted's mother. She couldn't help remembering the first dinner she had had with his family, how insulted and hurt she had been by his mother's criticism and ultimate rejection. She had hopes that the more peaceful relations would continue. But she still held her expectations in check.

Dinner started well, with Ted's Aunt Olivia helping her serve. Sophia had begun setting the table with Angela's new china plates. Angela was using a cream linen tablecloth. All the women were commenting on her well-set table. Ted looked on smiling. Angela tried not to be distracted by his charming self.

"We should make her a lace tablecloth!" Sophia said with enthusiasm after the first course had been served.

"That's a grand plan, Sophia!" Olivia said with equal verve. "We should add those to our inventory as well. It is most certain that the West is in need of more lace tablecloths." Olivia's grin was delightful and Angela couldn't help but smile.

"Here here. I second the motion." Ted added.

Angela laughed a little.

Nearly everyone was in a jolly mood when Amelia surprised them all by speaking too.

"You know ladies, I quite agree. With Angela's lovely house and table service could be the example of what young women should be doing in the West, which is to make a civilized home. We should certainly do our part to dress the ladies' tables with lace." Amelia smiled and gave a glance around.

Somehow at that moment, everyone knew the dinner would be a success.

Angela was so pleased; she couldn't explain how fully she needed to know she had Amelia's approval. She didn't want to need it. But after so much rejection in her short life, she wanted to make a fresh start here and now.

After assuring them that she would be glad to purchase the tablecloth a huff was heard by both Sophia and Olivia.

"Oh, hush now!" Olivia stated with a wave of her fork. "I should think as your soon-to-be family we should be able to provide that. For my part in it all that I ask is to come and stay here often. I have heard people raving about your neighbor Corinne and her fields in bloom over the summer months. Personally, I cannot think of anything grander than sitting in one of those rockers on your porch some mornings, seeing the purple fields in bloom."

Angela laughed and nodded. "I indeed am looking forward to that as well."

"Speaking of soon-to-be..." Olivia looked expectantly to Ted, who had been remarkably quiet throughout the meal. "When are you two planning to be wed?"

Ted coughed a little and a blush stained his cheeks. "Well, if I have a say I think it should be soon."

Angela met Ted's look and got lost in his eyes for a moment. She had so much she wanted to talk through with him. They just didn't get much alone time with his busy schedule.

"Well, I have a thought on the matter." Amelia spoke up. Both Ted and Angela snapped their heads to look at Amelia.

Angela felt her stomach flop in distress. *Was this going to be the beginning of more trouble?* She wondered.

"Yes, Mother?" Ted said with signs of tightness in his tone.

"I think perhaps you should wait a year or two." Amelia said with a tight-lipped grin. "Since you both are so young."

The table grew silent for a long minute.

"I can take that into consideration Mother. But I think Angela and I should decide together what would work best for us." Ted said, trying hard not to sound pushy. It only worked a little.

Angela gave her warmest look to Ted, hoping he knew that she appreciated his remark.

"No offense taken, just my thoughts that you both should court a bit longer, to be certain you know each other's personalities well enough." Amelia said, her tone was soft this time around. "I married young myself, and perhaps under the bloom of new love I did not..." Amelia paused, seemingly from emotion from the rise of pink in her cheeks. "Well, you both are of a quiet nature, which to me is a good sign of being thoughtful and level-headed. But I am just concerned from my own marriage that had I known better I would have taken more time to get to know my spouse-to-be a little more thoroughly."

Ted nodded quietly at his mother's reasoning.

Olivia joined the conversation herself a moment later. "I can attest to that myself, though I am not certain that two years would be necessary for these two. But I could say with my own experience that understanding the man or woman you are to marry with a greater knowledge of how they act in many scenarios and circumstances cannot be harmful." Olivia spoke softly.

Angela couldn't help herself but take these women's advice. She knew that both of them had ended up being unhappy in their marriages, in different ways. She felt even more that Ted and her needed more time together. She felt the loss of Dolly from her household even more. Feeling a sense of guilt, thinking about Dolly as a built-in chaperone. It did make things easier. Now living alone she would have less opportunity to have Ted over for dinner and visiting. She had to always think of her reputation.

"You are both sharing from your own wisdom. I cannot help but respect that." Angela said finally. "I do wish to make a good marriage, even if I know my heart belongs to Ted, I want to be certain that we are working within God's plan." It had been hard to say. As hard as the prayers she offered to God often, giving her plans over to Him.

There was a genuine peace that settled over the rest of the evening. Everyone involved somehow felt a little closer after the shared speeches. Angela said goodbye to them all after dusk with a renewed sense of family. Somehow if they all kept communicating she knew it would get even stronger.

Chapter 7

Oregon City

The rains came harder for the next several days in the valley, the river flooded their banks and the roads became awash with thick mud, making travel into or out of town impossible by wagon.

Families had their challenges to keep their essential garden plants protected from the heavy rains that worked hard at crushing the tender leaves and small stems that were only just starting to break free from the ground.

In town the Willamette River was swollen and the rapids quite dangerous for the men who were tasked with getting their logs downstream.

Business was halted for everyone who wasn't required to be outdoors, people were shut up in their homes.

It was a week before the sun came out after a long week of dark grey skies. With the sun came more challenges.

Grant's Grove

Corinne was wiping down the dirty glass windows of her greenhouse when she heard the sound of a wagon on the path behind her.

She waved and smiled when she saw her father John, with Marie behind him, Cooper jumped up to a standing position and waved happily. John had a handsome two-seater, all shiny black with big wheels with black and red trim. The small dog, Pepper, danced behind the wagon and then with a yip ran toward Corinne to say hello.

Corinne put her cleaning rag down and gave the dog a proper scratch on the head.

"We are heading to town, hope we can get through the mud, we are low on a few supplies." John spoke loudly so she could hear him.

Corinne nodded, "You be careful!" She blew a kiss and smiled as they left.

Corinne was back to cleaning the windows when she heard the horses distinct squeal of distress. Corinne dropped her rag again and ran toward the sound, hearing yelling and her father's voice yelling out "Whoa..."

Corinne rounded the corner of her lab building and saw the wagon on its side. Corinne felt her heart leap with dread.

"Father, Marie!" She yelled out and searched for her family.

Cooper ran from behind the wagon, his face was awash with fear. Pepper was barking. Corinne ran around the other side of the road, her father was bent over, kneeling on the ground.

Corinne was breathing heavy from her run.

"Marie is stuck." John said harshly, his brows slanted in worry. "Find baby Abigail!"

Corinne gasped and her eyes searched the area, the thudding in her chest painful as she jogged and ran around frantically.

She saw nothing but the shrubs along the creek, she ran down the creek bed, her feet slipping in the mud and she slid down fast and splashed into the deep water of the creek, the water ran past her quickly, the fear of the baby being lost a constant thudding in her mind.

"Please Lord Jesus, help me find her!" Corinne spoke aloud as she pushed herself to a standing position.

A moment later she saw a bit of white cloth in the water, she ran and sloshed forward.

Her hands found the fabric, it was a white lacey dress, and she pulled and realized it was her half-sister Abigail. Corinne had the girl in her arms a moment later.

Corinne wept as she carried the small child, sweet and pale to the side.

"Breathe baby girl!" Corinne coaxed. The child's eyes were shut.

She placed the girl against her chest and patted against her back, hoping to dislodge any water from the girl's lungs.

"Please baby." Corinne begged, she thought of how a baby was born and held the baby over her knees and patted her behind a few times, then her back.

Corinne sobbed as she held Abigail, too young to die. Corinne felt desperate and she gave another whack on the girl's back, harder than she had intended.

A small gurgling cough escaped and Corinne started, she kept patting the baby's back to encourage more coughing.

"Good girl Abbie." Corinne laughed when her sister coughed again, her baby cheeks were turning pink.

Abigail began to wail and squirm a moment later, certainly angry over the rough treatment.

Corinne did not even know that John and Cooper had joined her, her mind so focused on the baby in her arms.

"Thank you Lord!" Her father's voice was in her ear. Corinne felt a small sense of relief.

"Is Marie safe?" Corinne said as she handed the upset child to her father.

"She is sitting up. She got a bump to the head and some scrapes. Angela sent Warren for Doc Williams." John said thickly. He had tears in his eyes.

Corinne nodded and stood, and noticed she was soaked through with water and mud all over her, it mattered very little in that moment. She climbed the side of the creek bed, and walked around the bushes toward the capsized wagon. Marie was crying on the side of the road.

Corinne ran to her side and kneeled. "She is well, Abigail is safe."

Marie looked up to Corinne. "I heard her cries and was so thankful." Marie pulled Corinne close and kissed her stepdaughter on the cheek.

John and Cooper had joined them. John sat on the muddy ground beside his wife and they sobbed together. Corinne felt her own emotions rise, now that everyone was safe and let the warm tears flow down her own cheeks in relief.

Angela was next to her after a minute with a few blankets, she wrapped one around Corinne and placed a kiss on the top of her head.

Angela convinced them all to come to her house and get cleaned up, since hers was the closest.

John sent Cooper to fetch some clean clothes from their own house and then Corinne's and they all walked to Angela's porch up on the hill. John held a blanket and both Corinne and Marie changed out of their muddy clothes. Angela was there to wrap them up in blankets. Angela took baby Abigail and soothed the baby, who had begun to calm after her ordeal.

They all were clean and dry inside Angela's parlor a few minutes later. Everyone was relieved that the accident had not caused any permanent damage, but everyone was shaken. It was amazing how a split moment could change your perspective about things so quickly.

"The wagon wheel sunk into the mud along the bank." John said seriously once they were all settled. "The horses reacted and leapt forward, I think the axle broke." John rubbed his hands together in a comforting motion, they were still shaking.

"I should have reacted quicker. My shoulder got caught on something when I tried to jump out." Marie said softly, she bent her head forward, a few more tears dripped from her cheeks to the brown blanket that was around her.

Corinne ran a hand around Marie's shoulders to comfort her. It has happened so quickly for her as well.

"Does your head hurt?" Corinne asked.

"It is throbbing a bit." Marie admitted. Her hand went to the back of her head and she winced a little. "I have a pretty decent lump from when it struck something." Marie dropped her hand and looked to her husband. The look that was shared between the husband and wife was easy to understand. They were both so thankful that no one had been killed.

Cooper arrived with dry clothes and Angela had hot water ready for everyone to clean up a little before they redressed.

Doc Williams arrived by horseback and was pleased to see that no one had any serious injuries. Baby Abigail was declared to be fine, they would have to watch her for any signs of a cough or if any bruises showed up but her little body showed no signs of distress but for a tiny harmless scratch on her leg.

The doctor was a little concerned about Marie's bump but told her to take it easy for a few days and send for him if her vision has any spots or she gets nausea. John and Cooper had a few superficial scratches but they all were safe, they had a lot to be thankful for.

Everyone agreed to tell the neighbors to stay off the roads until they were drier. It was not worth the risk in a wagon.

By the time Doc Williams left the clouds were back and more rain was falling.

Dolly Bouchard

Dolly was feeling more comfortable now in the saddle after more than a week of travel. She was feeling confident that she could maintain the pace the men set before her. Each day they traveled a little further, mostly spurred on by Gray Feather, who was eager to make a good time back to the Wind River Mountains on the other side of the great mountain range.

Dolly was grateful for the valley they were currently traveling through, being an easier route. Her fears of traveling along thin mountain trails, trusting the able-footedness of her mount had been hard for her. Her stomach had been in knots for days through a particularly dangerous stretch a few days before. When she could look down from the side of her horse and see the cliffs drop off to treacherous rocky ravines had not been anything she had ever experienced. She prayed so much as she rode. Going through every single loved one she knew, praying for them to be blessed. It helped her passed the time.

She felt a bit like a prisoner with Gray Feather holding so much power over her. He was hostile at all times with her. Resenting her with every look in his eyes.

Bright Son was always trying to be a peacemaker among them, but it did little to help.

She kept repeating a bible verse to herself often when she wanted to lose herself into despair.

Fear thou not; for I am with thee: be not dismayed; for I am thy God. Isaiah 41:10

She missed her bible on these long days, but it was too precious to bring along the rough road. She thought of it often, the appearance of it where she had left it. Sitting on the bedside table at Angela's house.

Oh Lord, help me to get back to that place. She prayed often.

Dolly made efforts to enjoy the scenery, the rugged mountains being a kind vision. Each peak majestic, and making her feel the grandness of the world God had created; she felt reaffirmed in her faith in the Lord, He was *her* Lord now. Not to be thought of as white-man's God anymore. She was certain of that. It did not matter what these men thought of her faith, her time alone with her thoughts had made her more certain than she had ever been. Dolly was thankful for that part of this trip. But in every other way she wanted more and more to turn around. She wanted to be home. With every mile she traveled she was feeling further and further away from the life she felt called to.

Galina Varushkin

Galina's shoes were ankle deep in mud, and the warm rain splattered against her shoulders as she walked home from her work at Angela Fahey's house. They had to dry the clothes in an upstairs bedroom again, and it had taken many trips up and down the stairs. The clothes were always stiff when they were dried indoors. The sunshine and breeze did a better job, and they were both disappointed with the stiff clothes at the end.

The heat of the rain was an odd feeling and Galina struggled in the slick mud. She had been warned the night before that she would have to do more work in the field that afternoon, rain or no.

She heard the rumble of thunder in the distance and wondered absently if she would have the company of lightning as she worked. Her hair, dark and wet stuck to her head and the water ran into her eyes, irritating her further.

She looked at her shoes, now completely wet and coated with mud, the wet substance had overtaken the top of her shoes and it was sneaking down into her socks and shoes, rubbing her ankles abrasively.

The roads were a deep sloppy mess, and the grass was spongy and waterlogged, both treacherous and slippery under her. She knew it would not improve as she looked up to the dark clouds looming over her.

"When will things get easier, Lord?" She prayed aloud. The splat of the fat raindrops on her head was a funny sound and she smiled in spite of herself.

The trees around her said nothing in reply to her prayer so she trudged on. Knowing that God heard her was enough.

Corinne Grant

Corinne saw the sun shining through her bedroom window just after the sunrise. She felt a little cabin fever after the long rainy week. Knowing she had to break free from her confines and go to town. Lucas was getting dressed across the room. His dark brown trousers told her he planned to be in the fields, battling the mud to break more ground. He had busily kept at it all week, meeting with Mr. Varushkin, the man he had hired to clear out trees for future fields.

"You be safe out there today." Corinne warned him. She enjoyed the smirk he gave her.

"Don't fret so much, wife." His boyish grin made her heart warm.

"You know I cannot help myself." Corinne propped herself up on her elbows to see him better.

"I was thinking of going into town today." Corinne said with a hint of a mystery in her tone.

"Oh?"

"Yes, my husband. I was hoping to settle this matter of a certain mysterious feeling I have been having. I can stop to get our mail as well."

Lucas let his boyish grin slowly fade. "You riding horseback?"

"Yes, but with a promise of a walking speed. Absolutely no risk-taking." Corinne said with all seriousness. She would never take that for granted anymore. Not with the great desire she had of having a family.

Lucas's worried look softened. "I trust in you." He said in a soft tone, just above a whisper.

It was still their little secret, a promise of hope between them, that their dream of a family may have taken fruit again.

Corinne got ready, getting her long riding skirt, split up the sides to make for easier riding, she pulled out several petticoats, making certain they were all free from mud. This last week had been a busy laundry week with everyone's clothing taking extra time to clean.

Usually Violet and the young Galina, whom they hired to help with laundry, did it together, but Corinne had joined in to give a helping hand.

Her own work in the laboratory had been stunted since Dolly had left. She felt a sense of loneliness and sadness when it came to her work. She was frustrated with herself for letting her mood drop. She knew she was doing work that God had gifted her with, but somehow her drive had dropped off. She was in a funk of sorts.

Lucas was always encouraging, saying that with every change comes a new challenge to rise to it. He had said something wise the day before.

'You are grieving the loss of your partner; it will take its course. Then you must rely on the Lord to help you continue on.'

The phrase played over and over in Corinne's thoughts as she went through her morning routine.

She visited with Violet over breakfast, realizing that her housekeeper was also in her own grieving. It gave Corinne a new understanding, and perhaps a little levity on her own moods. Violet was adjusting to her new reality as a widow, just as Corinne must with her own situation.

The ride into town was longer than normal, Corinne taking her time to allow her horse Clover to take the river crossing and travel at a slower pace then normal. She figured that Clover was certainly confused over the restrained pace. She vowed to have Lucas give Clover a decent run, since Dolly was no longer here to do it. Clover was too spirited to be resigned to always being restrained.

Corinne settled her horse at her father's barn in town, where he rented horses and conveyances. The man running the place promised to brush and care for Clover for the day.

Corinne headed toward Doc William's place and saw Persephone sitting outside the office with her daughter. Corinne immediately had a grin for the mother and daughter. The little girl was giggling on her mother's lap with blond curls and rosy cheeks. Corinne noticed immediately how much that the girl looked like her mother.

"You are the most beautiful pair on this sunny day." Corinne said sweetly.

Persephone laughed and smiled warmly. "You are the sweetest thing, Corinne. How are you this fine day? I am so glad for some sunshine."

Corinne could not have agreed more. As the morning continued on the warm spring day felt more like summer.

"Well..." Corinne could not hide her excitement. "I had hopes of talking with your husband today if he is free. I am thinking that I may have news to celebrate over."

Persephone gasped and gave her squirming daughter an embrace in her own celebration.

"You really think so?" Her light blue eyes were instantly glassy with tears.

Corinne could feel the love shining through this woman's eyes and she felt emotions fill her as well. Corinne's throat got tight, so she just nodded.

"I cannot tell you how much I have prayed for you, sweet sister-friend." Persephone said, her sincerity so evident.

Just knowing how her church family had been so supportive had been such a soothing balm to Corinne since she had had her miscarriage more than a year before. But also knowing that her church friends and family had been praying for her and Lucas to be blessed with another chance to have children was more than special. She was flooded with thankfulness. That was real and she thanked God for it.

"I believe my husband is just reading, it has been a slow morning. He just got in a shipment of medical journals. He could probably use a break from his nose being buried in those books of his." Persephone laughed and was rewarded by her daughter joining in. She was trying to be just like her mama.

Corinne took a moment to caress the blond curls of little Charissa, the blond curls were soft as silk and warm from the sun. Corinne closed her eyes and felt a prayer rise up from her heart.

Please, Lord, bless my baby.

After a few minutes with a few more happy and hopeful tears she went inside with Persephone, they would tear the good doctor from his books for just a few minutes.

After visiting with the doctor Corinne felt at peace. He had agreed with her assumptions and he wanted her to visit him again in a few weeks. But he was certain that she was pregnant again. Corinne could keep her active lifestyle as long as she took more opportunities to rest. She was elated.

She walked to the post-office with a secret smile. Her petticoats swished as she walked, she knew she had a little bounce to her step today.

She settled the mail for her family and her father's household in her bag and set off for the Quackenbush fancy goods store. She wanted to look around, even if she didn't have anything in mind to purchase but she also wanted to see if Clive was around.

She felt such a kindred affection for Clive Quackenbush, having gotten close to him as a sort of spiritual grandfather on her journey west. He had been such a great leader to so many people, and Corinne had leaned on him for a lot of support during that tumultuous time.

Millie Quackenbush was at the front counter and Corinne said her hellos. Glad to have small talk, catching up on the community comings and goings after a long week of being housebound. Millie was happy to discuss her grandson and the announcement they received by post that she was going to be blessed again with another grandchild. Millie was in good spirits and Corinne felt a closer bond to her than she had in the past. Millie was very active in her church and community but she sometimes could get a bit forward in her opinions. Corinne had learned to forgive Millie's little outbursts, it had been a good test of her faith and forgiveness after her first miscarriage when Millie had blamed Corinne's choices to have worked outside of the home and perhaps it had been God's judgment to take her child. It had been a hard blow. But after apologies and a healing time Corinne and Millie had mended their feelings.

"Will you be visiting Gabe and Amber this summer?" Corinne asked politely.

"Amber and her little one are coming next month. Gabe will be running the store, but promises to come and stay a few days when he can." Millie was glowing in her anticipation.

Corinne couldn't help but congratulate her. She felt such a joy in her own heart that she blurted out her news.

"I will be so glad to meet Amber, I am also expecting a blessing myself." Corinne felt a blush burn her cheeks.

"Oh Corinne!" Millie exclaimed. She reached out a hand and placed it on Corinne's arm across the counter. "I have been praying for you to be blessed. I hope you know that."

Corinne could see that it was sincere and it made her grateful that she had shared.

"I only just confirmed it today. I told Lucas of my suspicions though."

Millie teared up and laughed with pure joy. "I will wait until church service on Sunday to share with the church, so you have time to tell everyone." Millie grinned conspiratorially. "Thanks for telling me though. A blessing shared..." Millie paused and put a hand over her heart. Corinne understood what she was saying. By sharing it, Corinne had shown the real forgiveness from Millie's harsh words from before.

Corinne nodded and looked around the store. She found a few baubles and a good selection of buttons and bows that she could not resist in buying, some for herself and some for her stepmother Marie who was extremely gifted at sewing.

As she purchased the items Millie gave her a recommendation.

"Be sure to stop by the lace store a few doors down, they have been making the most divine collars and shawls." Millie nodded with emphasis.

Corinne felt that the idea was an inspired one, since she hadn't been in the store since before winter. Certainly they would have a larger selection of lace goods available. She carried her bag of goodies with her as she walked a few doors down. A new sign hung out along the edge of the front porch railing.

Lady Greave's Lace

Corinne could see the start of landscaping out front. Her shoes thumped up the wooden stairs and the front door was changed, now being all etched glass. It was a beautiful entryway. It reminded her of a quaint shop she could have seen in Boston.

The bell rang and Olivia Greaves greeted her, whom she had briefly met before at church.

"Welcome Mrs. Grant." Olivia said politely.

"Oh, thank you, please call me Corinne, I have heard nothing but amazing things about you from Angela." Corinne smiled politely.

"Well Corinne, please feel free to look around. I do believe we will be having some fresh tea brought out in a few minutes. Feel free to join me, I would love a chance to get to know you better." Olivia was bubbling with charm and Corinne could not resist.

After agreeing Corinne took a few minutes to look over the lovely selections. Lace in every delicate and delightful form was on display: from bonnets to shawls, doilies, collars and gloves. Corinne stood over the selection of lace ribbon and could not resist grabbing a few spools, she knew Marie could use this lace to add a few touches to her Sunday finest. Lace could always spruce up a dress better than anything else. Her new baby sister could perhaps use some lace for a dress or two as well. Corinne was enjoying the shopping and felt herself on the verge of a splurge. She saw a lace christening gown for a newborn and felt obligated to inspect it thoroughly. There was something that melted her heart about the little white gown. She knew she would be back for it.

She gathered her selections and settled them on the counter when Olivia invited her to join her for tea and treats.

"I love your selections!" Corinne exclaimed and meant it, sincerely.

Olivia smiled her thanks.

"I feel like we are finally getting settled into our routine, and lace production is going so very well." Olivia poured the tea from a silver tea set.

Corinne thanked her and took a sip.

"Oh, this is good." Corinne was enjoying her day of freedom from being cooped up.

"I just had dinner at Angela's." Olivia shared.

"Oh, good. She is becoming a good little homemaker and cook." Corinne said.

"Yes, I feel badly about her losing her houseguest. She is feeling the loss of her friend Dolly."

"Oh yes!" Corinne's brow furrowed. "I think we all are, my prayers are with Dolly constantly."

Olivia placed a hand on Corinne's as a show of support.

"I am concerned that Angela and Ted will not be able to court with her gone. I was contemplating something but as Angela's friend I can ask if this would be a worthwhile plan."

Corinne was interested so she encouraged Olivia to continue.

"I was thinking of asking Angela if I could have an extended stay with her. So she could see Ted more, with the safety of her reputation intact."

"I think that is a grand plan, but aren't you the one who runs the store here?" Corinne asked, trying to think through any issues.

"I was thinking of hiring someone to run the counter, that way my sister can still focus on the lace-making. I will also be able to do work from Angela's home during the day, and keep Angela company." Olivia offered.

"I do know that there are some women at the boarding house that would be very responsible. With a nice dress they would do a fine job of greeting customers. With a little help from your mother and niece to answer questions." Corinne said, thinking it sounded solid.

"Oh that is grand!" Olivia chewed on her lip. Her eyes sparkled with her excitement. "That may work out in the long run as well. I have been missing my time with the bobbins. I feel a bit wasted at the counter."

Corinne smiled in agreement. "I feel that way about my business as well." This woman understood what Corinne did about having a calling.

After a moment Corinne got an idea. "If you make up a quick advertisement I could take it over to the Orchard House for you. Then I can talk with Angela tonight. Do you have an idea of when you would like to come? The roads are impassible with a wagon. So everything you bring would need to be by horses or mules."

"I would love to start as soon as possible. I am up for a little adventure." Olivia grinned mischievously.

Corinne let a giggle escape, Olivia was a charmer. Corinne was looking forward to getting to know her better.

The plan was laid and Olivia wrote out a short advertisement for a counter helper. Corinne made her purchase a short time later and made quick time up the street to deliver the notice.

Corinne and Lucas made time to visit and have dinner with Angela. Violet went to dinner with Marie and John Harpole.

Angela was overjoyed with Olivia's plan and was so pleased for a long visit with Corinne and Lucas. Violet had sent a note with Corinne for Angela, though, promising a long visit and a day of baking together. It was something that Angela and Violet did together every few weeks.

Every morning Angela said a prayer for Violet. She knew that it was going to be a little while before Violet was her joyful and bubbly self. Angela prayed for her heart to heal.

Corinne and Lucas were excited to share their pregnancy news and Angela felt somehow that she was going to be an Auntie, if not by blood than certainly by spirit. She felt that Corinne was so much like a sister, her child would always be treated like Angela's kin.

"Auntie Angela will certainly be there to spoil the baby as much as possible." Angela clapped her hands in delight.

"We certainly hope so." Lucas said with his own joy radiating from his eyes.

Once dinner was cleared and they had only just settled in Angela's sitting room they were surprised by a knock at the front door.

Clive was waiting there with a bag and a twinkle in his eye.

"Ha, I braved the mud to bring you gifts from afar!" Clive declared.

Corinne squealed and ran toward the door to give her mentor a squeeze. Clive was more than willing to share hugs with some of his favorite gals. Lucas waited to the end of the women's affections before the handshake was shared.

"Your mail, milady Red." Clive bowed and handed over a handful of letters. Angela settled them on her dining table. Certain she could read through them at another time.

Clive shared his adventures over the last week.

"A raccoon has decided that my fireplace is a lovely place to make a home. I thought I would die for certain trying to save the critter." Clive hissed out a few laughs. "I was standing in the pouring rain, my poncho failing ever-so-miserably at keeping the rain off once the wind had blown off the hood. I used my bare hands to try and scoop him out of my chimney top."

"On the roof in the rain!" Corinne gasped.

Clive laughed out again. "Not my wisest move, I know. But I didn't want to roast the poor fella with my fire. Better he or she make a better nest elsewhere. I finally caught the critter by the tail. I escaped falling off the slippery roof by only the slightest margin." Clive seemed pleased to see the shocked look from the females and the chuckles from Lucas.

Corinne and Angela took turns making Clive promise to be more careful in the future, both secretly knowing that it was a futile wish.

Corinne and Lucas shared their good news and Clive couldn't have been happier. After the congratulations he immediately asked to say a prayer.

"Lord, please bless these good folks. Knowing you always love us as your children, I ask for your divine protection over this little life." Clive's words filled the room and peace settled in as he finished his prayer. "May your wisdom and mercy cover this family as they are blessed with the greatest calling you can give us, Lord. To parent a child in the love of the Lord is the greatest occupation on earth. May you be glorified with this new life... Amen."

Both Corinne and Lucas wiped away tears and a group hug followed.

Corinne changed the subject as they sat down, thinking Clive's input would be advantageous.

"Clive, Olivia Greaves is wanting to come stay with Angela for an extended visit. Angela has agreed." Corinne asked. "Maybe you could help her get her things here, Clive?"

"Oh, certainly, I would never tell her no." Clive said with a smile.

Corinne explained her plan of getting help at the counter, and being able to be here and work on lace and be company for Angela.

"I would appreciate her company, but I have a feeling that she is coming to be a chaperone." Angela lifted an eyebrow suspiciously.

"Well, yes, but she wants to be certain your courting is not interrupted. But I think her desire to be a great Aunt is the main concern. She told me that Ted's mother has asked you both to consider a long engagement." Corinne shared.

Angela sighed. "Well, yes. I am praying about it, but haven't had much alone time with Ted to discuss it at all."

"Well, then dearie. Let's get his Aunt here soon." Clive chimed in. "I can help get whatever she needs here. I always have a few tricks up my sleeve."

Angela couldn't help but smile. Clive could make anything happen, she was sure of it.

Corinne and Lucas arrived home late, happy to see Violet was sitting by the fire, humming and knitting.

"Did you enjoy the visit?" Corinne sat next to Violet.

"Yes, I stayed just for dinner and came home, had some amazing time reading my bible and praying. I feel better than earlier." Violet's eyes were pink-rimmed but she was not looking as distraught.

"That is good. Do you need company?" Corinne asked.

"No, I am good, I feel like heading in to bed soon. I have Galina coming tomorrow for more laundry."

Corinne gave Violet a side-hug and went to join Lucas at the table. He had a kerosene lamp lit and was reading through agricultural journals.

Corinne grabbed the stack of mail and settled in to catch up on correspondence. She saw a letter from her Auntie Rose, another from the Boston greenhouse, the bottom of the pile was a thick letter from Sacramento with the bold letters of CAPRON at the top left corner.

She decided to begin with that one.

> "Dear Cousin Corinne,
>
> My daughter Megan has put in her heated request to make a visit with you in Oregon territory and after settling into Sacramento sufficiently I have acquiesced to her request. I understand from my mother, Ms. Rose Capron, that you are happily married and settled in nicely with a home and business

of your own. I send my deepest wishes of every happiness to you and your husband. I also wish to send greetings to your father, I am feeling inspired to correspond with him as well, feeling a kindred sense of belonging to the same worthwhile goal of settling the West with our own business ventures. I wish us all to have a prosperous future. I agree that every responsible man, and woman in your case, that has the gumption within them to bring their skills, faith and hard work to the West to make it a blossoming and worthwhile land. It is my goal to live as such.

With agreeing to allow my daughter to come for a visit I shall be sending her by ferry in a short while. With a telegram sent when the ferry departs.

I will agree to send her with a warning of her headstrong nature. She has promised me to be on her best behavior, but I give you full permission to return her at any time. A telegram is all I need and I can send a man to fetch her back. She has reached the age where she can be considered nearly a woman but not the maturity to match, I am afraid. I am hoping that between time with you and your father's household she can learn to settle her flighty ways.

My prayers will be with you. I hope to make a visit to your fine part of the country within a few years. I have heard much of the beauty of your Valley and hope to see it for myself. As I have fallen under the spell of the West and its many beauties here to the south of you I wish to see more of it.

I hope to be sending a telegram soon. Be sure to keep me abreast of Megan's activities and my thoughts will ever be with you.

Sincerely,
Arnold Capron

Corinne shared the contents with Lucas and they both were pleased and mildly apprehensive. They discussed it at length and knew somehow that it would be a challenge. Her cousin's claim that his daughter had 'flighty ways' made her nervous, she knew that God perhaps will allow some good to come of it all.

She sorted through the pile of mail and saw that a telegram had come a few days before. The ferryboat had left already with Megan.

The rain had kept them away from town. Whether they were ready or not, the gal was coming.

Corinne took a deep breath and settled herself. The winds of change had come.

Chapter 8

Angela Fahey

Angela stomped through the mud as she carried the bag of feed for her chickens to the coop. Her hired hand Warren had offered to carry it but Angela had insisted. He had been busy with gathering materials for a fence project.

I am more than capable of carrying feed. Angela thought stubbornly.

As the mud squished around her boots she realized how silly she must look. This spring has been so wet. The heat of the day was already feeling like mid-summer and the bugs were making their presence known. Her hands were full and the mosquitoes were swarming around her face.

The mud was six inches thick or more in spots. The ground must have been waterlogged and the moisture had nowhere to go.

By the time she was finished filling the seed barrel Angela was a mess. Olivia was arriving later in the day and she wanted all of her chores to be done so she could relax and enjoy a day or two of visiting before her schedule was busy again. Now she was certain to add a pile of muddy clothes to her chore list. Even if she didn't want to scrub them immediately she would certainly need to get them into a warm and sudsy soak. Once mud dried it was so much harder to get out.

Angela spoke kindly to her chickens, hoping somehow the bug swarms didn't bother them. She sprinkled their open area with some fresh hay to keep the wet mud down and put the feed down into a trough that Warren had built. Spreading out feed had been impossible in the wet weather and they had adapted.

Angela made her way slowly back up to the house, her skirts were heavy and wet with caked-on mud and with every effort she made the fabric would swing and slap against her legs with wet smacks.

Angela believed that every grumble she muttered on the way to her backdoor was well deserved.

Olivia Greaves

Olivia wore a short-sleeved dress as she prepared to leave. The heat of the afternoon was beginning toward a swelter. Every window in the townhouse was open, with thin cheesecloth to allow for some airflow but to discourage the mosquitoes.

She had everything she would need for a stay at Angela's knowing that she could ride back to town on any nice day to visit with her sister and niece anytime she liked. Olivia was so very excited though, she was thrilled to have a chance to be out of town for a while, to enjoy the quiet and to get to know Angela better. Angela was a darling young woman and Olivia was certain that they would get on swimmingly.

She knew that her heart was tripping along at an accelerated rate for more than one reason though and she fought hard within her self to stop acting like a young girl.

Clive was coming by to take her and her things to Angela's home. After making up her mind to pursue Mr. Quackenbush romantically she had failed to do more than say greetings of 'hello' or 'how-do-ya do.' She had been on better terms than that with the man but now that she had her cap set on him she had reverted to more formality. It was a silly female habit and she was angry with herself for it. But didn't know how else to overcome it.

With a promise to try harder she shook her hands out to get rid of her nerves.

Sophia came to fetch her a few minutes later. Olivia grabbed her leather satchel and walked arm-in-arm down the staircase with her niece.

"You must promise to let me come soon." Sophia pouted becomingly. She had been sad ever since Olivia announced her plan. Sophia had stayed a few days with Angela before but the thought of missing out on an extended stay made her moody for a few days, feeling left out.

"I certainly will, dear Sophie." Olivia gave her a kiss on the cheek when they reached the landing of the stairs. "I will hopefully be back to visit for an afternoon in a week or so, I will convince your mother for you to come and stay. You stay in her good graces until then and she may even agree."

Sophia took the warning well and nodded her agreement.

The ring of the front door opening got their attention and Sophia grabbed up a few bags to move closer to the door.

"Greetings, fair ladies." Clive removed his hat and gave a slight bow. His actions were polite but always had a sense of whimsy about them. Olivia couldn't help but admire his wit. She had a hope that she had outgrown blushing over a man's attentions.

"Thank you again..." Olivia started.

"No trouble at all, Ms. Greaves." Clive interrupted. He gave her a grin that triggered a stomach flip.

She could have chosen that moment to tell herself to stop being a silly schoolgirl. But she didn't. If this was the way it would be around Clive then she would just have to face it, head on.

"Well then, kind sir. Let us depart." Olivia said with a wide smile. She knew it was one of her best features, hoping that he would notice.

Olivia said goodbye to her sister, who had remained very quiet all day. She was not happy about the change but had to let her sister make her own decisions.

Sophia gave Olivia a long hug and shed a few tears.

Clive carried Olivia's belongings to the front porch and took a few minutes to load the pack mule he had brought along.

His horse had room for a few bags as well.

Olivia soon was boosted onto a gray speckled stallion, with a sidesaddle, and he glided into his own saddle with the ease of a young man a minute later. Olivia could not help but watch his every move.

Dolly Bouchard

The sky was a startling blue above, not a cloud to be found. Dolly braided her hair that had come loose, pulling the strands out and re-braiding with the ferocity she wanted to use in pummeling Gray Feather.

She watched Gray Feather work in front of her, his squinty eyes focused on his task of scraping dirt through the pot that had been used for their meal.

Dolly felt her anger rise up, her heart pounding in her chest. Gray Feather was impossible to please and after she attempted to speak to him again about treating her with respect she was greeted again with insults.

She had stepped away from the campfire and had found a large rock to sit on. She watched Gray Feather and Bright Son gather up their belongings, preparing for more travel.

She wanted to cry, she truly did, it was not her average response to confrontation and she knew she was near her breaking point. She wasn't sure she had been this angry for so many days in a row in her life.

She closed her eyes and took a few deep breaths. The air was warm and she focused on the sounds of nature around her. The birds and the wind calmed her. She wanted to let her heart be peaceful before she began to pray. After a minute of breathing she spoke softly, in a whisper in English so if the men overheard they could not understand.

"Father God, I need your wisdom and patience more than ever." She prayed. "I know I am your daughter, and you know my every trouble. Be close to me, Oh Lord, help me to walk in your wisdom. Keep me safe from harm as I travel away from the place I feel is my true home. I have so many regrets. Please give me peace in the company of these men. Or show me what I should do."

Dolly kept her eyes closed and listened to the sounds around her a little longer. Feeling like she was alone with God, no matter who may be nearby. They would be entering into a more barren landscape soon, and she felt the intensity of it creeping into her companions. The travel would become more difficult, and Gray Feather was losing his temper faster than ever.

Olivia Greaves

Olivia thoroughly enjoyed the ride to Angela's house, seeing the change of scenery quickly after getting out of town and into the rural landscape. The difference a few miles made. Spring was more apparent when she had the open views over the fields. The bluffs to the east of the valley were green and lush after all the rains.

Clive informed her that he had seen a black bear out with her cubs the day before. Olivia had delighted in the mental picture that formed.

"I hope to see more wildlife during my stay." Olivia said cheerfully.

"That is almost a certainty. The deer are active now that the rains are gone." Clive smiled as he spoke. Probably pleased to have an eager listener.

Her evening visits with Angela had mostly been after dusk, and seeing the Valley in the bright sunlight was better.

"I sure hope these bugs go away soon." Olivia said after swatting the pests away.

"I have hope fer' that as well. But I have a feeling with all the mud and standing water that we are in for an extended visit with the pesky things."

Olivia nodded and could see that Angela's house was just up ahead. The creek was swollen with water and the sides had washed away a bit. Clive led her around to the footbridge that had been built by Corinne's house. The horses could cross on it.

"The neighbors around here are considering hiring a stone mason to build a bridge. This crossing there is not looking good. May not ever be passable again in its current state."

"I didn't know there was a mason in this area." Olivia was surprised.

"Well, ya just never know what may be lingering around the corner in these parts." Clive turned and gave her a wink.

She just shook her head and laughed whole-heartedly. She could listen to him talk all day.

They reached Angela's house in short order and he helped her off of her horse. Olivia stood next to him as he unloaded the mule that had been tied behind his mount. She could have gone inside but she wanted to wait.

As he bent to pick up a few bags she halted him.

"Clive, I wanted to ask a favor of you."

"Well, I am certain I would do anything for the likes of someone like you."

She gave him a no nonsense look before she continued. "I would like to keep working from here. If you could stop by to check on my lace work every week or so. I would make sure to have tea on and you can keep me entertained with a visit or two."

Clive rubbed his chin thoughtfully. "I would never suspend the chance to visit with two fine ladies."

"You better not be using such sweet words with all the ladies in these parts." Olivia eyed him with mirth and a little suspiciousness.

"Well, Ms. Greaves, I may be a sweet-talker by nature. But I would never be anything but a gentleman. My mama done raised me right." He gave her another wink.

Olivia let out a slow sigh. It was very hard to tell with Clive when he was having fun or being serious. Time would have to tell.

Angela joined them by the front doors and gave an embrace to both of her guests. Clive unloaded the bags and helped himself to a cup of coffee that Angela had made fresh. After Clive made sure that Olivia was settled in he made a promise to come by every few days.

"I am going to hold you to that, Mr. Quackenbush." Olivia lifted her eyes over the rim of her teacup and made sure he saw her.

Clive chuckled softly and gave her a nod.

"I will Ms. Greaves." Clive waved. "I will go visit with my pal Earl Burgess for a bit before I head back to town. You let me know if I have forgotten anything."

Olivia pursed her lips and nodded. Once Clive had closed the door behind him Angela gave her a surprised look.

"Well, now what is that look for?" Olivia tried to take on the countenance of calm serenity. She was pretty certain that it did not work as well as she had hoped. Angela was soon grinning and rubbing her hands together, scheming.

"Ya know, Olivia, this may be a very entertaining visit." Angela couldn't stop her laughter from bubbling out. "He has shared with me his proclivity towards strawberry blonds."

Olivia huffed and then joined into the laughter. "That is interesting to know."

After the initial teasing Angela took charge and they got to work getting her things settled in. Her bag of bobbins, pins and lace-making utensils were put into the sitting room and the rest were carried up the stairs.

Chapter 9

Corinne Grant

Corinne waited in town all morning, she sat upon a stool at the general store and chatted with Clive, JQ and even customers as the morning passed. She shooed the bugs away that wanted to eat her to shreds. She had only known this kind of bug infestation when she had been on the Oregon Trail. Though this time it was the blood-sucking mosquitoes instead of the flies.

The steam whistle sounded just before the noon hour. Clive and Corinne walked to the livery across the street and quickly got the wagon to the landing zone for steamships just north of town. Several wagons were ahead of them. This was always an exciting time for folks, knowing that shipments and letters came with every ship. Communication was sought after more than gold here in the wilds of Oregon territory.

"I do hope my cousin had a decent trip." Corinne said to Clive distractedly.

Clive nodded and patted her shoulder with his free hand. The horses clopped along and kept a steady pace. The trip was made in a half hour. The area was flooded with people.

Corinne saw the crowds and searched for any young woman in the crowd. She wished she had a better idea of what Megan would be wearing, she had been a little girl the last time she had seen Megan.

A slow drizzle started and after a minute Corinne was wiping the moisture from her face as it threatened to drip in her eyes. She saw no person who looked the part of a young lady and she felt worry rise up in her belly. What if some foul play had occurred?

Clive gestured to Corinne and they both stepped down from the wagon perched and began milling through the crowd.

"Looking for a Miss Capron!" Clive started announcing.

Corinne sighed with relief realizing that Clive was so very thoughtful. She gave his arm a squeeze as she followed his lead through the crowd.

He announced it several more times until they made it to the exit ramp of the steam ship. There were still many people wandering the deck and Corinne wondered if they would have to go aboard to search.

"I am here... I am Miss Capron." A voice broke through the hubbub of the crowd.

A pretty gal with dark blond curls came to the edge of the deck aboard the steamship and waved, her other hand held a parasol more suited for blocking sunshine than any kind of moisture.

"Good to see you cousin!" Corinne stated warmly and waved back. "Is all your luggage aboard yet?"

"Yes, my father's steward came with me as a chaperone and guard dog. He wouldn't allow me to leave the ship or his protection until I was handed off into your hands." Megan huffed a little after her speech and glanced behind her and said something that Corinne could not hear.

A moment later a tall man came closer to the railing and gave Corinne a nod.

It was a few minutes later that Megan Capron and her many trunks were unloaded off the ship. The porters made quick work of loading the wagon full of luggage.

Megan made her way down the ramp like a queen, her flounces and taffeta far more elegant than necessary. Corinne wondered why Megan had not chosen to wear more practical travel clothing but kept her thoughts to herself.

Then Megan's steward joined them and handed a purse and a letter to Corinne before he even spoke a word.

"Thank you." Corinne muttered and looked to the items he handed her.

"I am handing her protection into your hands. Here are funds for her care. The instructions from her father are in the envelope. I must be back aboard." He nodded to Corinne and then turned to Megan. "Please behave gal." His voice had a hint of tenderness but his face was very stern.

Megan complained about the steward the entire way back to town.

"He was so very taciturn for almost every moment. Until he decided I was being ridiculous or mis-behaving. I do swear that he believed that I was a flibbertigibbet." Megan huffed.

To Corinne her huffing was already getting on her nerves. The heat, the bugs and the waiting had put herself into a mood so she had hoped that that was also the reasoning behind Megan's mood as well.

Corinne could hear the southern accent in Megan's speech and it made her a little homesick for her own years in Kentucky. She sounded a lot like her own mother, from Corinne's memory. In voice though, not in her speech.

"Well, Miss Capron, welcome to Willamette Valley. I just know you will love your time here." Clive said politely. Perhaps trying to steer the conversation to lighter things. "Do not mind the heat, this is warmer than usual for May."

"My goodness I hope so!" Megan removed her lace fan from her reticule and fanned her face vehemently. "Oh, sweet cousin Corinne, please read the letter to me from my father. I am simply dying of curiosity. Steward wouldn't let me see it the whole trip."

Corinne did not want to start on the wrong foot with her cousin, but she had no intentions of reading the letter to her before reading it herself.

"Oh no dear Megan, my head aches from the heat. I will read it at home with my husband Lucas. I have no desire to focus just now." Corinne felt the excuse was a lame one but Megan seemed to comply with her answer. "Your room is made up for you, there is shade on that side of the cabin so your room should stay cool throughout this heat wave."

Megan nodded with her pretty chin. Her dark blue eyes took in everything around her. "It sure seems like wild country out here."

"It is, young lady. But with enough civilization to keep the frontier growing. Not quite as fast as Sacramento to be certain." Clive said with his usual jovial humor.

"Will we be staying in a hotel in town or heading out right away?" Megan asked, her tone wasn't as sweet as it could have been.

"No, Megan, there is no grand hotel here. We are just a few miles out of town, but we will be driving through to get where we are heading." Corinne said. She was suddenly feeling tired and she wanted to be back at her cabin.

Megan made another of her huffs and let the topic drop. To Corinne's relief Megan seemed content to watch the road and scenery around her for a short while.

"Oh my, your cabin is so rustic." Megan said as they crossed over the footbridge in front of Corinne's home. They had left the wagon at the road, and the trunks would all have to be carried over the footbridge. The creek was not as high but the crossing was still pretty muddy.

Megan tisked as they got closer to the cabin.

Corinne knew her cabin was impressive and larger than most in the area. But her joy was robbed by the look on Megan's brow, like she was entering into squalor. Corinne was trying to keep her patience and judgment in check so she headed toward her home without saying a word.

"My father built us a brick townhouse in Sacramento. Had the bricks sent by ship before we even arrived. It looks straight from New York. It is quite a showpiece." Megan declared while wiping at her skirts.

Clive stopped and gave the young lady a slow look, his face frowning, he pursed his lips and made a clicking sound before he looked to Corinne. He was carrying a few of Miss Capron's bags a few feet behind them.

Clive and Corinne made eye contact for a brief moment. He wordlessly communicated to Corinne that she had her hands full with this young lady. They need not say a word.

"I see Lucas by the barn, and the young boy. You can ask for some help with the heavy trunks." Corinne placed a hand on Clive's arm. He placed a kiss on her head and then scooted the women to go inside.

Corinne took a deep breath, slightly regretting to have to take this young spitfire into her peaceful home. She shook her skirts loose and led Megan inside. Hoping the young woman could find her manners sooner than later.

Violet was at the door to greet both of them. Her smile brighter than it had been in weeks. Corinne was glad to see it.

"Welcome Miss Capron, please make yourself comfortable." Violet backed away from the door to allow them the space to walk in. The rag rug was at the front entrance for them to get the ever-present mud from their feet.

"Let's get you out of the bugs and the heat. It may be a big job to keep them out of the house." Violet smiled to Corinne.

Megan looked around the room without speaking. It was bright with all the big windows, rare for cabins on the frontier.

"Your room is set up for you. I will have your trunks sent in, we can get you unpacked later if you wish." Corinne stated, watching the young woman for any more signs of attitude.

"That would be grand." Megan said politely.

Corinne sighed in relief.

"This is Violet Griffen, she takes care of the home and the cooking while I work. She is like family to Lucas and I." Corinne smiled and placed her hand affectionately on Violet's shoulder.

"Nice to meet you Violet." Megan gave a head nod in respect.

The evening had moments of politeness off and on throughout the first day. Corinne and Lucas walked her over to visit with John and Marie.

Marie was recovering well from her bump on the head, and baby Abigail was giggling while playing with her brother Cooper, seemingly in perfect health. Corinne prayed a silent prayer of thankfulness that her baby sister was safe and well.

Everyone greeted Megan with enthusiasm; Megan was polite with everyone, even the new housekeeper, Celia Tally that John had hired from Orchard House.

Corinne had not met her yet so she took some time to talk with the mature woman, learning that she had a young son.

Marie fussed at having a housekeeper too, "I do not have a job like Corinne, and I should be fine for preparing my own meals and cleaning my home." Marie smiled and gave a sly look to her husband. "But I must say, Celia is a delight to have around here, especially now when my head still aches when I do too much."

Megan piped in. "An elegant woman should always have help in the home. Certainly your husband provides for you well enough, the least you could do is run a gentile home. In my experience, a woman ages so quickly when toiling over demeaning tasks."

Every adult gave Megan an astonished look, no one seemed to know how to respond.

"I don't necessarily agree with your opinion, young lady. But I am glad to know that my wife can rest and recuperate." John Harpole spoke gently to his niece. There was much more that could be said on the subject but they all dropped it. They had time to get to know the opinionated young lady and would get their chance to get to the bottom of her strange opinions.

They went back to Grant's Grove at dusk and Megan was ready to retire early, travel somehow wears a body out.

Lucas and Corinne read through the letter.

> Dear Corinne & Lucas Grant,
>
> I do pray for you as you take care of my headstrong daughter, Megan. Her actions lately have given myself and my wife several headaches over the last year. We ask you to join with us in trying to prepare our Megan for adulthood, she has many things to learn about life that she has not absorbed. Perhaps some time on the frontier will teach her more about the realities of life.
>
> Please send word if her actions are causing you any grief. I have provided funds for her well-being and care. Her mother and I have said many prayers for her to develop some wisdom.
>
> Be blessed and in good health. We look forward to steady correspondence.
>
> Sincerely,
> Mr. Capron

Chapter 10

Dolly Bouchard

"I would like to return to Oregon." Dolly said finally after a few weeks of traveling. She knew Gray Feather would not understand her reasons but she had the hope he would respect her wishes.

"You made a vow to your chief." He said while eating, his mouth sucking and chewing on his food loudly.

"I will honor my promise to the Chief in my own way." Dolly said with a firmness that was fleeting.

"I was promised you as a bride." He said and stopped his chewing.

"I made no promise, I don't believe we will suit well." Dolly searched for the words that would explain without insulting him. "My beliefs are different from yours."

"Yes, you have abandoned the ways of your people."

"I am half Hopi and half white." Dolly said with a little more resolve. "I have found a peace with the white community."

She was not prepared for his fist as it struck her cheek. He had leaned over so fast. She didn't even put up her hands to defend herself.

Bright Son was yelling but Dolly was on the ground, stars bursting across her eyes. She saw black for a moment and then her vision returned with a rush of sharp pain in her cheek.

"We do not hit our women." Bright Son said with more vehemence than she had ever heard from him.

"I do not want to hear from you. You would have allowed her to disrespect me and the Chief's wishes." Gray Feather spat back, his face a picture of the warrior he was.

Bright Son said nothing more.

"Bluebird you are of our tribe, how can you want to abandon those who have raised you?" He asked her from his standing position, he watched her try to stand and did nothing to help her.

"I am not of your tribe. I was in your tribe but not *of* it. I feel a calling to a new people." Dolly stood, holding her throbbing face. "I will find a way to honor my commitment to the chief but you are not my father or my keeper." Dolly was braced for another blow for her speech.

"You disgust me, your allegiance to the pale and thieving white people is a sign of your weak-mind. The chief was foolish to have sent you to learn, you are un-trustworthy for the task. Perhaps if he had sent someone more worthy we would now have someone OF the tribe who would help the tribe. Instead you will be a disgrace to those who fed and clothed you." He turned away and spoke to his companion, who was looking gray faced and disturbed, but silent. "She would be better off dead like her mother than to have dishonored her memory as she has done." He took two steps and pulled a hatchet from his bag and held it up.

Both Dolly and Bright Son yelled out, Dolly took four steps back and tripped over a rock. Her backside hit the ground and she scrambled back in an awkward crawl.

"I enjoy the fear in your eyes, Bluebird, if I were Chief I would rename you as a cowardly weasel." He laughed with frivolity in his voice. "Do not fret Bright Son, I will not take my hatchet to her today. But if she does not come along tomorrow I will not make such a promise. I am a warrior, not meant to deal with a weak-minded woman. If she cannot honor our tribe, then our tribe would be better off without her." He threw his hatchet and it hit the center of a nearby tree, proving he knew how to use the weapon. He laughed again as he saw Dolly's eyes filled with tears.

Dolly stayed where she was for a long while, ignoring the food she had been eating. Fear coursed through her and she prayed fervently for guidance.

Gray Feather was muttering about her being a weak female but Dolly was no longer listening. She knew she was in danger. She had no way of knowing how she would, but she had to escape. She would plan and pray.

She calmed her heart and stood again, she promised herself to remain quiet and cooperative until she could figure out what to do.

That night Gray Feather had her lay next to him near the fire. He tucked the blanket around her and settled the horse's harness over her legs. He gave her a glare for a solid minute letting her know that he knew if she moved that the harness's noise would wake him.

The night air was cold and she huddled under the furs and blankets, shaking and thinking. She had felt trepidation from the moment she had seen these men in Angela's yard. Why had she not listened to the small voice within her? She felt so foolish and trapped now.

Grant's Grove

The first few days of Megan's visit had been trying but not hugely eventful. Corinne had lost her inner patience with the girl's judgment of everything that she didn't find elegant.

The hot weather with intermittent rain showers kept everyone busy and irritable. Everyone, no matter how much effort they put in, were covered with bug bites wherever any skin was exposed, even indoors.

Corinne put dried lavender in every windowsill, and had fresh handkerchiefs with drops of lavender on them for everyone to tuck into their clothing to encourage the bugs to look elsewhere. It was not a foolproof plan but it did help.

By Megan's third evening with them she had been bitten so much that she approached Corinne to get help.

"I have tried ever so hard to stop scratching, I know you mentioned that it could spread infection if I do. But I must confess that I am miserable." Megan pouted and sat next to Corinne in the settee. Corinne took pity, she gave a glance to Lucas who tried to hide his smile.

"Let me see what I can do for you."

Corinne went to her bedroom for a minute and got out a salve. Corinne settled next to Megan and pulled out her jar.

"This has witch hazel bark, beeswax, aloe vera juice, lavender and tea tree oil from Australia." Corinne didn't mention the beef lard, almost certain that Megan would turn up her nose at having such an ingredient on her refined skin.

She let Megan smell the jar once it was open. "That smells very nice."

"It should help take the itching down, and any swelling or infection that wants to creep in." Corinne instructed kindly, she loved helping people and enjoyed seeing the respect in the young woman's eyes.

Corinne showed her how to apply on a swollen bite on Megan's arm.

"Feel free to apply this where necessary." She closed the jar and handed it over to Megan. "Just bring it back once you are finished."

"Thank you so much, Cousin. I can see why Auntie Rose spoke so highly of your skill." Megan said. The comment surprised Corinne, after having never heard such things from her critical Aunt in Boston, but Corinne let the comment go.

Megan scooted off to take care of any bites that needed privacy to deal with. Corinne gave a look to Lucas and he raised his eyebrows with shock and humor. Corinne chuckled.

"Little Miss Priss has a few things to learn." Lucas said softly, for her ears only.

"Indeed." Corinne said, trying to smother a grin.

"I may try and make some more of that salve in the laboratory tomorrow. I'm sure Doc Williams is seeing plenty of patients with swollen bites. Children are the most prone to ignore the instructions to avoid scratching what itches." Corinne said, changing the subject.

"Good idea." Lucas encouraged. His hands were busy, putting together a new harness.

Corinne sat back in the chair and watched him work, enjoying the quiet moment. Megan came back into the main room a few minutes later. She had the jar in hand.

"I think you should know, cousin. I think your housekeeper is ill." Megan said with a grimace.

Corinne jumped up from her seat.

"I could hear her retching..." Megan shook her head in distaste.

Corinne moved with efficiency toward Violet's quarters. She gave a knock. She waited a few moments before she heard Violet answer.

"You may come in." Violet's voice was weak.

Corinne saw her lying on her bed, with her hand on her belly and curled up, obviously in pain.

"How can I help you, Vie?" Corinne knelt beside the bed. Corinne took Violet's hand and felt her trembling.

"For now... just water." Violet said softly.

Corinne felt Violet's forehead and felt the heat of a fever present. Corinne fetched a pitcher and a glass to place near Violet's bed. Corinne poured, feeling a slight tremble in her own hands. She was worried to see Violet looking so pale.

"I don't want you near me Corinne." Violet said after she drank a few sips.

Corinne gave Violet a hurt look.

"The baby..." Violet explained and then cringed and pulled her legs up tighter toward her middle.

Corinne let out a sigh.

"I will take precautions Violet, I don't want you to worry." Corinne took a towel from the washbasin nearby and soaked it with water. She folded it and placed it on Violet's forehead.

"That is good." Violet closed her eyes, enjoying the cool rag.

Lucas joined them a few seconds later with a wooden bucket. He placed it next to Violet's place on the bed.

"Clive just came by. Yellow fever is making its way through town." Lucas said gravely.

Corinne gave him a worried look, he took his wife's hand and squeezed it.

"We will get you through this, Violet." Lucas said with conviction.

Corinne prayed that he was right.

Violet Griffen

Violet was ill a few more times that night. Corinne couldn't sleep well, so after helping Violet through the worst of a bad bout of stomach illness she lit a kerosene lamp and settled in at the dining room table and made a list of things to send Lucas to get from town in the morning.

She had seen that the local apothecary had feverwort before. She knew that that could bring down fever. She listed the things she had used to make that bug salve, knowing not to waste a trip to town. She wanted to make certain that Doc Williams knew about Violet's condition.

Corinne pondered the many medical journals she had read over the years. Knowing some scientists were questioning whether bugs or vermin were the cause of Yellow Fever. With the increase of hot wet weather had brought an enormous bug population to the valley. Corinne said a prayer for Violet, worry digging a pit in her stomach.

Corinne knew that Violet had only 3 to 4 days to beat this before the illness could turn more deadly. Corinne tried not to let her thoughts turn to morbid but she was so very concerned. Violet was more than just her housekeeper. She was a sister in Christ, she was a dear friend. Corinne also wondered if while in mourning over the news of her husband's death she would be more susceptible to the deadliest form of Yellow Fever. When the skin turned yellow and the body simply shut down.

Corinne did not want to watch someone else die in her lifetime. She had done it too many times. Corinne carefully ripped the page from her notebook for her husband to use in the morning.

She began a new page, writing down everything to feed Violet over the next few days. Within an hour Corinne was spent and she closed her journal and latched it. She peeked in on Violet and saw that she was asleep. She replaced the now hot rag with a fresh cool one on Violet's forehead. She placed a few drops of lavender on a handkerchief by Violet's face, knowing the scent was more than just a perfume, but had healing properties that could help a body fight off infection. Corinne based her life's work on this humble service. She prayed that this fever would not be too much for them to fight.

Corinne never went to bed but cuddled on the settee and fell asleep with prayer on her lips.

By noon the next day Lucas had been to town and back with supplies and news.

Corinne was roasting garlic cloves in the oven, to spread on bread toasted with butter knowing how well garlic was good for the body for fighting off any flus or infections. She had warmed up some chicken broth that Violet had canned over the winter months by boiling a whole chicken, with vegetables, then straining it all through cheesecloth. Her broth was delicious and Corinne knew that getting Violet to drink any of that would be helpful.

Corinne took the feverwort and the bonus of white willow bark the apothecary had included, and then made some tea by boiling the dried leaves. She added some honey and went in to visit with Violet. Violet was pale with dark circles under her eyes, her blond hair stuck to her face and shoulders from the long night of sweating.

"I brought some tea for your fever. I cannot promise that it will taste good but the tea should help with your fever and the aches." Corinne settled the brown mug on the table next to Violet.

Corinne took the back of her hand and pressed it to Violet's brow. Her skin was hot to the touch. Corinne sighed but kept her expression calm.

"I am boiling... I know." Violet said weakly and took a long minute to push herself up into a sitting position. Corinne leaned over her and helped.

"Once you drink that cup of tea and it stays in then I will bring in the broth and garlic toast."

Violet nodded a little, then took the offered tea. Violet closed her eyes as she sipped from the mug.

"The honey helps a little. But it is nearly dreadful." Violet only grinned for a half a second but Corinne was happy to see it.

Corinne had Lucas bring in an extra chair and Corinne sat with Violet off and on throughout the day.

Lucas came back home every few hours from his duties around the farm, to check in on how Violet was fairing. Corinne didn't have much good news, after the tea Violet felt sleepy, then she had sipped on broth, which brought on more retching and pain.

Corinne felt discouraged watching Violet suffer but knew that the illness would have to run its course.

Chapter 11

Grant's Grove

Corinne had caught a nap before the supper hour. Violet had fallen asleep again, which Corinne was happy to see. She kept her hydrated with the feverwort and willow bark tea. That seemed to do a little good, allowing for Violet to rest.

Corinne awoke when she heard the front door of the cabin, Corinne sat up in the settee to see Megan walking in, wearing a bright and flouncy dress that belonged at a party, not for a walk outside.

Megan's face dropped when she saw the frown on Corinne's face.

"I went to visit your father today." Megan said with an amused look on her face. Her cheeks were pink.

"I don't feel comfortable with you walking off the property alone, your father trusts me to keep you safe." Corinne said, trying hard to keep her patience in check.

"Am I not allowed to talk with my own uncle?" Megan said, her forever innocent expression growing wearisome to Corinne.

Corinne sighed and let the conversation go. Corinne stood and walked across the room, trying to decide whether she had the energy to be angry with Megan. Corinne grabbed one of her medical journals.

Megan watched Corinne and knew that she had worn her down. "I was insulted by the ranch hand. It was very disturbing." Megan sighed and sat in an armchair.

Corinne had sat herself on the davenport. "Oh? Perhaps that is why I wanted you to stay close to *our* cabin." Corinne was losing her patience.

"It was the man that Uncle John called Rey." Megan interjected, not caring that Corinne didn't really seem interested in hearing a story.

"Reynaldo Legales is the Ranch manager and a very good man." Corinne said bluntly.

"He was not crude in any way." Megan asserted. She paused and smiled coyly. "He just warned me to get on with my business and called me a little girl."

Corinne did look up from the journal she was pretending to read to avoid conversing with her cousin.

Corinne's raised eyebrow was enough to keep Megan talking.

"I had visited with John outside the house. Marie wasn't feeling well so he didn't want to disturb her. Afterwards I had wanted to watch the horses run in the yard. The men all so busy training and feeding them. They were breaking in a horse. Quite fascinating! My father's farm has dull cows. I have grown so tired of cows." Megan slumped her shoulders dramatically. "Anyway, I had only been there a few minutes before a few young men came to the fence to say hello. That Rey fellow had come around and bid them back to their work. They had only paused for a few minutes."

Corinne gave Megan a pointed look but chose to stay silent.

"He said, 'Go home, little girl and leave the men be.'" Megan said with her eyes slanted with her disgust over his words. "I said back to him that I was seventeen and a woman grown. He had the nerve to say that 'A woman doesn't need to entice every man from his work to prove she is a woman.'"

"He has a valid point. What was your purpose going dressed as you are to visit a horse ranch?" Corinne gave Megan a once over.

"You and that ranch hand imply that I had some sort of agenda." Megan put her innocent mask back on.

"Megan, there is so much you need to learn about the world. Can you not find some task to lose yourself into? In your letters you talked of painting. I have yet to see you bring out your paints or even a charcoal to draw anything. Do our mountains not inspire you?" Corinne asked and saw the momentary expression cross Megan's face, a look of irritation and then boredom.

"I need to go check on Violet. Please Megan, use your time here to find some peace. Must you always search for trouble?" Corinne was exhausted and her tone with Megan had crossed over into impatient and bossy. Corinne stepped away feeling a little defeated. She prayed for better words to use with her cousin.

Dolly Bouchard

The sound of something hitting the dirt beside her head startled her. There was a sliver of moon showing and in the darkness she saw the shape of Bright Son kneeling next to her.

The young man had his finger over his lips to warn her to keep silent.

She felt the heavy harness being lifted from her legs slowly. *Bright Son was removing it!* Dolly thought to herself. He was playing a dangerous game if he intended what she thought he was.

A long agonizing minute passed until she felt that her legs were free. She turned to see that Gray Feather was still sleeping. He was so very close, how would he react if he woke?

Dolly grabbed the blankets and slowly removed them and slid her legs out. Her heart was beating fast in her chest and she had to work hard to keep her breathing shallow and soft. Gray Feather shifted a little on his bedroll, Dolly held her breath and halted her slow escape from the blankets. She stayed still for a count of thirty before she moved again.

She was kneeling next to Bright Son a moment later. He wordlessly pointed at an object on the ground. In the dim light she could see it was a thin knife. She picked it up and followed Bright Son's steps away from danger.

He grabbed the pack that Dolly had been laying on. It had her extra clothes and her journal.

With her feet in moccasins her steps were close to silent through the loose gravel of their camp. She followed the shadow of Bright Son's form for what felt like an eternity. The night sounds were muted in her head competing with the thudding of her heartbeat.

Bright Son finally stopped, Dolly nearly collided into him.

"You go south, there is a river. Use the river until you come to the mountainside." He spoke softly. Dolly scooted close to him to listen to his whispered words. "There is a cave you should find by morning. Only light a fire if you must, none for two days if you can." He handed her the pack she had been using as a pillow. He handled several items to put them inside another pack and handed it to her.

She could barely tell what they were by sight, but she felt some sticks, something that felt like round metal, a length of rope, and a tin cup. She packed it all slowly and carefully in her pack, trying desperately not to make a sound. He then handed her a thick wool blanket tied with rope around the middle and a loop to tie to her back as she traveled.

"Why are you helping me escape?" Dolly whispered, she could not help but ask.

"You do not belong with us, Gray Feather is not safe to travel with. He is punishing you for something the chief has done. He intended to marry someone else. The chief instead gave her to his own son as a bride. Then sent him away to do this errand. I believe you are in danger." Bright Son told her. He placed a hand on hers in a gesture of friendship. "You stay in the cave tomorrow. I will leave a trail for him to follow. Let me do one thing..." Bright Son took his own knife and bent down to Dolly's feet. With a quick flash he cut a thin strip of cloth from the hem of her dress. "I will make certain that he thinks this is you. I will try to convince him after a day or so of searching to give up and go back to our tribe. The Chief will not be happy, and many will talk, but I do believe you will be safer where you were. If you want to come perhaps Mr. Quackenbush could bring you safely back to the Shoshone, he is a good man."

Dolly knew what he was saying. It was the same thought she had had many times a day since she had left her home. That she could come back when she was ready. Not when forced.

Dolly was amazed how well Bright Son had planned this escape for her. She had been plotting every night but had not thought of a way to get away from Gray Feather without him being able to find and torment her more.

"I somehow believe I belong in Oregon now. I will make it up to the chief. Please tell him that I will return one day to share my knowledge." Dolly was relieved to see him nod.

"Will you be able to survive?" Bright Son asked.

"I will never forget how to be in the wilderness. No matter what new direction my life takes." Dolly said, though she was suddenly very afraid. The night was dark and the cold air was stealing her warmth away.

"There is some dried beef in those things I gave you, enough for a day or so, I hope you remember how to use the sling."

Dolly could see the smile light across Bright Son's face. "I was always a good shot when I was young." Dolly said, remembering the days of her youth, chasing down birds and squirrels, competing with the boys over who had been the best shot.

Dolly saw Bright Son stand tall. He turned to look and pointed Dolly in a direction to go.

"I will lead Gray Feather away. But be careful about leaving spore to follow. He will be very angry."

She thought about everything that had happened so far this evening and knew God was watching out for her. She knew he would not understand that. "I will be careful. Thank you Bright Son." She whispered, hoping he felt the sincerity.

He took her hand and squeezed it once and was gone a moment later, silently about his own journey.

Dolly watched his steps for only a minute, realizing that she would not speak her native tongue with anyone again for a long while, if ever. The enormity of her freedom hit her like a heavy stone. She was free to be the woman she wanted to be, but she had to survive the journey home, on foot. She turned back to face south, she saw a tree in the distance that she would use to keep herself on course. Before she took her first step she knelt on the ground and thanked God for her freedom.

She found the river after an hour of walking, lamenting the loss of her horse. Her eyes had grown accustomed to the low light. She didn't hear much beyond the sound of her own footsteps. The area was pretty flat with only a few scrubby trees to speak of. She knew she would have to backtrack over the mountain range to the west of her to find more fertile grounds, but that was tomorrow's problem. She sat on the ground at the river's edge. She put her hand in and felt the chilling cold, this was definitely from snow melt off in the mountains. She took several mouthfuls and forced herself to stop. The cold water would steal her warmth away. She was glad for her sturdy wool coat. It was dingy from the weeks of travel and sleeping so close to the ground but she was not worried about her appearance at all. She turned to face west and stepped a few feet away from the river's edge. She didn't want to step in fresh mud and leave footprints if possible. She was counting on Bright Son to do his part to steer Gray Feather away from her trail, but she had to be cautious herself.

She walked through the night, praying the entire way.

Ted Greaves

Ted Greaves listened to the talk about Yellow Fever as he went through his morning errands. He had stopped by the grocers, getting a few things for his mother's pantry, hearing from several people who were arguing over what caused Yellow Fever, one gentleman saying it was surely a judgment from God for sinful living, another swearing it was carried by the bugs, another in tainted water.

None of this talk helps anyone. Ted thought to himself. He felt frustrated over those who spoke of such things. He was a practical sort. However the fever was spread it was most important to take care of your friends and neighbors.

When he had picked up the mail at the post office he overheard the plans of the town council meeting that was scheduled for the day. With over forty people showing signs of the fever they were considering closing down all public activities. The word quarantine was whispered around.

He delivered the mail and pantry goods back home and planned to ride out to visit with Angela and his Aunt, glad to have the freedom to spend time out there, now that his Aunt was there to chaperone. Ted felt that inner frustration return, wanting to be married and finally settled in with his bride.

The warning from his mother to take time for a longer engagement had given him a moment's pause, wanting to be reasonable and listen to her advice. But another part of him felt that waiting was going to be difficult. He was hoping that he would get a good chance to speak with Angela today. They needed to talk over these things.

The day was already scorching hot and the sun hadn't reached the midway point. He wore longer sleeves despite the heat to keep the bugs from feasting on him. If some were to be believed that the bugs carry this deadly fever than he did not want to risk catching it. People were scared and had every right to be.

Ted rode toward Angela's house on horseback....

Chapter 12

Violet Griffen

Violet's head burned, the hottest part being right above her eyes. The aches throughout her body were intense, it was always the worst right before the nausea forced her over the bucket. She wallowed in her bed, kicking off her quilts one minute to shivering with aching chills the next.

She was so weak now after two days of fever. She wanted so desperately for the heat to leave her body. The cool cloth felt so very good. Corinne mentioned that she could give her a cooling sponge bath. Violet had finally agreed to it, she dreaded the lack of privacy, thinking of the mortification she would feel at being so exposed. She had told Corinne that she would like the bath in the morning. Perhaps on the third day her fever would break. Violet tried to pray and not worry but her mind was so muddled, she couldn't put many coherent thoughts together in any kind of sequence. She knew that another day or two should finish this dreaded illness, hoping it did not go further, knowing that after four days that she could be in danger.

A dark part of her wondered if that would be best. After learning of Eddie's death she knew a part of her wanted to join him somehow. The weakest part, she mused. She was still young and she had fought through too much in her life to give up on her fight to live.

Her dreams the last days had been strange and horrible. A part of her enjoyed the good memories, but her body and mind worked together with the fever to take her dreams to places that she preferred to leave buried in the past.

She could see the small two-room cabin, next to the watermill, the sound of the gristmill ticking and the swooshing of the stone on the grain. The days of pounding out bread dough with her mother, seemed like almost all of her childhood was at the table in the kitchen, baking bread and learning from her mother. Those were the good memories. The darker parts of her dreams were the parts that drove her into the despair that she remembered so well. Her fever made her body hurt so badly, it translated so well into the old nightmares.

Violet woke the first night several times, in pain from the nausea but the worst pain was the memories. How many years she had spent to push those thoughts away? She cried weakly and curled tighter under her blankets, allowing the chills to decrease only to fall back into the same dreams.

Her father's voice, stern, yelling at her laughing younger brothers, who were always underfoot when their mother left for town to sell bread, every Monday and Thursday.

The boys would always be put to work outside chopping wood. They had to make two piles as tall as their heads on those days. Her father's attempt to keep them busy. He would take them out behind the cabin and tan their hides if they came in before the task was done.

The dark deeds done in that cabin replayed through Violet's dreams. The threats and secrets kept in those dark years of her life. She had prayed so much and dedicated her life to God so many times since those years to erase the shame and horror of what had been done.

Violet woke again and again from her fever dreams, wondering if she should die from the shame more than the fever. She prayed pitiful prayers before she bent over the bucket again and again, feeling her energy leave her so violently.

She lay in her bed, not asleep but spent and lost in thoughts and memories. Reliving the day she turned fifteen, her heart pounding as she sat with her mother and told the secrets. Knowing the threats her father made, hoping that her mother would protect her.

Tears ran down Violet's cheeks, surprised she could even still cry over the memory, replaying the shocked look on her mother's face, then the accusations that came forth. Being called a liar and a charlatan, wicked and deceitful.

Her father taking off his belt to punish her for her 'lies'. Her mother's screams for her to leave. After everything that had been done to her, the accusations felt better than the secrets had. She had lived in fear enough.

She had run up the ladder to the loft and pulled it up to keep her father away. His hoarse yells had scared the boys and they cried holding onto their mother.

She packed a small bag and escaped through the narrow window, jumping to the ground and twisting her ankle a little when dusk fell. She left a note to her mother and brothers saying goodbye.

She had run all night through the woods and out of town. She knocked on the door of the Whittlan's, the pastor and his wife took her in. Mrs. Whittlan and Eddie were the only people in the world who knew her darkest secrets.

Violet heard Corinne come into her room, Violet looked up to see her friend in the candlelight.

Corinne set the candle on the table, and handed her a mug full of the warm tea. She had grown use to the flavor, it was earthy and not very pleasant but the benefits outweighed the unpleasantness, usually giving her a break from the aches.

"You look worn down, Vic." Corinne said soothingly.

"Yes, bad dreams." Violet said with a whisper.

"I am sorry friend." Corinne knew there wasn't much she could do to help with that. "It is a few hours before dawn, I can get a cool bath ready for you by then."

Violet nodded and realized that she was embracing the idea.

"I will wash your hair too, being clean helps a lot to keep your spirits up." Corinne said practically.

"That sounds good." Violet finished the last of the tea and settled back under the covers. Corinne went behind Violet on the bed and massaged her shoulders as she had done several times that day. It was so comforting to be touched with so much kindness. Violet felt more tears escape as she accepted the gesture.

She felt a calmness come over her. She thanked God for her friend and prayed for healing as Corinne massaged the ache from her shoulders. It was the closest thing to peace she had felt in several days.

Soon Corinne left her to sleep as the tea did its work. She slept peacefully until dawn, the dreams stayed away.

Dolly had found the cave after walking all night. She settled in and wrapped in the blanket and slept. The morning was quiet, the area barren of trees. The creatures were still as she slept. The cave was small and had no scent of animals. Bright Son must have been planning to help her for a few days, looking for a safe place for her to rest before she began her escape.

As she woke she walked out of the cave, the sun was in the western part of the sky only a few hours from escaping over the rocky hill she had found shelter on. The brown rock walls of the cave were cool to the touch as she peeked around the edge of the cave, looking for any sign of Bright Son or Gray Feather.

Dolly planned to stay put. She pulled out the two bags she had, the one from Bright Son and her own and spread out everything she had.

In her own bag she had, flint, a piece of refracted glass, a few small squares of char cloth, bits of dried beef, a round tin of mints, a hunting knife, a thin rope, a bottle of lavender oil from Corinne, her journal, a small tin with a sewing needle and colored thread, bandages and a glass jar with ointment, a few shirts, a tin cup, and two long skirts.

She looked through the bag that Bright Son had given her, finding many practical things, a hatchet blade, a sharpening stone, a wool blanket, a bundle of tinder, a wound piece of braided string, a small cooking pot, a leather bag canteen, and another hunting knife with a sharp thin point.

She was thirsty, the leather canteen was mostly dry, she didn't want to risk a fire at this point, and the stream water was a little too silty to drink. She undressed to her underclothes and washed in the stream though, to keep herself clean. Bugs were drawn to unwashed humans, it was always wise to keep as clean as possible.

Dolly ate a few bites of the dried beef. Making plans for the next day to get over the hill to more wooded territory, she needed to plan her journey, whether she would take a southern dip for the next few days and try and find a different route over the mountain range that would take her back to Oregon City. She wondered if she could find part of the wagon trail. She could easily follow their path over the mountains, the wheels leaving good tell-tale signs of their direction. She was pretty certain that she wouldn't be able to handle the terrain she had traveled with Gray Feather and Bright Son without a horse. She knew that beyond the ridge to the west she would find better terrain, they had been in that valley for days, and she knew that she could make shelter in the trees and fish in the streams. She had a daunting task before her. She prayed for the strength and wisdom to survive. Wondering if she had been foolish again, had leaving Gray Feather and Bright Son been the wrong decision? She knew that Gray Feather was angry and volatile, but would leaving on her own lead to her own death?

She took a deep cleansing breath, determining herself to focus on surviving and not worrying over every unknown. She would do what she could, use her wits to survive and get back to her real home.

She repacked her belongings, being able to fit everything including the spare cloth bag into the bag that Bright Son had given her. It had a good angled strap that she could use over her back to carry.

Dolly went back into the cave when the sun went down. She had miles to travel the next day. She wanted to be rested. She was thankful that the blanket was warm and the nights had not been as cold as they could be. She would survive the night without a fire.

Galina Varushkin

Galina bent and scooped up another basketful of her family's laundry in the early morning light. She had been awakened before dawn to scrub the clothes. Her father had put up posts in the yard, and hung a wire-line to dry the clothes. She felt an inner rebellion rising up over his orders to do the family laundry after she had been washing laundry all week for pay. Her hands were sore and chapped from all the water and soap her hands had been subjected to. Today was the only day she had to rest her hands from that kind of labor. Her mother understood but her father was the loudest voice in the house again.

His absence for months last year had been a blessing and a curse to her family when he was in California. They had nearly starved and were living in a thin tent when the winter snows threatened. Galina remembered the first earnest prayer she had ever said was when she was certain her family would die of exposure. That very day had brought their salvation, and a new home, with the help of the local church outside of town. To her it had been the proof her heart needed to know that God was there. Her father was harsh and had left them to fend for themselves. But God had never abandoned her.

Galina took a deep breath and prayed for a peaceful heart. Knowing the resentment she carried around for her father had burrowed in deep. She did not like feeling that way.

The cabin was crowded later that morning with her younger brothers playing rowdily. Her mother looked a little ragged, she scolded for them to go outside numerous times as Galina helped her mother with dinner preparations. They took turns holding the youngest family member, Radimir, who was cranky.

Galina shifted Radimir on her hip. His grabby hands tugged at her and pulled on her hair, Galina tried to be patient and find something for his little hands to do.

She found a wooden block on the floor and with a grunt she bent carefully, holding her brother, then scooped up the block. He grasped onto it cheerfully. She placed a kiss on his curly head.

"Be good, Radi." Galina could not help to grin a little at the sheer joy her baby brother had over the toy.

She walked back to the kitchen and grabbed a few plates to get a head start on setting the table. It would be an hour before the meal, but she could get started.

"Boys, if you do not exit this house immediately I will have your father deal with you!" Her mother's exasperated tone carried well. She muttered something in Polish as the two boys took the hint and ran out of the front door of the cabin. The door slammed behind them with gusto.

Her mother sighed and continued her work.

"Those boys..." Her mother muttered.

Galina agreed with her mother's exasperation. A big breakfast was served after a while; the boys came in after their father, who had been outside.

Galina slipped up to her room before she joined the family at the table and rubbed some salve on her hands, they were stinging smartly.

After the meal a messenger came from the Harpole horse ranch. They were hoping that Galina could help out with baby Abigail, Marie was feeling sick.

They had all heard the rumors of a fever spreading around. Galina was happy to help out. She took some extra clothes with her in case she was asked to stay overnight.

Her mother gave her a kiss on the cheek before she left.

"You bring your pay to me when you get back, girl!' Her father said harshly. Galina's mood always seemed to drop whenever he spoke to her.

Galina nodded to her father and left quickly before she said something she would regret. She wondered when she would be allowed to keep some of the pay she earned with her work. Would she ever be out from under his thumb?

She made her way quickly across the fields and then the footbridge, the dew on the long grass was still clinging to the plants, and the heat of the day was rising fast. She waved to Lucas Grant who was chopping wood at the woodpile.

"Is Violet recovering?" Galina said when she was closer.

"The tea Corinne gives her helps some. Hoping today will be a good one for her." Lucas answered.

Galina could tell that he was trying to stay positive. Galina told him that she was heading to help out at the Harpole's, he sent his own greetings to them.

Galina walked on toward the ranch house next door down the path. She prayed for Violet as she walked. Violet had been such a dear friend to her. She was not certain she could imagine a world without her.

Chapter 13

Grant's Grove

Corinne helped Violet back into bed after the cool sponge bath. Violet was clean and dry except for her hair, and in a dry nightgown. The bed made the slightest of squeaks as she sat, she was thankful that the bathing part was over. Violet sighed, feeling so much cooler and relieved. The pounding in her head was better, and she had a glimmer of hope that it would be the end of her illness.

Corinne sat with her for a few minutes to keep her company.

Violet felt peaceful but something was bothering her just a little bit.

"Corinne, I want to ask you something..." Violet said quietly, she seemed unsure of herself.

"Anything... Violet." Corinne answered quickly.

"I need..." Violet stopped. She took a deep breath. "Would you check on Mrs. Whittlan? If she is well and can get away could you ask her to visit with me?"

Corinne gladly agreed and was pleased to see some of the worry leave Violet's countenance.

Violet relaxed and drank more of her feverwort tea. She was asleep shortly. Corinne left Violet to her quiet room, praying for her complete healing. Knowing that there was a chance for Violet to fully recover. Yellow Fever had a one in four chance to kill. Corinne tried not to consider that fact. She prayed for her community, hoping that the death toll would not reach too high. Corinne's face showed her concerns when she walked into the parlor.

Lucas was waiting for Corinne at the dining table. Megan sat in the settee looking irritable and bored.

"Heard from town, they have placed the whole valley on quarantine, no public events, no school or church services. The paper promises to have a list of the townsfolk that are affected by the end of the week." Lucas said. His green eyes searched Corinne's. "They are just taking precautions that people will not pass it around."

"Yes, I can see that." Corinne sighed. "I have a gut feeling that the coincidence of the bugs is no coincidence at all. Several well known in the field of medicine are suggesting that several of the plagues and fevers are carried by creatures. Not a punishment from God or spread by demons." Corinne huffed.

Sometimes Corinne just despised the assumptions made by superstitious people. She wanted to huff again at such things that went around as gossip, when it did no one any good.

"I agree with that statement!" Lucas smiled conspiratorially. "I have some bad news, I believe Marie is sick now too. I am heading over to see what can be done." Lucas sighed, hating to share bad news.

Corinne gasped and held her hand over her mouth, new fear filling her for her beloved step-mother. Also realizing that a fever like this had made her father a widower years before, with Corinne's mother Lily. She tried not to think how much her father would hurt to lose another wife.

"Let me have a moment before you go." Corinne ran to the kitchen and parceled out a selection of the feverwort and white willow bark. She wrote down instructions on a notepad feverishly, her hands shaking a little as she wrote.

She came back to Lucas a moment later, her eyes red and her cheeks wet with tears.

"Please tell them I will come by later." Corinne said sincerely.

"I will darling." Lucas placed a hand on his Corinne's cheek to sooth his worried wife.

"May I come along?" Megan asked from across the room.

Corinne gave Megan a questioning look. *Why would she want to go?* She wondered and was almost angry with her cousin. *What mischief can she be up to now?*

"I was thinking of young Cooper, perhaps I can be a distraction for the boy while the grownups talk. He promised to show me his favorite fishing spot a few days ago." Megan said. Her cheeks were red and she looked as upset as Corinne felt.

Corinne relaxed her shoulders and nodded. "That is kind Megan, thank you."

Lucas placed a hand on Corinne's face again.

"You do not fret, dear wife. God has us all in His hands." Lucas kissed Corinne sweetly and her lips trembled as he let her go.

"I will pray." Corinne promised.

Corinne watched her husband and cousin go a few minutes later. Praying for mercy for those that were affected by this dreadful fever. She also prayed for strength for everyone that was caring for the sick, knowing the worry and fear in her own heart was being felt by so many.

She checked in on Violet who was still sleeping, she wrapped her self up and headed out the door soon after. She had made a promise to seek out Mrs. Whittlan and see if she could come and talk to Violet. She could use the walking time to pray and calm herself.

The day was not as warm as it had been but the bugs could be heard around her. Her lace shawl pulled over her head to keep them away. She thought of the little one she carried and wondered how the worrying could affect her pregnancy. She prayed for peace to settle her heart. She felt a sense of calm overtake her as she walked. A bible verse from Joshua 10:25 helped her on her way.

Fear not, *nor be dismayed, be strong and of good courage: for thus shall the Lord do to all your enemies against whom ye fight.*

She knew that God knew the things that troubled her thoughts, her enemy was the fear and fever that traveled across this Valley. She felt instantly that God was fighting with her against these things.

Chapter 14

Violet Griffin

Her eyes were closed but she could feel the morning light coming into the room through the window. Just a hint of it since the window faced the West. The soft sheets were smooth against her skin and she felt a moment of relief, realizing her aching pain was gone. She reached her hand up to the underside of her pillow and felt the coolness. She shifted her weight just a little to cuddle into the comfort of sleepiness, wanting to relish that feeling for just a few minutes more. She was enjoying the release from the crippling pain she had felt for days.

A few minutes were bliss, just lying there, but Violet felt her body give way to wakefulness. She fought it half-heartedly, wanting to enjoy the sensation for just a few moments more before she would open her eyes and see what the day would bring. A soft rumble of hunger roared from her stomach, proof that she had eaten so little for days. It roared again to make its point. Violet chuckled and opened her eyes, knowing the time for rest was at an end.

She sat up and stretched long and with a few groans. Her muscles were stiff from the violent sickness but she felt the urge to get up and move around. She stood up and took a few steps around the bed to test herself, quite happy to see that she had no leftover dizziness or weakness. She took in a deep breath and sighed, content. She was herself again.

Galina Varushkin

The Varushkin Cabin was quiet today. Her mother quietly mending socks by the hearth, no fire burned today. The air was full of moisture and her brother slept fitfully in the new pen that had been built for him. Galina's wages had been taken to town and the carpenter Amos Drays had designed it and delivered it. Galina was glad for the convenience for her mother's sake, but she resented the funds had been spent from her own money. Her father never was willing to allow her to keep any of her earnings, and it chaffed at her relentlessly.

Galina counted the hours, every stir of the spoon through the thick porridge, every swish and pull she made with the broom, and every scolding word from her father's pursed lips made her wish to be away.

The beatings were becoming more frequent, she was not certain why, Galina tried not to dwell on thinking of it. There was nothing she could do to stop them, he was a big and strong man, with a will of iron. His work as a lumberjack was a good job for him, and he seemed happier for a time when he first came home from his failed mission to find gold last year. Lately his temper had returned, always claiming that his family, especially her, caused him distress.

She had made a promise to herself, and God, that she would obey and honor her parents, even her father. Her eyes, her mother informed her often, still held their resentment, even if she had gotten control of her runaway mouth.

In many ways Galina felt her father did not deserve her respect and honor. But somewhere deep inside Galina desired that evasive peace, that place hinted at, but so very hard to find. She knew that forgiveness was the way to this place, forgiving him for abandoning them, forgiving his temper.

Her ability to continue on, with her mouth clamped down tight on the things she wanted to say, instead she would do her work. She worked in four households doing laundry, then the rest of her time working until the sun went down for her parents.

Her hands were rough and chapped from the soap and laundry duties, lately they were blistered from helping to break the ground for the large garden. Her chapped skin on the rough wood of the hoe would rip and bleed, then would crack and split even more after more laundry, her brother teased her that her hands, at 14 yrs old, looked like an old man's.

Her envy over her brothers' days, the schooling being the hardest to see, and then the easy chores they did, pushed her hard towards that resentment that she desperately tried to keep under control.

When she worked for Corinne & Lucas, Violet would have Galina read aloud to her on their breaks, then at Angela's home she would practice her writing skills. It was the only part of her life that was happy. For that main reason she did not mind the work. To get away from her house was the main objective.

Galina had spent a full day at home, not having any outside work. She watched the long grass sway in the slight breeze, the heat was impressive and she could feel sweat dripping down her back. She instantly thought of how much extra laundry the heat was causing for her. She swung the hoe into the dirt and kept her motions rhythmic and steady, if she didn't think about it the pain in her hands were less. She thought about her reading while she worked, she just read a book of poems that Violet had loaned her, she did not know all of the words, she had received a little pocket notebook from Angela to write down words and she could look them up in the dictionary when she went back to Angela's house to do more laundry.

Her brothers were still at school at this time and her father was busy at Grant's Grove clearing trees for more future crops. Galina knew her father expected a certain amount of ground to be prepared to plant the garden, and if she didn't get a good few rows prepared today she would feel his wrath. She considered him to be watching her, somehow her father would know if she took any unreasonable pauses. The sting of his belt strap was a strong memory and she had no desire for fresh bruises, so she continued. The crunch of the dirt and rocks underneath the hoe was the cadence, she would not stop until it was time to help with dinner.

By midday her head was scorching hot and she knew her skin was burning. She put on a sunbonnet to protect her face, but the heat made her head sweat and several times that day she felt light-headed, she imagined several times about how cool the water of the creek would feel, wanting to take a walk and dunk her bonnet under the cool water, if she had been younger she would have just climbed into the creek and let the cold water soak her thoroughly. She knew at her age that would be considered indecent, but she wished for it.

She sang a song that she heard at church services, singing about the goodness of God, it helped her to pass the time as the pain increased in her hands, she could see that a blister had broken and the gloves she wore were getting wet with sweat and blood. She pushed through the pain, it was all she could do.

"Go on home, girl!" She heard her father's voice carry over the sound of her work. She stopped after hitting the dirt and swung the hoe over her shoulder. She turned around a full circle to see where the sound came from.

Galina saw her father on the far side of the property. He was pointing toward their cabin and Galina nodded dumbly. She glanced up to the sky, seeing that it wasn't the usual time for her to quit. She felt her stomach clench in apprehension. Something must have happened for her father to have to stop her work early.

Her feet carried her swiftly over the ground, she was thankful for the dry heat for one reason at least, the mud was clearing from the ground and it was much easier to get through the field. Last week had been terrible, the mud was ankle deep in some places and she had fallen more than a dozen times. The creek had been so swollen that the creek crossing on the road was no longer possible with the ground falling away at the sides.

Her father was excited to announce that he was helping at Grant's Grove with getting the lumber for the bridge project underway. He had spent all of the previous evening talking about it, working with some prominent members of the rural community had him all puffed up with pride. Galina watched her mother encourage his behavior by making all sorts of comments.

'You must certainly have earned their trust to work on such a grand project.' She had said.

Galina wanted to roll her eyes at his boasting, she instead focused on her plate and helping her mother with Radi, her baby brother, while he spoke.

Now as she headed into the house after the hot and uncomfortable day in the sun she was glad to be under the roof.

"Mama, Pa sent me home." Galina said as she removed her dirt encrusted shoes at the door, she hung her sweat soaked bonnet on a peg on the wall. She felt the state of her hair and knew she must look a bedraggled mess.

Galina heard a distressed cry from her brother. Galina took a look around the dark cabin and was concerned, she couldn't hear anything but the crying.

"Mama?" Galina walked over to the crib where Radimir lay, his head was sweaty and his cheeks an angry red. Galina reached in and felt the heat radiate from his skin.

"Awe, poor little thing." She placed a kiss on his sweaty forehead, his head was sweltering hot. Her heart jumped in alarm, he was hotter than he should be.

"Mama!" Galina exclaimed, her hand slipped under her brother's backside, his nappy was dry. He had been changed, but where was her mother?

She held Radi against her chest and for a moment he ceased his cries and cuddled against her, obviously needing to be held. She heard a rustling from her parent's room and she walked a few steps to the door.

Galina gasped when she opened the door and saw her mother on the floor.

She knelt quickly to the floor and her brother did not appreciate the jostling, his wails started back up with vigor.

Galina stroked her mother's cheek and saw her eyes flutter open.

"Mama?" Galina said softly, worry lines creased across her brow.

"Oh..." Her mother sighed and sat up, her dark hair falling out of the pins. Her cheeks were just as red as her young son's.

Galina used her free hand to help her mother sit up.

"I sat down, my head was spinning about." Her mother's accent was still thick with her polish upbringing.

Galina used the back of her arm to feel her mother's head, she was also scorching hot. "You are sick mama. So is Radi..."

Her mother nodded.

Galina heard the front door open, the heavy steps of her father across the floor, he had a limp, from a lumbering accident a few years before, but he was healthy.

Her father had a towel in his large hands, he was wiping his face.

"Why is Magda on the ground?" He looked at Galina, his eyebrows accusing her of foul-play.

Galina opened her mouth to answer but said nothing.

"I got dizzy and fell, Slava, do not blame the girl." Magdalena stood slowly, holding a hand to her brow. Galina shifted the baby on her hip and leaned into her mother's side, worried that she would get dizzy and fall again.

Radimir began to whimper. He reached for his mother. Galina tried to hush him and she walked away to allow her father to help her mother. Radi did not like being further away from his mother and began to wail again.

"Radi is very sick too, Papa." Galina finally said when all her efforts to calm the child were in vain.

Her father, Slava, got her mother settled onto the davenport and grabbed a throw pillow and placed it under her head.

"I can take him." Slava reached for the boy. "I want you to go to the Grant woman... Mrs." He paused, the cries of the baby filled the air. "Corinne, she has a gift for herbs and such. Perhaps she will know a way to help them."

Galina took a deep breath, "Yes father." Galina thought of the talk she had heard everywhere she went this week. That yellow fever was going around. She wanted to be scared, and stop to pray but she went into action, not thinking about anything. As she ran across the field toward Grant's Grove she had the tiniest concern about her appearance. She shook the thought away, knowing that Corinne would never judge her, they were kind people, when she knew that her mother was sick she would do all she could to help.

She got to the footbridge that crossed the creek and looked to the clear water trickling underneath the wooden planks. She was reminded of her thirst but she continued on. She thought of her baby brother with his head burning with fever, his dark blond hair plastered to his head and how dreadful he must feel.

It was a minute later that she was knocking on the door of the Grant cabin, finally having a moment to think she sent up a prayer for her family.

Violet Griffen answered the door. Galina had heard that she was sick and was glad to see her.

"Is Ms. Corinne here?" Galina asked softly, she was still out of breath from her run. Her head was spinning and for a minute she was worried that she was ill too.

"She should be home any minute now. She went to see Mrs. Whittlan." Violet made a gesture for Galina to enter.

Galina paused, wondering if she should just go back home, or wait. She didn't want her father to go into a rage for her taking too much time away.

"You sit, you look like you may have heat sickness." Violet pointed to the table.

Violet grabbed a mug from the nearby kitchen cupboard, she scooped a few ladles-full of water from the bucket on the counter.

Violet sat next to Galina after she handed her the mug.

Galina thanked her politely and sipped on the cool water.

"Slowly, not too fast."

Galina nodded and settled the cup on the table. The cool water felt heavenly on her tongue.

"I heard you were ill." Galina said after she took another small sip.

Violet nodded. "I am feeling better today, but weak. Corinne would scold me if she saw me cleaning the dishes."

Galina smiled weakly. "I will not tell on you."

Violet reached out a hand to pat Galina on the shoulder. They had grown closer over the last months, having spent at least one day a week together. Violet had been so encouraging to Galina and the young girl counted Violet as a friend.

"My mother is sick now, baby Radi too." Galina said through a throat that was tight with emotions.

Violet didn't speak but her eyebrows furrowed with concern.

"My father sent me. Hoping Corinne had something to help."

Violet pressed her lips together in thought. "She helped me with a tea, she has ways to help, but I know it is not a cure. That is in God's hands."

Galina nodded, she picked up the mug and sipped it, trying to swallow the lump that had formed in her throat.

"It is frightening, yes?" Violet asked, squeezing the shoulder she still held.

Galina nodded and two fat tears escaped down her dirty cheeks.

Violet stood and got a rag from a drawer, she dunked it into the washbasin water and gave it to Galina.

"I was outside all day, getting the garden ready for planting." Galina said as she wiped her hot face with the cool rag. "I wish I had known, that they were feeling unwell." Galina said, trying not to cry anymore but failing.

Violet spent a minute, trying to soothe Galina. She was practical, and knew the stern nature of Galina's father. They had spoken of it on a few occasions.

The door opened and Corinne came through with a large round basket. Corinne was surprised to see Galina.

Galina stood and watched Corinne settle the basket on the table. The basket was full of bright white wildflowers.

"What brings you to Grant's Grove?"

Galina took a step forward, "My mother and baby brother have the fever." Galina said through a tight throat.

"Let me get you some water, Cori." Violet said and stood up.

Corinne's eyes widened. "Not a chance Violet, you sit! You are lucky I let you out of bed today." Corinne spoke with a smile but her tone had a hint that she meant serious business. Corinne turned to Galina who was looking more and more distressed as she stood there.

"I just picked some White Yarrow in the woods, to bolster my stock. I can put together some tea for you to make for your mother." Corinne wrung her hands in thought. Worried about so many people, wondering if she could do anything to help more than she was.

"I have a little more of the fever wart herb for making a tea. I am wondering how well Radimir could handle it." Corinne chewed on her bottom lip.

"Let me make some notes..." Corinne went to the parlor to get her notebook. Her dark eyes serious and thoughtful. She sat back down at the table and invited Galina to join her. Instead Galina got a mug of water first and settled it on the table next to Corinne.

"It is hot outside, I'm sure you are thirsty." Galina said. She needed to focus on not crying.

Corinne muttered a 'thank you' while scribbling in her notebook.

"The tea I will send you will help your mother with her fever." Corinne wrote and spoke disjointedly, a little distracted. "A few times a day. In between she must drink a lot of water. You can try to feed her when she is willing, but she may not be." Corinne held onto her chin for a minute, then wrote some more. "Has she or your brother vomited at all yet?"

Galina nodded, her mother had said as much before Galina had left.

"Your brother will be more difficult. He cannot drink his mother's milk when his fever is high, it will curdle in his tummy." Corinne's brow was creased in worry, knowing the baby was in danger.

"I would give him several luke-warm baths throughout the day or night. You will need to keep a close eye on him. You have your father and brothers all help. This is a lot for one person to do."

Galina was absorbing as much as she could, glad to know Corinne was writing everything down. She wanted to thank her friends, Violet and Angela, again and again for helping her learn to read.

A knock came to the door that very moment. Corinne got up to answer it.

"I do hope I came at a good time." The sweet voice announced.

Galina could see that it was Mrs. Whittlan, the pastor's wife. Galina had always found her to be a kind lady, though she didn't know her well. She had a reputation as a woman with a generous heart.

Violet rose from the table and gave Mrs. Whittlan a warm hug. Galina noticed the tears in Violet's eyes. Galina was certain that there was a strong bond between these two women. It warmed Galina's heart to see it.

"You ladies chat away. I will gather up some things for Galina to take with her." Corinne went about her work after she gave Mrs. Whittlan an affectionate pat on the shoulder.

Galina and Violet chatted with Mrs. Whittlan for several minutes, Galina spoke only a little. The discussion about how yellow fever was spreading through the valley had sobered her dramatically. She was more than a little concerned. Her shoulders were tight from the work she had done in the heat all day, and now the stress of her family's illness was making her tighten up even further in her distress.

Corinne came back to the table a few minutes later with a basket and her notes.

"You can feed your mother and Radi the broth I have included. Have your father send one of the boys over tomorrow. I will have some more ingredients for tea by then. I am going to send Lucas into town for Doc Williams, and also to the apothecary." Corinne stood patiently while Galina said her goodbyes.

Corinne gave Galina a tight embrace, Galina felt a little relieved from the concern of Corinne. It helped to know that someone was on your side.

"I will follow your instructions implicitly." Galina nodded as she spoke to confirm her resolve.

"We can only do what we can humanly do Galya." Corinne held her hands protectively on Galina's shoulders for a long second. "This fever is serious, do not despair when things look bad. Send for me if you need a hand."

Galina felt emotions boiling to the surface but tried to swallow them back. She had to be strong now. She left with a promise to send a brother if she needed help. Her steps were fast as she made her way the long mile home.

Dolly Bouchard

Dolly had traveled a few miles, up the steady slope of the hill just south west of the cave she had spent two days in. She felt the ground under her moccasins, some rock and sandy soil that was shifty underneath her. She looked ahead of her, seeing a few trees higher up before she saw a flat plateau.

She would get a vantage point there to see if she could find an easy way over this ridge. She knew the other side had a good potential to be a better place to shelter and find fresh water. She had just been on the other side of this ridge a few days before. It was greener with better survivability. She knew this was going to be difficult, but heading back was renewing her mind. She was heading in the right direction, back toward home.

An hour later she was still climbing, a few steps had been treacherous and she had leaned forward to bear crawl up a spot near the plateau. She had a few roots and small trees to help her keep her balance. She did not want to fall, even at this incline, she could be hurt and that could be deadly.

The plateau was a bit greener with rock and moss showing up underfoot. Thicker trees were ahead of her and she got her bearings.

With the sun shining brightly overhead she had a good view of the lay of the land. She was between two mountains. This spot that Bright Son had led her too had been a divine choice. Her escape down the plateau was an easy elevation to manage. Lots of trees sprouting up and only a mild incline to climb down. She saw the forest below, knowing in that thicker woods she could see a well defined break, meaning that something, probably a stream or river broke its way through. She needed to drink and knew it would be a few hours to reach that tree break. She began right away to find the best course down. She only had to turn backwards once, using trees and a vine to keep her footing as she climbed down the large rocks. She was happy that she hadn't had to climb a mountain to get over the ridge. She was feeling blessed as she got to the nearly level ground. She saw that the forest she was in was getting thicker and more abundant with life. Little green plants shooting up through the fallen leaves from the previous autumn. Proof that life and water was here.

She found the tree break within a few hours and could hear the water trickling as she made her way through the thicker brush. Birds and wildlife were active around her and she knew she could find a good place here to settle in.

The stream was clear and flowing fast, Dolly removed the bags from her back and settled them behind her. She knelt down and scooped up the water, it was shockingly cold and she took a small sip from her palms. The water was clean and felt wonderful on her dry tongue. She took a few small sips, not wanting to make herself sick and she lay down on the side of the stream. She prayed as she laid there, her mind wanting to think of the many things she had to do. She forced her mind to clear and she looked above her, the canopy of trees swaying, the green leaves waving sweetly.

"Thank you, my God, please help me find my way home." She spoke softly to the air around her. Her voice sounded strange in the stillness. She felt a peaceful calm fill her.

She drank more and more until her belly was full. She walked along the edge of the stream until she found a good place to make a shelter. A few trees with nice forks were near each other, she settled her bags near them and began to make a plan.

Chapter 15

Galina Varushkin

Galina arrived home to a house full of chaos. Her brothers were home, pouting because school had been canceled until further notice. Her father, Slava, was bellowing out orders to the boys for overdue chores that they were grumbling about doing. Baby Radi was whimpering in his own misery, alternating between standing and sitting in his wooden playpen.

Galina was shocked to see him alone, her father sat across from the room bellowing his orders, not concerned with his youngest boy needing attention. Galina sighed and settled the things she had gotten from Corinne onto the table. She wondered where to start. Her father gave her a task, almost reading her thoughts.

"Your mama got sick on the floor in the bedroom. Go clean it up." He gave her a look that would frighten a small animal.

"Is there boiling water?" Galina asked without considering his response.

Her father's glare said that she had been foolish to speak. "You want me to fetch and carry for you girl? Anything else you would like?" His mocking tone cut through Galina's inner strength. She had given herself a pep talk on the walk home, to ignore her tired body and take care of her mother and brother. Dealing with her father's animosity made her feel every ounce of exhaustion with fresh force.

Galina grabbed a brother and told him to bring in fresh water. Milo, still grumpy from being yelled at by his father, wanted to baulk at the chore, but Galina silenced him with a pinch to his shoulder. She was not going to take any nonsense just now.

Galina grabbed a rag and headed into her mother's room. Hoping the mess would be manageable. The room was hot and thick with the smell of the sick on the floor. Galina had to fight off her own nausea as she saw and smelt it.

"Hey Mama." Galina said softly. She stepped around the mess and sat on the bed to give her mother a moment of comfort.

Her mother's dark brown hair was plastered to her pale face, her forehead was burning hot with fever still. "I'm sorry..." She spoke, her voice was weak.

"Awe hush now, Mama." Galina soothed. She wiped away the film that was drying on her mother's chin. She got the worst of it wiped away, her mind busily making plans to get the tea on, get the floor scrubbed and check on Radi. She was trying to fight off how alone she felt in this battle. Her father obviously hadn't even thought to get a bucket for her mother, just allowing her to get sick over the side of the bed.

Well, if he doesn't have to clean up the mess what does he care where the vomit lands? Galina thought with anger.

Her mother moaned and turned on her side, bringing Galina out of her thoughts.

"You going to be sick again?" Galina asked ready to dash outside to find any bucket she could.

"Not yet... just hurting." Her mother's whisper was harsh and Galina felt a rush of sympathy.

"I am going to get this place all cleaned up and get you some tea, Corinne gave it to me. She said it may help a little."

Her mother's smile was tiny, only a half-second of the lift of the corners of her mouth. "You are so strong child."

It was an odd thing for her mother to say at such a time but it helped Galina to embrace her inner strength again. She placed a kiss on her mother's hot forehead and got up. She had work to do.

Milo had two full buckets of water on the wooden table.

"Go fetch me an empty bucket, if it has anything in it then clean it out." Galina said firmly. "Pavel?" She called out, looking for her other brother. He popped his head down from the loft on the second story of the house.

Galina gave him a look, wondering what he was doing up there at this time of the day.

"You get started on getting all the windows open, we need fresh air in here." Galina said.

"But the bugs?" Pavel pouted. "They will come in."

"The place smells of sickness. Would you like to get sick too?" Galina spoke as she poured water into the largest kettle they owned.

She heard her young brother huffing but she heard his feet climbing down the ladder from the loft with soft footfalls.

She reached into the top cupboard and found some cheesecloth and settled it on the table. She took her mother's best scissors and cut pieces big enough to fit in the window frames. The boys could hammer the cheesecloth into the frames if need be.

She got another pot going with more water to clean with, it wouldn't need to come to a boil but just be warm enough to help her scrub. She pulled out the washbasin they used for dishes and contemplated, she could use this to clean up the mess. Or she could leave this next to the bed in case her mother got sick again. Either one would contaminate it, giving her something else to worry about. She searched through the pantry for other large bowls and came up with one that would work to use for cleaning. She muttered a prayer that her brother Milo would find a suitable bucket in the shed.

"Radi needs a nappy change." Her father announced. "Starting to stink in here."

Galina stared at her father, dumbfounded.

"He is your son!" Galina said with a little bit too much edge to her voice. She tried to remedy it with more talking. "I am really trying to get the tea made to help them feel better, and get the mess cleaned up in your bedroom."

"That'll keep." Her father's tone was cold, his eyebrows low and menacing. She could not imagine the depth of someone's hatred to look at a person like that. She really felt his contempt more and more every day. In the midst of this crisis, the house full of sickness and fever, she pondered the loss of her father's love and felt it deeply. She could not recall the last time he had spoken to her with any affection.

She walked to her baby brother, fighting off the lump in her throat, her eyes blinking rapidly to keep any tears away.

She scooped up her brother, realizing he had sweat through his clothes. She stripped him bare, taking his urine-soaked diaper in a free hand, then balancing her naked brother on her hip she went outside the door and dropped the dirty nappy in the soapy water bucket they kept just for this reason.

Galina patted her brother's back and hoped fervently that her brother wouldn't pee all over her dress. The messes she had to clean up were adding up quickly and a dirty dress, and clothes change would just be more things to deal with.

Galina heard the kettle start its whistling, trying to figure out what to do, holding a naked baby and handling hot liquids and pans was not wise. She scrambled. She put Radi in the playpen again. He started crying immediately.

She dashed to the stove, with the thought of removing the kettle and dipped her elbow into the water to test it. She didn't want to touch anything, since she had handled the dirty nappy. She let the whistle shriek and it competed with her brother's crying. She noticed the washbasin was almost empty and wanted to throttle her brothers for skipping their chores. She poured what was left over her hands and wiped the lemon soap over her hands and scrubbed. She had nothing to rinse them off so she wiped the suds the best she could with her skirts and grabbed the full bucket of water and filled up the washbasin. She rinsed off the residue on her hands and dried them off.

She removed the screaming kettle, then the hot pot of water. She placed them on the hot pads on the counter. She grabbed the towel she had used on her hand washing and dipped it in to the hot water on the stove and took it over to her brother. She was surprised with a baby brother urinating like a fountain all over his belly and the pen. She flipped the towel over her shoulder, scooped up her brother, let him drip the remainder into the bottom of his playpen and then moved him to a clean part of the kitchen floor.

With the lemon soap and the warm rag she cleaned up her brother, who was very content to be touched and cuddled when it was all finished. He was back in a dry nappy, and a clean and dry shirt.

She had done all of this under the watchful eye of her father, who hadn't lifted a finger to help her.

Oh Lord, Galina prayed in the quiet of her mind, *please help me.*

She was too overwhelmed to think of any eloquent prayer, but she knew from her bible lessons and reading that God heard her cries.

It took her hours to get everything done, the floor in her parent's bedroom being the biggest challenge. She had made tea and broth for her mother, who had sipped the tea with more enthusiasm than the chicken broth.

For her brother she made warm water with a little honey in it, suggested from Corinne's notes. Baby Radi couldn't drink his mother's milk but he needed to replenish his moisture. Milo and Pavel had done the chores, with further urging by both Galina and their father. They enjoyed the task of nailing the cheesecloth in the open windows, any excuse to bang or pound on something was a delight. Each pound worked to strengthen Galina's impressive headache.

Galina finished cleaning out her brother's wooden pen and then held Radi in the soft chair for a few minutes, trying to sooth his whimpering. He had thrown up on himself while Galina was scrubbing the floor. She had to leave one job to clean another, then returned to finish.

Radi's cheeks were pink but after the last wash down he had settled into a more calm state. Galina's stomach growled as she rocked her brother.

Her father had gone outside after her baby brother had vomited. Galina wondered what would get through to him that she needed his help?

She prayed and cried as she rocked her brother, not knowing what else this day would bring, but feeling so very overwhelmed.

Angela Fahey

Angela read the headlines to Olivia who was tatting some lace in the seat across the parlor. Ted had just been by to check on them bringing mail and the newspaper. Usually the paper only ran once per week but with the sickness running rampant they ran another edition mid-week.

"Yellow fever is sweeping through the Willamette Valley. Oregon City, Portland and Salem being hit the hardest. The apothecary and the doctors are overwhelmed with the patient load and encourage every family to be diligent." Angela read, she looked up to watch Olivia work for a moment then continued. "All church and school functions are canceled. Each city council agreeing that though the illness did not seem to be spread by human contact it was better to move forward with caution.

The governor, John Pritchlan has asked the paper to publish all the names of the sick, encouraging neighbors to keep watch over each other, as is our Christian duty."

Angela took a deep breath. "You want me to read the names for Oregon City?"

Olivia looked up from her work and nodded.

"Persephone Williams: recovered, Violet Griffen: recovered, Russell Grant: recovered, Gemma Caplan: recovered, Greta Jamison: recovered," Angela continued on reading ten more names of those who had caught it early and beat the fever. She read through the rest picking out the names she knew and the ones that sounded familiar. "Magdalena Varushkin, Radimir Varushkin, Reginald Garner, Sarah Grant, Marie Harpole, Reynaldo Legales, Earl Burgess, Amelia Greaves, Sophia Greaves, Clive Quackenbush."

She said all the names of those she cared about so deeply with a tight voice. Olivia looked up and met Angela's gaze with moisture in her eyes.

She hadn't been surprised by any of the names, for the word spread as quickly as the fever itself through this small town but seeing them in print had been difficult.

Ted had been by and shared that his mother and sister were fairing better, but still suffering with a low grade fever. They seemed to be on the mend. Ted was heading back to town to check on Clive, who had been poorly the day before. Millie Quackenbush had sent for more of the fever tea from the apothecary.

"So many to pray for." Olivia said weakly. "My heart is overwhelmed."

Angela nodded, not having any words to speak, her fear at the forefront of her mind. She hadn't read through the names of the deceased that were listed, she hadn't the courage to speak the names aloud, knowing a few from church and even a few from the school where she had visited before.

"I feel the need to confess something..." Olivia settled her hands in her lap as a few tears ran down her cheeks unchecked.

Angela raised her head from her prayerful stance and gave her a look to continue.

"I am so afraid for Clive, and I have such a sense of guilt about it." Olivia gulped, and reached up and held her throat. "So many suffering, and I am worried so much about one man that I cannot think outside the fear that he may be lost."

Angela had that same fear but she had many on her list. "Why Clive?" She finally asked, feeling foolish because she already knew the answer.

"I do declare, I believe I may love him." Olivia stated. She dabbed at her tears with a lace handkerchief but didn't say anything else.

Violet Griffen

Violet tightened the lid of her last jar of fresh homemade chicken broth, having spent a good chunk of her day with Corinne working in the kitchen. She had gotten tired a few times and took lots of time for rest but she had little spurts of energy and wanted to use them efficiently. There were so many sick people in the valley she felt that she needed to do something to help.

Corinne had spent the morning searching the woods, she had left at sunup. She was on a mission to find spearmint or peppermint plants. She was planning to do this search with Dolly but now that yellow fever was spreading so fast she wanted to see if making mint tea would help people through the worst of the nausea.

Violet pushed all the jars to the edge of the counter and sat for a while, they could cool for a little bit. Corinne had done a test round with the peppermint leaves and decided the best method for making the tea. She then spent time separating leaves into envelopes and writing instructions for each one.

Violet was feeling so much better, the fever had gone, she would need to get her strength back, but she felt like she had been given a new chance to live.

Mrs. Whittlan had stopped by a few days before, and her and Violet had sat in Violet's small sitting room and talked for hours. Mrs. Whittlan had known about her past more than anyone else and it helped to talk through the painful dreams. Somehow the pain of the dreams had done more damage to her heart than the death of her own husband. Violet was processing how she felt about that.

She had gotten up with Corinne but had stayed in the kitchen while Corinne was out on her plant search. She prepped all the vegetables, garlic, onions and spices for the broth they would make for the neighbors who were ill. She knew that other kitchens across the valley would be doing the same. While Violet prepped she thought about her conversation with Mrs. Whittlan.

'We cannot expect people to behave in the way we want them to.' Mrs. Whittlan had said. 'People with evil in their hearts cannot fathom the way of the righteous. Sometimes evil men exist and we have to live among them. I am not certain it is wise to allow them to continue to do evil.' Mrs. Whittlan looked so serious as she spoke. Her eyes, which usually were always filled with calm joy, were troubled.

'How do I obey the bible, to honor my parents, if I tell people of the evil that he has done? Would that not disparage his character?' Violet had asked, fighting the same thought she had felt for years. She had been trained up since she was little that you never speak ill of your elders, especially your parents. It was ingrained as a part of her.

'I will never believe that God would have us protect someone whose intent is to harm a child.' Mrs. Whittlan had said wisely. 'The time may come when he must not only pay for his sins on judgement day in heaven, but also pay for his deeds here on earth.'

They had talked long and hard on this and then the subject changed to how she was dealing with her husband's death. She thought of Eddie often but since she was ill he has played less and less through her mind. She was feeling unburdened by the grief this week, feeling that having survived the fever that had more than likely killed him, she had finally settled it in her mind. She was still alive, and perhaps God had a purpose for her life. She was more determined than ever to move forward. She was beginning to feel that small seed of acceptance within herself. She had survived much in her short life, but she had a lot to live for as well.

Violet came out of her heavy thoughts when Corinne announced that her mint tea packets were ready for delivery. Lucas was out in the barn, taking over duties of the young lad who took care of the stables. His parents were both sick and he was taking care of them the best he could.

Corinne leaned out of the front door of the cabin and gave a call for Lucas. Violet could see that Lucas had a wagon ready for the deliveries. Corinne and Violet would tag along and make notes on who needed anything. They would pass along needs to the church body and neighbors. Anyone who was able-bodied and could help a friend or neighbor would do whatever they could to make sure everyone was taken care of.

Earlier in the day he had been by his brother's home, his brother Russell seemed to be bouncing back, and Sarah the youngest was sitting up in bed. They all had breathed a sigh of relief that their house had been spared the worst outcome.

Lucas handed Corinne the newest newspaper as he prepared to load the wagons. Corinne immediately handed it to Violet.

"You are not to load anything, I want you to read this and sit while we load." Corinne pointed a finger at Violet with a glint in her eye. "I do not want you to overdo it. The fever could still come back."

Violet nodded and stuck her tongue out playfully. Corinne laughed and joined her husband, he made a similar gesture with her, that she had done enough for the day.

Violet read through the list of people who were sick in town, feeling sad over so many of her dearest friends who were still in a fight for their lives. She gasped and dropped the paper to the table when she read the names....Meredith & Timotheus Smithers, in the names of the sick. Their faces had haunted her fever dreams and in so many thoughts over the past few days.

The Smithers name was stamped on every bag of flour that anyone purchased in Oregon City, and Violet had grown accustomed to it, eventually, but seeing their names in the paper had been a blow. They were not very active in town life, with quiet, preferring the life off the main street, only her mother came to town on Mondays and Thursdays, Violet had avoided contact with them since she was 15 yrs old. Until a few months ago when she saw her mother in passing. She had not handled it very well, going into hysterics in front of Corinne.

Violet wondered if God was preparing her for something, having them spring up so often in her mind. Could her path and theirs be crossed again? Violet would pray to her dying day to never see their faces again. But she would not deny what God would do in her life. Even if it was painful.

Chapter 16

Dolly Bouchard

Dolly sat for hours with her knife whittling on a stick, late into the twilight of the evening, the fire crackling beside her. Her stomach was satisfied with the dried beef she had nibbled on but she was longing for fish. The river beside her had them, she could see them under the sparkling water. Today she had walked along the shore heading toward what she hoped was a mountain pass. Her strength was running out with her lack of food so she settled on a spot for shelter earlier than she should have, certain the amount of miles she had traveled had not been as many as she would have liked.

She found some inner strength to make another shelter. Using a large rock and two trees that were close to latch a roof over her. She pulled dead leaves from the ground and made a soft and dry covering for the ground and called it good. She would make a big fire and try to keep the animals away. The night was alive with animal sounds. In the valley she was in the sound carried and the calls echoed far and long. The scream of wildcats brought gooseflesh to the back of Dolly's neck several times the night before.

Corinne Grant

Corinne sat with Marie Harpole and chatted about the little things. Marie was recovering, but very weak. Marie had kicked off the pink floral quilt and was sitting up in her bed, sipping on some peppermint tea that Corinne had made for her.

"I was praying so much for you while I was in the midst of the fever." Marie said with sincerity.

"For me?" Corinne was slightly shocked.

"Well, I was thinking of your little one, so helpless and small in there." Marie got a bit misty in her confession. "He or she needs a fighting chance."

Corinne nodded, starting to feel a rise of emotions herself. Marie was a sweet and caring woman, and had made a good companion for her father. But Marie was more than that, taking a supportive role for Corinne too, who needed a mother in a new way. She may be grown and married but a Mama is good for many times in a life span.

"I talked to Clive last night." Corinne changed the subject, wanting to keep from crying. "Just briefly while delivering tea and broth. He thinks he will be up soon. Though his fever was still medium-high when I checked him. He shooed me away with gusto, it gave me hope." Corinne smiled warily. Still feeling that small trickle of fear when she thought of a loved one in danger.

"Clive is a scrapper, he will fight this as much as he can." Marie said in response. "I have found a deeper understanding of how I feel about living. A few days ago, there were a few dark moments and I thought about my mortality." Marie said with a serious look. She closed her eyes for a moment, almost like she was in pain. "I hurt so badly in that moment, the nausea and pain stabbing through me. I thought I might die. I wasn't afraid of it, but I thought of John, Sarah and Cooper, and prayed for God to take care of them. I imagined how sad they would be and that hurt more than the pain in my body." Marie opened her eyes but she still frowned. "Not sure how I survived that night without God with me. I repeated many verses as I suffered. John tried to soothe me but it was almost like I was alone with God, battling to keep my strength."

Corinne knew only one night like that herself. When she had lost her child. Even with people around her she had felt alone with God. Corinne nodded but kept quiet. Letting Marie speak if she had more to say.

"I know many folks in my lifetime have questioned God, and how he allows the innocent to suffer. Or how death comes to the righteous and the unrighteous. I guess I believe that God has allowed us each a life, and in the world there is disease, and evil, and disaster. I will never believe that he sent this fever through this valley as a punishment. But the fever did come, and He allowed it. I do not believe that God wished me any harm. But while I was suffering He was with me. In the sweet quiet and rest I heard him whisper inside me that my time was not yet come. When it does finally come and I get to go to Glory I will praise Him, whether it be tomorrow or many years from now."

Corinne smiled and felt encouraged by Marie's faith. She had a way of stating things so simply. Her own mother had felt similarly, and had praised God with her dying breath.

Corinne's throat was tight when she finally spoke. "I am so very glad... your time has not yet come." Corinne was sincere in her statement and wished that she could express better how she felt about her step-mother. Perhaps Marie would just know. Corinne hoped so.

Chapter 17

Galina Varushkin

Galina watched the curtains flutter in the breeze, the weather was cooling down and the fresh air was calming as it hit her cheek. She held her mother's hot hand and kept silent, listening for her mother's breathing. Her mother's cheeks were sunken in and she wasn't responsive to Galina's requests anymore. Her eyes, the last time Galina had seen them open, had a yellowish tint where the whites should have been.

The morning had come, her father had stayed up with her brother Radimir while Galina stayed with her mother. They finally, after several days of sickness, began working together. Perhaps the visits from others had spurred her reluctant father into caring. Galina wasn't certain what had stirred his heart into finally helping, but she was glad for it. Least as much as she could will herself to be glad. Her anger at him had reached new levels over the last few days.

Galina had reached her breaking of exhaustion and she had been openly weeping the day before when Violet had come with Lucas Grant for another check-in. She had not bathed or slept in days and her sick patients had only gotten worse as each day progressed. The tea had done nothing to soothe her mother's tempestuous stomach. Radimir had cried non-stop since that first day in-between vomiting and high fevers. Galina was beyond herself to know what to do. Her father had taken every opportunity to leave her alone with both her mother and brother, taking Pavel and Milo with him.

One time had been to till the garden patch, another to plant. In the evening when it seemed he should be there he spent as much time outside the cabin chopping wood.

Violet and Lucas helped Galina get things clean, then Violet spent some time at Galina's mother's bedside, cooling her fever with a wet towel.

Galina was able to lie down for a few hours to get some much-needed rest. Lucas put the boys to work. Showing them how to care for Radi for when Galina needed help. Lucas and Slava spoke for a while, Galina overheard some of the conversation and was surprised by her father allowing Lucas to speak to him in such an authoritative way. Lucas had challenged him to take over duties so that Galina could rest more. Galina could not help but feel protected by Lucas Grant. He was a good man, even if he was younger than her father he was still his employer. It was a brief moment of calm in Galina's heart. She had fallen asleep with a smile on her lips.

Now she looked to her mother, so beyond hope in her inexperienced eyes. The fever burning through her skin, like she had hot coals in her guts. She had sent her brother for Corinne, but she was beginning to fear the worst.

Corinne arrived within an hour, her face serious and she came with a purpose. Milo and Pavel joined Corinne and they all piled into the bedroom. Both Milo and Pavel were shocked by their mother's appearance. Pavel began to weep.

"She will die!" He dropped to the side of the bed and wailed.

Galina fought back the urge to join him in his weeping, for she felt the same way.

"Will she drink?" Corinne asked over the sound of weeping.

Galina shook her head. "Boys, please watch Radi." Her voice was raspy, she heard the desperation coming through every sound she uttered.

"He finally sleeps," Milo said.

Galina dropped her head in relief. "Let us have some room to talk in here. Go and be with Radi and pray for Mama." Galina saw her brothers' nod, both teary-eyed and red-faced.

Once the boys were gone Galina looked to Corinne for any sign of a plan. She was not comforted by the look that Corinne expressed.

"We can try to get some fluid in her. It is the only hope." Corinne said softly, grabbing a clean wash rag and dropping it into the water bowl that was on the nearby table.

"Try to get her mouth open." Corinne gave instruction as she squeezed the cloth to the right consistency she required.

Galina touched her mother's cheek, the color of her skin had changed so much in the last few days, from a healthy pink, to the fiery red, now pale and yellowed with ashen cheeks.

"She has eaten nothing since yesterday, and only a sip or two of broth." Galina shared as she gently pried on her mother's face.

"Mama, can you open your mouth for me?" Galina begged, hiding the sob that wanted to escape.

Galina succeeded to get her lips parted open just enough and Corinne held the cloth over her face and squeezed the cloth and a few drops made it to her mouth and inside. Galina rubbed any spare drops around her mother's chapped lips, her finger gently coaxing water into her.

They repeated this until a raspy gurgle sound alerted them. Magdalena had reacted eventually to the water in her mouth and made a heavy swallowing sound, a gulp that gave Galena hope.

Corinne and Galina stayed at this for more than an hour, coaxing every drop they could into her mouth. Slava visited them once briefly but left just as fast.

"I cannot watch this." He said through a thick voice and stomped away. The front door of the cabin slammed hard and soon the sound of chopping wood met Galina's hearing.

"Thank you for staying Corinne." Galina said through her exhaustion. So very glad she wasn't alone.

"I am here as long as I need to be." Corinne said, her face pale with worry.

Violet Griffin

Violet sat in prayer, she had so many lives that she thought of as she poured her heart out to God.

Corinne had just left an hour before to go and help at the Varushkin house. Violet had seen the scared look of the young boy as he pleaded for Corinne's help.

His description of his mother had placed a fear in her heart for this family. Yellow fever was known to be deadly when the skin or the eyes began to yellow. It had gotten its name from that deadly symptom.

Violet thought of Galina, who had worked so tirelessly to help her brother and mother survive this dreadful malady. She knew that Galina would blame herself if her mother did not survive. An anger welled up within her when she thought of Slava Varushkin, and his cavalier attitude when she had seen him the day before.

When both she and Lucas explained to him that he was putting too much on his young daughter's shoulders. His actions had disgusted her. His words even more so.

"She is my child, and the eldest. It is her duty to care for all of us at my whim." He had stated so coldly.

Violet could tell it bristled him severely to be scolded by both her and Lucas.

It was only because he relied on his work with Lucas to provide him with work that he hadn't lashed out with his temper.

Violet knew from small things that Galina had shared with her that her father was one to take his frustrations out on her. Violet knew that kind of father-daughter relationship herself.

Her thoughts for Galina and her mother were fervent as she prayed.

Violet wiped a few stray tears that had traveled down her cheeks. She stood, wanting to think on something besides this illness that had affected so many lives in her world.

She wandered through the kitchen trying to think of anything to do to keep her hands busy when a knock interrupted her thoughts.

Her shoes clicked across the floorboards as she made her way to the front door.

She was shocked to see a young man she knew, one she loved and had lost, staring back at her.

This blond young man seemed as shocked as she.

She looked him over, drinking in his looks, the straight blond hair, cut short but with long sideburns beside his ears. His tall frame looking so much bigger than the last time she had seen him. He had been no more than ten years old the last time she had clasped eyes on him.

"Timmy." Was all she could say.

"You look well, sister." He replied back to her. His voice sounding like a man, a bit like her father.

Violet swallowed and paused, she was locked into a trance, recalling memories of playing along the riverbank with him, hide-and-seek in the mill near dusk. Where had all the time gone?

Violet finally remembered her manners and stepped back, welcoming him to come in.

"I saw your name in the paper. I snuck away and asked around. The folks at the fancy goods store told me where to find you." Tim said, he stepped through the doorway and followed her to the parlor.

Violet nodded at his statement, thinking how strange this moment felt within her. Like visiting a past life.

"You look well. I am glad you recovered." Tim said.

Violet murmured a thank you, but she could not think what else to say. He was here, her brother, flesh and blood shared between them, and she did not know him.

"I know this is odd, seeing me like this." He said and sat in the chair she gestured to. "You work here as a housekeeper?" Tim asked, probing her to speak to fill the empty silence of the room.

"Yes, the Grants are good to me." She wanted to say they were her family. But she felt that would be insulting somehow.

"I am glad you have a good placement." Tim was rubbing his hands together. Violet remembered that gesture from his childhood, he had done that when he was nervous.

Violet nodded and searched for something to communicate.

"I was married." Violet stated and felt foolish. "He died in California."

Tim's face showed a pained look.

"I am sorry Vic." He said sincerely, using the name he had said a thousand times or more as a child. It sounded odd and comforting to hear to Violet's ears.

"Yellow fever..." She stated flatly. Then laughed without mirth.

Tim's frown was deep. He didn't seem to have a reply.

"You are 18 now?" She asked.

"Yes, only just." Tim said with only one side of his mouth shooting up in a half-smile.

"Yes." Violet did grin. "May 3rd, I recall."

The silence grew heavy for a minute or more. Violet felt it grow within her as she struggled with her feelings and thoughts.

Why was he here?

"I came to see you, because when I saw your name..." Tim was rubbing his hands together again.

Violet chewed on her lip while she waited for him to finish.

"I just saw it and knew I had to try. To know you were well. That you survived after all this time." Tim met her gaze. His pained expression broke her heart.

"We live outside of town and rarely leave the watermill. We were never allowed to speak of you." He looked down at the floor, his shoulders slumped forward.

Violet reached out to him, filling the empty space between them and touched one of his shoulders.

"Harold and I missed you. We spoke of you when we did chores." Tim looked up at her again. It was painful to see the agony in his eyes.

"Is Harold well?" She asked, thinking of her youngest brother, with his mop of blond hair and endless energy.

"Yes, He is almost 16, he is even taller that I am." Tim smiled a little fuller.

Violet saw his smile and rejoiced inside herself for seeing it, but instantly felt a sense of foreboding.

"What are your plans, Tim?" Violet's tone sobered, wondering what good could come from this visit.

"In life?" Tim sat up a little straighter.

"Did *he* send you here?" She didn't want to even say her father's name or even call him her father.

"No!" He stated emphatically and put up his hand in a sort of surrender. "I read the names in the paper aloud and skipped over yours. I didn't want to stir them up." Tim sighed deeply.

Violet joined him with a sigh of her own, in relief. "I am just confused. I don't know what to do here." She said softly. Feeling at a loss again, with an even deeper sense of guilt over some unnamed feeling.

"I really just wanted to see you happy." Tim finally said and met her eyes in an intense look. "And to know you are loved."

Violet's cheeks felt hot and she felt a warm rush envelope her. This was unexplored territory and she didn't know how to move forward. "That is kind of you."

"I didn't come to make you feel uncomfortable or anything like that. I guess I had this hope of seeing you taken care of and..." He paused, trying to find the right words. "That you escaped to a better future."

Violet silently watched Tim, seeing his face and the strong jaw, his features like her father and mother combined. She saw that his nose had a slight curve to the left, just a slight variation on her own nose. She didn't know that she did it but she reached out toward his face.

"Your nose..." She said and pulled her hand back. Feeling like an utter fool for speaking thus to him.

"Ah... well," Tim laughed softly. "Father and his fists. He does like to toss them around. I got a broken nose for pulling him off of m...." He stopped and his smile dropped to a frown.

"Off of Mama?" She finished for him.

Tim only nodded.

She had felt his fists many a time in the alone time he had set aside with her. To force her to his will. He would never leave marks where others could see, but she remembered them well. Violet closed her eyes and tried to will the memories away.

"You could leave." She offered, wanting to apologize for him having to stay under that roof, but she couldn't say it then. Her tongue felt heavy and stunted, unable to say what her heart wanted to.

"I won't leave as long as Mama and Harold are there." Tim said simply.

Violet nodded, seeing the man that he had grown into, better than his father already at eighteen than his father would ever be.

"I'm glad you came." Violet finally said and lost the battle of her emotions. A sob escaped her lips and Tim filled the space between them and embraced her. They both cried together.

Violet felt her brother's arms squeeze her tight and felt so comforted in a way that she hadn't in a long while. The connection had been lost for so long she thought with certainty that she would never play the role of a sister again. She thanked God for one more chance. Whatever storm came, she was glad for this gift.

Before he left, more than an hour later, she invited him back anytime he wished. He had said that he would talk to Harold in confidence, perhaps he could come with next time. Violet had whole-heartedly agreed. It was a first step. She knew that her parents must never know, but she was certain it was the right thing. God had brought this together, a blessing would come out of it, she was confident in that.

Corinne Grant

Corinne had indeed stayed throughout the worst of it, after getting water into Magdalena she had made some fever wart tea. They had coaxed her mouth open a little more and had spooned dribs and drabs into the sick woman. They would wait until she swallowed then continue. It was tedious work.

Galina left her mother's bedside only to check on her brothers, seeing that they were doing better at keeping her baby brother cleaner than she expected. His fever was high but the boys took turns wiping him down. She had never seen Milo and Pavel so dedicated and was more than proud of them.

Her father had sat with the boys throughout the evening. He came into the bedroom after dark. Galina and Corinne sat on each side of the bed, watching for any signs of improvement. So far they had seen none. Magdalena was looking worse by the hour.

"Mrs. Grant?" Slava's voice was just above a whisper.

Galina looked to her father to see his tear-stained cheeks. Corinne stood and walked to him.

"Yes?"

"My son..." His head gestured to the left of him, beyond the room.

Corinne wordlessly left and Galina heard soft voices and more tears from her brothers. Galina's heart dropped.

Corinne came back in, holding Radimir, she took the cold rag and handed him to Galina.

"Take everything off of him!" She ordered, her voice tense.

Galina quickly followed the orders. She heard footsteps and knew that her brothers and father were just behind her, watching from the doorway.

Corinne pointed to the bowl and Galina placed Radi in it. The cool water lapped over the sides and splashed on the floor and Galina's dress.

"Breathe Radi.... Breathe sweet baby." Corinne massaged the boy's limbs gently. Trying to will life into them. She lifted him up and scooped a hand full of water and smoothed it over the top his head. She forced a finger into his mouth and dribbled water in, but there was no response. She repeated these things several times until there was no more cause. His skin no longer flushed with pink, but slowly turning ashen. Baby Radi was gone.

Galina never heard the wailing of her brothers and her father. She never heard her own cries. The world was soundless and empty to her. She gasped for air as the room spun slowly.

Corinne wrapped her brother up, ignoring her own tears, and placed the boy on his mother's chest. Time stood still for a long while until all were certain. Magdalena Varushkin and the child were gone.

There was no such pain as this. The emptiness and numbness washed over Galina and she was lost to it. Her mother who was her guide and sweet escape from the harshness of the world was gone, along with the sweet cherub who had only just begun to live.

The sight of her mother's body holding her brother in that moment would stay with her for the rest of her life, the coldness of the moment a sweet agony.

Chapter 18

Dolly Bouchard

Dolly tripped over a root and nearly tumbled over, the area was hard to walk in, so many close trees and knobby roots sticking up, some hidden under dried leaves from the previous autumn. Dolly was tired and ready to stop but she knew it was just past midday.

She needed to push through her apathy. This journey was harder than she expected, being alone out in the wild was the loneliest she had ever felt.

The sounds at night kept her on edge and she never slept as soundly as she needed to. She felt dirty and lost, not knowing if she had picked the right direction half the time. The sun hid behind the clouds for most of the day. She was heading toward an area that she hoped would allow her easy access between the hills. She was on a dangerous trail, whether the path was easy or not, wondering if all her efforts would be wasted if she picked the wrong way and ended up trapped with mountain cliffs or a water feature that would make her turn around. She had seen a few potential caves along her way always looking at the bluffs to the west of her, but the potential to be a bear or mountain lion den was just too great. She heard the big cats every night, knowing this was their hunting grounds and they would be active, probably providing meat for newborn cubs. Dolly shuddered at the thought of coming face-to-face with a predator.

She made a spear a few days before by splitting the top of a long pole, stripping off the branches and tying one of her knives into the split then tying it tight. Her hands had burned for an hour after she tugged and pulled on the string to make certain it was tight. She had tried out her spear a few times a day, working on her aim. She wasn't certain it would do much to scare a large animal but she had something to fight with if it came to it.

She stumbled on through the day, her feet sore from the uneven ground. Her moccasins were not as sturdy as a good pair of regular shoes.

Dolly encouraged herself every few minutes to just keep moving forward. Only a few more hours and she could stop and set up a quick shelter. Then she could rest before she set up a snare or two. She needed some food.

Angela Fahey

Angela barely was able to get her one horse buggy through the creek bed near her home, with the drier weather she had seen others use the road through. It was a bad idea. The washout had eroded the sides and the huge drop when she went into the normally smooth creek bed just did not work like it had before the spring rains. The buggy slammed down hard off the edge and Angela fell off her spring seat and slammed her hip and leg into the side. Feeling it shake her to the core before she righted herself and got back in her seat.

She had to slap the reins on her horse's rump to get the animal to move. Angela fought off her nerve as the pain radiated down her leg. Her old bruise from her injury letting its presence be known.

Once she was back on the road she kept the pace slow. Feeling perhaps she had made the wrong choice to take the buggy. Everyone on her side of the road had complained about the creek passing, knowing there was a plan in place to build a bridge, but her desire to go into town was too great and she ignored the warnings. She now wondered how long her leg would hurt because of her decision.

Angela tried to ignore the pain as she rode along, a part of her enjoying the beauty around her. It was the first of June and the weather was perfect. The other part went to the ones that were suffering. She had found out the night before that Galina's family had suffered two losses in the space of a few minutes. Corinne had sent for her after she returned home. Angela arrived at Grant's Grove to see Corinne in tears, utterly spent.

"I left when Doc Williams came. He had nothing to do but cry with the family. He told me before I left that with the Varushkins that made five deaths in one day, just in Oregon City. He claimed that there were at least ten more people that were in the later stages of the fever." Corinne said with her heart so heavy that Angela could feel her pain from the doorway.

Angela had spent the evening comforting Corinne. Angela was glad that Megan had chosen to stay a few days with her Uncle John and Marie Harpole.

Angela had gone home and talked for a while with Olivia, who was such great company. They prayed for the Varushkins and even shed tears together. The loss was felt and carried by everyone.

Angela had woken up with a determination to see Clive and Ted. To be close to the people she loved.

Angela's thoughts were jumbled as she rode. Thinking about the deaths of Galina's family and wondering how she could express her thoughts to Ted. She wanted to be married to him. She felt like the time had come. She did not want to regret not having every day they could have together.

Angela delivered her buggy to the livery, deciding to board it there until the bridge was built. She walked across the street feeling the pain in her leg intensely. After two steps the pain took her breath away. That old deep tissue bruise in her leg was aggravated.

She limped into the fancy goods store and saw Millie and JQ at the counter.

"Oh sweet Angela." Millie exclaimed and made a few steps toward Angela and then she saw that Angela was limping. "Oh my heavens." Millie placed her hands over her ample bosom and frowned in sympathy.

Angela was hoping to avoid anyone noticing her in pain but she knew it was a foolish hope. "My buggy and the creek crossing had a disagreement, and I lost." Angela smirked sarcastically.

"That doesn't sound good, Red." JQ said. He had started to call her Red like Clive did and she found it comforting.

Angela let them fuss over her before she asked to see Clive.

"Oh, so good of you to come. Clive needs a distraction. His fever has been gone since yesterday but I made him stay in bed today. Took all my threats to get him to stay there. I thought I may have to board the door shut." Millie laughed good-naturedly and led Angela up the stairs. JQ wouldn't allow her to resist his help up the stairs.

Clive was sitting in an armchair in the parlor. Millie huffed at his being up.

"I only took a few steps to get here, and then stayed put. I was gonna get bed sores iffen' I stayed in that bed one more minute." Clive said with a wide grin for his visitor.

Angela limped into the room and immediately had to explain her injury.

"I swear I'll be right as rain in a few days. Just jostled it a bit." She promised him after she explained.

"Jed, son, can you find a solid cane for the fair lady." Clive gave his son a look.

"Our minds are of one purpose. I was thinkin' of the same thing." JQ left and his chipper ca-thump ca-thump down the stairs could be heard, as well as the tinkling of the bell from the front door.

"Oh that is my call. You set down and rest yourself." Millie patted Angela's shoulder.

Angela couldn't resist giving Clive a kiss on the cheek before she sat down in the chair next to him.

"You cannot know how glad I am that you are well." Angela said will conviction.

"Me too dear girl. Never will underestimate yellow fever." Clive said and grasped her nearest hand in his. "I heard about Mama Varushkin and her youngest."

Angela nodded, feeling the pain of it run through her flesh. "I have no words." Angela took a deep breath, willing herself not to tear up. She felt so deeply for Galina and her family.

Angela shared everything that Corinne had told her the night before, and Clive shared his news from town.

"Portland has had more than 12 deaths already, and Salem more than ten." Clive said soberly. "But the good news, iffen there can be any of that with such a thing, is that Doc Williams claims there are no new cases in the last two days. We talked of it this morning when he checked in on me. I think he just wanted some of Millie's cream puffs, more than my sour company."

"You are never sour company." Angela squinted at him and grinned.

"I was after he told me to stay abed today." Clive winked at her and her mood lightened.

"I am glad he did, you are so stubborn that tomorrow you will probably be off on one of your adventures. I wouldn't be able to catch you, especially now." Angela looked at her throbbing leg with an accusatory glare.

"Nah, young lady, I am changing my ways." Clive confessed, with his hands up in surrender. "I feel an urge from the Lord above to stay put more. Cannot say exactly what that entails, but knowing that the Lord is still willing to give me that soft voice of His to me. The stubborn old coot that I am. I am feeling obliged to listen."

Angela nodded, amused that Clive was considering staying closer to home. She knew that would be a great challenge for him.

"I've been having some thoughts and prayers answered like that myself." Angela shared her thoughts about her relationship with Ted. He had been a witness to the first days they had met and courted. Now she was counting on his wisdom. "His mother wants us to wait a few years."

"Well, Mama's do tend towards long courtships, especially when it concerns their baby boys. Not certain why they spend so much time trying to raise up a man, then resort to drastic measures to keep them a boy." Clive cackled happily.

Angela was happy for the subject change. Not certain her heart could take more talk of yellow fever.

"I will talk to him today, Lord willing." Angela smiled, hoping that Ted would be receptive to her idea.

"I think you are a wise woman." Clive smiled back at her.

"Clive, if this all works out... would you walk me down the isle?" Angela felt his hand squeeze hers affectionately.

"Awe, Red. I would be honored." He placed his other hand on top of the one he held. Angela closed her eyes and sighed. She was so lucky to have Clive in her life.

Millie came back upstairs. "Don't mind me, just going to make some tea."

She rattled around in her kitchen. To Angela this place reminded her of the place in San Francisco when she had stayed with Gabriel and Amber Quackenbush. It was spacious and homey, with all the lovely touches.

Millie served them tea and cookies and went down when the bell rang again, taking her tray of tea with her to serve JQ.

"I was thinking of doing something fun next week." Angela said while blowing on her hot tea.

"Oh, do tell." Clive was in high spirits, glad to have a good visit.

"Well, I want to start a betting pool about a certain lady and a certain gentleman." Angela's eyes were wide with her secret.

"Oh really, I do love this game. I do recall losing badly once when Ted had his eye on you, Red." Clive wiggled his eyebrows at the memory. As if it still smarted.

"I remember that fondly." Angela sighed dramatically and enjoyed Clive's exaggerated eye-roll.

"I've been ill so you must fill me in on the players involved." Clive took a sip of his tea and scooped up a cookie. "I may be an old coot but I do enjoy watching young love sparking. It is very entertaining."

He finished his cookie in two bites.

"In most cases I would tell you and be glad to share the details. But I just now realize that telling you about it could greatly affect the outcome." Angela sipped her tea innocently.

"I cannot reckon to yer meanin'." Clive gave her a sideways look, he seemed disappointed that she would give nothing away.

"You may not reckon..." Angela said, she couldn't hide her smile. "But I am hoping you catch on sooner than later."

Clive looked baffled.

Angela grabbed a cookie and nibbled while Clive pestered her for details. She laughed a time or two but said little about the subject again.

JQ came upstairs with a dark wood cane that he made Angela try out. It did help with putting weight on her leg and she thanked him.

She kissed Clive again before she left, and he promised to come for a visit soon.

"Indeed, I expect that." Angela smiled wistfully at him again before she made her way slowly down the stairs.

Ted was on the front porch swing with a glass in his hand, casually resting on the arm as the swing moved back and forward. He grinned widely when he saw Angela approached.

Angela felt the familiar feeling that she always had when she saw Ted, that sense of safety and love that he gave her. His blue cotton shirt crisp and clean, he was looking rather dapper. His blond curls tumbled over his forehead.

"Hello, my Angel." He said sweetly and gestured for her to join him on the swing.

Angela sighed in spite of herself and jumped up each step with enthusiasm.

"I wanted to enjoy this fine day." Ted said and offered her a sip of his lemonade.

She shook her head 'no' but plopped next to him, the swing swayed erratically for a moment before settling itself.

He saw her leaning on the cane as she walked up the steps.

"I bumped it in the buggy." She said and he nodded. He seemed to sense that she didn't want to talk about her leg. Instead he welcomed her to his side with his smile.

"Could I just keep you on this swing with me forever?" He leaned over and kissed her on the cheek.

"I think that could be arranged." Angela finally spoke, feeling like her heart was ready to spill out of her chest.

He put his arm around her shoulders and she leaned against him, closing her eyes and just enjoying the nearness. It was a quiet minute this way, just being together that spurred Angela to speak again. She didn't even open her eyes but spoke from her place against his shoulder.

"I have a thought, Ted." She said quietly.

"I am sure it is a brilliant one." She could hear the smile in his voice.

"Well, I have thought much about what your mother said last week about our courtship, and I do despise going against anyone's advice, but I feel in my heart that I do not want to wait two years to be your wife."

Ted stopped pushing the swing forward with his feet. Angela finally opened her eyes and looked at Ted who gazed back at her intensely.

"I could not agree more." He admitted. "I have wanted to speak with you about this every day since then. I held back though."

Angela nodded, knowing how difficult it was to have a serious discussion with people always around them.

"Are you certain you do want to marry me?" Ted asked, he didn't seem to doubt her, but maybe just making absolutely certain.

"I am beyond certain, Ted." She said with all sincerity.

"Why am I the one who has earned your hand?" Ted said and leaned back, smirking.

"You are fishing for compliments Mr. Greaves." Angela poked him playfully in the ribs.

"Well, yes..."

"I think you are the kindest, strongest, best man for me. You love the Lord, and you love me." Angela leaned against his shoulder again. The motion of the swing began again.

Eventually the talk went on to other things, the loss of Galina's mother and brother, of his family and their recovery, but mostly they spoke of a wedding. It was decided by the end of that long swing visit that a wedding would come to the valley by mid-summer. Ted and Angela had found their happiness in each other. It was a good thing.

Chapter 19

Dolly Bouchard

Dolly stood on the rock, looking down the edge of the ravine, her mind pondered the danger of a fall but she had to risk it. There was no good way back but days and days to find another route. She was seventy-feet away from safety, she just had to survive this part.

She was committing herself to her set course with one simple action. She held her pack for a long second. Considering and reconsidering her plan. Once she tossed her bags over the side to the landing below she would have to make the climb, whatever the consequences may be.

She took a breath, smelling pine and earth, and let the bag go after a swing. She picked up her knife pole and also tossed it with gusto. She watched it turn and dance through the air before thudding unceremoniously into a heap of dried leaves and earth.

Her ankle was still just sore enough from a twist she received from a clumsy jump off a boulder.

She had found a good hill to climb and get a vantage point and it seemed to be a perfect spot to move between ranges. Dolly felt a bit silly but wondered if anyone had ever used this place before as a pass. It was not really wagon safe, but a nice clear view and a smooth way for as far as she could see.

Once she got through the thick woods settled at the apex of the hill and mountain junction she saw a few obstacles, but nothing that made her consider turning around.

After twisting her ankle the little bit she had taken a break and sat on the mossy rock and thought about her quest for home. She thought of Chelsea Grant with her children scurrying around, she thought of Corinne and their many excursions into the woods, all these thoughts moved along to others until she settled on Reggie, his black hair and serious eyes staring into her, seeing through the walls she had put up around herself.

The thoughts had clung to her as she had traveled that day, her hardest day yet.

She now stood on the edge of her sanity and strength, the rocks and boulders had taken every ounce of focus and concentration to climb and scuttle down. Now she must move forward and she let the fear go.

The large tree fall was leaning on the rock she stood on, a great rock that was a chunk of the mountainside. The tree was solid and had been there a few years and the vines and branches of other plants and trees had attached itself to the tree and the mighty rock. It was where Dolly placed her hopes of reaching the bottom. She saw as she reached for the tree's trunk the state of her hands, scratched, and bruised, she looked down and the state of her clothes was not any better. Dolly knew there was nothing for her vanity today, she would survive to take a bath in the stream later. She reached for the tree and with a careful and cautious stance she swung her body over the fallen tree and let herself off the safety of the edge.

"Oh, Lord protect me!" She said loudly as she made her way down.

Her knees hugged the trees and her feet searched for ledges, she tried to always keep at least three parts of herself touching an edge at all times. Her left foot found a spot that was solid, her hands were clasped upon a vine, each thicker than her own wrists, her right foot went lower and found a crevice, it was solid and she lifted her left foot out of it's safety and searched for a lower spot. On she went, painfully and methodically, her skirts catching and tugging on every thing they could, her sleeves and hair trying their hardest in the game to compete for the largest nuisance award.

At one point her legs were tired and her muscles cramped from squeezing her body closed to the tree. She took deep breaths, wishing for cool water and to lie down. She still had at least twenty feet to go before she could safely jump off. She stopped moving and hugged herself against the tree, praying and breathing deeply, catching her breath and willing herself to find her second wind.

The journey downward continued, her feet and hands ever-searching for its next hold. Dolly had never felt more exhausted. She slid a few feet downward when her foot slipped and fear clutched her but her wits were about her and she grabbed tight to the vine that was near her and was able to stop before she plummeted. Two minutes later she was only five feet above the ground and with what energy she had left she pushed out and jumped. She bent her knees when she landed and let herself tumble safely and harmlessly to the ground.

Dolly lay on the ground, she looked about and saw her pack nearby and the pole as well, she was safe and alive. She enjoyed the long moment she spent on the ground, she sang out sweetly a song from the Spring Creek church, perhaps not as prettily as her friend Violet did, but she felt a praise enter her heart and had to let it out. She was alive, and one step closer to home.

She waited a few minutes before she stood. She laughed merrily as she shook a pound or more of dirt, bark, dead leaves and debris from her clothes, promising herself to never wear a skirt again while shimmying down anything. She'd rather be caught climbing in her under things than do that again.

Her arms were rubbery and legs shaky as she picked up her pack and pole from their landing spots. She knew she would be no good for any more travel for a while. She saw the creek she had spotted from the giant rock and headed toward it, knowing that she could make a place to rest. Then she could fish again. She felt accomplished and knew some good was coming her way.

Violet Griffen

Violet sat with Galina for a long while after the task was done. They had cleaned and prepared Magdalena and Radimir for burial. For Violet it had been harder than she thought, originally offering to help to take some burden off of Galina's shoulders. Knowing the young girl would have a hard time doing it alone.

Corinne had given Violet some perfumed oil and then Marie Harpole had given Violet some instructions to make the burial process easier, as well as some white linen she had in her sewing pantry.

Violet had shown up in the early morning and Galina had welcomed her warmly. Her father, Slava, couldn't bear the thought and had taken the boys out early, he had mumbled something about fishing. Violet had stood with Galina watching the males leave and was glad at least Slava had lifted the body onto the table for them.

Violet set herself to getting hot water on to boil and Galina stared at the table for a few minutes, her eyes red-rimmed but tearless. She seemed lost in thought. Violet figured that Galina was imagining her life without her mother. Violet had spent many numb moments this way imagining life without Eddie. It was a part of the process and Violet wouldn't stop Galina from doing it. She was here if Galina needed her.

Galina finally came out of her stupor, "Do you know what to do?"

"I was told by Marie." Violet said simply.

"So you never have?" Galina asked and looked to Violet with a haunted look.

"No..." Violet said but had a strange thought, she pondered whether or not she should share it. She decided to let the words out. "I wish I had... with Eddie."

Galina took a step forward and grabbed Violet's hand.

Violet continued. "To say goodbye, and do one last thing for him."

Galina nodded vigorously, understanding the depth of what Violet meant.

Violet offered up a sweet prayer before they started, asking for God's blessing to be over them as they cared for two precious children of God. Galina was moved and ready to start when she uttered 'amen.'

The duty set before them was at times unpleasant and difficult. Galina felt many moments of overwhelmed emotions, and took several breaks to cry or to go outside the door to get fresh air. Violet always joined her, they were in this together.

Violet had been moved to tears a few times herself. Washing baby Radimir, then drying his tiny fingers and toes had been profound to her, her heart a broken and shattered stone by the time it was done. Seeing the pale cheeks and lips had nearly done her in. This sweet child, no longer to squeal and wiggle and be.

Violet had held Galina's shoulders as Galina brushed her mother's freshly washed hair, Galina's sobs were tearing at Violet's soul but she kept her own composure. Violet felt that a few tears was alright, but she did not feel right to lose herself in her own grief, when she was trying to lift Galina up.

After the cleaning, Violet anointed each body with the perfumed oil, the heavy rose scent was thick and powerful in the small room but it did a lot to hide the smell of death that was lingering.

They took turns to dress the bodies and get them wrapped in the white linen, only their faces showing. Galina and Violet were both tired by the time the task was done, but both relieved to have been the ones to do it.

The woodworker was set to come at noon and he was one minute early, his knock at the door was welcomed.

"I brought the casket, ma'am." Amos Dreys, the carpenter said softly, his soft brown cap respectably in his hands.

"Thank you, Mr. Dreys." Violet said and opened the door to allow him in. "We just finished here."

He took a few steps in and bowed slightly to Galina. "I am sorry Miss, for your loss." His words felt more than perfunctory; there was a deeper sense of sincerity from this soft-spoken man.

"They will be placed in together, yes?" He asked, going about his business.

Galina nodded. Violet stood next to her to give her support. Galina was looking a bit overwhelmed. Violet wished that Slava Varushkin would have not been such a coward.

"I've brought some lads with me to help. Should we do this in here or outside?" He looked to Galina. Galina in turn looked up to Violet.

Violet saw that there wasn't enough room to maneuver with so many people and a large casket.

"Perhaps just outside." Violet offered.

"I am prepared for that." Amos spoke and went out the front door, leaving it open.

Violet and Galina stood still, waiting in place to watch the young men work.

Violet could see that Mr. Dreys was setting up a short table, the legs on hinges and he pulled each leg down and settled the casket with the help of the two lads he brought along. Violet was surprised to see a nice casket, with scrolling work on the sides, not the plain pine box she had expected.

Galina had looked confused and had walked to the door unexpectedly.

"Mr. Dreys?" Galina spoke quietly, "I thought we were to have a plain pine casket."

"The church in town paid for this one." The man said simply, he bowed and continued on with his work.

Galina had fresh tears on her cheeks.

The three young men came in and took Magdalena, a man at the head, foot and midsection, they shuffled their way through the house and out of the front door. They gently set her in the coffin, instead of watching as Galina gently scooped up her brother and carried him to the door. Mr. Dreys took the small body and placed him in his mother's arms. He pulled the linen over there faces. Their faces pale and beautiful under the sheer weaved fabric.

Violet joined Galina and watched as they settled the lid on the coffin. The funeral was later in the day, and Violet invited Galina to get ready at the Grant's home. Marie had promised a black dress to be laid out for Galina's use. Galina agreed.

They put the house back in order and put away everything. Galina left a note behind for her father and gladly left.

Galina Varushkin

Galina had been embraced by nearly two hundred people as they left the church cemetery. Galina had been surprised by the numbers that had come to pay respects, her father had commented more than once how honored he was that so many had come.

Galina was a bit numb but she held together better than she expected. She felt the time in the afternoon had been her final goodbye.

Clive had bravely come out of his sickroom to be there early, and he had given Galina a bear hug that she had needed so badly.

"I risked the threats of a daughter-in-law to be here today. But I wanted to be here for ya." Clive had a way about him. He smoothed a hand on her shoulder and said the thing she had so wanted her father to say. "I heard you did a good job in caring for your mama and brother today. I am so proud of you." She soaked in his praise and it warmed up the coldness that had settled around her heart.

Pastor Whittlan had spoken sweet words over her mother and brother and many hankies were dabbed at cheeks. Slava had thanked everyone for coming and Galina had said a few words when she stood over the casket. Her words were stilted and not eloquent. She was not feeling poetic just then. She was just broken.

She watched her father and brothers, with a few of the church men, lowering the casket into the ground. The air was quiet and Galina thought of all the words that she wanted to say to her mother the most.

I miss you Mama, so much already. I promise to take good care of my brothers. I will try to sing to them all the songs you taught me from the old country, so they will never forget you. I will mind my tongue when talking to Papa. I will never lose sight of God or forget all the blessings He has given me. I will try so hard to be good. Please be proud of me Mama.

Galina began to weep and turned away from the grave. Her shoulders shook and she wrapped her arms tightly around herself. It seemed only a second like this before she was surrounded by arms. A handkerchief was thrust into her hand and the group around her rocked with her as she continued her weeping.

Corinne, Violet and Angela all stood with her when she had the strength to look up. They didn't say a word but each woman there was holding onto her. It was enough to make her stronger. God had provided the comfort she needed to get through this day. If He could do that, he could do it tomorrow.

Chapter 20

Corinne Grant

Corinne was dressed in a simple brown skirt and white blouse, her dark brown shoes laced up tight around her ankles. She had asked Megan to join her on a walk through the woods to gather plants and starters for her greenhouse. Megan had scoffed at first but agreed to it finally, after realizing that she needed to get out of the cabin. Corinne had convinced her cousin to wear simple clothes.

News had spread that there were no new cases of yellow fever in Oregon City. Everyone was feeling a need to get out and socialize again. In many peoples minds it was a desperate need to remember that they were still alive. So many funerals in the past few days had brought people to a deep sense of gratitude if their own household hadn't been visited by death.

Corinne and Megan started toward the road, where the men were starting their work on the new bridge. It was a happy thought for all those who lived on spring creek road, the bridge would make travel by wagon available again.

Megan gasped when they reached the road and saw so many men, digging in the creek bed, shirtless in the sun.

"Oh my!" Megan stated, her eyes were wide. "I should have worn a nicer dress." She muttered only loud enough for Corinne to hear.

Corinne couldn't help but laugh. She was pleased to see her husband, also shirtless, working hard alongside the other men. She may have taken a moment to appreciate his form, he was her husband after all.

"They will be in work mode dear. They won't notice us that much today." Corinne said and they walked closer when she saw her husband wave her over.

"Speak for yourself." Megan exclaimed and patted her hair absently.

Corinne ignored her fretting cousin and took in the scene around her. The creek bed was dug out on the sides with six heavy posts leaned against the muddy sidewalls. On the opposite side of the creek a team of four workhorses was pulling a stack of small logs all cut the same length. Corinne hadn't seen the schematics of the bridge but her mind was putting the pieces together to see how it would form.

She looked down into the creek bed again and her husband was climbing the sides with some effort. He popped up at her side and gave her a sweaty kiss on the cheek.

"Hello my bride." He smiled charmingly.

"Oh, you are at your most handsome and boyish while digging in the dirt." Corinne flirted, her smile was broad.

"Ah, yes... us boys do love to play in the dirt." He chuckled. "We will get the posts in today. I have to bring over the rocks to stabilize them. We have a good work crew." Lucas pointed over to the men across the creek to where Corinne could see her father standing with Reggie and a few other men.

"I heard that a few men from town were coming by to help out as well." Corinne said.

"Oh yes, I expect it. People like getting involved in a project like this. It reminds us of when we were young and would build anything with sticks and rocks." Lucas wiped at some crumbly dirt on his breeches. It was a hopeless gesture, he was caked in dirt and mud.

Corinne saw Reynaldo and Russell still digging in the creek bed. "Your brother looks some much like you. I hope I never get confused and grab ahold of him." Corinne giggled at the thought.

Lucas gave her another kiss on the cheek. She dismissed him.

"I'll be off to the woods." Corinne waved and blew him a kiss.

"Enjoy your scrounging." He called back and he climbed back into the creek bed, his bare feet splashing in the water and muck.

Corinne walked over to her cousin who was pestering Reynaldo. Megan was talking and flirting at a fast rate, Corinne tried not to laugh when Reynaldo rolled his dark eyes around at Megan, like a man who was tired of a pestering sibling.

"Let's go and leave the men to their work." Corinne took hold of Megan's arm as a cue to leave. Megan shot Corinne an angry look, her mouth tight and her eyebrows squished down unpleasantly. She relaxed her face a half-second later and gave her a fake smile.

"Yes, cousin." Megan said with a tight voice.

It could have been a delightful walk in the woods, the air was warm, the breeze gentle and the fragrant woods offering up its many delights, but Megan made the trip nearly unbearable. Corinne had to coax the girl along often and then when Corinne found plants she wanted to transplant and took more than a few seconds to dig up their fragile roots Megan would get impatient and chastise Corinne for moving like an old woman.

Corinne thought about Dolly and prayed for her as she progressed through her morning. She missed having her enthusiastic partner and it made Corinne reminisce about how her mother and Grandmother had spent so many years in the woods and mountains of Kentucky when she was young. Corinne tuned out her cousin and thought instead of her childhood and the many things she had learned from the women of her family. By midday Corinne had the urge to go back home and dig out her journals from them and begin working again on the book she and Dolly were writing. She had put it off since Dolly had left but the urge was growing within her with those little nudges that told her that the Lord was leading her there. She was ready to move forward on that project, she had mourned Dolly's leaving long enough. She had to except that Dolly would come back in her own time, and Corinne had to do what she was called to do.

Corinne stretched a healthy stretch of her arms and back, having bent over a little more than her back enjoyed. "Let's head back."

"Oh good." Megan huffed and smiled in a way that annoyed Corinne.

Corinne wondered if there was anything in the world that Megan enjoyed besides being a nuisance and flirting with men who weren't interested.

They made it home in time for lunch with Violet, Corinne was glad for the sane company.

Clive opened his cabin door and heard the indistinguishable sound of something scurrying. He muttered under his breath, then chuckled softly.

The ride from town had been slow. His body had taken quite a beating from that darned fever. He was sore and tired in parts of his body that he didn't enjoy much.

He was pondering his visit with Angela as he walked through his cabin, looking for tell-tale signs of any kind of rodent infestation. The sunbeams came through the windows and shown light into the darkness of his cabin. He got to his usually tidy countertop and found the evidence. Mouse droppings and a hand towel with a corner that was tattered with obvious chew marks.

"Stupid critters." He muttered again a bit.

He rummaged through a nearby drawer and found a piece of wire and then a piece of moldy bread in his breadbox. He reminded himself to clean out his cupboards well or the critters would take over the place.

He concentrated on setting a snare to catch his 'visitor'. He used the knob on a cabinet and strung the wire up just right. He contemplated as he was setting the snare, wondering again at getting a new place. He had thought of buying a townhouse closer to the fancy goods store. He would still want to keep his land, but he didn't know if he wanted to stay way out here anymore. The place was a bit too quiet for him these days. He liked being around people more, he noted, it was nice to have company around.

Clive wove the wire expertly, having decades of practice and got the snare set and tested it. It worked like a charm, he reset it with ease and backed away. Thinking that he would need to go visiting with someone to get a good meal for supper. He wasn't sure if he trusted anything that came out of his kitchen until he did a thorough scrubbing. He wasn't sure he had the energy for that yet.

Perhaps Angela would be up for a visit and pick her brain on the mysterious conversation she started earlier. He knew she would have had her visit with Ted, he thought of her for a while after she left. Praying for the future of that young couple. He knew that Ted would treat her well.

Clive took a seat in his parlor and found his pipe. Within a minute of puttering he found some pipe tobacco in a tin. With the scratch of a match and a few puffs he was happily lounging, enjoying the rare treat of his pipe. After two puffs and a little contemplation he figured out what Angela was hinting at. His jaw dropped in shock for more than a half minute. Then he just laughed.

He spent a few minutes puffing away then he got up to get cleaned up. He was inviting himself to dinner.

Olivia Greaves

Olivia sat on the porch, with embroidery in her lap, her eyes focused on the task set to tat out some fancy white flowers she was making as a surprise for Angela. She was rejoicing in her heart as she worked, hearing Ted and Angela inside the house laughing and flirting happily. It was a joyous sound after such a week full of bad news and sickness for so many. This happy thought of romance was a brief respite from the pain, even if it still lingered inside, it was pleasant to let it go for the smallest little moment.

The breeze was delightful and the sun sparkled on the world around her, catching on the water of the creek, and shining defiantly along the white picket fence of the horse ranch across the road. Olivia was glad she had come to stay for a time here. It was good for the soul.

The clip-clop of horse hooves alerted her to a visitor but she didn't look up, assuming it was Earl Burgess coming back from his visit to the Orchard house. She focused on finishing up the lovely piece she was working on, imagining it on Angela's dress. She would make lots of little flowers and attach them to the bodice of the dress, it would be stunning. Olivia smiled to herself, pleased with her surprise.

"That is a mighty pretty secret smile you have there, milady. Mind sharing your secret?" Clive Quackenbush's voice shocked her out of her thoughts and she looked up to his clear eyes just a few feet away from her. He was wearing a bright blue shirt and a bowtie, had she ever seen him in a bowtie? His smile was ever charming and a little sarcastic, which she found so very alluring.

She had forgotten what he had asked and she hoped beyond herself that she wasn't slack-jawed and staring at him. The question finally came back to her and she recovered her senses.

"My secret is only from the youngsters." She said softly enough for only his ears. His raised eyebrows were the only sign that he heard.

He walked quietly up the stairs his black boots shining, he had on dress slacks and black suspenders.

"You look dressed for Sunday meetin'" Olivia said with a little flair, proud of herself for getting her wits back.

"I wanted to get spiffied up." Clive sat in the chair next to her, he seemed in no rush for anything.

"Glad you are feeling better?" She asked and settled her hands in her lap and looked over to Clive, trying not to be unnerved by his closeness.

"Indubitably." He said and winked at her.

Olivia shook her head with a grin, he was incorrigible.

"Has anyone ever called you Olive?" Clive leaned in a little closer.

"I wanted to be called that when I was younger, but it never caught on, my parents were quite formal and despised nicknames." Olivia shared, she grinned at a memory.

"Well, I don't think I shall ever be stamped with formality as a character description."

Olivia laughed and agreed. "No, I think not. But that is part of your charm."

"So if I called you Olive would you mind so much?" He asked.

Olivia wrinkled her brow and gave him a long look. "I don't think I would mind. It is a rather nice thing to have a nickname, I think."

"Well, I would consider it a pet name in my mind." Clive sat back to watch her. It was making her nervous.

She paused and considered his words and would not let her mind carry them away into anything that was more than just his way.

"You have many pets?" She finally asked.

Clive chuckled and rocked a few beats in his rocking chair.

"I have a reputation for championing the female line. I never was one to enjoy the opinion of some men to say that women are the weaker sex." He started and gave her a sly look when her eyebrows rose in a moment of defiance at the thought. No woman likes that notion. Clive continued, "But I draw the line in my attentions to women at a certain respectable distance, perhaps not enough if you hear the gossips, but I always enjoy seeing my female friends succeed and go beyond what the world expects of them. Perhaps it's a hobby or even take it so far as a passion." He stopped rocking and looked at Olivia intensely, drawing her gaze until she wouldn't look away. "So I guess I need to be forthright in asking your permission to call, Ms. Greaves. So you don't confuse my attentions for my usual friendly banter."

Olivia was indeed shocked, she had placed that whisper of a hope in her heart for a new romance in her life. But to have it actually happen was another scenario entirely. She had no idea what to do with herself. Should she blush or grin or stammer and act like a foolish girl? She had no concept of what she was getting into.

"I would like that." She said lamely. The minute passed quietly, and Olivia felt her face heating up, like she had when she was sixteen and getting her first bit of male attention.

"I am a bit rusty at this." Clive finally admitted.

"As am I." Olivia laughed. She looked up from her lap and saw that Clive was grinning and relaxed, he was feeling a bit foolish too. It helped that she wasn't the only one in new territory.

"So now, I suppose I should go talk to Angela and invite myself to supper. Would you be up for a walk later? We can bring the youngsters along to be our chaperone." Clive gave her a wink and she nodded. Enjoying the way her heartbeat was tripping along at a new beat.

She heard Clive go into the house and the greetings and conversation and enjoyed her moment alone. Pondering the thought of having her very own gentleman caller. She sighed in relief of starting this new adventure in the relative privacy of Angela's home, without her sister and her ability to interfere. That was a problem for another day. For now she could spend a few weeks here and receive a few visits with little to no outward meddling.

She was certain that with Clive calling she was in for a bit of fun, and some adventure thrown in. Olivia hid the project she was working in her bag and got up to join the others in the house. She was happier than she had been in a long while. She was thankful.

Chapter 21

Oregon City

The town was abuzz with happy news and it was a good time for it. June had come in mild with warm sunny days and cool breezes. Sickness and death had blown through but many were glad for the reprieve and church activities and summer planting was on everyone's agendas. Garden's were growing with fresh starts of green plants, and summer romances bloomed. The biggest news was of course the wedding of Thaddeus Greaves and Angela Fahey, who were the darlings of every woman's conversation. Her houseguest was having her own rumors, the pert and pretty Olivia Greaves was seen several times on the arm of Clive Quackenbush and though the age difference of twenty years was a definite gap, it seemed a good match in everyone's mind but for the few naysayers. The general consensus was that Clive was a man with a young heart, and that wiry constitution that could keep up with a younger wife. She was smart and attractive and would keep Clive on his toes, they all reasoned, and that is where he should be.

The first weeks of June brought about the talk of the Spring Creek Bridge and the progress was shared over every sales counter and bench as men and women gathered in their daily errands.

The lumber mill kept buzzing through its many logs and the river flowed with many more as the weeks passed along. As all the families got about the business of summer the days of the yellow fever passed behind them and the only reminders in the sad faces of those it affected harshly.

Angela Fahey

Angela settled her tea into the saucer and gazed across the table at her fiancé. His hair had grown a bit over the spring and his long curls were hanging below his ears and even longer in the back. He looked handsome and manly and she couldn't help but admire her catch.

They had discussed the plans for the Sparks cabin to be built on the property. Knowing they had left Fort Kearney back in April she felt that ever present deadline looming closer and was glad to have Ted on board.

Since Edith and Henry Sparks had adopted three orphans from an earlier wagon train, Angela wanted to make sure the cabin was spacious enough for all of them. She envisioned a covered back patio, with an open yard for Edith's garden to the East. Mama Edith would enjoy sitting and watching over her precious vegetables and bushes.

Angela was not using the walking cane anymore after her accident in the buggy but she had it nearby if the throbbing returned. Doc Williams had told her that bruise may pester her off and on for a long while. She had accepted that, to live through such an ordeal, that dark night in the ravine, she was glad to have survived and was happy in her new life. She was not going to dwell on it.

Ted had grand ideas for the cabin and they discussed it at length. He promised to head into town in the afternoon and seek out Clive with ideas about hiring someone to help him get proper dimensions and then purchase the materials. Ted was excited for the task, and perhaps an excuse to be on the property every day.

"This place is beginning to sink into my bones, as ours." He told her over breakfast. "Does that bother you?"

Angela laughed. "Of course not. When I purchased the land I envisioned you with me. Even if we hadn't a full understanding of a future. I had the hope of it." She stood and kissed him to seal her words.

They had many days like this in June, talking about their future. Usually his Aunt Olivia, in her favorite place, in the rocker on the porch overlooking the southern valley.

As Ted was getting up to leave Angela heard talking on the front porch. Ted opened the front door and was surprised by Millie Quackenbush.

"Oh, having lunch with your betrothed." Millie smiled and patted Ted on the shoulder.

Ted grinned. "Cannot keep away. Just making plans and schemes."

Millie clapped her hands together in mirth. "Oh, young love is a thing to behold."

Angela joined them all on the porch. Ted kissed her on the cheek for his audience, it had the desired affect of ladylike snickers.

"I will come by later. Going to talk to Earl for a few minutes before I go." Ted said as he plodded down the porch steps.

"He is planting almond trees to the East." Angela pointed beyond the apple trees.

He nodded and waved. All three women watched him walk away.

"He is a good lad. I see him almost everyday, being such a close neighbor." Millie sighed and gave Angela a sly look.

"It is good to see you, Millie. What brings you out?" Angela had wanted to ask since she saw her there. Her politeness made her wait until just then.

"Well, there is news coming out in the paper but I was given an advanced copy. Mr. Hines at the paper is a friend of JQ's." Millie explained and Angela gestured for her to sit in the other rocker on the porch. Angela excused herself and grabbed a dining room chair and dragged it out. It was a habit when she had guests.

Angela settled the chair so the small group was a circle and sat, once she faced Millie then she continued.

"Well, I have already spoken to the Christian women's fellowship in town this morning and wanted to share with you and the rural community as well. But especially you, Angela." Millie took in a deep breath and a sad look came over her face.

Angela was worried by the look but had no idea what the fuss was about yet.

"Well, dear, I'll just spit it out. It started last week in Salem, a few members of the town council there met with a few in Portland, and I was told by Mr. Prince, whom you know is still the head of the town council here in Oregon City."

Angela huffed and grinned over her experiences with Mr. Prince. They were on speaking terms only, barely civil.

"He explained that he, nor the other members liked the idea but was pressured to agree, he wanted you especially to know that up front." Millie made eye contact with Angela to make sure he heard that part.

"That is fine, but what is the problem?" Angela was still confused.

"Due to the death of so many over the last month from yellow fever, between the three communities there are more than twenty orphans." Millie said and gulped. Angela sat up straighter, she felt a tensing in her stomach as Millie continued. "Salem and Portland have put forth the suggestion of building a Work Orphanage. They have pressured Oregon City into agreement, there were threats of cutting off the new mountain road construction if they didn't agree to it. Jed Prince was adamant that the agreement was only a temporary solution and he is seeking counsel from the governor and the church to see what can be done."

Angela felt ill, her years growing up in a work orphanage had been a travesty, and she wished for no child to ever experience that kind of degrading lifestyle again.

Two fat tears ran down Angela's cheek. "This will not be." She said firmly and swiped away the tears angrily.

Millie reached for Angela's hand. "It will not be!" She promised.

Millie told her all about the discussion in town, allowing Angela to absorb it all.

"I swear, this has the town's women in an uproar. The men will be too if us women put our minds to it. I believe a town meeting will have to be called to discuss ideas. But I have a simple one that I want to put forward." Millie offered.

"Do share." Olivia piped in, she was feeling the cause within her heart as well and didn't want to be left out, even though she was only a new member of the community.

"Well, in Oregon City there are seven or eight orphans from the fever. Certainly we could find good Christian folks to take some in here. We would have to be certain that each family was a good one, if funds were needed to clothe and feed we could, as a town we could provide that. Someone could be put in charge of that easily and then families could go through them to formally adopt the children. There is enough generosity in our hearts to do this. If we show the example to Portland and Salem, and perhaps a few well placed articles about it in the paper, you never know what the Lord could do." Millie grinned and both Angela and Olivia agreed. It was a good plan. It would take work to get town councils to agree but they have overcome other obstacles with town councils, they would succeed with this one as well. Especially knowing that the decision was one that was against their will.

Angela agreed to pass along the information to Corinne and the other women of Spring Creek Church; this would need to be a community effort to make a difference.

Dolly Bouchard

The water glistened as Dolly splashed herself with huge handfuls of water. She had come across a trapper cabin the day before, and knowing the rules of it, told to her by Clive in one of his many stories, she knew she could stay there and not be trespassing.

She had the feeling that she was getting nearer to civilization but she had no knowledge of exactly where she was. Her wandering took her over several mountain ranges and she always just used her knowledge of her childhood to find different routes. She had not come across any thing that was more than a game trail in days. The trapper cabin had given her a boost of energy. Inside she had found a decent cot, a few tins of beans, a wood stove and even a bar of soap.

Today she began with plans of a thorough bathing. She scouted around thoroughly, making certain there would be no witnesses beyond the squirrels and birds nearby of her cleaning ritual.

She laughed to herself as she enjoyed the water, she had her traveling clothes soaking in sudsy water and she cleaned her self and her hair several times. She brushed through her long dark hair, and spent a long afternoon in the sun, letting her self feel human. She had saved a set of clothes and not worn them to travel in, hoping when she saw signs of habitation she could change and not look like a vagabond savage. She had a worry in the back of her mind that if she came upon nervous strangers that they would think her to be something she was not. Her mind played through many scenarios.

She used the fishing tackle in the cabin to catch a few trout, and had a hearty dinner of fish and beans, glad to have a full tummy for her evening plans.

She hiked up the big hill to the East of the cabin and caught a glimpse of the valley before her. Her heart skipped a beat when she saw Mount Hood ahead of her, a few miles and mountains between but it was there. It was unmistakable. She jumped and clapped her hands in glee and celebrated with a whoop. She felt silly but she was so close to home, it was so very possible that she would survive this journey that had started as a mistake.

She hiked back down the hill, careful to keep her clean clothes clean, her other things were still drying back at the cabin. She spent her evening in prayer of thanksgiving, she braided her hair and repacked her bag before bed, ready to begin her journey early, with the sunrise, to get herself home. It would be days but the end was in sight.

Chapter 22

Galina Varushkin

Galina settled the pot on the stove and stared at it, not seeing it but deep in thought. She would be going back to her regular work the next day. Her father had insisted and Galina had agreed to it willingly. She was certain that her father didn't know how much she had really longed for it.

The community was generous in the last weeks since the funeral and each day a family had brought over food and supplies for them. Violet had been over several times a week to visit and bring over fresh bread and biscuits, she had even brought a few dried apple tarts that had cheered the boys up dramatically. Her home was quieter than usual, her brothers not themselves since their mother's death.

Galina actually missed the sound of their rowdy play, the cries of her baby brother were also noticeably absent. She was stuck in this strange new reality.

She helped some in the garden but her father hadn't asked her to do it. His demeanor was quiet also, dealing with his grief in his own way. He had barely spoken a word of it to her but she had overheard him talking to the boys. Mostly that they would have to be responsible young men now, and to remember to behave the way their mama raised them to be. Galina hadn't had to do much to keep them in line. Any word from her and they had obeyed immediately, Galina was not foolish enough to believe that this phase would last. Time would march on and they would return to their boyish ways as the weeks and grief passed.

The dinner table was the worst part of the day, everyone solemn and missing those that should have been there.

Her plans were to get back to living, even if it was just putting her focus on work and learning how to deal with the drastic change her life had taken. She spent a few hours of every day in tears that was unavoidable. She would not avoid the feelings, Violet had shared with her that the best way through the grief was to let it exist when it needed to, especially this early on. Later, Violet shared, she could learn to set aside time to mourn, and the body would adjust to the pain. At least that was how Violet explained it. Galina was learning to lean on Violet more and more as a mentor, and though she loved her many friends, Violet was becoming the one she could rely on the most. Galina said many prayers, thanking God for the friendship. It was the best thing she had in her life right now.

Galina had spent the last week putting away all reminders of her brother, his clothes, rocking bed and toys. Her father had taken the wooden pen and bed to the nearby church, telling them to find a good home for them. Seeing them on a daily basis had been a dagger to their hearts and had caused them all to bursts into sobs on many occasions, the reminders had to go.

Galina packed her mother's things and kept a few dresses and coats with her father's permission. Her mother did not have fancy things or jewelry to speak of, but the little things would keep her memory in Galina's heart fresh. The bedroom off the side of the kitchen was now her father's bedroom, with no reminders of the woman who shared it with him. Slava seemed to want it that way.

Galina set the table for dinner after a while, dreading the quiet house and being stuck in it alone. The lack of sound an ever-present reminder of those that were gone. The boys were in their last weeks of school, having to make up for the weeks that the school had been closed.

She had spent the day doing little jobs around the house, sweeping the floor, and scrubbing every particle of dust from the fireplace. The place was spotless and Galina was glad to keep her hands busy. She would need some sort of hobby to do at night so she would stop going stir crazy. She wondered if Corinne or Violet had any books she could borrow. Perhaps her father would no longer yell at her for reading. If ever there was a time to test the theory it was now. He didn't seem to have the energy for anger any more, Galina knew that too would only last for a time.

Dolly Bouchard

It had been two days of solid hiking when Dolly got her first glimpse of a road. She took the path of least resistant in most cases and was heading North of Mount Hood, She knew if she reached The

Dalles that she had gone too far. Her experience from the Oregon Trail had given her a good sense of where the major landmarks could be. She thrilled when she saw the signs of the road while resting on a hilltop. She nibbled on the fish she had caught that morning, she cooked them quickly over the fire and wrapped them in a handkerchief, and she ate as she walked.

She was more than ready to be back in civilization again, knowing how much work it had been to travel so far. She dreamt of a soft bed and a roof over her head.

She changed into her good blouse and green skirt and took care with her hair, despising the time it took but wanting to look like she belonged in the White man's world as much as she could with her light brown skin.

She was happy when her hair felt to be in place, she made a straight line toward the road and made a quick pace, her legs were ready for the travel as her many days had strengthened her body. The green leaves of the treetop rustled and cheered her forward. She was hoping today was the day.

The road was smooth dirt with a few wagon ruts showing constant travel. She saw the area ahead was opened up from the dense trees of a forest and she could see signs ahead of farms and fields. After an hour she crossed a footbridge and knew she was getting closer. She saw a house after another half hour of travel and was pleased to see a few young children at play in front of the cabin. She waved when one caught sight of her.

The other ran into the cabin. Dolly's breath was caught in her chest, a prayer escaped her lips as she hoped for the best.

"Hello." Dolly yelled when a woman appeared at the door with a large bowl at her hip.

The woman waved with the wooden spoon in her hand. It seemed a friendly enough gesture and Dolly made quick time toward them. It took her a few minutes to reach the yard. Dolly swallowed back her fears and went forward.

"Greetings." Dolly said smoothly, despite the pounding in her chest.

"Hello there." The woman said easily. She was tall and thin, with an easy smile. Her light green apron was lightly smudged and she had a young girl hiding behind her grasping hold of her skirts.

Dolly had been practicing what she would say for the last week of traveling. Hoping that she wouldn't alarm anyone. "I got separated from my traveling party in the mountains a few weeks ago. I am in Willamette Valley, correct?" Dolly said smoothly, so glad she had worked out so hard on her English.

"Oh yes, you poor dear. We live on the outskirts of Portland." She spoke, she had a few freckles across her cheeks.

"I know Clive Quackenbush very well, I believe his grandson owns a store in town." Dolly offered and saw the look of recognition on the woman's face.

"Oh, I met Clive once er' twice. Yes, his grandson Gabriel and his pretty wife live in town by the coast." She motioned for Dolly to come inside the cabin. Dolly followed mutely. So relieved that this woman was allowing her in.

"My name is Evie Brown. You come on in. You have been weeks alone in the mountains. My goodness you must be a strong gel'." She settled the bowl onto her small countertop.

She leaned out the door.

"Jessie!!" She yelled out the door and leaned in. "I'll send out my son to get my husband."

"I'm Dolly." Dolly said and saw her nod.

"I am happy you stopped. I am glad to help out a friend of Clive's. A good man all around."

Dolly nodded fiercely. "He is a very interesting man." She thought for a moment, choosing her words. "He has lived many lives." She said finally.

"Yes he has." Evie chuckled.

"Yes, Mama?" A young boy with dark red hair stuck his head in the door.

"Go fetch yer Papa. We have a guest for lunch." Evie instructed. The boy took off from the doorway at an impressive sprint. Looking happy to be put to task.

"It isn't nothin' fancy but some fried pork and bread and butter." Evie offered.

"That sounds like heaven." Dolly said and sat down at the table where Evie gestured. She settled her pack behind her.

While they waited she shared a summarized version of her story, and how she came to be alone. Evie seemed interested and sympathetic to Dolly's problem.

"Sounds like that Gray Feather was an angry young man. It doesn't matter what race or upbringin' sometimes. I am glad you made it safely away." Evie said as she sliced up the load of fresh bread for the table.

"I just feel really blessed that I survived. It was a hard journey. I felt like I was praying every moment." Dolly said feeling open to share. Evie was easy to talk to.

"You are a believer in God?" Evie asked, looking up from her chore.

"Yes, that is the biggest change within me, the reason I really don't belong with my old tribe." Dolly said simply, hoping that was understood.

"That makes sense, the verse where it speaks of not being unequally yoked with unbelievers. It can easily apply to anyone once you think of it. When you are with those that try to pull you away from your faith, it can be very destructive. Coming west was a way for us to live out our faith. To believe that God has called us to this simple life was why we came." Evie went back to her work.

A minute later Jessie and a man came through the front door.

"Oh Jamie, this is Dolly. A friend of Clive's." She said simply.

The tall man with broad shoulders and dark brown hair reached out to her with a big hand and an even broader smile.

"Good to see ya." He said, his voice low and husky.

Evie went into a speech that quickly explained Dolly's situation. Dolly felt the warm acceptance immediately. Knowing Clive Quackenbush had proven to be a great relationship; not only for his friendship, which was excellent, but his ability to have friends wherever he has gone.

Three children joined them at the table and the conversation was lively as Dolly polished off a large portion of bread and fried pork.

Jamie was impressed with how well Dolly had done through the mountain passes. She told him about some of the close calls she had had. Even the children were impressed with her stories.

They finished the meal and made a plan.

"We can go into town and talk to Gabriel, he will know when the next ferry is headed towards Oregon City, usually it goes every few days. Only takes a few hours." Jamie offered. "You can stay with us until you have to go."

Evie liked the plan and got the kids working on getting the spare cot ready in the loft.

Dolly thanked them over and over for their generosity.

Jamie called Dolly out when the wagon was hitched up, the kids were happy to tag along into town. They thought the whole thing a great adventure that they could brag about later to their friends. An Indian woman alone in the mountains, it was all so exciting.

She sat quietly in the wagon and listened to the young children tell her stories about all their favorite places.

"My friend Joe, jumped out of the barn just over that way and broke his foot. His pa was so mad that his face turned red as a tomato." Said young Jessie.

The small girl, Lynnie, did not want to be outdone. "My mama said that her friend was stomped on by a horse and her toe fell clean off!"

Dolly showed the appropriate reaction to each story as they took turns trying to impress her. She was just so happy to be safe and close to home. Seeing the fertile valley around her made her ever aware that she was soon to reunite with her family, the one that counted.

They arrived to the Portland Fancy Goods store and Dolly got a good look at the busy street, it was bustling a little more than Oregon City and she knew this port town was growing fast.

The store had a clean and bright look to the outside, similar to the store in Oregon City, but when she saw Gabriel Quackenbush she instantly saw the resemblance to Clive. He had a stockier build but his eyes and chin were so much like Clive.

"Hey Gabe, we have a task to set before you." Jamie said as he pushed his hand forward to give Gabriel a firm handshake.

"Well, I will always take on a worthy challenge." His smile was broad.

Dolly couldn't help but smile, it was like seeing her old friend.

"Well, this young lady here is a friend of your Granddad, Clive, she has had quite a journey." Jamie introduced Dolly.

"Oh." He gasped. "You were living with Angela until recently. We had just gotten a letter from her, she was missing you something fierce." Gabriel declared and shook her hand.

Dolly was usually pretty reserved but tried to force herself to be more forthright.

"Yes, I should have stayed put. Would have saved me a lot of trouble." Dolly admitted.

She told a brief account of her travels through the mountains.

"I am glad you are safe." Gabriel said after hearing the story. "You will probably be wanting a quick way home. Let me talk to the Port Manager and see what is going out that would be safe for you. Don't want you riding along with any ruffians or hooligans." He chuckled at his own humor. Just the way that Clive did.

"She can stay in our loft, we got room for her. May take a few days to fatten her up. She was probably livin' off of twigs and berries for weeks." Jamie said with a smile.

Dolly laughed. "And fish, lots of trout to be exact. I made a fishing stick with a sewing needle." She gestured the shape of it and how she caught them with it by spearing them.

The men were impressed that the girl could catch fish that way. They had seen the local natives do it that way but it took a lot of practice and patience.

"She is quite the woman of the wild." Gabriel chuckled.

Jamie agreed and they hatched the plan.

"Let me find out what can be done and get passage for this adventuress and we will come by tonight or tomorrow afternoon to let her know." Gabriel offered. "I am sure my wife Amber will want to meet ya. Angela talks of you often in her letters. She and Angela were like sisters in San Francisco. She is achin' to get to Oregon City for a visit. Now that Yellow Fever has moved out we are planning a trip."

Dolly was surprised to hear about Yellow fever and wanted to know more. Worry struck her hard as he explained.

"The whole valley was affected. My Granddad Clive was sick for days, and almost every household was touched by it. Let me get the paper from Oregon City. It was from a few weeks ago." Gabriel dug around under the counter and came out with the folded newspaper. "Here ya go. You can read it when you have a spell."

Gabriel made a note on a small pad he had on the counter. "I will send a quick telegram to my gramps, letting them know you are coming. They will be relieved to know you are safe."

Dolly thanked Gabriel and smiled warmly, her hands were clasped around the newspaper, nervous jitters in her stomach to think that her friends were in danger from a terrible illness.

Jamie and his two children were looking around the store and Dolly joined them after saying another thank you to Gabriel. She was so very happy that they all were taking care of her. She promised to repay him for the cost of the ferry but as she expected he hushed her, just the way that Clive would have.

"No bother Ma'am. You are family." Gabriel was a good egg, as Clive would say.

She spent the night at the Brown's cabin and was fed well for dinner, after supper she sat outside on a hollowed log bench with the sun setting behind her and read the newspaper. She had dreaded it, wondering if anyone she knew was in danger.

She read that Violet had been ill and was recovered which made her anxious but relieved, but when she came across Reggie's name as ill she felt the world stop.

She had left him behind, with no word of her feelings for him. Not certain when she left exactly what she felt beyond flattered. Her time with Bright Son and Gray Feather had been plenty of time in the saddle to think on it. By the third day on her own she had settled in her mind that Reggie Gardner was the kind of man she wanted to marry. The feeling in her chest now, knowing he could be gone, made her certain that if he was still in this world and still interested, she would put away her shyness and tell him... What would she tell him, though?

She wasn't certain... but she needed to know he was safe. She said a long prayer for him as she sat in the quiet, and for all her friends back home.

She read through the article again, pausing at each and every name listed, whether she knew them personally or not. That was her community and she cared for them all.

She slept well that night, happy to be in a warm bed and a roof of protection. No sounds of wildcats or animals to scare her in the night, no rain to fall on her head, she was safe.

Breakfast was a boisterous one at the Brown cabin and reminded Dolly of Chelsea Grants house, with the three children, Jessie, Lynnie and little Annabelle all competing for attention.

"Ach, be gone with ya." Their mother finally said with an exasperated smile and shooed them out into the yard after the food was all eaten. "Jessie, watch over yer sisters while Dolly and I clean up."

Dolly loved helping in the kitchen as she had done with Chelsea and Angela. She had learned something from every woman she knew and Evie Brown was no slack in the kitchen.

Dolly told her all about the work she did with Corinne and Evie prodded gently into talking about Reggie, whom she had told about the evening before.

"Do you think you love him?" Evie asked as she scrubbed the dishes.

"I don't know." Dolly pondered. "I know I care about his well-being. Perhaps that is the start of it." Dolly dried a dish and settled it on the towel on the counter. "I have a lot of regrets with how I left things." Dolly sighed. "I have been too... is shy the right word?"

Evie gave her a look. "You do have a quiet way about you. But he must know that if he cares for ya."

"Maybe because I knew I would be returning to my tribe I held back more than I should have. I am determined to work harder at being who I want to be, and not what others want me to be." Dolly said after a minute of quiet between them. "In the long time alone in the woods I had a few thoughts. Reggie never asked me to be something I was not. Nor did any of my friends. But I got myself all confused with things all by myself."

Evie chuckled and slipped a soapy hand around Dolly's shoulder, Dolly didn't mind at all. "Don't we all get in our own way sometimes?" She laughed again.

Dolly felt laughter rise up from her chest too and she let it out. Feeling light and free in the kitchen of a near stranger. She felt her heart changing. She was free to make her own mistakes, and be alright with them. It was a new freedom and she enjoyed it.

Angela Fahey

Light blue paint dripped over the side of the paint pail as Angela patted the edge of the paint brush on the edge. She smoothed the paint onto the wooden siding of the west side of the house. She had done several hours of painting and had only a small section completed. Clive and Ted had spent a few days grinding the zinc oxide and the colored powder that had been ordered from England. They mixed it in a large vat with linseed oil. Both had covered their faces with two kerchiefs to keep from coughing and breathing in the fumes. It was a labor of love for certain. She loved the light blue color, a few shades lighter than a clear blue sky. Angela was very pleased. She was just wondering how she could ever keep up with the men who painted with so much more expertise.

She watched Clive and Ted cover twice as much siding in the same amount of time, and they were on ladders. She was pretty sure that they had less drips too. She loved the color and was happy again at her choice. There was a lot of work to be done but she had a lot of hands helping. Earl and Warren, her tireless helpers, were on the East side of the house getting a good start. Earl had gotten a few almond trees planted early but had come over afterwards.

Reggie, Lucas, Russell, Reynaldo, and John Harpole all had promised to come by after they were done with the bridge work for the day. Corinne and Violet promised to come by with dinner and coffee later too.

The house was going to be a light blue with crisp white shutters and a dark blue trim around the windows. It would look beautiful and she wanted it to be lovely by the time she would be married. She wasn't sure why it mattered, but it did.

She was promised that the lumber for the log cabin for the Sparks family would be delivered in a few weeks and she knew once that was delivered the house painting would seem a bit trivial. The Sparks were coming by in September and she wanted the cabin to be ready. They would be tired from the overland trail and need a warm place to call home. Angela was so very excited to see them. She couldn't wait for the surprise of being married when they arrived. A part of her sad that they wouldn't be here for the event, but she didn't want to wait any longer than July or August at the latest. She was ready to be Ted's wife.

She daydreamed as she continued to paint, ignoring the pinch in her shoulders and the dull ache in her leg as she swished the paintbrush over the smooth wood. Even if she wasn't as deft as the boys she was making slow progress.

Olivia was busy working on her secret project from her favorite seat on the porch. Olivia moved her rocker on Angela's wraparound porch to visit with the workers. She said that she had always dreamt of having a wrap-around porch. Borrowing Angela's was the next best thing. Olivia had promised to show her the 'secret' project when it was all finished. Angela couldn't even get a peek. Olivia talked often about her love for Angela's porch and everyone enjoyed seeing her there, rocking away doing her work. She was a lovely sight.

Ted had been making plans alongside Angela all week, she had challenged him to talk about every idea he had for the farm he had always dreamt of.

She coaxed until she finally got him talking. He loved her long-term plans with the almond trees, already having a buyer for future almonds was a grand scheme. But he was finally brave enough to mention that he had a love for animals and talked about a few things on his wish list too.

"I once worked for a farmer in upstate New York, in the summer in the evenings to make extra money for the family. They had goats, chickens and a few pigs. I learned a lot from that farm work." Ted shared. "His wife always made goat cheese from the goats' milk, it was so delicious." Ted had beamed at the memory.

Angela had whole-heartedly agreed and Ted made enquiries. He found a local farmer with a male kid for sale and the name of another who just had two females. Ted had happily reported when he arrived just that morning that he had purchased one of each. Angela was thrilled to see Ted getting a part of his dream accomplished. He said he would wait a year before acquiring the pigs. He wanted to get used to a little at a time. The two kids were going to be moved into the barn yard in a few days. Without the bridge the kids would be delivered and carried over the footbridge. Angela was looking forward to watching the whole thing play out.

Angela settled the paintbrush on the side of the pail after another hour of painting. She stretched out her arms and shoulders and even bent over to get the kink out of her back. She was thirsty so she padded up to the steps around to the front, she inspected her feet to make sure no stray drips were on her work shoes. It looked safe so she went up the steps and dipped out of the water bucket on the porch into one of the mugs she left there for everyone to use. She gulped down the cool water and was refreshed. She must have had a good idea because she saw Clive come around the corner a few seconds later.

"Ah, I see I was not the only thirsty soul." Clive winked at her.

"Yessir, water is here. Only ten cents a cup." Angela teased.

"Well, a bargain price from a pretty gal." He whistled merrily and she handed him his own cupful.

He sipped his own and sighed heartily.

"She is going to be a showpiece, Miss Fahey." He looked up to the house, not close to even a quarter of it painted.

"I believe it will be." Angela beamed at the praise.

"I am thinking about painting my place green in the fall." Clive said with a twinkle in his eye.

"Your cabin?" Angela gave him a quizzical look.

"Well, Red, you don't know everything." Clive laughed. 'This old coot is up to somethin'." His laughter was contagious and Ted and Olivia were rounding the corner of the house.

"We are missing out on the garden party, Ted." Olivia said as she walked across the porch, her burgundy taffeta skirts swishing around her.

"Oh yes, it is the social event of the season." Angela declared.

Angela filled two more mugs and handed them out. Ted rewarded her with a kiss on the cheek as she handed him his mug.

Clive Quackenbush

Clive went to town after his lovely evening with Angela, Ted, and Olivia. He was growing fonder of the witty and charming Olivia and he wasn't afraid to admit it to himself. He chuckled several times on the way home as he felt his chest swell with those old feelings that rekindled a lot easier than he expected.

What was it to be in love three times in one lifetime? He wondered. Every woman he had married had been special and had taken a piece of his heart when they had died. Could he trust that he had enough pieces left to be in love again? He was growing more and more certain that he could.

"Lord, you are a mystery." He said to God while his horse trotted along at a slow clip. The dark sky was showing off. The stars in their radiance would dare any unbelieving heart that there was no creator to all the magnificence that Clive could see. An owl hooted in the distance and a few night birds sang sweetly. Clive was at peace, thankful for another chance for companionship. Life was certainly bringing him a new adventure.

He went to stay with his son Jedediah, having a spare room set up for him when he wanted to stay in town. Millie and JQ were sitting in the parlor and were pleased to see him.

"How was your dinner?" Millie smiled at him knowingly. She had begun guessing that there was something to his many visits to Angela's home now that a certain lady was visiting.

"Excellent. Angela is turning out to be an accomplished cook." Clive winked at her. Seeing the glint in her eye for what it was.

"And the lovely Lady Greaves?" JQ interjected and looked up to Clive with a gleam and a grin that meant he was in on the scheming too.

Clive laughed and hung his hat on the hook by the door.

"Ya meddlers." Clive huffed out without any malice.

Millie and JQ were amused greatly to get under Clive's skin a little. He told them about the evening.

"I have something for you on the table. A telegram from Gabe." JQ grabbed a nearby pipe and ignored the huff from Millie who didn't approve of the pipe smoking.

Clive got up from the comfortable seat and retrieved the telegram and went over to the kerosene lamp to get a better look at it in the dark room.

Clive Quackenbush, Oregon City

Dolly arrived in Portland, safe and alone. Sending her home via ferry.

Gabe

Clive felt a jolt. Dolly was alone, and safe. His mind raced over how that could have occurred but he was so very thankful that she was safe.

He would be certain to keep his ears open for news of any ferry coming in the next days. He wanted to have a good chat with that girl to know how she had survived alone. He knew she would have a few stories to tell.

Millie and JQ gladly talked with him about Dolly and they wondered conversationally how well they would survive alone in the wilds.

Corinne Grant

Corinne was ready to lose her patience again with her houseguest. After more than a dozen arguments and rude remarks by the ever-critical Megan, Corinne asked the Harpole's to take the young lady again. There was simply no making that girl happy.

Corinne read through some of the early letters she read from her cousin and saw a genuine desire to focus on art and painting. Yet Megan had yet to touch her drawing or painting supplies. All she seemed willing to do was flirt with the ranchers next door and criticize the life that everyone led in the entire territory of Oregon.

A few weeks before Megan had insulted Marie when they were visiting.

"The women in town have been all abuzz talking about you Marie - saying how you are hoping to give Mr. Harpole a passle of girls iffen you can. That way your son Cooper can inherit the Ranch."

Marie had dropped her jaw in astonishment. She blustered for a minute.

Corinne had jumped in. “Megan that is absurd and rude.”

Megan fluttered her hand and ignored any protest. “I was just sharing the local gossip.”

Marie, wisely, remained mute on the subject.

Then a few days ago, while visiting with Angela, Megan piped into a conversation after being petulant and quiet the whole visit with...

"It's a good thing that Ms. Greaves is staying with you Miss Fahey because being alone you are apt to draw unwanted attention from men with divisive intentions. Mr. Burgess or even lumberjacks traveling through could sneak into your place. My thoughts that even married men get strange ideas about a woman living alone. I have always been told that women who live alone have loose morals. But I would never think that of you, of course."

Olivia had snickered at the absurd comment. "You make friends easily, I am guessing."

Megan had given Olivia a glare that could have curdled milk.

Since then, Megan had declared Ms. Greaves to be bad company. "No wonder she is divorced." She had said when they got back home.

Upon more than one occasion that Lucas, though he seemed very intelligent, "was really just a glorified farm hand with the way he got so dirty every day."

Corinne was fed up with her uppity attitude and ever-flowing criticism.

The ranch manager next door, Reynaldo, had forcibly removed her from the fence line of the ranch several times for repeatedly making attempts to distract the ranchers. They were not on good terms.

Corinne knew Reynaldo to be a good manager and a fun-loving guy when the time was appropriate. But a flouncy female hanging about when dangerous work needed to be done was not safe. Reynaldo's easy humor was tested.

Corinne felt guilty after Megan left for the night. Feeling let down that she had allowed that young lady to get at her. She had lost her patience. She wondered how well she could handle being a mother if she felt so lost with Megan.

She spent some time with God that night. Praying for patience.

Corinne knew she had been a challenge at times with her father. She had to remember that when dealing with her cousin.

Chapter 23

Dolly Bouchard

The noon hour came and so did the visitors. Gabriel and Amber, showing with child and with little Silas in tow.

Evie welcomed them in and sent her son off to fetch his Papa.

"We have you on a ferry for first thing tomorrow. Iffen you'd like to stay closer to town we could save you the trouble at leaving so early." Gabriel offered.

Dolly was glad to accept.

"I have read so much about you in Angela's letters." Amber said after she had given Dolly a warm embrace.

"She told me stories about you." Dolly said, looking over the woman who stood before her. "She was right. You look like you could be sisters."

Amber laughed and they all sat at the table. Amber had brought dried apple tarts. Evie set about making a fresh pot of coffee to enjoy with them.

Silas sat on his Mama's lap but wanted to be released when he saw the other children playing nearby.

"I've got my eye on them. You folks visit." Evie said with a smile.

Talking about Angela and Clive with Amber and Gabriel Quackenbush was a blessing and it made Dolly's heart long to be home even more. To see her home in the valley again was within her grasp.

The children played and the adults chatted away for several hours. Dolly was learning to share more. Knowing her quiet nature didn't mean she had to be so silent. The solitude of her time in the mountains had taught her a few valuable things about herself. She was certain she had so much more to learn. But she was more confident within herself. She was discovering her person, and her soul.

After the visit Dolly prepared to go back with the Quackenbush family. She hugged Evie for a long while, promising to write and keep in contact. Each of the Brown children gave her a hug and she promised to send them sweet peppermint treats that she would make herself. They cheered and wished her off with smiles.

Dolly sat with Silas in the back of the wagon, she watched Evie Brown wave from the side of her cabin. Dolly felt blessed to have made that connection, though brief. Evie had helped her talk through some things that had been dancing around like cobwebs in her mind. She was forever grateful for this experience.

The ferry left early the next morning. Dolly was wearing a new coat that Amber had given her, her wool coat was a bit of a mess from the hard journey. They refused to be paid for the ferry passage or the new clothes and coat. It was just not their way. Dolly promised herself to send them a nice gift at some point.

Dolly felt the fresh air of the sea breeze and prayed a blessing over the people she met in Portland. Knowing her experience could have been so different. Someone could have seen her light brown face and assumed any number of things. The thing that settled into her mind was becoming clearer. She had had so much fear of strangers because there were still so many who put so much emphasis on the color of skin. She was determined to move forward with a new understanding about that. Good and bad people were not determined by their shade, but by their hearts.

She felt her heart swelling with the absence of fear. She wondered if people would let go of fear if perhaps they made more room for love. It was an interesting thing to ponder with the blue-green sea around and the sun shining brightly. She would be home soon and she spent every moment aboard that ferry being thankful that she had lived.

Dolly gathered her leather satchel, another gift from Gabriel and Amber and walked down with the other passengers. It was a lovely day and the mountains were singing in their own way a welcome home song to Dolly. The breeze allowed the leaves to rustle and wave hello on the shoreline.

Dolly wondered how her day would go. It was only early afternoon according to one of the men aboard she had overheard. A promise of a day at home. She wanted to see everyone.

Dolly walked down the plank when it was her turn and headed towards the road. She had only brought along the satchel, having thrown out all the unnecessary or filthy items. The satchel was a little heavy but she knew the mile walk to town would not be too bad. She could go to the bank and get some of her money deposited there and rent a horse to get her home.

All her plans flew out of her mind when she saw Clive and JQ waving at her from near the road, standing at the front of JQ's wagon.

Dolly leapt up, dropping her bag and waved furiously, she felt that her smile had never been so broad.

She scooped up her satchel again and with a near sprint she weaved through the crowd. Clive had jumped down and was ready to receive her in one of his famous bear hugs.

She cried and laughed simultaneously.

"You are one brave gal, Bluebird." He called her by her real name. It was so rare to hear it anymore and she loved it again.

"I flew home." She said as she leaned away from his hug. She looked Clive in the eyes and smiled again.

"Let's get you to town." Clive helped her into the front seat with JQ and settled in with her satchel in the back.

She wanted to tell them everything but she shared her last few days with them first. Talking about the Brown family and JQ's Son and wife, and she promised that she had letters to give to JQ and Millie too.

"They are coming here to visit in a month." Dolly shared and was pleased to see JQ's smile.

"Millie will be beside herself." He said and wiggled his eyebrows to make Dolly laugh.

It was only a short ride to town and Dolly got settled in quickly with Millie upstairs in the parlor. JQ put a worker on the front of store and joined in with Clive and they all enjoyed some fresh tea and cherry preserve tarts.

Once the tea was served Millie joined them in a chair that JQ had pulled up in the parlor.

"You tell your story. We have all been dying to know how you managed." Millie said with emphasis.

Dolly told them how Gray Feather had acted in those first weeks. She shared about how Bright Son had tried to keep things calm but it wasn't enough to make it safe.

Clive had gotten tense and cleared his throat in discomfort when he heard that Gray Feather had struck her. Millie had reached over and settled her father-in-law with a hand on the shoulder.

"God was watching out for me, Clive." Dolly soothed and continued.

She spoke of that first night and the cave, sharing how well Bright Son had helped her escape. Understanding what Gray Feather was feeling from his jilted courtship and then this journey could make any man a little resentful. Dolly was more forgiving than Clive was at the moment and Clive reminded her of that.

"Oh, Clive, it is much easier to be forgiving once I was over the mountains. That first night back under a solid roof with a full belly my forgiveness came a lot easier." Dolly smiled, remembering the kindness of Evie and Jamie Brown.

Clive sipped his tea and listened. He nodded though when she looked at him with concern. He didn't want to make Dolly uneasy.

"When I was exhausted and huddling under a crude shelter in a drizzle I was not nearly as quick to forgive." Dolly laughed.

She told the men about her fishing spear and how she had made her own char cloth, they had all been impressed, Millie especially.

"I probably would have died, child. I cannot tell you enough how brave you are. To trust in God in the wilderness all alone. It makes me want to trust in the Lord even more in my little troubles." Millie said sincerely with a few misty tears in her eyes. She dabbed at her eyes with a lace handkerchief and her husband soothed her with a supportive hand on her back.

Dolly knew she would be telling this story to everyone again but she felt such warmth from Millie it reminded her to never give up on people. She would have never guessed that she would feel such genuine friendship from Millie Quackenbush. It confirmed her place in Oregon City as her true home.

"I sent Ted ahead when I heard a ferry was on the way. Everyone by Spring Creek should know by now. Whenever you are ready I can deliver you back wherever you like."

Dolly pondered where she wanted to be and decided on Angela's for now. She would settle in there, but definitely have a long visit soon with Chelsea Grant as well.

Dolly was surprised at the bridge being built over Spring Creek and marveled at how much was done. *Had she been gone long enough for that?* She wondered and felt a pang at missing so much in the Valley. She had asked Clive on the drive about the fever she had read about in the paper. Clive told her who had recovered but kept the bad news for another day. He didn't want to mar her homecoming with anything but happy tears.

They parked the wagon along the side of the road and walked to the footbridge. Dolly walked past Corinne's cabin regretfully and saw the greenhouse and laboratory and was relieved to see them unchanged. Had it only been a month? It felt longer in her heart.

Angela's home was ahead and Dolly and Clive walked at a brisk pace to get there.

Dolly could see as they neared the road that the small orchard of apple trees had lost there blooms but the green leaves were plentiful.

The weeping willow along the side of the riverbank was sweetly swaying in the breeze and she saw that a log had been settled underneath it, inviting her to come back some fine morning with hot coffee and her bible. She would listen to the quiet gurgling of the creek as she reconnected with God's word.

She saw the start of color on the sides of the house.

"Oh what a lovely blue!" Dolly gasped.

"We started a few days ago." Clive shared and pointed to the front door. "We are about to be bombarded." Clive chuckled as both he and Dolly watched the swarm of people poring out of Angela's front door.

"Dolly!" Chelsea was at the front of the crowd, her arms wide.

Dolly received her hug warmly and felt more pile on as Angela, Corinne and Violet joined in.

The group swayed and a few released for another to move in for a private hug, this lasted a few minutes as they all fussed over her. Brody and Sarah Grant had hugged her around her middle, telling her how much they missed her.

"When Ted told us that you came back alone I…" Corinne said with a muffled voice through her hug. She never finished her thought but just hugged her more.

Dolly was finally shuffled in. Everyone, including Russell and Lucas, all told her in their own way that they were glad she was home. Olivia had embraced Dolly when she got inside. Letting the others have their chance first but wanting to build on their friendship.

Dolly was just settled at the table when the Harpole's showed up and Cooper burst through the door and charged into her for an exuberant embrace. Dolly felt tears on her cheeks by the time he let go.

"Never leave again, Dolly." Cooper looked up to her with red cheeks. His eyes were a mix of happy and sad.

"I will do my best Coop." Dolly said and thought of the multitude of times they had been fishing together and shared long walks in the woods.

Marie was radiant as usual and patted Dolly's hair, then shoulders. It was her way of making sure Dolly was safe and sound, a mother's way. She planted a kiss on Dolly's head.

"You scared us!" She said in a half scold.

Dolly nodded, she had been a bit scared herself.

Marie had brought a pound cake with berry preserves, and Violet had made fresh sourdough bread and Angela had coffee brewing. It looked like an impromptu dinner party was about to unfold.

Dolly told her story again, sharing all the main details since she had left.

She noticed the few absent ones, Reggie and Galina, and she felt a bit of worry sneak in. But she knew she would find out more as the night progressed. Until then she would enjoy her company.

Corinne Grant

Corinne had been so pleased about seeing Dolly safe and sound and she had a lot of energy when she came home from the welcome back party. She and Lucas had taken Megan, and the young lady had complained about going, she didn't know Dolly after all. Corinne had coaxed her patiently and Megan had agreed finally and had worn a near formal dress for the occasion.

Megan had muttered a few inappropriate things to Corinne while they had been there.

"I think Olivia is a fool for courting that old man." Had been the first. And "Marie could look so much nicer if she would just wear a corset."

Megan had very strong opinions about corsets and proper attire for civilized women and the fact that many women in Oregon opted out of wearing the restrictive corsets for casual events was disgusting to her.

As they left, still on the porch near the open windows of the house Megan blurted out. "The half-breed girl dresses much nicer than I expected. She has handsome features- it is really too bad for the tone of her skin. Otherwise I would call her a beauty. Though, she's not as dark as some savages I have seen since I have been in the West."

Corinne bit her tongue, but Lucas had had enough. As they were walking into the cabin Lucas had his say.

"Young lady. May I be so bold as to ask you to keep your critiques to yourself while you are in our company? I may live in the frontier and not be refined society, but my mother trained me to be polite at dinner parties. I do not consider your actions appropriate behavior for a well bred young woman." Lucas hung up his hat on the hook and gave Megan a long look. Daring her to challenge him.

Corinne wanted to laugh but watched while working on controlling the corners of her mouth, to keep the smile down that desperately wanted to come out.

Megan took a long slow breath, not backing down from Lucas's glare. "I apologize." She said simply and left the room.

As she reached the hallway toward her bedroom she announced. “I am changing into more comfortable clothing.” Her door shut behind her a few moments later with an extra oomph.

Corinne let out the smallest chuckle and looked to Lucas.

“You had enough?” Corinne asked, her smile finally free from the constraints.

“Yes.” Lucas sighed and walked to the parlor and sunk into his favorite chair. “How long is she staying?” Lucas said and grabbed the bridge of his nose with a hand and closed his eyes in frustration.

“I was considering writing to her father. I think the visit should be done soon. I don’t see any reason to keep this on when she is obviously so unhappy.” Corinne said.

They let the subject drop and Lucas found a book to read and Corinne buried her head in her Grandmother Trudie’s botany journal.

Megan joined them a while later, wearing a nightgown and a large robe.

“Before I go to bed I want to say that I do not appreciate how much you both judge me!” Megan announced. Her hair was still done up fancy and the few sausage curls bounced around her face as she spoke.

Corinne had pulled her head from her book to look at her cousin in bewilderment.

“I am sorry that you feel we are judging you.” Corinne said calmly. Trying to remember the patience that she had prayed about.

“Well, you do.” Megan huffed. She stood there, not attempting to join them but to stand where they had to crane their necks around to see her. “You make no effort to know me. You think that everything here is so wonderful but you all are simple-minded and mean to me.” Her sausage curls were swaying again.

Corinne was distracted by the girl’s hair and nearly giggled. She forced herself to listen and try to contemplate any kind of reasonable response.

“I am sorry you feel that way.” Corinne said simply, not certain that anything else would help the situation. Everyone in the room was unhappy. Fighting and throwing a tantrum was what the young lady wanted. Corinne wasn’t sure she wanted to give her the satisfaction.

"Is that all you have to say to me?" Megan's voice grew louder. She huffed again and stomped her foot three times in rapid succession.

Corinne stood up slowly, setting the book on the space next to her. "Well, yes." She spoke calmly.

"You are the most infuriating..." Megan was now yelling. "You think you are so above everyone else." She paced a few steps and turned to face Corinne again.

"All you do is talk about plants, and Lucas is dirty as a common farmhand." She pointed to Lucas, perhaps hoping to get a rise out of him. "I just can't get over how drab you all look. I know fashion isn't as practical here but the only one of you that looks smart in the least is Angela, and she used to be the scullery. Well, the Greaves dress very well but Olivia is insufferable." Megan tossed her head again.

Corinne was silent, allowing Megan to blow her top if she wanted to. Megan glared at Corinne with a scowl, expecting Corinne to say something.

"All I expect from you is to be respectful of the people who are taking care of you. To be kind and respectful to my friends and family." Corinne said calmly, not to allow Megan to push her into a frenzy.

Megan stepped back, offended. "I do not see that speaking the truth is offensive. These people that you set in a place of importance over me are no better than me. Everyone thinks these things... I am just brave enough to speak my mind." She looked to Lucas who was sitting with a calm face that showed no emotion.

His calm demeanor bothered her and she spat out, "If you think I will abide by the simple-mindedness of all of these people here you are more foolish than I think."

Corinne folded her hands in front of her body and pressed her lips together. She refused to talk to Megan while she was yelling.

"I question the sanity of the whole lot of you, leaving civility behind and coming out here in the wilderness to struggle. To my thinking the western expansion is a grand plan to evacuate all the eastern nitwits to a place where they can stop their complaining about all the things that are wrong with the world. You all can pretend you are creating a society out here, to me it just seems like an excuse to struggle and all become religious zealots. At least in California territory some men are seeking financial gain. Here in Oregon all you do is work and die in an unnecessary struggle." Megan stated finally and waited.

"You done?" Lucas asked, he actually smiled the tiniest little smirk that Corinne found very humorous and she lost her control for the briefest of seconds and a half-cough half laugh escaped.

Corinne quickly covered her mouth to control her mirth but Megan had heard it.

Megan stomped her feet again and turned and ran back to her room. The door slammed and thumping could be heard in the parlor.

"I hope she doesn't tear down the walls?" Lucas said then started to laugh finally. He lost control and bent over laughing.

Corinne joined him and laughed along with him. Getting angry didn't work and calm seemed to make it worse. Laughing seemed like the best remedy and they enjoyed it thoroughly.

Chapter 24

Angela Fahey

The next morning Angela awoke with a spring in her step. She had two houseguests and she was thrilled to have Dolly safely back in her bed. Olivia had moved to a spare bedroom when she heard that Dolly had returned. The new room had only a four post bed, but Angela knew that a dresser, bookcase and wardrobe was coming from the local woodworker. Her rooms were filling up. It was her dream after all.

Angela felt her world was coming together. She wanted to go into town and check on her furniture and make certain it was coming along, and talk to Millie about squashing the orphanage.

Angela felt the heaviness of her heart last night as she had lain down, she had stayed up talking to Dolly after everyone else had left. Dolly had been devastated when she had heard about Galina's mother and brother and Angela had joined in more tears in the retelling. Galina had some hard days ahead and they were all going to help her through as much as they could.

Angela prepared breakfast and was satisfied the house was awake by the mild creaking of the floorboards overhead.

Dolly and Olivia both joined her soon after, with fresh morning faces and their long hair down their backs. There was something special about a table full of women. They shared their plans for the day and each set off on their own paths, Olivia to her porch chair and lace making, Angela to town, and Dolly to a few special visits.

Dolly Bouchard

Dolly had walked through the woods a while after she had tidied up her appearance and put on her dark blue skirt and jacket that she had left at Angela's house. Her frame was smaller from the weight she had lost and the sleeves were a little loose. She knew with all the good cooking she would put those pounds back on soon. Her cheek bones had been a little prominent in the mirror that morning and she smiled at herself for picking out all the ways she had changed. She would be back to normal soon enough.

Her walk in the woods was peaceful and she reflected on Galina and her loss. She picked wildflowers as she walked, letting them gather in the wide basket she had brought along, bright yellow arnica, golden columbine, light purple aster, larkspur, some pink thistle, and some flowers she had no name for. She considered every flower she saw, wondering how she could learn about them all, and discover their mysteries. It was a blessing to have Corinne's knowledge and other books and journals to look through and she hoped to spend her life in that pursuit. It was a good life she had in mind, she prayed that now she could focus on it without worry about leaving. The heaviness that had settled on her was gone. She was doing more than learning about plants for one tribe in one place, but instead she would share this passion with anyone who wanted to know.

With a basket full of many flowers she headed toward Galina's cabin first. Hoping to share a bit of beauty from the flowers to brighten the sadness that was certain to be in her heart.

Galina was surprised to see Dolly at the door. She welcomed her in and they sat at the table.

"My brothers are out with Father, they never want to be here but to eat or sleep." Galina said as she sat with Dolly.

"I am so sorry Galya." Dolly settled the basket on the table. "I brought these for you."

Galina smiled, her eyes were red. Dolly could tell she had been crying.

"It is Saturday, I have no work outside the home today. Neighbors delivered meals today, so I have so little to do to keep my mind occupied." Galina shared, she stood and gently touched a few of the blooms. She walked over to a shelf and pulled out a large mason jar.

Dolly stood and joined her in picking through the blooms. Dolly cut off some off the long stems and they started to arrange the flowers together.

"When my mother died I was kept busy, it had been in the fall and we harvested berries and smoked fish. Keeping my hands busy didn't stop my tears but perhaps it had slowed them. It is hard to know." Dolly put an arm around Galina's shoulders. Galina leaned against her and let more tears fall.

"I am glad you are home." Galina said sincerely.

Dolly was glad too.

They arranged flowers and talked for a long while. Dolly couldn't think of anything better to do than that. Today she was a shoulder to cry on.

Dolly and Galina talked for a long while, her brothers and father returned for lunch and left just as swiftly, all of them eager to keep working on the bridge. John Harpole and nearby neighbors were paying for all extra hands to help sand and nail the boards to the top of the bridge. Pavel and Milo were getting paid to bring extra nails and supplies to the men at work. Galina and Dolly waved them off after they ate.

Galina grew tired after a while and Dolly encouraged her to nap.

"I haven't been sleeping very well." Galina confessed to having nightmares.

Dolly nodded. She had had similar issues when her own mother passed.

Dolly left Galina alone to sleep and looked to the sun. She wondered if Reggie would be with the men at the bridge or if he would be at home. She walked toward the bridge figuring the most likely scenario was that he was there. It meant that they wouldn't have much of a chance to talk but maybe she could invite him to visit Angela's after he was done. She had already had Angela's permission to invite him so she hoped that she would have an opportunity. Her stomach flipped a little at the thought of seeing him but she wanted to push all those thoughts away. She had done much harder things to get nervous over inviting a man over to talk. Dolly smiled to herself and her own self-scolding. She would figure out this adulthood thing eventually. Until then she would practice as much as she could.

She swung the empty basket at her side as she walked to the bridge, the high grass swayed as she walked by. The basket tapping on the tops that were heavy with seed.

She heard the commotion of hammers and pounding and saw the gathering of about twenty or more men all working together. The flat part of the bridge now almost covered the expanse. A few men now adding a railing on the sides, it had only a few feet started but Dolly could see how the completed project would look. It was quite an accomplishment.

Dolly stood a safe distance away, watching a few men work. Reynaldo, the ranch foreman for John Harpole's ranch walked over and greeted her, glad to see that she was in one piece. Rumor had already spread about her heroics and he patted her on the shoulder for making it through the mountains. His handsome smile and charm was sweet and Dolly blushed at his praise. Reynaldo got back to his work and Dolly waved at a few others who were working hard, Ted, John, Lucas, Russell, and Clive, her eyes traveled over every man she could see, there were some she didn't know by name. She finally got a glimpse of Reggie crawling up the side of the creek bed, his pants were wet and muddy up to his knees. She couldn't help but smile at the sight of him. She had been more than relieved to hear that he had survived yellow fever, but seeing him healthy and working had completed her thoughts on his full recovery. She had some regrets about not being there for him while he was ill.

"Hey there." Reggie called out. He waved and was shaking himself off.

Dolly smiled and felt heat rise to her cheeks. "Hi."

He walked over to her, laughing at himself and shrugging over the mess that he was in.

"You look like you had a mud bath." Dolly said, finding words somehow.

He laughed again, full and from his gut. It was a happy sound. "Well, just a little."

"A little dirt never killed anyone." Dolly said with her smile glued to her face.

"I heard your story from John Harpole this morning. Wow, Dolly, you really made it alone over the mountains." Reggie ran a hand through his dark hair, some mud from his hand smeared across his forehead in a charming and distracting way.

"With God's help." Dolly said and tried to look away from his forehead, not very successfully.

Reggie nodded. He looked back to the bridge. Dolly could see that he needed to get back.

"You can go, I just wanted to invite you to come by after you are done. We could catch up on the porch, have tea?" Dolly offered.

"Oh…" Reggie looked at his appearance nervously. "I'm not sure I should."

Dolly must have shown disappointment because he spoke up after Dolly tried to form a reply.

"I can get cleaned up and come by, iffen you'd like." Reggie offered with a grin.

Dolly nodded in relief. "That would be grand." She sighed in relief and he turned and waved. She watched for a few minutes more, enjoying the entertainment of the project coming together. It would be a lovely wooden bridge and she marveled at the minds that could build such a thing. Someday soon the muddy water underneath would be clear and trickling under those boards and beams, and fish would swim by. It was a beautiful thought.

Dolly went home and spent a good few hours primping and getting ready for a gentleman caller. Olivia helped her do her hair extra fancy.

Dolly was pleased when she heard the knock at the door. Angela had come back from her errands and she and Olivia were talking in the parlor. Dolly had been too anxious, waiting for Reggie, to sit still for so long.

She answered the door and after he greeted Olivia and Angela she invited him to join her on the porch. He obliged.

She gestured to a chair and then sat after he did. Her heart thumped happily in her chest.

"I am glad that you weren't injured on your trip." Reggie said simply. He was rubbing his hands over his knees nervously.

"I prayed a lot. It was hard but my childhood was spent learning about living in the wilderness. I didn't forget." Dolly fidgeted with a piece of lace on her skirt.

Reggie caught her gaze for a second and smiled. Dolly took a deep breath and found some bravery.

"I am sorry about..." She started and faltered awkwardly. "I mean when you asked to court me. I wanted to say yes... and I should have." She spit it out and felt relieved.

Reggie was still, his face unsmiling.

"I appreciate you saying that." He said finally. His face was calm but not as happy as Dolly would have wished.

"Have I waited so long that you have no wish to return those sentiments?" Dolly asked, forcing a fake smile that hurt her cheeks.

"That is not my feelings. I genuinely was sincere. A part of me still wishes that." Reggie said. He stood and paced in front of her.

Dolly looked down to the floorboards of the porch feeling lost. She had waited too long, she had left and snuffed out his affections.

"While I was sick I had a lot of quiet time with God. Even before that I had been praying for you and about you for weeks." Reggie said. If he was looking at her Dolly didn't know it, her eyes were glued to the porch.

Dolly could see Reggie's shoes in front of her and knew he was looking at her, she looked up and caught his gaze. The seriousness in his eyes made her change her posture. She wouldn't look away again.

"Sometimes change makes us look at things differently. I saw you as a beautiful young woman, intelligent and spiritual. That is the truth. But I am not certain that I am your intended. I have a few things hidden away in my heart that I had been pushing away." Reggie reached for her hand then pulled back, realizing that touching Dolly wasn't wise. "I have held several jobs as a man, and a few were necessity and one found it's way into me. I left it behind to come here and mostly I have made a way here by accident, working for John Harpole and some for Corinne. I am good at numbers and ledgers."

Dolly nodded but didn't shy away from his look.

"While I was sick I had a dream that I was back on the sea. It was so vivid that I awoke with confusion. I missed being there and felt that tug again at my heart to go back." Reggie confessed and broke the contact to her face. He sat down next to her again and waited a minute to talk.

"I have gone over and over this with God and come to a conclusion. I am attracted to you for many reasons, but the most compelling thing about you is your passion for what you do. Both you and Corinne have found your calling. Any man or woman who can find their purpose is blessed. I want that so much for myself. And when I recovered I had rediscovered that."

Dolly smiled weakly and felt resigned.

"I do not want you to mourn the loss of my affection. Because you never will lose it. But I really believe that God has someone for you that can work with you on your life's pursuits. I cannot believe that I am that man." Reggie removed a letter from his pocket and unfolded it.

"My former boss is requiring my services, I received it a few days ago. I will be moving to Sacramento to help my old friend in his merchant business. Traveling to China, Russia and India to purchase goods for the west."

"That is incredible news Reggie." Dolly said sincerely, swallowing her disappointment but not doubting his sincerity. The thing she liked so much about Reggie was his kindness. He would never intentionally hurt her.

"I want to be certain that you understand what I feel. I don't consider you a loss but a beautiful and passionate friend." His eyes were intense, hoping she would respond in understanding.

"You will never lose my friendship." Dolly replied and fought off a few tears that threatened at her eyes.

"I want to help you in your passion too. I plan on sending medicinal plants back to you and Corinne. Your thirst for knowledge knows no bounds. Imagine all that you will do in your lifetime, Dolly." Reggie smiled and finally took her hands. "I pray so very much to have my own legacy to leave."

Dolly understood that well, realizing she finally had the freedom to be her own woman.

"I cannot thank you enough for showing me, through your own heart, what it is to be on fire for a purpose." Reggie kissed her hand.

Dolly felt it down to her toes but pushed away the romantic thoughts. Reggie was not for her.

"I will pray for you." Dolly said softly.

"And I you..." Reggie promised.

"You will come see me again before you go?" Dolly asked, knowing he was getting ready to leave.

"I will indeed, and I will write about my travels. You will write back, sharing with me about your own adventures." Reggie smiled broadly.

Dolly tried to capture his face, his dark hair stubbornly falling over his forehead, his eyes fierce and dark in their resolve.

"I will indeed write." Dolly smiled wistfully.

She stood, almost bumping into him. He backed up a few paces and the tension of the moment was felt by both. This union was not meant to be but their closeness created that spark that both could not deny. Standing for a long few seconds staring at each other. Their breaths held in that anticipation of something happening that shouldn't happen but could.

In one agonized instant Dolly leaned into him and let him decide how to say goodbye. She would let it be whatever he was willing to give her. She would never say aloud that she hoped for a kiss to remember him by but she did wish for it.

Instead he pulled her into an embrace. He kissed the top of her head and whispered a goodbye. Dolly was waving at his retreating form a minute later. Feeling empty and full at the same time.

She wanted to pray but instead she just took deep breaths. What might have been...?

Chapter 25

Oregon City

The women's fellowship from the two churches of Oregon City gathered together to discuss plans for the orphanage shared between Salem, Portland and Oregon City.

Millie and several wives of the town council members were at the front, and many women of the community were in attendance.

"First of all I believe we are all in agreement that we do not believe the answer for the orphan issue is to build this atrocity." Millie announced when the meeting started. Many women clapped and cheered their agreement.

"In many private discussions we all came to the agreement that we should find homes for these children and make official adoptions. As Christians it is our duty to provide for our widows and orphans as it says in our precious bibles." She said and more clapping erupted.

"Since our petition for statehood is still in question we must act on our own conscience. I hope we can come together with the best plan and go to our own town council. If we can set the example perhaps Portland and Salem will come to an agreement and adopt our strategy." Millie announced, her face beaming at the agreement of the women there. "I open the floor to suggestions."

Millie sat and was happy to see hands in the air. She pointed to Mrs. Whittlan, the wise and lovely pastor's wife of Spring Creek Church.

"I have prayed long and hard about this. Being a woman in these cases is a challenge when our voices are seldom heard but by nagging our husbands." Mrs. Whittlan paused when the crowd snickered behind her. "I believe we should treat this as the men would, it is the best way to get attention. We should put our own committee in charge of the names of the children to be adopted. Anyone willing to come forward to meet and adopt them should put their names in to be considered. We should make certain that the parents of any adoptive child should be happily wed, for more than a few years, with a reputation of caring for their property and a solid foundation of morals and integrity. Once the council agrees that the adopters are agreed upon and the children are introduced and agree to be adopted by them we can have the town council agree to the assigned adoptions." Mrs. Whittlan paused.

The crowd agreed heartily and it was put forward by more than one woman that Mrs. Millie Quackenbush, Mrs. Prince and Mrs. Whittlan, should form the adoption committee. Together they would decide and gather names of children to be adopted and with the help of the community seek out adoptive parents.

The women gathered offered a few more ideas that were added to the notes of the meeting. That the list of adoptive parents be shared publicly and it was agreed upon. They wanted safe and happy homes for children. Every woman there had read the stories in the newspaper about adopted children being used solely as labor by unscrupulous parents. That would not be tolerated here. A child was to be loved and nurtured, taught to work hard and be respectful, but never to be abused or used as slave labor.

The women departed the meeting slowly, as women were known to do, socializing and visiting long after the meeting had ended. Every woman there was proud of what they had agreed to. It was the right thing and the Christian thing to do. They were certain that God was smiling down on them.

Angela Fahey

The bridge over Spring Creek was built and it was a pretty site over the creek, the large Willow tree sitting companionable beside it to the north and some stately pines guarding it to the south. Beyond it lie the open fields where lavender and jasmine would bloom over the summer and fall. The town was abuzz talking about the bridge and the women's plan for the orphan children. News came that telegrams were received that new members of the community were coming by wagon train in the fall and people were excited about the growth of their small town.

The days after the final nail that made the bridge complete were filled with the sticky job of sealing the wood. With linseed oil and tree sap a few men stayed behind, they applied the sealant in many layers to prevent wood rot over time. The posts that held up the bridge had been sealed before they were put into the ground, but more was added, just in case.

Angela brought sweet tea to the workers, keeping them hydrated throughout the hot days. Her own workers on painting the house were busy at work too. Making her house transform into a showpiece.

Ted had made a small batch of white paint and was working on the porch and the white railing that surrounded it. He took down all the shutters and painted them the bright white as well.

Angela rewarded Ted's hard work with a few well-deserved kisses. He felt paid in full.

Angela set herself to keep busy, deciding her painting was not benefitting the project, having to sand away her drips, so she left the work to those who did it better. No one wanted her on a ladder anyhow. Her leg grew stiff and achy whenever she overdid it. Angela had gotten a new furniture delivery the day before and had pleasantly filled Olivia's room and another spare room with furniture. Marie Harpole had made some delightful curtains and the rooms were looking better.

She planned to surprise Ted's sister with an invitation to come and stay a few days, to help plan the wedding with Angela and Olivia over the visit. She just knew the young lady, only fifteen years old, would be delighted to be involved in the planning.

Angela stayed busy cooking and making her house a home, while going through everything that was needed for the Sparks arrival in the fall. She had a large cook stove, furniture, rugs, a dining table and chairs in storage in town. She also had hired Marie to sew curtains and linens so they would be welcomed home with clean and fresh beds for all. The carpenter in town had the task to make beds and bureaus for each room. Angela would add more to the busy woodworkers list as she planned and schemed. It was a lovely thing she thought on throughout her days. There was so much in her life to be thankful for. She felt so very blessed.

Dolly and Corinne met for lunch and discussed plans for the future. Corinne had made Dolly promise to take a week or more to rest and recuperate from her journey that first night Dolly had been home. Dolly had reluctantly agreed but this meeting was a compromise. Dolly had so many thoughts and ideas in her mind and she needed to be able to talk about them with Corinne. It was easier to focus on that then Reggie's announcement.

She had talked at length with Angela and Olivia, who were good listeners, but she was rather unwilling to broach the subject again after that night. She wanted to move forward. Reggie had been right about her in many ways, and she was determined to focus on her purpose rather than a failed romance.

Corinne began the meeting with a long hug, and the smallest of a scolding.

"You really scared us all, young lady." Corinne said as Dolly finally sat at the table in Corinne's home. Violet laughed from her spot at the nearby kitchen counter where she pounded out dough.

Dolly didn't want to apologize anymore and knew it wasn't really needed. They knew why she had gone, and God had seen her through the worst of it.

"Let's focus on what we can do." Corinne started finally at the business at hand. "I do apologize for interjecting my fear into this. I missed you dreadfully." Corinne pouted playfully.

"I missed you all as well." Dolly laughed and reached a hand out to her friend.

"I had made inquiries months ago to the Boston greenhouse and some publishers in New York. There are interested parties in our research and we are promised an audience with our work should we complete it in the next few years. It is a big project we are undertaking." Corinne offered.

Dolly nodded. "I am more than ready to move forward."

"Ah, good." Corinne sighed and pulled out some papers. "I was thinking, that your drawing is far superior to mine. I would like for you to focus on your plant drawings and choose what plant groups you want to focus on. It is a big list and I am not certain they all will fit in one book." Corinne looked over some of her notes.

"I was thinking of that as well." Dolly offered. She bit her lip in thought. "If we plan on a set of guides. Starting with thoughts about the most common problems that plague us. The simple remedies that every households suffer with. Certain plants and flowers are common to many areas. Apothecaries carry a lot of diversity when it's available. We could focus on that first, then bring awareness to other plants that are lesser known."

Corinne nodded and made a few notes.

"This could be a lifetime pursuit." Corinne said with her eyes wide.

"Oh, yes!" Dolly agreed, smiling wide her eyes sparkling. "Won't it be a grand way to live?"

They both laughed and agreed excitedly, they talked for hours about plants and who would write about each one. They would lose track and discuss future endeavors, or things they had heard from articles or from others in their past who had shared wisdom about remedies. The afternoon was well spent.

Violet teased them as she was doing her own work. They were like schoolgirls giggling and at play. So very excitedly talking about things that most people knew so little about.

They stood and stretched and went to the greenhouse. It was bright with the summer sunshine gleaming through the glass. The air was sweet and fragrant with the many blooms and plants growing. Dolly got reacquainted with the plants she had left behind, she muttered her many apologies to them sweetly. Knowing the plants would forgive her easily enough.

She saw the small almond trees growing in the section meant to provide Angela's orchard with a fruitful harvest in years to come. She saw that Corinne had transplanted a few spearmint and peppermint plants from a nearby woods and was pleased to see it. She knew she would get to go hunting through the forest herself and add her own finds here. She was filling up on her passion and it was pleasant and rewarding. She and Corinne talked over more plans and Corinne pointed out a few ideas she had. Dolly left later with her heart fulfilled. She was where she needed to be. It was enough.

She prayed out her thanks to God as she walked back to Angela's home. With plans of a wedding she was certain to be moving back to Chelsea Grant's for a time. She was happy about it. She wasn't quite done with her nomadic ways.

She felt secure within herself now, someday God would send her a reason to stay in one place. Until then she was free to be Bluebird with her own wings to fly where she wanted.

Chapter 26

Oregon City

Progress was slow but the women of Oregon City made their way to every household in town and some on the outskirts. Everyone knew about the plan that the women came up with and names of children in need of permanent homes was gathered, as well as a few people talking with family and friends about adoptions.

Millie made it known that she was available to talk to anyone and she was working in town, an easy target for anyone who wanted a chance to meet some of the children involved. The pastor of the church in town had several staying in their crowded house, they had four children of their own and not a lot of extra room but cots and quilts were used in the meantime to give them shelter.

The Pastor of the Spring Creek church had taken in two children but they were also crowded in their small cabin. One little girl was staying with a family in the Boarding house but the widow taking care of her neighbor's orphan child was struggling. She wanted to help but had two babies herself and the task was difficult.

Many prayers had been prayed over these young lives that had been so tragically affected, hearts were opened. Certainly there were enough families with room and open hearts to help.

Millie was pleased that in that first week she had more than four families ready to adopt a child. They only needed three more and God would be glorified, indeed.

The newspaper ran a large article about the orphanage and had many opinions and points of view. It had meant to be an open look at the issue, but it was very swayed to side with the women's committee in the end. Three different communities could at least try their hardest to take care of this handful of children. It was the Christian thing to do.

The Oregon City town council was eager to agree to the plan and as long as the children had a home. Then Oregon City could back out of the work orphanage with its head held high.

It was everyone's desire to see it to the finish.

Dolly Bouchard

Dolly was back to work after more than a week of being back in Oregon City. She was ready. There was so much to be done and she was eager to put her full energy towards her work.

Corinne was happy too and they spent much of that first day back just getting the plan for the summer discussed. The green house was going to be expanded when more glass came in from a glassmaker in Sacramento. Corinne ordered more than she needed, knowing how difficult it was to get glass from place to place. Now that the bridge was complete, travel was so much easier and she was excited to have her husband back to building the frame for her greenhouse expansion. There were more trees and flowers to plant.

Dolly worked some on tidying the laboratory getting back behind the large pots and cleaning the ashes from the fire pits. They would have bottles delivered soon for the next batch of lavender and pine oil. She hoped in a few years to have almond oil to ship too. Having a carrier oil on hand would give them a lot of opportunity for more ways to make medicines. They had so many ideas.

Dolly kept her thoughts on Reggie to a minimum; she was counting the days regardless to his leaving and wondered if he would keep his promise to visit with her before he left.

She dreaded and longed for it. She knew he had been right, if his path led away from her than there was not much sense to pursue any kind of attachment. But she felt still somehow, that she was at fault. Her reserve had not helped matters. Olivia had given her a good bit of wisdom that she was stewing over, it made her think long and hard about the whole situation.

'If you did fall for him and he for you, would this still have come to him? This longing to be somewhere else? It is better to know before any heart need to be thoroughly broken.' Olivia had shared about her husband's wandering ways. Never happy or satisfied. It had given Dolly a pause. But the pain lingered still in her heart at what could have been.

Violet Griffen

It was a lovely Wednesday and Violet set herself toward town. She wanted to stop by the butchers, the grocers and check the Fancy Goods store for any ideas for a wedding gift for Angela. It was a month or more away but she wanted some inspiration.

She borrowed the one-horse buggy and headed off. She had worn a fine dress that was a pale green and she had taken extra care with her hair that morning. She had been cooped up for a while at her own whim. She was feeling better about her place in the world, being a widow would not be the end of her, just a chance for a new start.

She started at the grocer, finding a crate of lemons that had been shipped from California. She snatched it up and walked back to the livery to place it in the back of her buggy that was being kept there. She waved politely to the man who ran the livery who was mending a harness and whistling merrily.

She stopped by the Greaves Lace Shop and couldn't resist on splurging on a new lace shawl to wear on Sundays during the summer months. She was happy to see the new counter worker, Francine Havers, working at the counter. Violet remembered her being a widow who had moved into the boarding house over the winter months. It was good to see her looking so well. They struck up a good conversation. Francine, who had heard about Violet's husband, was quick to give her condolences. They spoke a little about widowhood, not in a negative way but bonding a little over the feelings and how best to move forward. It had been a good conversation and Violet added Francine to her list of friends in her mind. She would have to make time to visit her again.

Violet went next to the Fancy Goods Store and saw several customers in the process of purchasing goods, chatting away with Millie Quackenbush who was excellent at customer service. Violet overheard them talking about the list of potential parents for orphan children. Violet made a mental note to write down the names to tell Corinne and the other nearby neighbors, she would ask Millie to show her if she decided to purchase anything.

Violet looked through the fabric seeing some beautiful chintz and cotton prints that were new. She pulled out a few bolts to consider when she overheard a name she hadn't expected.

She stopped and almost dropped the bolts, she moved slowly to a nearby table to set them down before she spoke up.

"Pardon me, Millie." Violet spoke louder than she had intended and the four ladies in the store all turned to look at Violet in surprise.

Violet felt her cheeks flame but wasn't going to quiet herself. "What was that last name you mentioned for adoptions?" Violet's voice was loud but it cracked a few times as she spoke.

"The mill owners, the Smithers, are putting themselves forward for Delilah Sparver, she is seven years old." Millie said with no hesitation.

"No!" Violet yelled.

Millie may have been shocked but she didn't seem affronted. She just looked at Violet with curiosity.

Violet felt ill. "Timothious and Meredith Smithers?" Violet grabbed her throat after she said their names.

"Yes, the very ones. They own the watermill south of town." Millie said with a smile.

"No, no, no!" Violet grabbed herself around her middle, stabbing pain going through her. *It could not be!* She said within herself. *He could not be so bold!*

Violet tried so very hard to gather her wits. She truly did but she was beyond that. She had worked so very hard at putting her past behind her and now it was all rushing at her like wild horses on a stampede.

"Pardon me…" Violet said weakly. "You should perhaps reconsider."

Violet waved, knowing her face was purple with mortification and she was breathing strangely.

She pushed her self through the door, the bell tinkling behind her and five faces watching her as she walked disjointedly across the street to the livery.

After she got to the livery manager she asked him weakly to hook up her buggy. Within a minute she was riding back. Only after she was most of the way home did she realize that she had left her new shawl in the Fancy Goods Store.

Chapter 27

Violet Griffen

Sweat dripped down her back as she walked, thinking and breathing deeply. Violet wiped at a horsefly who was buzzing near her. She had gone back to her home and put the horse and buggy away in the barn but she couldn't go inside. She just started walking.

She felt out of her depth. She had made a scene at the fancy goods store and now she was certain that half the town knew by now that she was half-crazed.

"Or fully crazed!" She muttered to herself.

She swatted at the tall grass and pondered what to do. She could not allow her parents to adopt a seven-year old girl. It was impossible for her conscience to allow. Righteous anger flooded her again as she thought of what fate was waiting for that little girl if she said nothing. Young Delilah... Violet wasn't sure she knew her, but she already felt a solid instinct to protect her.

Her childhood had been a strict one, 'you do not ever speak to people about family matters', was drummed into her from a young age. There were people in and out of the mill every week, but it was usually men and Violet had never been allowed to speak to them. She had been schooled at home, her father always nervous about the school prying into their personal business. It had been a lonely childhood until her brothers came along. By then she was her mother's full time helper. She had never had anyone to talk to about what her father had done to her. His threats always loomed over her.

She contemplated heavily what to do. Knowing she would have to break the vow to herself to never speak of what had happened at the watermill. She would have to confide in someone. The fear of it gripped around her throat, she felt a headache coming on and she fought the fear bubbling up through her. She wanted to pray but felt surrounded by her fear, like weeds choking out the air around her, making her tongue feel thick and her thoughts clouded.

She dropped into the tall grass, settling in and letting the quiet surround her, clearing her mind as she listened. The afternoon was calm, there was no breeze to speak of. She closed her eyes and heard the buzzing of flying insects and far off birds chirping. It seemed so peaceful here but her heart wasn't allowing the peace to settle in. The storm inside her was coming alive. The part of her that was never ready to face her abuser was coming to life and she had to allow it. She had to free herself to this part of her if she was going to save this young girl from her own fate. She finally allowed the tears, and with them the prayers came out.

Violet wept in the tall grass for a long while, letting the memories come and the pain that came with it. She was going to start a war, and she needed to be ready for it.

Chapter 28

Violet Griffen

Violet stood at the door of Clive's cabin, it had been a long walk but she knew she had to speak with him. When her tears had run out she had felt the peace of God surround her. She prayed in the quiet and was led to Clive's door, knowing what she had to do. The walk was a long one and the time flew by as her thoughts formed into a start of a plan. She saw his small cabin and went forward knowing she couldn't turn back.

"Clive?" She said softly and then knocked.

"Come on in." Clive called out jovially. He was always up for visitors. He was nothing like her father who was suspicious of anyone that came by in the evening hours.

Violet entered and saw Clive seated on the floor with a few crates around him.

"You packing?" She asked.

"Why yes, Miss Violet." Clive grinned but he saw the look on her face and his smile faded.

"You are lookin' a fair bit troubled." He said softly and stood, he gestured to the two soft leather chairs next to the dark fireplace. No fire was needed in this heat.

Violet wordlessly sat down, willing herself to do what she had come to do. "I am in a fair bit of trouble." She used his own words to start.

Clive nodded and reached out to her. She allowed him to squeeze her hands supportively and then he scooted the chair closer to her and sat.

"I need some counsel. I see no other way to move forward." Violet said, looking at the floor, she bit her lip to keep control of her emotions. She needed to try and avoid sobbing and hysterics just now.

"I am here, and I will offer what I have and trust God for the rest." Clive said quietly. He was then silent, letting her have the floor.

"Today, I found out in town that an older couple are offering to take on a seven-year old girl in adoption." She paused. "Delilah

Havers, for the women's council project." Violet started, she looked up to see that Clive was listening intently, watching her carefully.

"The couple I speak of is Meredith and Timothious Smithers, they are my parents." Violet said.

Clive lowered his eyebrows and frowned. "The Smithers that built the watermill?"

Violet nodded.

"Met Timothious a few times when I set up my Hudson Bay Store. I am surprised that I never saw you with the other school kids." Clive offered.

"They never let us go to school in town, Mama schooled us from home." Violet said stiffly. "He wasn't much for having folks around. He liked that we lived outside of town, down river."

"He gave that impression." Clive said simply.

"I have fought off talking about my family with anyone but the Whittlan family for a long while, but I need to know how to move forward so I can do this without sin or regret." Violet said, feeling heat rise in her cheeks as she prepared herself. She took a shaky breath and began. "I cannot allow my parents to adopt that little girl. There are things that I know that I have hidden from everyone since I left the watermill when I was fifteen. Mrs. Whittlan is the only person who knows the whole truth and she vowed to never tell a soul. She would never break that promise. But now I fear I must break that silence myself."

Violet wrung her hands together and felt panic race through her. "My mother baked bread and delivered the ground flour and cornmeal every week to town on Mondays and Thursdays. My father started when I was very young to spend the afternoons that she was gone in the house with me." Violet stopped, breathing heavy and trying to stay calm.

Clive stood and got her a mug of water. He handed the mug to her and sat back down, his face grim.

"As I got older it got worse, he would force my younger brothers to do chores outside under threat of a beating if they came in. He would threaten me into silence about what took place on those days."

Violet looked to Clive and saw the sickened look that crossed his face as understanding dawned. She didn't want to go into details.

She never wanted to say those words aloud. She felt that shame again, now deeper than she had ever felt it before, because it was out. A man she deeply respected now knew the darkness and depravity that she endured.

"I was abused that way until I was fifteen. It was either on my birthday or a few days after, it is hard to remember now. I told my mother." The fat tears could not be contained when she thought of the betrayal from her mother, to her that pain was worse than the other sometimes. Violet continued, her voice thick with emotions. "She called me a liar, I was threatened by my father. I climbed into the loft and eventually jumped out of the window and escaped. The Whittlan's had visited our house once, they had gone door to door letting people know that they were holding services in the school outside of town. My mother had visited with them and they seemed like kind people. I ran through town and asked for directions to their home. They took me in."

Violet finished and bent over, putting her head on her knees and let the pain of the memory go through her. She was sure Clive heard her and would think while she dealt with trying to breathe.

This was the simplest version of this story, the whole truth being so much darker than that short tale. But Clive could glean from what she had said to help, she hoped.

She heard Clive get up and walk a few steps. Violet sat up but kept her eyes closed. She wasn't sure she was praying or just breathing but she felt that God was holding her through it.

The sound of Clive's steps came closer and she heard him take a seat.

"Matthew 18; 15-17. If thy brother shall trespass against thee, go and tell him his fault between thee and him alone: if he shall hear thee, thou hast gained thy brother."

Clive took a hand and touched her shoulder. She opened her eyes and saw Clive staring at her with sincerity. "You went to your parents and confronted them back then." He looked back down to the bible in his lap and read. "But if he will not hear thee, then take with thee one or two more, that in the mouth of two or three witnesses every word may be established." He looked to her again. Violet gulped and he continued. "And if he shall neglect to hear them, tell it unto the church."

"I will go and be a witness for you. We can confront him and your mother. It need not go beyond us if he will concede to his sin." Clive closed the bible and pressed his hand upon it. He took her hand and laid it over the top of his. "God's ways are the best ways. You do not have to fight this battle alone."

Violet climbed out of her chair and laid her head in Clive's lap and sobbed. Relief and regret mingling as her heart was lightened. She had a wise ally and he would go with her.

Clive's hand soothed over her head like he would have a child's.

"Dear Father God, bless your daughter Violet, she has survived so much with a joyful spirit. She has sung your praise amidst all her pain. Give us the strength to do your will and to overcome the evil that was done to her."

Violet felt a tear splash on the hand that was held by Clive. She looked up to see tears on his weathered cheeks.

She whispered, "Amen," and he nodded with her.

Chapter 29

Violet Griffen

Violet knew she could never be well prepared to enter this battle. It was one she had fought off in her head for more years than she wanted to admit. To face down the abuser and the betrayer in a single stroke would take some inner strength she wasn't certain that she had.

The bridge on Spring Creek Road was mostly finished but it was closed to allow another crew to seal it with linseed oil. Violet stood waiting on the other side. Holding her hands and wringing them nervously waiting for Clive to come by wagon to get her. She watched the men working absently, inside her own head, her thoughts whirling in a painful tornado. She wasn't sure what to say first. Who would she see? Her father or mother? Would her brothers be there? Would she have to make her accusations in front of them? She played out every possible scenario and none of them were good.

She wanted to hide from this but she knew for the sake of the little girl that she couldn't. She had not been able to save herself from the fate she had survived but she would never allow those atrocities to be suffered by someone else while she had breath in her body.

She had made polite small talk with John Harpole when she had crossed the footbridge and walked up to the road. He had talked about the lovely weather and she had participated but she was very glad when he went back to his work.

After a few minutes that felt like an eternity Clive's wagon came around the corner from the direction of town. He waved his hat at her and plopped it back on his head. She smiled wearily and walked toward him as he pulled off the side of the dirt road.

He lent a hand to pull Violet up into the seat.

"You ready?" Clive asked. His face was more serious than his usual wit.

"No, but I need to get this done." Violet said with a shrug.

Clive waved to John Harpole and the men working. He got the wagon turned to the position he needed and clucked the horses forward. The trip through town was quiet, both deep in their own thoughts. As the headed down the path toward the watermill he finally spoke.

"I am here to back you up." Clive said. "All you need to do is tell them the situation. They should not move forward with the adoption or you will have to talk to the town council. You do not have to make them like the idea. You just have to let them know there will be consequences. If they assure you they will drop the adoption attempt no one else should need to know." Clive said thoughtfully.

Violet nodded, feeling better somehow. The way he said things made it seem simpler.

"I am sure people will be talking already because of my actions in town."

"People will always talk. But things can simmer down in time." Clive assured her.

The wagon stopped a few minutes later, the watermill was a few miles outside of town along the rocky banks of the river. The sound of the water wheel brought back memories. She saw the cabin and felt her stomach clench in fear. She had never thought to come back to this place.

She saw her mother, tall and a little thicker around the middle than she had been when Violet had left when she had only been fifteen. It had been seven years since she had looked at her mother for more than those few seconds she saw her at the market. Seven long years and her mother made no effort to find her. Violet felt it go through her like a bitter poison. The betrayal of that last day here replayed and Violet nearly lost her nerve.

Violet fought the fear welling up in her and stepped down from the wagon. She had been so still she hadn't noticed that Clive was already on her side of the wagon, he was helping her down. Violet noticed that Clive had a revolver on his side, she had never seen him with any gun besides his hunting rifle and she was shocked to see it. *Would they resort to violence if they saw her?*

He walked beside her as she numbly walked toward her mother, who was hanging wet laundry on the line.

"Mother?" Violet said aloud. Feeling the word as bitter on her tongue.

Her mother turned, looking so much like an older version of herself. The recognition came across her mother's face. She didn't looked pleased.

"You are not welcome back here." Her mother said and frowned.

"I have news." Violet said. She stopped walking and she yelled across the expanse. It was a good thirty feet between them.

He mother put down the shirt she had been shaking loose back into the basket at her feet.

"Then say it." Her mother said as she looked up.

"I know that you and Timothious have put your names to adopt that girl." She hadn't planned to call her father by his name instead of saying father. But she felt it was right somehow, for herself anyways.

"That is none of your business." Her mother said with a bite to her tone.

"It is my business if he hurts her. Which he will. Like he did to me." Violet said, her heart pounded in her chest. This was just like reliving that day.

Her mother threw up her arms dramatically. "It's all lies."

"You can believe what you want. But if you go forward with this I will tell the town council what he did. Then they can decide." Violet said when her anger rose. Being called a liar again was expected, but how could her mother believe after all this time that her daughter would just make those things up.

A rifle shot rang through the air, the boom made Violet jump and Clive jumped in front of her.

"Get off my property!"

Violet whipped her head around and held a shaky hand over her heart.

"We will leave!" Clive announced.

Violet saw her father with his long-barreled rifle pointed at the sky. Her brothers stood behind him, both looking confused and on edge.

Her father hissed at them. "You boys get in the house."

"I don't think so." Her oldest brother Tim said.

Her father turned and shoved Harold and he went into the cabin. Tim stood his ground.

"I came as a witness for Violet. She wants you to withdraw your adoption request. If you agree no other action will be taken." Clive yelled across the yard.

"You have no say in my business, Mr. Quackenbush. Kindly take that woman and turn yourself around and leave." Timothious spoke harshly, the veins on his neck standing out. His face was red and his eyes were glassy. Violet had seen this look on her father's face a thousand times. Usually violence followed that look.

"Let's go." Violet put a hand on Clive's shoulder.

The pain in her heart had traveled down to the pit of her stomach, knowing that they would never change their minds. She dreaded it but she knew she would have to move forward and accuse her father of his atrocities. By doing that she would bring all that shame on herself, to everyone in town.

Her mother ran over to her husband, her lips were moving but Violet could not hear her. She watched her mother wave her arms and try to push her husband toward the front door of the cabin.

"They have heard what they need to." Clive said and turned to face her. Violet took a few steps backwards, not wanting to turn her back on them if her father planned on trying anything.

She watched her brother Tim try to talk to Timothious, he wasn't having any more luck than his mother at moving him from his stance.

Violet felt her bravery swell up and she had one final thing to say. "I will not let you hurt another girl, Father. You drop this adoption now or everyone will know." Violet yelled out fiercely.

His face registered her words and he dropped the rifle to the ground. His face was free of the anger, instead he was shocked. She had never seen that look and she memorized it to think upon at a later time.

Violet thought of turning around and walking back to the wagon but she stayed for a moment longer to see her father's anger return.

"You better close your mouth, girl." He yelled, his eyebrows drawn together in ferocity.

"Never! You will never rape another girl again." Violet yelled and meant it. That look he had, for so many years of her life had pushed her past her fear. No girl would cower before that man again.

Tim finally looked at his sister in shock and took several steps away from his father. He held his hands to his head in surprise and tears filled his eyes.

"No..." Her brother yelled and never looked away from Violet. "Oh God..."

Tim broke his gaze from Violet and looked at his father, who had calmed and was standing still. Looking to his eldest son. He was talking too low for Violet to hear but she could tell he was trying to back away from her accusations. Tim pushed at Timothious and stormed into the cabin.

Violet felt Clive pulling her toward the wagon. She walked backwards until she was stopped by Clive. She climbed into the wagon seat never looking away from her parents.

Clive clucked at the horses to try and get them turned around in the yard. Before he had the wagon facing north to leave on the road Violet saw her eldest brother with a satchel in his hand.

"Wait!" Tim yelled. He ran like a bullet and threw his satchel in the back. "May I have a ride to the boarding house?" He asked, his breath ragged from running and emotion.

"I'll do ya better than that, Lad." Clive said and nodded, giving his permission.

Tim climbed in and they left the watermill behind them.

A minute went by with only the sounds of horse hooves on the dirt road before Clive spoke. "I got an extra bed at my cabin iffen you need a place to squat."

"I'd appreciate it, kindly." Tim said hoarsely. His face was red and he had tears in his eyes still. Violet watched him but he hadn't looked at her. He was looking to a far off place. She would let him be.

They rode through town in silence.

They were nearing the bridge project when Tim finally spoke, he got Violet's attention away from staring into the distance with his hand on her shoulder.

"How long had he hurt you?" Tim's voice was still ragged.

"I was seven when it started." Violet said flatly. Not wanting her brother to think of such things but knowing she had to tell the truth.

Her brother turned away from her and sobbed against his hands. She heard him saying he was sorry through his outburst but didn't know how to tell him that he was just a little boy then.

Clive stopped the wagon in sight of the bridge. "You'll be okay from here?" He asked, his face in serious contemplation.

Violet nodded.

"I got him. You talk to Corinne and Lucas tonight. I will come by tomorrow. We started this war. We need some reinforcements. I'll talk to the Whittlan's." Clive looked her in the eye.

She climbed down from the wagon numbly. Hearing her brother's agony was harder than she would have ever thought. She knew somehow that Clive would get through to him. He was in good hands.

She walked away towards her home, the safety of Grant's Grove called to her like a beacon and she longed to be there in the peaceful life she had made there.

She couldn't think beyond that thought. Just get home.

Clive Quackenbush

Clive was bone tired when he finally laid his head to rest. The young man had been calm when they finally ended their talk.

Clive had warmed up some stew and sat for hours talking with Tim. Knowing there would be more words in the coming days. Clive knew the ripple effects of today's activities would be felt by more than just this one lad.

Clive laid his head on his pillow and his thoughts would not stop. How could a man…? Clive didn't want to consider finishing the thought. It was unthinkable.

He had seen many a father beat their kids, and had stepped in a few times when he felt he could do some good. But to cross that line that should never be crossed was beyond Clive's understanding. So many people were going to be angry and Clive could not see any other way then to play out this scenario. People would have to know.

He wondered how Violet would be able to bear it. His heart ached and he felt bile rise in his throat when he thought of everything she had had to bear. He sat up and lit a candle. He stared out of his small cabin window and prayed for a long while. He just wasn't sure anyone but the good Lord could unravel this tragedy.

Corinne Grant

Corinne felt safe in her husband's arms that night. It was well past midnight and Corinne had cried so much her head ached. The talk with Violet had been such a shock. Violet had tried to just make it simple, not wanting to upset them but to let them know what she would be doing in town.

Both Lucas and Corinne had forced Violet to share more of the story than she wanted. That they couldn't let her be alone in this fight.

Corinne laid in bed, hours later just trying to let her sadness go. She wanted to comfort her friend but she knew she had to rest, the child within her needed her too.

She had been angry before, that burning righteous anger at her first husband when his foolishness had gotten Angela nearly killed on the Oregon Trail years before. This anger had surpassed that day.

What punishment was enough for a man who would do that to a child? She couldn't fathom that anything man could come up with would be enough to be any kind of justice.

Corinne wanted to talk more, she felt she needed to... To hash this out until some kind of solution could be agreed upon. The hour of the night was a quick reminder that she couldn't and Corinne laid in the safety of her husband's arms until she could do nothing but pray. Finally after a long while and more than a few more tears she slept.

Angela Fahey

Angela was absently counting the logs and lumber that was piled high on her property. The wagonloads of goods had arrived to start on the cabin she was building for the Spark family. A part of her had rejoiced to see them but her heart was so very heavy.

Corinne and Marie had come while Angela was frying bacon and eggs for breakfast for Dolly and Olivia. She had been dreaming about her wedding and thinking on the pleasant summer it would be. Sophia had gone home the day before with a pretty pout or two but with a promise to come again soon it had all smoothed over.

The knock had been surprise and Angela wiped away the bacon grease from her hands on a towel as she went to answer the door.

"Come in, I have breakfast on. Come to the kitchen." Angela saw that their faces were sad and serious and she felt that drop in her stomach, certain that there had been some kind of accident or something.

"No one is injured!" Marie spoke quickly as she walked in, she must have seen panic on Angela's face.

Angela sighed and walked briskly to her eggs. She scooped them out of the pan and onto the plates.

Just then Dolly could be heard coming down the wooden stairs in her bare feet. She was carrying her shoes at her sides by their long laces.

Angela finished making breakfast; both Corinne and Marie had already eaten so Angela didn't need to throw extra on for them.

Dolly set the table and Olivia came down, as the last plate was set. She was surprised to see the visitors so early but she sat at the table with everyone.

"We came to talk about Violet." Corinne started and shared the tale as the women picked at their food. It was not the best conversation for a meal but it had to be done. Everyone at the table was crying soon thereafter. The news was not what anyone wanted to hear, especially about a beloved friend but as the shock wore off they prayed together.

Corinne and Marie had left a little while later, still with heavy hearts. They were going to talk with Chelsea Grant to make another ally for Violet for what was coming.

Dolly left to go to work, but she wanted to go talk to Violet first, making sure that she wasn't losing her mind alone. Angela and Olivia stayed in the parlor for a long while, trying to make sense of what they had heard but not able to. They prayed again, needing some peace.

Olivia finally went to her spot on the porch with her string and bobbins. Angela went to work on the milk pails delivered earlier by Warren. She separated the milk and cream and set aside some of the cream to churn butter for later.

As Angela looked to Olivia as she had for the last weeks she did not see her friend and soon-to-be Aunt making lace but instead weeping as she rocked. Angela felt her throat tighten as she felt overwhelmed again.

It was a few minutes later that Angela had to wipe off her face because the wagons were there with the lumber.

Angela had finally signed the sheet with all the lumber and logs accounted for. Clive had delivered the long nails and spikes needed a few days before and everything was here but for the roofing shingles, which were being readied by the lumber mill. Angela should feel overjoyed but her heart was just too heavy.

Chapter 30

Harpole Ranch

That evening everyone involved gathered at John Harpole's house. Violet looked weak but when she saw her brother Tim and Harold arrive with Clive she had enough energy to bolt towards them. The embrace was intense and her younger brother cried as they held her.

Everyone else stood around them in support but feeling at a loss to help them through the quagmire of pain.

Marie took charge of all the little ones and Dolly helped her corral them to a separate room. Cooper and Brody were told to go outside and play with the dog, Pepper, and they gladly obliged, ecstatic to get to play outside a while longer.

The meeting wasn't long but it had a few interruptions as people had questions.

The general consensus that Clive and Violet would go to Millie and tell her about the complaint, knowing that the town council would have to be brought in. Corinne and Lucas wanted to tag along in the morning with them. Even just to be there for support.

When it came to talking with the town council others wanted to be there as a sign of support. Before it was all done Harold Smithers, the youngest brother spoke up.

He was quieter than his brother and he had left his home the morning after the confrontation when he had overheard his parents talking. He knew Clive a little and after talking to the man at the livery, who knew where Clive lived, he walked all the way out to Clive's cabin. Harold came to the front of the group, his hat held tightly in both hands. His blond hair and cornflower blue eyes looked so much like Violet there was no denying he was her sibling.

"I am working through all of this the best way I know how. I was nine years old when Violet left and I was always a bit confused about how it had happened. My father was a brutal man about many things. I can attest to that." Harold swallowed hard. "When it comes time to talk to the town council, I need to speak with them..." His cheeks turned red and he bit down hard on the side of his cheek with emotion. "I saw something long ago, it was years before and I was too young to understand it. But I understand it now. I will confirm Violet's story for them."

Every woman gasped and several men shifted uncomfortably. Everyone had discussed amongst themselves that a woman claiming abuse was sometimes considered a liar, just because of her sex. A witness in the crime committed against Violet would go a long way.

Harold went back to his sister and she buried her head in his chest, sobbing hard and ragged.

No one knew what to say but the announcement rung through all of their hearts that night.

They were now armed with stronger weapons in the battle to come.

Clive Quackenbush

The next morning Clive came by early to pick up Violet and Lucas and Corinne followed behind them. Violet wanted to visit with her brothers after meeting with Millie.

Everyone was quiet as they rode to town. Clive took a chance every few minutes to reach out and rub a supportive hand down Violet's shoulders. She felt numb and wondered how her life had come to this.

What would Millie say when they told her the truth about her parents? What could she say to her brothers later, who had left everything behind for her? Would they stay by her side when they were disinherited?

Violet felt sadder today than she had ever in her life. A part of her wanted to save that little girl and run away, move somewhere far away so that no one would know her. Could she do that? Could she leave her new family behind and just start again?

The wagons parked at the livery and the short walk across to the fancy goods store was painful. Every step Violet wanted to turn back but knew she couldn't.

The bell tinkled again and Millie met Clive and Violet with a bright smile.

"I have your lace shawl!" Millie spoke brightly. She didn't comment at all about Violet's strange behavior. Millie's brows dropped a moment later. She must have noticed their heavy countenance.

"We need to talk with you Millie. You mind handing off your responsibilities?" Clive asked in a low voice.

Millie shook her head, and called for JQ.

"I need to chat with them. Can you mind the counter?" She asked and patted her husband companionably on his arm. He nodded and kissed her on the cheek affectionately and Clive and Violet followed her to the back room.

Clive's old office still had its round table and chairs and they sat quietly.

It only took a minute to tell Millie the basics. Millie was as shocked as everyone else was. She teared up too, and settled a hand on Violet who was pale and tired looking.

"We know the town council will have to be informed." Clive said. Millie nodded and a few more fat tears tumbled down her rosy cheeks.

"I will strike through their names this moment. God help you child." Millie's voice was tight.

Clive went to stand up but Millie spoke again, with her hand still on Violet.

"I may be a shallow woman sometimes, quick to spread gossip and talk more than the good Lord wants me to. But I know what my Lord desires for me, to act justly, to love mercy, and to walk humbly with God." Millie sniffled and dabbed at her face with her free hand and handkerchief. "My lips shall not talk of this until the moment is right, but only to call for justice for what has been done. That should never have been done to this lovely girl." Millie stood and saw Clive nod in agreement.

"I couldn't have said it better."

Violet stood and without warning hugged Millie Quackenbush.

"Thank you." Violet said after she broke from the embrace, her eyes red and swollen and her cheeks bright from crying and grief.

Millie promised to immediately go to Jed Prince, the head of the town council, and begin the process of removing the Smithers from the list.

"I will send a messenger your way about when they will want to meet with you." Millie promised.

Clive and Violet joined with Corinne and Lucas, only a short discussion was needed and Clive and Violet left. Corinne and Lucas stayed in town to finish up the shopping that Violet had been unable to finish. Her work was not as important now. They would all pitch in together to keep the household going in this time of need.

Corinne clung to Lucas's arm all that day. She was more than a little bit lost.

Clive Quackenbush

Clive left Violet at his cabin to have alone time with her brothers. Marie and John Harpole were just leaving as they dropped off some food for them to have lunch when they wanted to. Clive smiled to see Marie living out her love in her own way. Every woman was a little different in the way she loved best. Marie Harpole was a good woman and he felt that tug on his own heart while thinking how John had needed a good woman to be a companion after he had lost his wife before he came to Oregon.

He knew where he wanted to spend some time after such an emotional few days and he saddled his horse and headed there.

Olivia was seated prettily on the porch working on her project as he came closer to Angela's house. He slid off his mount and tied him to a nearby post.

He watched as Olivia lifted her head and acknowledged him. Wondering why he had waited so long to court this woman. She had made no secret in her actions since they met that she was interested. He wasn't sure what he had been thinkin'.

"Greetings, Ms. Greaves!" He said with a small smile.

"You get things settled in town?" She asked as he walked up the steps.

He nodded and took the rocker next to her.

"Good." Olivia looked him over and sighed. "Tough business that."

Her hands were settled in her lap, lace was pooled around her legs.

Clive nodded again. "For today it is done. Tomorrow will bring its own trouble." Clive said wisely.

Olivia patted the hand that was resting on the arm of the rocker.

"I have been doing an enormous amount of thinking lately and most of it on things that are just dreadful. But amidst those unhappy thoughts I had one constant thought that wasn't so awful." Clive said and placed his hand over Olivia's.

"Oh?" Olivia didn't look away.

"Well, I know this seems like a strange time for courtin'. Going through this tragedy. But sometimes the hard times make decisions a little easier." Clive cleared his throat and continued. "You don't seem to mind much that I am 61 years old." It wasn't a question but he paused for a response.

"No, Clive, I do not mind so much." Olivia said sincerely.

"You are 20 years younger than I." Clive countered, a little of him in disbelief. She was very attractive, and young enough to get a younger man.

Olivia nodded and smiled becomingly. "I never would have thought you to ever doubt yourself, Clive." She lowered her head and looked at him through her golden lashes.

He wasn't certain if she had meant that look to be flirtatious or not but it did a number on him nonetheless.

"I could continue to court you for months and see where this goes, but I suddenly feel... After so much sadness has come over me from recent events, how foolish that sounds." Clive rubbed his chin with his free hand.

Olivia smiled again looking him in the eye seriously.

"Would you consider being my wife?" He asked simply. He felt foolish for holding his breath a little but he did it while his heart drummed a little faster.

"I have waited a long while to be happy again." Olivia had tears spring to her eyes and she looked down for a moment. "Could you truly want to be with me?" She asked.

"Well, it may seem quick, and folks will be certain to talk. But I have fallen in love, Olive." He said, trying out a nickname he had called her a hundred times in his head.

She smiled over his words. "I have always wanted to be loved."

"I have never been shy on loving deeply. I promise to be there with you for the rest of my life." Clive announced and couldn't help but lean forward to kiss her sweetly.

"Yes." She whispered as the kiss ended.

He held her hand for a minute before he spoke again. "I know that this can be our secret for a bit. Not bein' the time to announce it yet."

Olivia nodded and couldn't hide her smile.

"You know, I needed something good to lift my heart up a bit." Olivia chuckled a little.

"Oh, Olive, me too." He let the nickname slip again.

She chuckled again louder.

"Olive..." She grinned and gave him that look again through her lashes. "I like it."

Clive sat back in his chair and watched Olivia blush and sort through the lace that was tangling in her lap. They sat for a long while, rocking and talking on the porch. Letting their little secret sink in.

Corinne Grant

Corinne packed up some fresh bread that Violet had poured herself into baking the day before. Corinne had watched Violet cry through pounding out the dough and her heart went out to her. There was more than a few breaks to talk throughout that day but Violet would go back to her work to keep her hands busy.

Corinne had come back from her errands in town, Megan was petulant and moody and Corinne hadn't want to deal with the young lady's moods. She visited with Dolly who was taking her grief out on cleaning the lab from top to bottom.

After leaving the lab and spending a little time checking on her plants in the greenhouse she made up her mind to take some of the loaves of bread to Galina and see how the young girl was faring.

Corinne wasn't sure if the visit would lift her mood but it would be good to talk to her young friend. So much pain in the valley in such a short amount of time. On a whim she grabbed an empty journal she had purchased in town to give to Galina. Perhaps the girl could find time and space to use the journal. Corinne would be praying for that.

The walk was only a mile or so and the breeze was kind. Corinne wore a bonnet to keep the bright sun from her face.

The Varushkin cabin was close and Corinne saw Galina outside with wet laundry by the laundry line that hung from the side of the house and connected to a tall post.

Galina saw her and waved and even smiled which immediately lifted Corinne's spirits.

Corinne gave her a warm hug when she reached her.

"Let's go in, the laundry will wait a bit." Galina offered, still smiling.

Corinne nodded and peeled out of the bonnet. The bonnet kept the sun from burning her cheeks, but the heat under the bonnet was stifling.

Once they were inside Corinne pulled out the bread and the journal.

"Violet was baking up a storm yesterday. I just thought the journal might allow you to write out your thoughts a bit." Corinne looked to Galina's face searching to see how she really was doing.

"Oh, that will be wonderful." Galina exclaimed and held the journal close to her. "I have so much more time now to read since my father wants to be gone so much."

Corinne nodded and sat down at the table.

"Are you doing well?" Corinne asked.

"Some days yes, I've had lots of visitors, and so much food delivered. That will end eventually. I am not really looking forward too taking over everything if I am being honest." Galina sat down but held on to the journal like a treasure.

"I hope you know that we will all be here to help. I want you to promise to ask for help." Corinne was sincere and Galina nodded that she would.

"Knowing that will help." Galina confessed. She looked thoughtful. "The house is so very quiet. I will grow used to it. But sometimes it overwhelms me." Galina was clear-eyed but the pain was still in there.

Corinne and Galina talked for a long while, just reconnecting and planning for the future as much as they could. Corinne didn't tell Galina about Violet's trouble, not feeling it was the right time yet.

After the visit Corinne helped Galina hang the rest of the clean laundry and they spoke of lighter things. The coming 4th of July picnic at the Spring Creek Church was something to look forward to.

Corinne left with a lighter heart than she expected. She saw that John and Marie were riding past her cabin, as she was closer to the property. She turned to go and talk to them before she returned home. Lucas was going to be busy with stump removal on the property and she wanted to keep busy. A visit with Marie would be perfect to pass the time until Violet came home.

Before she got to the Harpole home she saw Megan sitting under a tree, dressed like a butterfly in a colorful tea gown and full skirts. A young man that Corinne recognized as a ranch-hand for the Harpole ranch was seated next to the young woman, leaned in close. Corinne sighed, not certain what she should do next.

John Harpole was ahead of the situation and was walking towards them. Corinne watched without hearing what was said. The young man bolted up from his spot next to Megan and spoke briefly, with contrite posture. He took off in the direction of the barn and then John was talking with Megan. Megan stood and absently brushed away any leaves or debris on her large flouncy dress.

It looked as if Megan was heading back to Grant's Grove thankfully and Corinne kept walking, thankful to avoid her own chance at an argument for now. She would spend a portion of the evening preparing a letter to Megan's father. It was time for the young lady to go home.

Marie was still watching her husband walk home, baby Abby was in her arms, sleeping happily. Corinne reached her and they waited together.

"We have news to share." Marie said softly, as not to disturb the child sleeping.

"More news..." Corinne whispered with a sigh and a smile.

"Good news to balance the bad only a little." Marie said and understood Corinne's exasperation. So much to absorb lately...

Marie looked back to her husband that had a long walk still across the fenced-in horse yard.

"We are adopting Delilah." She said simply.

Corinne let the words absorb into her. Her first thought was gratitude and relief, knowing the young girl would be safe, thinking how generous it was to open their home. Corinne and Lucas had considered adopting, but knew that their marriage was still new. They would have probably not been considered a good candidate by the town council. The next thought Corinne considered that brought tears to her eyes is that she would have a new sister.

Corinne reached over to Marie and they shared a wordless gaze. Corinne felt tears prick at her eyelids and she looked away. Letting the happy emotion fill her. After so much pain this was such a blessing.

"I will be praying extra for Delilah." Corinne finally spoke. She watched a young horse prance in the nearby corral near his mother. She prayed that Delilah would be happy here, and never, ever know about the trouble surrounding the near adoption that almost took place.

Marie stood with Corinne, holding her child and they waited for John, both settling into the idea of change and a blessed future.

John jumped over the fence of the corral and they all went inside. Cooper was whittling with his knife sitting on a half log bench that was in front of the Harpole cabin.

"Hey Sissy!" He saw Corinne and waved with the piece of wood he was carving on.

Corinne roughed up his blond hair and then placed a kiss on his head. He was getting so big already. She wondered if Cooper knew yet.

The visit was so much needed, John brought Cooper inside and while Marie served fresh lemonade they told Cooper about Delilah. He had cheered out a little 'whoop' when he realized he would get to be a big brother again.

"I do hope she loves to fish!" He said with wide, excited eyes.

John chuckled and gave Cooper a poke in the side playfully. They discussed that Delilah may be sad for a bit, but they would shower her with love and give her plenty of time to get used to them.

Marie and John plotted out what to do with their last spare bedroom. Marie chuckled as she realized that some of her fabric would have to be moved, since her addiction to sewing had overflowed into so much of the house.

"I will now have more dresses to make." Marie was excited about her own little projects.

"Oh my, more dresses!" John teased her. "How will you ever cope?"

Marie handed the sleepy child to her husband and stretched out her back. "I will cope just fine."

Corinne wondered about how God works. She had been so very shocked that first day she arrived in Oregon City, she hadn't seen her father in nearly three years and he had been remarried. She had a new step-mother and step brother in an instant. It hadn't been a hard adjustment, but it had taken her a little while to get used to the thought of her father loving another woman. Now she thanked God for Marie daily. She hadn't replaced her mother, Lily, but she did fill in the void left behind a little bit more each day. Lily would have loved to see John happy. Now Corinne, who had spent most of her childhood as an only child, would have three siblings, no matter the relation by blood. They were her brothers and sisters in her heart. She was so very thankful.

Chapter 32

Oregon City

The next day at 1:00 in the afternoon the town council met with quite a crowd. The meeting was at the Methodist church in town to have enough space. A table was set at the front with Jed Prince and the other members of the town council, the new Sherriff, Harvey Worth, had joined after hearing about it from Millie Quackenbush.

The crowd in the pews was all there for Violet, more than thirty people in total. She sat near Clive and her two brothers, with the Grants, Harpoles, Ted, Angela, all of the Greaves family, including Amelia, the Quackenbushes and the Whittlans.

Galina had been asked to stay at the Harpoles house with Chelsea Grant and Sophia Greaves to watch the gaggle of children that didn't need to be a part of this.

The meeting was long.

The council had questions for Violet, who had made the claim that the Smither's family was unfit to be adoptive parents. The sheriff took over and had more questions. Violet did her best to avoid talking about some aspects of her claim, but when her brother Harold shared his witness testimony the whole crowd had been shocked.

The sheriff's wife was there and she wrote down every word that was said. Finally after a short recess for the town council, the sheriff made the announcement.

"We appreciate the way you have all come today. We can never know fully what goes on behind closed doors, no matter how well a family is known. The Smither's name will be stricken from the adoption list of course, the other family, the Harpole's, will be signed as the official adoptive parents of Delilah."

The crowd murmured their approval.

"The town council is very concerned with the accusations of Timothious Smithers. Since we are not yet a state we have no official system to move forward with formal charges. But we will be investigating the crimes done against Violet Griffen. We will be moving forward as best as we can to..." Harvey Worth cleared his throat, then coughed uncomfortably. "We will deal with this swiftly and justly."

There were more than one shocked individuals in the pews. Making certain they couldn't adopt and harm a child had been the goal. But the shocking nature of the accusations had pushed the council into action. No one that left that day was certain what would happen. But it felt like a dark shroud had covered them all.

After the meeting the crowd inside the church spent a while talking outside. Each had their own pondering of how the future would look.

Violet watched, huddling next to her brothers. She was still numb. Having to share the darkest part of her life to the town council had been hard enough, now she was certain that the rest of the town would know within a matters of days.

Who am I fooling'? She asked herself. *It will be within a few hours.*

Her brother Harold held her hand; she looked to him in sympathy. They had stood by her side and she could not fully express how good it felt to know she had family supporting her. It was all a good feeling, she admitted. A part of her wanted them to be as far away from the accusations and darkness as possible. The guilt that swam through at moments was nearly unbearable. But as her brother Tim had told her. 'They had made the choice.'

The crowd eventually dispersed and Corinne and Lucas invited her and her brothers to come back with them. Lucas had purchased a whole goat at the butcher and the men could roast it on the spit. The Harpole's would be joining them after a while. They were picking up Delilah first.

It wasn't too long before the Grant's wagon wheels creaked noisily over the wooden bridge near Grant's Grove.

Angela and Ted were just ahead of them and waved as they past.

Corinne Grant

Corinne settled her bonnet on the peg by the front door. Lucas had Tim and Harold already excited to get started on the goat roast. Lucas shooed the women away from any part of the cooking.

"We have this one under control. There is already bread made, Marie is bringing lemon tarts. We will put potatoes on the fire outside. You women have the day off." Lucas had shared with his mischievous grin that Corinne could never argue with.

Violet had sat down quietly in the parlor and Corinne went looking for Megan, who had not wanted to be a part of the town council meeting.

Corinne changed into a cooler, light cotton dress, she grabbed Violet up to take her for a walk to keep her busy. Corinne didn't want to see Violet sitting alone too much today, knowing the young woman was struggling within herself.

They walked peacefully over to the Harpole's cabin, Corinne saw Cooper and Brody playing with the dog Pepper and informed them about the men roasting the goat. They took off like a shot with an energetic shadow companion nipping at their heels.

Corinne checked in with Galina, Chelsea and Sophia, who had the children handled well.

"Did Megan come by to help?" Corinne asked Chelsea, who was resting lazily in the chair with a sleeping baby.

"No, I never did see her today." Her sister-in-law spoke softly and shook her head from side to side.

Corinne pursed her lips. She let Chelsea know about Cooper and Brody leaving and Violet and Corinne shortly left.

"Let's walk to Angela's and invite them over. There will be more than enough for a large gathering." Corinne said to Violet, looking her over as she spoke.

Violet was paler than usual and had not spoken more than a word or two since they left the meeting. Corinne felt concern rush through her but had no idea how to help her friend.

Angela and Ted were sitting with Olivia on the porch already, soaking up the beautiful day.

Angela walked to them and gave Violet a big hug. No words were said but Angela seemed as concerned about Violet as Corinne was.

"Violet, come and sit with me." Called out Olivia.

Violet nodded and excused herself from Corinne and Angela. Corinne talked with Angela and Ted who had joined them in the front yard. They sat on the hill and looked over the valley as they talked over dinner plans.

"Dolly went to walk along the creek. She seemed to need to get some fresh air." Angela said.

Corinne nodded. Everyone was a little somber after the things that were said at the meeting.

Corinne looked over her shoulder and saw Violet and Olivia talking. Violet seemed to be conversing and she was glad to see that Olivia was able to get Violet past her silence.

They spoke in soft whispers, all sitting on the grassy hill. Trying to think of anything they could do to cheer up their friend. They really didn't have any good ideas, but they would continue to think on it.

A short while later John Harpole's wagon rolled over the bridge to announce their presence. Everyone jumped up and headed over to see the family arrive. Seeing Delilah was a happy thought that they all needed.

The group caught up with them to see Cooper standing next to his parents, he shook Delilah's hand and grinned.

Delilah was a thin wisp of a girl, a few inches shorter than the eight-year-old Cooper. Her hair was a light brown and she had pink cheeks and a shy smile.

Marie had a hand placed on Delilah's shoulder, mothering already. Corinne felt a warmth spread through her as she saw John pointing her way. Corinne walked faster to reach them, her heart skipping along in anticipation of meeting her new sister, nervous about overwhelming her.

Corinne watched Delilah turn around to face her as she got close. Her hazel eyes bright and curious.

Corinne knelt before her, looking in her eyes directly.

"I'm Corinne." She said simply and put her hand forward.

"I'm Lila." She said with a smile.

"What is your favorite thing in the whole wide world, Lila?" Corinne asked not even thinking.

Delilah's eyes were even brighter when she whispered. "Horses!" She grinned and pointed toward the nearby corral.

Corinne couldn't help but smile at the girl's enthusiasm. "You have come to a good place for that."

She won their hearts swiftly and after introductions the girl took off on a sprint to the tall fence of the corral. With a boost from John she stood up on the fence railing and watched the horses. Cooper joined her and named off each one that he knew personally. Marie went inside shortly after to save Chelsea from her child care duties, but Lila and Cooper were stuck together for a long while on that fence, learning to be fast friends, as it should be.

Corinne walked back to her group who had all enjoyed watching the newest family member being introduced. Violet's cheeks were red and eyes swollen.

Corinne walked to her to see if she needed anything.

Violet reached for Corinne and sobbed into her shoulder, holding on tightly. Corinne let her cry, hoping the woman needed to release something that had been locked up tight.

"I could have never dreamed... such a way for God to show me his goodness." Violet said as she pulled away. She may have stuttered through it, but Corinne understood every word. Violet smiled as she wiped away her tears.

The young girl was the proof that God could work through the worst of situations and find some good.

Grant's Grove

The dinner went well, every extra chair from the Harpole house and Corinne's home was settled in the back yard near the creek. Lucas played his violin. Cooper sang a silly song they had made up at school. It was a celebration for Lila. She seemed very delighted and pleased over how everyone tried to make her smile. Dolly came when the goat was done roasting and had a basket full of plants and flowers. She weaved a few together and made a sweet little tiara for Lila's head.

Clive joined the party as well, just in time for the eating, as if he had planned it. He checked on Violet and was pleased that she was fairing better. He spent a lot of time next to Olivia and everyone noticed how often the two whispered to each other. It was a pleasant distraction from any heavy thoughts that tried to sneak into anyone's mind.

Once everyone was full the older children played by the creek and the adults gathered there chairs closer to talk.

Clive waved a hand after a while of visiting to make an announcement.

"Since you all are so dear to me, I thought I should tell you that Olive and I are going to be married." He sounded so casual that it took a moment for everyone to respond.

Angela cheered first, followed by everyone else. They clapped as Clive scooped Olivia up from her seat and planted a kiss on her cheek.

"Oh, you crazy man!" Olivia sputtered through her laughter.

Sophia jumped over and gave Clive a big hug. "My new uncle!" She giggled and kissed her aunt on the cheek too, to finalize it.

"Not yet... Sophie." Clive wiggled his eyebrows at her. "But soon."

The mood was far more jovial than Corinne had ever expected the night to go. There was so much good to be thankful for.

As the dusk fell, some of the younger children getting cranky and needing sleep, the adults started to go their way towards home, Megan was seen crossing the footbridge nearby. Some of her hair tumbling out of pins and her cheeks red.

Corinne was joined by Lucas as Megan walked across the yard.

"You are not supposed to be gone so long." Lucas said simply.

"I was out walking." Megan said with an edge to her voice.

She walked past them and around the side of the house. Corinne looked to Lucas in bewilderment.

Clive said his goodbyes and wished them luck. "That girl will take a bit of work to be tamed." He shook his head and headed toward the barn to get his horse.

Grant's Grove

It is a truth well known to many that a tragedy will never truly thrive on its own without bringing a few more troubles into the mix.

Corinne woke in the morning and found her own trouble had landed on her doorstep, or to be more precise, escaped out the window.

A single white sash dangled outside Megan Capron's bedroom window was the best evidence Corinne saw when she went to check if Megan wanted breakfast. She was going to attempt to make peace.

Corinne's thoughts were ahead of her, thinking of the day's events and not on the empty messy bed she saw. It took a long moment for Corinne to see the room for what it really was. Empty...

The small argument that blew over the home of Corinne and Lucas was brief but mildly explosive. Megan declared herself old enough to be alone without them hovering over her like a mother hen. Corinne had argued that she was under their guardianship and not yet an adult. It was said on deaf ears. The only answer was Megan's retreating form and another slammed door.

Corinne looked at Megan's empty room with an undercurrent of anger that she was going to work hard to control.

A neat little note was on the small desk in the room, sticking out from under the inkwell. A stubby quill sat beside it, the knife and shavings scattered across the desktop.

Corinne picked up the letter, she took some deep breaths to calm herself and opened it.

Dear Cousins Corinne & Lucas,

I have long overstayed my welcome in Oregon, I can feel it in all the angry stares, especially from Corinne. I cannot remain here under this strain any longer.

I have my own life to lead and vow to start it now. Perhaps I have not been as honest as I could have been with you from the start. I never intended to stay as long in Oregon, but have been planning my escape nearly since I arrived.

I have no intention of leading the life my father wants of me. I desire to be more than a rancher's daughter, married off to some boring business associate of my father, which I am certain he eventually intends.

My desire is to go to Europe and be an actress on the stage. The young man I met recently is willing to take me. First to

California, probably a port town like San Francisco first then forward from there.

I will confess to taking the money my father sent forward to you, it was for my care so my guilt is small. But I intend to borrow money from your accounts as well for my passage. I do need to travel in a style that befits my station. I do promise to have the money wired back to you when I reach my final destination.

I do intend to visit with Auntie Rose in Boston before I go all the way to Europe. She will certainly be generous to me when she sees me. I have always been a favorite of hers.

Stewart Ferrill, the rancher who is accompanying me is a small bright lad, and good company and promises to keep me safe. I do say he is far more desirous of me than I am of him. I believe he intends to marry me. I can assure you that is not my intent.

I will pay him well for delivering me to the East coast. After that Aunt Rose will certainly get me a proper escort to London or Paris. Perhaps she will even come with me. She has always encouraged my desire to see Europe and promised me on many occasions to take me. My father would never allow it, though.

I am regretful of the strain that was between us Corinne, I do hope you forgive me for all our disagreements and wish me well on my journey. You were younger than I when you headed west. Certainly you can understand my desire to be my own individual.

I will certainly be gone, sailing away before you can try to stop me. I wish you well in your life, and ask that you wish me well on mine.

Sincerely.

Megan Capron

Corinne read through the letter a few times before she went to find Lucas, hoping he was still lingering over his breakfast, or talking with Violet.

Lucas was washing up when Corinne found him with the letter. Lucas wiped his face and hands with a towel and read through it quickly.

"Do you know of the ferry scheduled to leave." Corinne asked.

He shook his head. "I have not paid as much attention lately." Lucas offered with a shrug.

Corinne skipped eating but gave Violet a brief description of the letter before she rushed to her room to dress. Perhaps the ferry hadn't left and she and Lucas could stop her.

Corinne was dressed and ready, standing next to Lucas a few minutes later, trying to figure out if they should go to town first or straight to the ferry port.

A pounding at the door interrupted their discussion and without a moments pause it opened wide and crashed against the cabin wall.

Timothious Smithers stood at the door, his dark eyes searching. He glanced through the room and saw his daughter at the kitchen counter. Violet's jaw was dropped and Corinne could only stare as he took a step into the house.

He yelled out a curse but it ended in an 'oof' because Lucas reacted quickly and shoved him out of the door. The angry man landed with a thud on the ground in front of the door.

Lucas stepped out and stood in the doorframe, his body rigid. Corinne watched in horror as Timothious stood and came toward the door with force.

"You will let me talk to her!" Timothious yelled.

"I most certainly will not!" Lucas yelled hoarsely. They shoved at each other for a long minute. Lucas was younger and stronger but Timothious was angry. Corinne ran to the side of the room and grabbed for the rifle, but had no idea where Lucas kept the bullets. She searched around frantically and said. "Dear God, help me!"

Violet grabbed a frying pan and stood behind Lucas in a warrior pose, her face pale and angry.

"You lied to the town council about me. A friend came and told me. I am a town-founder. I have friends in this town." Timothious cursed again, he was spitting and grunting while Lucas kept his arms in an iron grip. Timothious kicked at Lucas and they both went down to the ground.

Corinne screamed and ran out of the house to call for help. She held up the rifle but with the men rolling around in the grass she couldn't swing it without potentially hitting her husband.

Clive Quackenbush

Clive was riding fast toward Grant's grove. His head still shaking over the news from the local banker who had come to him a short while after the store opened its doors. He hadn't planned on working much, but was going to come and help Ted get started on the cabin they were building for the Sparks. He was looking forward to visiting a little with Olive too. Just a few minutes of her smiles and witty conversation could keep him going all day. He felt younger in his heart knowing she was going to be his bride.

The banker had given him a note and left swiftly.

A Miss Megan Capron attempted to withdraw a large sum of cash from Mr. Lucas Grant's account when we opened at seven. We did not allow her the money but I thought that they should be informed.

B. Rollins - Bank Manager

Clive was nearing the bridge when he heard yelling. He clucked and kicked his horse's flanks and his horse lurched into a faster sprint. Clive could see that two men were scuffling in the front of Corinne's cabin and he sped towards it.

After a long few seconds Clive got down from his horse in a rush, he tied his horse to a nearby tree, his hands fumbling nervously to get it secured.

He ran up and tried to grab for the shirt collar of Timothious. The shoving and cursing by the man was not making the job easier. Corinne stood nearby holding a gun, Violet was brandishing a frying pan, both ready to take him on.

Clive yelled out, "Stop this madness Tim!"

Lucas grabbed hold of Timothious's wrist and twisted his arm back painfully. Timothious grunted and held his other hand up in surrender.

Lucas held him down for a few seconds, uncertain if the man truly intended to cease his struggle. Lucas was covered in dirt. Timothious looked the same. He had a few scratches on his face and arms, blood trickled down his face and was creating a dark crimson mud on his cheek.

"Get off me!" Timothious bucked. Clive put his boot down on the arm Lucas was holding. It freed Lucas to stand up.

"You stop acting like an angry buffoon, and I'll let ya up." Clive said, his heart raced a bit just from watching the little he had seen. From the state of the two men the scuffle had been surely exhausting.

Timothious nodded, his face against the ground, his chin pushing the dirt around with his actions.

Clive pondered for a moment and let his foot loosen on the man's arm, the boot-heel left an impression behind.

Timothious stood slowly, probably to ascertain if his body was damaged. His face was still angry but the color under the muck was not the purple of rage.

"You had no right!" He said as he whacked his hands on his dirty pants, sticks, leaves and dirt fluttered to the ground.

"No right to what?" Lucas said, taking charge.

"I am speaking to Violet!" Timothious hissed through his teeth. He rubbed the spot on his forehead that was still bleeding. He hissed again and pulled his hand away.

"I had every right. I followed the good book. Confront, bring a witness, go to the community." Violet said slowly, her tone implied that perhaps her father was a bit feeble.

The affect of her speech did nothing to sooth his temper.

John Harpole and Reynaldo were running behind them.

"I see you are more than a little outnumbered Mr. Smithers. I think you should make yerself scarce." Clive said, the smothered grin didn't hide his mirth.

"You have disappointed your mother." Timothious said venomously.

Violet raised her eyebrows but her lips were pressed together until she spoke. "Well, I guess we all will get used to life's little disappointments." She put her free hand on her hip. She was not going to back down. Clive felt a swell of pride. She had been looking rather frail the last few days, now she seemed ready to face this monster head on.

"You are going to pay for what you did!" Timothious spat on the ground in her direction.

Lucas took a step forward, now holding the shotgun as Corinne had, ready to swing at the man.

John Harpole and Reynaldo joined the circle around the man, hedging him in.

"Time for you to go or we will have to make you go." Clive said seriously, he was afraid that another fight would break out.

"I think you better mind your own..." Timothious turned and took a step toward Clive and Violet. Clive jumped in front of the girl. Lucas stepped forward to swing the rifle at the man. Timothious, with faster speed than anyone expected swung his right fist and connected to the side of Clive's head just as the butt of the rifle clipped Timothious in the shoulder.

Clive slumped to the ground and the world went black.

Chapter 34

Galina Varushkin

Galina arrived at Grant's Grove to see Clive fall to the ground and another man scream as a rifle hit him along the side of the head.

Galina ran and yelled out as she approached the scene. Lucas was covered in dirt, Violet and Corinne both huddled over Clive, while John Harpole and Reynaldo dragged the other man, who was hollering every word that her brothers got in trouble for saying, even if her dad said them all the time.

"He is breathing!" Corinne announced and checked the side of Clive's head.

Galina did not like to see Clive thus, sprawled out, his face slack. She took deep breaths, as if taking them for Clive, willing him to open his eyes.

Violet ran into the house, still gripping the frying pan she held.

Galina turned to watch John Harpole and Reynaldo, who were threatening to hogtie the man.

Corinne gasped a second later, Galina whipped her head around to see Clive blink his eyes a few times.

Clive opened his eyes fully. He grimaced a little and looked at Galina and then Corinne.

"Well, iffen that wasn't the poorest showin' I ever had in a fight. Didn't even get my licks in first." Clive smiled weakly and attempted to sit up.

"None of that now!" Corinne scolded and pushed on his chest.

Clive huffed and wiggled his jaw a little, wincing at some pain.

"Hope I didna lose any teeth!" He said as Corinne probed the side of his face. "I always did have a pretty smile." He winced again as Corinne pressed on the swollen cheek.

"I think you may have been in danger if he had hit you an inch higher." Corinne said and frowned. "You can try to sit up." Corinne sat back and let the man have some space.

Galina grabbed Clive's hand as he slowly pulled himself up.

"Thank you, Galya." He said, using her nickname sweetly. "No dizziness yet. I may live." He muttered and touched the side of his cheek that was swelling.

Corinne and Galina chuckled at his ever-present humor.

Violet came back with a chunk of red meat.

"Well it's a good thing we have fresh meet from the butcher." Violet announced and skipped ahead when she saw that he was awake.

"I have always loved a good steak." Clive tried to smile broadly but winced at the action.

"You may look a fright by tonight." Violet handed over the meat and Clive unceremoniously slapped it against his cheek.

"It's a little rarer than I like it." Clive went to stand, and Galina put all her weight into helping him get to his feet.

Corinne and Violet took charge and Galina stood in the front of the house for a long moment. Watching John, Lucas, and Reynaldo drag the other man off to the side of the house.

"If your horse isn't over there you can walk home, you fool." John Harpole said as they pulled the man along.

The man went along with them, but he seemed angry. "It's just beyond the footbridge." He grumbled.

Galina could have no idea what was happening and she went into the cabin to see what she could do. She had come today to do laundry; she had not expected a spectacle.

Soon after she went inside she wordlessly watched Corinne get Clive settled in, still holding the red meat against his cheek.

"Galina, could you run over to Angela's house and let Angela and Olivia know that Clive is okay but injured?" Corinne smiled and asked.

"I'll be fine!" Clive bellowed from his spot on the settee. "Just what I need is more women fussing over me." Clive chuckled and winced.

Galina nodded and took off on her errand.

Olivia Greaves

Olivia ran from the breakfast table when she heard the young lady's news. She had just been thinking about Clive, he had promised to show her a surprise today. She was wondering while she nibbled on her eggs what he could be up to.

The news shattered all her happy thoughts and she was just glad she had dressed before breakfast. Her hair was not done but she really wasn't concerned that her strawberry blond curls hung down her back like a young girl's.

She reached the Grant's cabin and heard Clive teasing someone and felt better. If he could tease he would be fine, she mused.

"You better be well." Olivia said with a bit of force.

"Oh, Olive, I will be fine. Just may turn a few colors before the day is done." Clive said. He waved his free hand for her to join him on the settee.

Violet went to grab Olivia's arm. "He defended me from my father, who showed up to make us all pay." Violet sighed.

"I didn't see him swing until I couldn't get out of his way." Clive said as Olivia sat next to him.

"No more fighting!" Olivia declared and Clive nodded.

"I will try." Clive said.

"I love you." Olivia whispered when she leaned against his shoulder.

"I love you right back." Clive said.

Both Corinne and Violet said "Awe..." in unison.

Everyone laughed.

A few minutes later the house was full. All the men had seen Mr. Smithers off the land, and Angela, Dolly, and Galina had arrived too.

Clive pulled out the note from his pocket and explained about how Megan had tried to take a large sum of money from the Grant's bank account.

"If they were going on the steamship that was leaving this morning, it should be long gone by now. It was leaving by 7:45." Clive said. "It was the Marie Star, I believe. You should get to the post office and send a telegram to Megan's father. He might be able to intercept the Marie Star in California before we could ever hope to catch it."

"I had two horses missing this morning, what you wanna bet they are tied up near the steamship dock outside of town." John Harpole said. He was grimacing. "What a mess, Megan was under our care and we have let this happen."

"I was the one who should have been more watchful." Corinne said. Her cheeks were pink and she looked on the verge of crying.

"That girl has been a handful for all of us. She is beyond willful and headstrong. How were any of us going to thwart her plans unless we tied her up in the barn?" John offered, grinning a little.

Clive laughed, the others just smiled.

"She would make a pretty little prisoner in her fancy dress gowns." He chuckled again.

Corinne couldn't help herself and laughed along.

Reynaldo spoke up. "Stewart Ferrill has been paying her a lot of attention."

Corinne took a minute to read everyone the letter Megan had left.

"Well, there ya go." Reynaldo said something in Spanish. "Ten compasión."

"Should I ask what that means?" Corinne asked.

"Oh... have mercy." Reynaldo said and blushed. "That girl is like a train headed for a crash. I will pray she does not succeed much further."

The group dispersed shortly, both John and Reynaldo promised to help in any way they could. Lucas was determined to get out of his dirty clothes, Corinne was beginning to fuss over checking him for injuries.

Olivia and Angela wanted to take Clive back to Angela's house where they could fuss over him for the day.

Corinne declared the laundry a silly plan and instead she would use the water that was heated to get her husband cleaned up.

Violet invited Galina for a long walk to clear their heads.

Galina Varushkin

Galina had been horrified and shocked to hear Violet's story, knowing how much she worked to forgive her own father for so many injustices. The anger and violence had made the last few years unbearable for her at times. When he had left them penniless to go gold-hunting a few years ago they had ended up in a threadbare tent near the shacks outside of town. No food, down to their last match to make a fire, filthy and the snow had been soon to fly when the local church had gotten them this warm cabin, and a job for Galina. She was still working on forgiving him fully for that. Since he came back the beatings have been worse. Now with her mother and brother gone she felt this small reprieve, her father sad but not angry.

She had listened to Violet and wondered at it, how Violet could have survived such abuse and have turned into the sweet and loving woman that she was. Violet exuded joy, even after husband died she had a peace about her most days. Galina was struck by that small voice inside her that whispered the ways that she could have that peace too.

Galina finally got brave enough to ask Violet a question after they stopped under a swaying willow tree along the edge of the creek, the shade was nice and they sat on the large rock at the edge of the water.

"How do you forgive him?" Galina asked.

"I spent many years forgiving him everyday, over and over. I pushed the memories away after a while. I suppose it sounds too simple but it took so many days. It was the hardest thing I have ever done." Violet said as she untied her shoes. She smiled and tossed her shoes behind the rock and plopped her feet into the cool water and sighed dramatically.

Galina followed Violet's actions by removing her own shoes. The water was cool and decadent as it trickled by.

Violet pulled the pins from her hair and let her blond wavy locks tumble down her back. She placed a hand on Galina's shoulders. "I can see how you struggle with your father. I know the feeling of being powerless under the broad shoulders and intense anger." Violet said. "I wish I could ease that for you, but the violence and most intense pain can be overcome. Trusting in Jesus and leaning on God is how I learned to day by day renew myself. Trusting that God is my father, a better father. It took a long while to remember that."

Galina nodded and knew she had a long way to go, but felt more peaceful but yet heartbroken that Violet had had to suffer through such horrible things.

"Thank you Violet." Galina said. She wiped away a few misty tears.

"Thank you for asking. I needed a chance to remember how I got through those years. Confronting him and reliving that pain has stirred it all up within me. I needed to say those words aloud to remind myself what Jesus did for me." Violet smiled and switched her feet around. She stood and pulled up her skirts to her knees and with a smirk she slid off the rock and stood in the creek.

"Perhaps a little riverside baptism is in order." She laughed and surprised Galina down to her toes by plopping down on her behind into the water and leaning back to dunk her self back to get fully wet. She came out and yelled. "Thank you Jesus!"

Violet splashed in the water like a child for a minute.

Galina saw the stress that had formed across Violet's brow was gone. She looked renewed. Galina felt that pressure on her heart, the heaviness that had been there for so long had just lingered and suddenly she was overwhelmed.

Galina wept on the rock. Violet let her have her time to feel what she felt, knowing that was the only way through the pain. You have to feel it and then you can let it go, easier every time.

Galina wiped her tears and jumped into the water as Violet had done.

"I was baptized when I was a baby. But I would like to do it again. As my choice... Will you help me through it Violet?" Galina asked. She felt so raw and ready. She wanted that joy that Violet had.

"I would be so very happy to..." Violet said and smiled broadly.

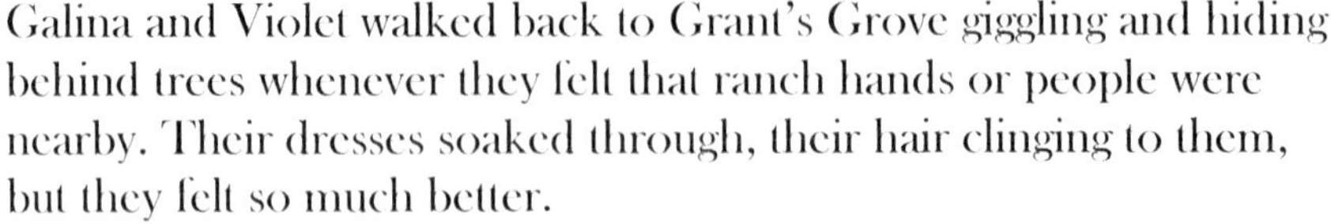

Galina and Violet walked back to Grant's Grove giggling and hiding behind trees whenever they felt that ranch hands or people were nearby. Their dresses soaked through, their hair clinging to them, but they felt so much better.

"Well, we may have gotten a little undignified today but I just bet that God loves it when his people put aside the formality sometimes and just do what it takes to be in his presence. That is what we did today Galya!" Violet said. "I feel so light and free, again."

Galina smiled and agreed. "I wish I could feel this way every day." Galina smiled so much her cheeks hurt a bit. She felt as if a heavy weight had been lifted from her.

"Sometimes it isn't in the grand gestures but in the quiet moments. I love to pray while I'm cooking or pounding out my bread dough. I have always had this joke between me and God, that my bread is so good because I pray while I make it." Violet said as they walked.

"You have jokes with God?" Galina gave her a sideways glance, doubting that was possible.

"Well, God made us, and we like to laugh!" Violet explained simply.

Galina giggled and shrugged. "I guess so."

They made it back to the house and managed to sneak in without anyone seeing them. They changed into fresh clothes, Violet shared a cotton skirt and blouse with Galina.

They ended up working together on laundry after all, only getting a small portion done, but after Corinne came by she promised Galina full pay and asked her to come back in a few days to help Violet finish.

"With all the drama going on an extra hand made the work a little easier to manage." Corinne had said.

Corrine shared that her and Lucas had gone to town and sent Mr. Capron a message about his daughter's escape, and details on how to find her, and the man she traveled with.

"It was the longest telegram that I have ever sent." Corinne laughed.

"That girl is more trouble..." Violet sighed and didn't finish the thought. She had never gotten on with the girl. Being stuck with her for days on end had been unpleasant. Violet had worked hard on ignoring Megan's many character flaws.

Galina and Violet worked through the next hour. Hanging the laundry, their long hair down and drying in the breeze.

Galina went back home with a lighter heart and wages in her skirt pocket. She felt so blessed.

Chapter 35

The Watermill

Dusk was soon to come over the land, the sun was trailing and the hills and rocks to the west of the Willamette River were welcoming the evening with yellow streaks through the wispy clouds above.

The water of the river flowed by with its usual vigor, some waterfowl floated by, happy to have the summer insects to feed on as they landed near the birds.

The watermill was quiet, the day's work done. It had taken Timothious longer than usual without his sons helping.

The husband and wife that were alone in their cabin were not getting along well. The last week had wreaked its havoc on both of their nerves. All their children had abandoned them, and the bitter pall of the empty cabin was felt by the parents.

Meredith and Timothious Smithers were certain that any day he would be arrested. They were no longer in the good graces of any of their long-time friends. It was only a matter of time now.

The Smithers had been in another argument, it seemed they were endless now. Meredith was beginning to wonder about her daughter's accusations and she questioned Timothious everyday since her boys left. Rumors had made it to their door, from an old friend the day before.

"The youngest boy has made a witness statement. I just came to let you know. Don't expect me to darken this doorstep again." The friend had said.

Timothious had come back that morning with cuts and bruises and his knuckles bruised. He was angry and had confessed his actions after Meredith pressed him. Her doubts were rising to the surface, wondering at how her youngest boy, so very soft-spoken and quiet could have done such a thing as say he saw something if he had not. All her children gone had made her think more than she had ever had need too. She was a simple woman, she couldn't reason on one hand how her husband could have done such a thing. He was a hard working man, who declared that he feared and loved the Lord. But on the other hand her children were never one to telltales, not being the tattling kind. What on earth could posses them to say these things unless there was an ounce of truth to them?

Her husband was a mystery now to her, so very angry and bursting with rage over the smallest provocation. He had never been that way with her before. He was a harder man on the children always, declaring it was his job to punish and admonish them. But she was trying to find the truth behind his angry eyes now. Had she been mistaken for all of these years?

Her confusion had no end as her husband continued his denials, calling all their children liars and ingrates. Meredith was at a loss.

A few night birds began to call as Meredith cleaned up the supper table, the stew in her bowl barely touched. She sighed over the two settings at the table, feeling the empty house like an echoing shell around her. It took her back to those first days after Violet had left and she had cried so many tears for the loss of her sweet girl. It had been sadness at first but the anger had stayed permanently after the sadness left. Now she felt the sadness again. Wondering now if she had been wrong.

Timothious was outside, chopping wood to keep himself busy and out of sight of his nagging wife.

She heard the grunts and chops, the high-pitched scrape of the wood splitting, the rhythm was comforting in its own way. She tried to focus on the sound and not think anymore. The thoughts tormented her and she wanted to escape them.

The chopping abruptly stopped and she heard voices far off. Her heart thudded and she lifted a hand to her cheek, wondering if now the time had come.

The grind of wagon wheels on the rough road that led to their door could be heard through the open windows.

Meredith ran to the door. She saw nearly twenty men, all ages, were marching toward her husband.

"You sir are an abomination to the Lord!" A tall, broad shouldered man marched in front. Several men held rifles, a few just carried torches, in preparation of the light that was failing quickly.

"Get off my land!" Timothious yelled but the men ignored him. The largest man snatched the axe from Timothious' hands. The others nearby piled onto him. He was helpless against so many. A man then came with thin ropes and bound Timothious' hands in front of him, then his ankles.

Timothious yelled out and struggled against the ropes. They shoved a cloth into his mouth and tied a kerchief around his head to keep it in placed.

Meredith watched in horror as they carried her husband away. She had no concept of what to do. She couldn't send for help, her boys were gone.

"Where are you taking him?" She yelled out to any man that was listening.

"Woman, you stay out of this. You are lucky we don't tie you up along with him. You have betrayed your children!" The tall thin man proclaimed over her.

Meredith took a staggering step back into the safety of the doorway, dread and fear filled her. The world had gone mad. Her heart dropped when she saw them tie her husband to the back of the wagon. They were going to drag him behind it!

Clive Quackenbush

Clive was settled into Angela's plush couch, a few lanterns lit nearby, Olivia sat in a rocker across from him, looking lovely. Earl had just left after dropping off a half bottle of whiskey and visited for a bit. They had shared a few glasses and Clive felt a bit warm and loose from the spirits.

"I did intend on taking you to town milady." Clive said.

"I am a patient woman." Olivia declared and winked at him.

Ted, Angela and Dolly sat on the front porch, chatting after supper. Clive was thinking about leaving but he felt no rush. He was enjoying his time. Even with the throbbing that was thudding in his cheekbone.

The windows were open and the evening breeze was sweet, the smell of grass and summer flowers floated through. Corinne had planted a few lilacs along the road and their blooms this year were magnificent and perfumed the air, even up the hill to Angela's house.

The sound of a horse crossing the bridge interrupted the quiet. Olivia had replaced his empty glass of whiskey with some sun tea that Angela had made. It was sweet and refreshing.

"Is Clive here?" Clive heard the sound of his son's voice.

Clive stood up slowly, checking himself that he didn't do it too swiftly. The thudding in the side of his face intensified a little but it was bearable.

Angela let JQ in the house and Clive walked over to him slowly.

"I heard about the ruckus this morning. Everyone in town is talking. Things escalated." JQ said a hello to Olivia quickly and nodded in politeness.

Clive sighed.

"You look a fright, Clive." JQ took a step to get a closer look at the mean and swollen bruise on Clive's face.

Clive ignored the comment. "What happened in town?"

"Well, Timothious Smithers is in the town jail. He was going to be arrested tomorrow anyhow... but a mob of men went to get some justice on their own. Everyone heard about what happened at Grant's Grove today. People were getting all worked up. Trying to strike out at Violet and then clocking you in the face has done nothing but fan the flames." JQ grimaced and looked at his father's face again. "The mob went and grabbed Timothious at his home, trussed him up and dragged him for a bit before the sheriff got wind of it. They were forced to put him in the wagon and take him to the jail under the watch of the sheriff."

Clive grunted. "Is he conscious?"

"Yep, but scratched up to shreds." JQ grimaced again. "I think everyone in town was standing on the main street watching the parade going by. It was a spectacle all right, men with torches, a trussed up man, and people crying out for justice."

Clive's face was impassive but he was struggling with his own thoughts. The part of him that was disgusted by Timothious' actions was warring with the reasonable man that knew that the law could handle this.

"The sheriff promised that the man was going to stay behind bars until his trial was announced. That was the only thing that settled the crowd. People were yelling out to tar and feather the man, and hang him." JQ shuddered. The scene was obviously still fresh in his mind.

"What a mess?" Clive muttered, the throbbing in his face was uncomfortable and now his stomach churned from stress as he considered how this whole situation would turn out.

"It is that..." JQ agreed. "Want me to stop by the Grant's? Let 'em know?"

"Yea. I should be headed home." Clive said.

"No, sir. You are sleeping in Dolly's room. We all agreed." Olivia piped in. "She will head over to stay with Chelsea, she will be leaving soon."

Clive shrugged toward his son.

"I guess you are well taken care of then." JQ smiled.

"Yayup." Clive said.

Oregon City

The town council and the sheriff worked feverishly to work on a timetable for dealing with Mr. Smithers and the charges that were coming together against him.

A town meeting was called for three days later to hear the testimony and allow for any witnesses; character references and discussion of the crimes could be decided together as a town.

John Pritchlan, the state governor made a special trip from Portland and arrived at the town council meeting to be a part of this momentous decision.

The local paper ran a special edition to announce to the community all that would be taking place.

In the Oregon Gazette:

June 20th 1851- Special Edition

On June 19th the meeting of city council members, joined by the good Sherriff Worth, John Pritchlan, Governor and several town founders was held to decide the best course of action for the arrest and trial for Timothious Smithers on the charges of indecent behavior, perversion and assault on the person of Violet Smithers Griffen. Due to the graphic nature of the crimes the paper refuses to comment on the severity of these charges.

A witness, young Harold Smithers, has come forth with damning testimony corroborating the brave young woman's claim.

The story has come forward because of the local women's attempt to allow the orphan children to receive good homes after talk of a work orphanage. The unfolding events and attempted adoption of a young girl had forced Violet Griffen to come forward with the gruesome and disturbing tale of her childhood horror.

After reviewing all the evidence and witness statements, from Harold Smithers, Violet Smithers Griffen, Pastor Whittlan and wife, and Tim Smithers Jr, the town will be allowed a chance to hear the statements and without the formality of the federal or state courts to decide the verdict of Timothious Smithers.

With the town meeting acting as a jury of his peers the fate of the man, Timothious Smithers, is at the mercy of the town of Oregon City.

Many citizens are shocked and horrified over the charges, and with witness statements to corroborate, makes this case a terrible and tragic case for this small wholesome town.

We all will be praying for the young people involved in this tragic case. There is no justice sweet enough when a child is treated thus. May God have mercy on Timothious' soul.

- Writer and editor of The Oregon Gazette, Gomer Hynes

Violet Griffen

Violet settled herself in the back of the meeting, held in the Methodist Church in town. The stained glass windows shown the bright sunlight through the colored glass with a dazzling brilliance that Violet stared at absently. Corrine and Lucas sat at her side with her brothers on the other side of her. This week had brought about many opportunities for them all to spend time together and they had a reluctant eagerness to have it over. Each wanting to avoid it but also wanting the talk to die down and be done with.

Her morning walk with Galina a few days before had been the best thing for her. Talking through her healing was a deep reminder how God had gotten her through this before. She knew, with time, that she could get through this again. The talk in town was something she had been afraid of since she was young, never enjoying the spotlight. But she knew that she had done the right thing.

Seeing Lila running and playing at the nearby Harpole Ranch made her more certain that it was the right course of action. But living through it would test her in ways she had never imagined.

The meeting came to order, with Jed Prince bringing out the accused. Violet watched her father strode angrily to the stage at the front, standing near the solid oak pulpit, his body a battered mass of scabs and scratches from his ordeal with the mob. Violet had dreamt of the mob coming for her after she had heard of it, she had woken in a feverish state of fear. It had taken all the morning, a few days before, to shake off the feeling.

She had done her part, never having asked for justice, but only to stave off any more suffering by another girl. To know that her father may be punished, and harshly, was something that she couldn't comprehend yet. She wasn't certain that she wanted justice more than she would have appreciated an apology. That seemed silly in her own mind. That stubborn excuse for man ever stooping to an apology would seem as ridiculous as taming a bear for a house-pet. The town was perhaps more furious than she was, she wondered how that was but it was true.

Jed Prince and the Sheriff introduced the accused and then read through the statements. The crowd was vocal and gasped and yelled out frequently, insulting and condemning the man still bound by the wrist.

Violet squirmed through the reading of the witness statements, knowing that her shame and mortification was being trampled as the majority of the town heard the horrific details of the worst possible atrocities. A local man stood and walked up to the edge of the stage and spit on her father and had to be forced back to his seat.

Violet felt a hot rush go through her, reliving the shame again and again.

Corinne kept squeezing her hand on one side, and her brother, Tim, did the same on the other. She looked to Harold as his testimony was read and saw the hot flush of emotion on his cheeks as well. Anger, or shame, certainly. Violet wished with every part of her she could escape this.

The testimony of the Whitman's came next as they recounted her story as it had been told to them years ago, having never changed over the years, with any added embellishments.

The sheriff spoke and explained the charges they were bringing against the man and how they were using the town meeting in lieu of a jury.

The sheriff then asked for Clive to speak before the town would vote.

Clive Quackenbush

Clive wore a dark grey suit, his salt and pepper hair trimmed and his beard shaven down to a neat little mustache and long sideburns that nearly went down to his chin.

He took the stage and began, his face grave and serious.

"I greet you all with a heavy heart. Knowing we step into this trial, not as an official state, doing what we can in this troubled time to do our best to provide a fair trial without the backing of the U.S. Government and the elaborate court system. I come forward to remind us all of our sacred duty. To consider the evidence and witnesses and decide with justice and under God's watchful eye and to decide this man's fate."

Clive wrung his large hands nervously then continued.

"It may be easier to cast the responsibility solely on his shoulders and want to exact a harsh punishment because he is an unrepentant man. Even with a witness and a hurting daughter he is unwilling to admit his guilt."

"We all have the ability to do evil. And sometimes we do in small ways, then over time we may realize our mistakes and make a recompense. To apologize or confess is the way the Lord gave us to get those sins out of the dark hiding places in our souls. His forgiveness is always available, but without confession of guilt we fool ourselves."

"We live in a world of rules and laws. He has broken those, according to the witnesses, and though he may be forgiven by the Lord, that is between him and God. He also sinned here on earth. His sins are heinous and a despicable act that violates the trust that God gives us as a parent."

"If we are commanded to respect and honor our elders, and obey our parents, then what should become of the one who betrays that trust in such a way?"

"I have never been a fan of mob law, it is a violent and destructive force that usually begins and ends without justice but is a knee-jerk reaction of vigilantism that is based on bias or hate. In this case it cannot be stressed enough that we move forward as a community. Using the wisdom from our founding fathers to guide us. We do not have a circuit court, but we do have the gathering of this man's peers. Let us go forward in prayer and wisdom. If the man be found guilty he should be able to have his say, we should consider this man's crimes as not only a crime against one person, but also a crime against the decency we all strive towards... To forever snuff out this kind of sin and lawlessness as an example to others. No harm should ever be done to any child in this manner. As we vote let us remember why we came here. To create a safe home for our families, to foster a community we could be proud of. To allow this kind of crime in our midst would be a double tragedy."

The crowd clapped and cheered for Clive's speech but he didn't stand in front of the crowd but instead quietly sat in the front row, his face a show of shadows and sadness.

Reverend Whittlan stood and took the front.

"Let us pray together before we start." He sighed and began. "Lord we come before you, as a community in pain. The ripples of this devastation has been felt through all of our hearts. We go forward with heavy hearts and minds full of confusion. I believe that our children are one of the greatest gifts you have given us. We cannot protect them if we do not have a boldness. In your word it says that love is patient and kind. No actions this man has been accused of were either of these things. How Lord do we move forward in judgment? Give us wisdom and guidance. Let us all know with certainty that we are standing firm in our righteous anger, not with bias or hate, Lord, but in our desire to do what is right. In Jesus name we pray." The reverend kept his head bowed as the people gathered said 'Amen.'

Soon after Timothious Smithers was brought forward again, rubbing his hands and looking angry and battered.

The sheriff came to the front and introduced him, and announced his crimes.

"Timothious Smithers is being charged with assault on his daughter Violet Smithers Griffen, in a sinful and corrupt nature. He is charged with sexual perversion, assault and rape. How sir do you plead?"

Timothious Smithers' face was hard and he gritted his teeth. "Not guilty!" He stated emphatically.

"There has been witnesses come forth and have seen you perform these foul acts."

Timothious grumbled then spoke. "It is all lies!" His neck bulged in his intensity.

"Due to the lack of an official state appointed judge or jury I put it to the community gathered today to act as your jury of peers. All the evidence has been spoken of. Today I ask this comment of Oregon City. All those who believe that Timothious Smithers is guilty of his crimes say Aye and raise your hands."

The crowd loudly proclaimed 'Aye' and many hands shot up, filling the room. The sheriff counted the hands for a long few moments; he scribbled the numbers on the notebook in front of him. Tim and Harold Smithers had both raised their hands and shouted 'Aye'.

"All those that believe that this man is innocent of his crimes say nay and raise your hands."

A few weak voices spoke out and three hands shot forward. One being his wife and a few that were still uncertain.

"By the gathering of your peers and me, the sheriff of Oregon City, I pronounce you as guilty of your crimes. Your sentence shall be decided within forty-eight hours, and shall be carried out within three days."

Chapter 36

Violet Griffin

"I will not be attending the sentencing." Violet announced later at dinner.

Corinne and Lucas nodded, letting Violet have the floor.

"I had enough with the meeting. I am not certain how to feel and I am not certain I could watch without having an outburst." Violet sighed and took a bite of her food reluctantly.

"Would you like me to stay with you?" Corinne offered. "I am not certain I want to be there either." She gave Violet a lopsided grin in support.

Violet grinned back, "That would be nice."

"We could go for a walk." Corinne offered. "I'll bore you with details about every plant I see."

Violet snickered and agreed. "I will try not to be bored. I promise."

Oregon City

The town rippled with talk and rumors as the Sherriff and town council decided on the sentencing. Hearing from many members of the community throughout the day who wanted to have a say in the sentencing.

It was decided on the afternoon of the 24th and announced that evening at the Methodist Church with over a hundred town members in attendance. Timothious Smithers stood bound before the meeting angry and seething.

The sheriff announced his sentence.

"Timothious Smithers is found guilty of his heinous crimes and will be executed on June 26th. In the front of the jailhouse, a gallows will be built, and he will be hung by the neck until his death. May God have mercy on his soul."

The meeting erupted in cheers that overwhelmed the wailing of one woman in the front row.

The announcement that followed shook the shimmering woman to her core.

"The watermill, being built by the town founders is owned by the town. The death sentence cancels the ownership of Timothious Smither's property to his eldest son Tim Smithers Jr. At this juncture the resident, Mrs. Meredith Smithers is at the mercy of Tim Smithers Jr., to be decided on at his whim whether she be removed from the property. Tim and Harold Smithers promise to keep our grist mill running from this day forward to provide that much needed service to our community."

A cheer went through the crowd again.

The next day was a Saturday and almost every family on Spring Creek Road past the bridge and congregated at Angela Fahey's house to help begin the cabin for the Sparks family.

Everyone needed a distraction so the proper gear was gathered, men, horses, winches and many tools were needed. The men were all gathered at the building spot that was cleared and leveled with the floor and foundation already built. The stone fireplace location was set and outlined and would be laid out by brick masons in the coming weeks. The heavy work of settling the floor and the sidewalls of the outer shell of the cabin was measured out and the heavy labor began early.

The women gathered in the kitchen and the visiting and cooking would take all day to feed such a crew. Young children were watched over in the parlor and the dining table was covered with all the good food that was already made, or would need to be heated throughout the day.

It was a gathering for certain and everyone tried to keep Violet entertained and distracted from too much thinking. Her brothers were happily helping with the men to keep their minds from thinking too much of the coming execution.

Angela was fussed over as talk of her wedding was a pleasant diversion from the heaviness of all the recent dramatic events. The ladies, after the lunch was ready were introduced to the two newest members of her farm, Cookie and Hattie, the two goats were in their new pen. Cookie got his name on the first day when he stole a fresh baked cookie out of Ted's hands when he leaned against the fence and the sneaky fellow snatched the treat from Ted's hands.

Angela had teased Ted for carrying a cookie near the goat pen. It made a good enough name so it stuck. Hattie was a spotted brown goat with a circle of white around her head and ears, almost like she had tied on a little hat.

It was a simple thing, goats, and not as much excitement as she fussed over them, but it was proof of their 'settling in'. Ted was going to be her husband and this was their farm. A very pleasing thought to ponder.

Marie went into great detail on how Angela's wedding dress was going to be, a pale cream dress with big skirts and lots of lace provided by the Greaves family.

The ladies sat on the hill for a while, watching the men go about their work. Allowing the young ones to run on the grassy hill, it was a good distance away from the construction but they could see the progress in between their cooking. John Harpole brought a few tables and benches, by in the wee hours of the morning, usually reserved for the harvest season, and at the bottom of the hill they were going to be laden with a feast for all at the lunch hour.

By noon the walls of the cabin were higher than two feet on all sides and the men were ready for the vittles. Clive was the first in line, his cheek an angry mix of purple and blues in the healing from Mr. Smither's flying fist. His smile was wide as he settled on the bench next to Olivia who was waiting until after the men ate to get her own plate.

"You are pretty as a picture milady." Clive said softly.

"Even with your painted cheek you are a handsome fellow." Olivia countered and kissed him on the cheek. By then the town was well aware of the relationship of the two and many were guessing that another wedding would be ringing the church bells soon. "I do like the new shave!" She said enthusiastically and rubbed his smooth cheek.

Clive winked at her before biting into his fried chicken.

Across the yard Ted and Angela locked eyes as they enjoyed each other's company. Married couples watched the gazes and smiles between them and they were reminded of their own days of being young and in love.

The work resumed after the men ate and by the end of the afternoon the walls were nearly high enough for a roof.

An evening meal was set out and the visiting commenced at the tables as the tired men refueled. Chelsea rode back home with her wagon a bit early, with a fussy toddler who was in need of a nap. And Marie came and went as her youngest needed rest away from the ruckus of the pounding and building noises.

The sun was far in the western sky when the tallest pole in the middle of the structure was being used to pull up the support beams for the roof. While strong men and horses used the clever pulleys to pull up the beams, other men nailed in the windows. A good-sized paned window would be facing to the south, and all the ladies were pleased with the window that would shine light over the kitchen. Every bedroom and even the loft would have good light. It was going to be a grand cabin.

Angela remembered the way that Edith Sparks had loved her summer kitchen with an outdoor overhang roof and a wood stove that she could cook with in the summer months. Angela wanted this place to feel like a home for Mama and Papa Sparks. They may not be her parents by blood but were truly loved like they were family. They were only in their forties and Angela imagined many good years they could spend living out their days in the Oregon Valley. It was a fond thought imagining them there, with their three adopted children underfoot.

By sundown the roof was on and the windows in. The men were exhausted and happy, doing a good deed for a neighbor and a cabin well and started that they could all be proud to brag over as they passed it in their day-to-day lives.

The open space for the large fireplace was covered by a linen tarp with a few nails tacked in to keep the rain and critters out. The rest of the house should be able to be finished by Ted and any other helpers who had free time to pitch in. It was a job well done.

Chapter 37

Violet Griffin

The gallows were built in front of the jailhouse as the announcement had said, the lumber gleaming bright in the morning sun. It was a small platform with the high bar across the top and the hangman's noose dangling ominously from the bar and tied tightly to the side. The floor had a clever little trap door that would drop when the time came, but Violet couldn't see the door from her vantage point.

She wasn't sure why she had come, the pit in her stomach was deep and hot, and had been all morning. She had relived this moment in her dreams and watched her father's execution play out several times in her dream from the night before. She wasn't sure she needed to see it.

The small town had all gathered, being the largest crowd she had ever seen in her life. The crowd was quietly waiting, all her friends and neighbors nearby, being supportive but leaving her to her thoughts and not pestering her with a thousand questions. They knew her well enough by now to know that she would process everything later. For now she wanted to be left alone.

The Sheriff came out with Timothious Smithers and the crowd cheered and called out to him. Too many words yelled out to separate them out as individuals.

Violet noticed that a few of his scratches and scabs were healing from his night with the mob and the wagon. She saw her mother at the front of the crowd, dry-eyed and frowning. She couldn't read her mother's thoughts but wished she could. A part of her wishing somehow that she could know if her mother had ever, in the smallest way, believed her.

Violet saw that her brothers, standing in front of her were rigid, standing both with arms crossed in front of them and a part of her wanted to stay, to watch the justice play out in full.

The sheriff made his announcement, the repeat of the crimes he was charged with and the decision by the town declaring him guilty. Violet watched her father's face, looking for any sign of shame or remorse but saw none.

The sheriff allowed Timothious to have a moment to speak his last words.

Timothious shook his head in denial. He would say nothing to clear his name or any sort of apology to those he had hurt.

Violet took a deep breath and sighed, letting the moment be absorbed to be thought of on another day.

She watched them move her father to the middle of the platform. The executioner, Jed Prince, grabbed the noose and began to slip it over the head of her father.

She saw the slightest flinch crossed her father's face, the anger was slipping away in the realization of the fate that was befalling him. With seeing the fear Violet had seen enough. Remembering her own fear as she cowered before her father so many times. It was enough for her and she turned and quietly slipped away, wordlessly and walked a few blocks away.

She sat on the bench outside the fancy goods store. She stared unseeing the world around her, trying to tune out the crowd behind her.

"You need a ride home?" A voice said to her after a minute of being alone.

She looked up and Reynaldo was looking down at her.

She shook her head in the negative.

"You want me to leave you alone?" He asked simply.

"No..." She said softly.

Reynaldo sat down next to her on the bench. The crowd was loud and the sound could not be ignored. It swelled and then the unmistakable sound of the scraping wood from the trap door was heard. The crowd gasped and cheered.

She looked at Reynaldo for a long moment. Her eyes asked why he was there without saying it aloud.

"I'm not much for hangings..." He offered simply. "A little too close for comfort."

She nodded, not fully understanding.

"I was foolish once in my youth." Reynaldo said and held his neck and shivered.

Violet turned toward him on the bench. "Do tell. I need a distraction."

"I was seventeen, my English was still only fragmented. A local mission outside of what is now San Francisco was near my family's ranch, they were teaching all the local boys English." Reynaldo added. "My brother who was a few years older than I had dared me to go down to the trapper camp outside of town. These French trappers had built a ramshackle saloon. It was not much to look at then, but on Saturdays they played poker." Reynaldo brush a hand through his black hair.

"My brother had taught me the basics of poker but I was woefully out of my depth with these hard men. I stumbled into a few hands of beginner's luck and won a big pile of cash. The men had not taken it so well." Reynaldo smiled weakly.

Violet watched and waited for the rest of the story.

"The men were ready to steal the money I had won, and I reacted with a fist flying or two. I was overpowered, robbed and dragged out behind that shack and one of the men produced a rope." Reynaldo frowned and grabbed hold of his neck again. "If my father had not already left to come and fetch his foolhardy son, I would have probably died. Though the thrashing I got when I got home had me wonder whether I should have stayed with the poker players. I couldn't sit for many days without discomfort." Reynaldo grimaced.

Violet nodded. "That doesn't sound pleasant." Was all she could say.

"I have never been a gambler since. And hangings always remind me of that night." He shook his head, his eyes a little distant.

"Are you still willing to give me a ride home?" Violet asked after reconsidering.

"You bet. Just have to share my horse, if that's okay?" He said.

"Yes, would you tell someone back there that I am going home with you. If you don't mind going near the... scene." Violet shivered, trying not to picture what was happening there.

"I will manage." He placed a comforting hand on her shoulder and walked away.

He was back in short order.

They walked to the livery, there was no attendant but Reynaldo plunked down a few coins on the counter and went to retrieve his horse that was stabled nearby.

He walked the horse outside, a tall brown and white horse.

He got the saddle settled properly and climbed on, he took Violet's hand and with a yank pulled her up behind him.

"Let's go." He clucked and they were away.

Reynaldo kept the pace slow and the summer air was thick with the smells of summer. He urged him to a steady trot and they made it back to Grant's Grove in good time.

He dropped her by the door and stood outside with her for a minute.

"I know it seems like the world may be shattered for a while. But we are all here to pick you back up if you need it." Reynaldo said. He tipped his hat to her and headed toward his small cabin on the other side of the Harpole Ranch.

Violet went into her kitchen and saw that her bread dough she had set out to rise had done well and she had some good prayer time as she pounded out the dough.

Once the dough was ready she placed it in the oven she took a solid moment to look around, her eyes not seeing the kitchen she was in but seeing instead the cabin of her childhood.

Imagining her mother putting bread in the brick oven to bake, her father at their small family table, talking to his young sons. The image was Violet's undoing, realizing that that family was so shattered. The man who had threatened and abused her was even now dangling from a rope in town.

Violet lost her resolve and allowed the tears to come, shaking off the shroud of numbness that she had allowed herself. She let the pain flow through her. Her sobs rang through the empty cabin, her heart broken into pieces.

Chapter 38

Clive & Olive

Clive picked up Olivia Greaves on the 1st of July from Angela's house, her strawberry curls pulled up neatly and wearing a white and green Chintz dress, her skirts were full around her and Clive could have declared she looked no older than twenty-nine in her current state. His chest puffed out at the thought of having the third chance at love. God has truly been good to him.

He held her hand as she climbed up onto the handsome black buggy and they road to town in style. He was proud of his purchase and glad he had invested in the sleek and light buggy to travel around with his lady.

The secret plan he had for the day had been too long a secret and he was eager to let it loose. He was just outside of town when he turned on a barely noticeable road to the south. The buggy climbed up a hill slowly, the incline not great, but the land opened up when they got past a group of tall pines and he turned sharply to the east for a ways.

"Close your eyes, Olive." He bossed her with a smile in his voice. She obeyed and for the last minute she stayed that way.

When he finally stopped the buggy he let her down, guiding with her eyes closed still.

"Open them my love." He said, waiting with excitement coursing through him.

A green house sat before an open field, with the land to the East laid out before them. There was a neat porch around the front and side and two rockers on one side and a porch swing on the other.

Olivia looked to Clive with a question in her eyes. Clive grinned and grabbed her hands.

"Iffen you like it, Olive, I would be glad to live out the rest of my days with you here." He said and kissed the hand he held.

She leaned in for a proper kiss and as she pulled away she smiled with misty tears in her pretty blue eyes. Clive was pleased to see her happy tears, knowing from his years of life experience that happy tears were the best kind.

"Oh, Clive, I do love it. Let me see the rest." Olivia said breathlessly.

Clive was more than happy to oblige.

"I have owned this property for a while, but just this last year the renters vacated and moved on to Portland. God was rustling through my heart that a change was coming. These last months I have been fixing it up for you." Clive said with pride. "I added on to the porch."

"You know my weakness for a good sized porch." She grinned wide, showing her pretty smile and his heart swelled again with love. He was such a lucky man.

He gave her a grand tour of the place, strolling through each room and commenting on the additions he made. The chairs in the parlor were soft and welcoming near the stone fireplace. He pointed out the basket he had beside one chair. "To placed your bobbins and string while you work inside."

He showed her the new cooking stove. "I promise to bring you a cook if you wish so you don't have to stop yer work."

"Perhaps a few nights a week I can cook for ya. I set a pretty good table for a working woman." She boasted.

He showed her all the rooms; a few spare bedrooms were there for any potential visitors. "I figured your niece Sophia will be pestering you often for a visit, and I got me a collection of family around that may come and see us sometimes. I know, the house is bigger than we need but it was such a nice open place. I thought it fit you." Clive finally said to finish. They walked out to the front porch and looked over the land and sat on the rockers.

"I do believe it fits us." She finally said in agreement as she gave the rocker a few test 'rocks'.

Clive beamed and sat with his betrothed. They left soon after, driving the mile toward town and they had dinner with JQ and Millie, his grandson Gabriel and Amber were still visiting and he got to bounce his great grandson Silas on his knees after supper.

It was a grand time.

Chapter 39

Tim Smithers

The cabin at the watermill was full of grief and tense feelings. Harold and Clive had helped him that first day after the hanging. They had gone to the cabin, they carefully knocked down the western facing wall and removed the wall of that side of the house, tearing it down and putting up support beams. They had spent days discussing this over the last weeks, and with Clive's help came up with a plan to change the cabin.

The second day Harold and Tim cleared out every item that had belonged to their father, including the bed and any furniture from that bedroom. They had started at dawn and the pile was ready quickly. They started a bonfire and the brothers held each fiercely as the items burned. A few townspeople had come by when Clive spread the word about the Smithers boys and their plan to cleanse the cabin.

Pastor Whittlan had invited some of the elders, and the pastor from the Methodist Church in town joined in, and while the young men watched the fire burn the town's men came.

Tim wondered how it could have come to pass, that so many would have shown up in support.

Pastor Whittlan prayed with Tim and Harold, and the elders of the churches walked around the property with them, praying over the evil that had been done. Then they prayed that Peace and God's Love would fill that place. Tim had been moved to tears on more than one occasion. His emotions were raw.

After the prayers and the bonfire burned low the men rolled up their sleeves and helped to prepare the cabin for its addition.

It had taken three days but the addition was complete. The house inside looked so very different, as the boys wanted it.

There was now a parlor, a second fireplace and two small bedrooms added.

His mother, who had stayed with an old friend for a few days, was invited back. Tim and Harold had discussed it at length. Tim was concerned about his brother, who was even more withdrawn and quiet than usual, but he knew that his brother had his own thoughts to get through. They would all carry scars from everything that had happened.

Harold had agreed that their mother could come and live there. They weren't certain how it all would work. But making their mother homeless was not something they were able to do.

Meredith Smithers came, with her head bowed and a broken countenance.

There had been no embraces, or well wishes, just Meredith's tears and a nod to her sons when she walked in.

Tim had shown her the room they had built for her, a simple bed and dresser with her things folded neatly on top.

"I have a wardrobe ordered, should be a few days to get it from Portland." Tim offered.

His mother looked pale. "Thank you." She said quietly. It was the first time she had spoken to him in weeks.

He left his mother alone and went to sit in the parlor. The chairs and loveseat were a nice addition and changed the feel of the place. It was less rustic and Tim found it comforting, to see a different place. The air still smelled of fresh lumber. The fireplace was only just finished, and the low-burning fire was lit to help dry the grout between the bricks.

Harold was working in the gristmill, trying to catch up on orders from the last weeks of inactivity. Tim would join him once his mother was settled in.

His heart was so heavy, and the unknown hung in the air. He wondered every other moment whether he had done right in inviting his mother back. He thought of Violet often, knowing he didn't want her to feel unwelcome here.

He prayed that they had done the right thing.

His mother had joined him in the parlor, she looked around, her sad eyes taking everything in.

"You did good." She said simply. She looked to the chair opposite of Tim and looked to him for permission to sit.

"Please mother, sit." Tim offered, and felt a pang. She didn't feel welcome yet.

"I don't know how to be just yet." His mother said weakly.

Tim nodded in agreement. He felt the same way.

"We have a long road set before us." Meredith said a little stronger.

Tim clasped his hands together, his shoulders ached from the stress he felt weighing down on him.

"I have a lot to learn from you, Tim." Meredith said while tears raced down her pale cheeks.

Tim looked up to her, quiet but searching her face.

"I realize, after years of being so very wrong in every way, that my sons and daughter are my greatest accomplishment. I betrayed you all. I am not certain I can live with the shame." Meredith put both hands over her face and sobbed harshly.

Tim felt hot tears escape and he brushed at them gruffly. He watched his mother cry with a pit in his gut. This was so much harder than he could have ever imagined.

The front door opened and Harold's boots scraped at the rug. Tim saw him and gestured him into the parlor.

It took a while before all the tears were spent, but it did come. The apologies and first steps of forgiveness was started.

Tim wondered by the end of that first day how soon the healing would come. He thought of Violet and her sweet smile, and remembered her as the young girl who always had hugs for her baby brothers. She had lived under that monsters thumb and still become a strong woman.

Tim had a small faith, barely more than a passing belief in God. Listening to her wisdom over the last few weeks had changed something in his heart.

At dusk, after Meredith had made a simple dinner, and the light was fading in the world around them, Tim led a bible reading. Meredith sat and let her tears flow. Harold watched the flames in the fireplace as the words were read.

1st Corinthian chapter 13

Though I speak with the tongues of men and of angels, but have not love, I am become as sounding brass or a tinkling cymbal.
And though I have the gift of prophecy, and understand all mysteries and all knowledge, and though I have all faith so that I could remove mountains, but have not love, I am nothing.

And though I bestow all my goods to feed the poor, and though I give my body to be burned, but have not love, it profiteth me nothing.

Love suffereth long, and is kind; love envieth not; love vaunteth not itself, is not puffed up; doth not behave itself unseemly, seeketh not her own, is not easily provoked, thinketh no evil; rejoiceth not in iniquity, but rejoiceth in the truth; beareth all things, believeth all things, hopeth all things, endureth all things.

Love never faileth.

Chapter 40

4th of July
Spring Creek Church

The Spring Creek Church held its Fourth of July picnic on a partly cloudy day, the morning was cool and the morning mist clung over the ground as the festivities began.

The two long tables had pies and preserves to be judged by the town council, who were lucky to get to sample every treat laid out.

Another set of tables had the feast brought by nearly every family in town. Families brought blankets to be spread and they would all share in the feasting and celebrate the day of independence for the great country they lived in.

Young boys and girls were excited for the races and contests that would have grand prizes throughout the day. Older teens had the chance for a day off from helping at their family farms and get a chance to visit with their peers.

The grownups were busy keeping the little ones happy and making sure they all could enjoy the fun.

Angela and Ted were a popular couple to talk to, their wedding only a week away.

Angela had tried on her dress only the day before and it was declared the prettiest dress of the West by Olivia Greaves. Angela's color was high as she was so very happy.

Millie Quackenbush provided fresh pies to the winners of the contests.

Brody Grant, only 7 years old beat out the other runners in the boys' race for the seven to eight year old males. His shock of red hair zoomed past his competitors and his fast legs got him the win. He promised to share a few pieces of cherry pie with his family but said he could eat the whole thing himself with ease.

Lucas and Russell Grant won the log-sawing contest by only a half second in the fiercely competitive contest. Slava Varushkin won the log-chopping contest with ease though, his swing of the axe was impressive.

A few souls were missing but the close friends of Violet knew where she was. They all enjoyed their day but many prayers were offered up for the meeting happening today at the watermill.

The Watermill

Violet felt her pulse race as she pulled into the yard. Tim had come by a few days before and they had had a long talk, so she expected the cabin to look different. She sighed and tried to keep herself calm, but a part of her wanted to run away.

So much of the last week had been difficult for her, and she felt raw and vulnerable.

She dismounted from her mount, Clover and tied her to the new hitching post.

Tim and Harold came out of the front door and they joined her on her walk toward the house. She hadn't been inside since she was fifteen years old. They both held her hands silently, letting her have the time to think and cast off the painful memories.

Her mother peeked outside of the door when Violet neared it, Violet fought off the urge to take a step back protectively. She dropped her head and looked at the ground, she took a few deep breaths. She wondered for a moment if she had made a mistake in coming. Her mother's words just a few weeks ago had been angry.

'You are not welcome here!' She had said.

Violet felt her cheek flush and she fought off a moment of panic.

"Don't go." She heard her mother's voice say softly.

Violet finally looked at her mother again, her mother's face was covered in tears but her eyes weren't angry.

"There was a day seven years ago, that I made a terrible mistake. My daughter came to me and shared her heart with me. I can never undo that day." Her mother said in the doorway.

Violet listened, and paused. "No you cannot." She said truthfully.

"I will live with that shame until my dying day." Meredith said simply. "I am so very sorry."

Violet nodded, and approached her mother, letting her mother embrace her. Her mother's sobs had reached her. It was the start of something unknown.

Violet went inside and smelled her mother's fresh bread cooking, reminding her of her many years baking together.

The place looked so very different, even the kitchen cabinets had been painted. The parlor was grand and with a few touches that place would be elegant.

She shared hugs and conversation with her brothers and her mother. Though, it was stunted and awkward at moments.

Her mother apologized again and again. Violet was relieved to hear the words but a part of her heart was numb.

Violet watched her brothers interact with her mother, they had a better way with her. Having never been apart for longer than that last month. Violet grieved a bit that she had been denied that.

She felt quiet and watchful, letting some of the routine of the lunch help through.

After a while she felt overwhelmed again, wishing for the quiet of Grant's Grove on a normal day, where she could have her thoughts to herself.

She said a few little prayers in her head, wishing she felt something more than confused.

Her mother finally pulled her aside.

"I know this is hard for you. Probably more so than any of us. I will give you the space and time you need. I don't deserve any kindness from you. If you decide that this is all too hard…" Her mother's voice broke a little before she continued. "Iffen it's just too much. You can go. I will not pressure you, nor blame you."

Violet put her hands on her mother's face. Held it in her hands and searched her mother's features. Her cheeks pink from the warmth of the kitchen, her eyes sad and a little darker blue than her own.

Violet had nodded and kissed her mother on the cheek. To Violet it was a gift to give her mother, just one act of kindness that she felt free to give her.

The day was full of many emotional outbursts, but by the end of it Violet felt better. It hadn't been more than a try for a new beginning. She knew she had a lot of praying to do but this had been a good start.

July 15th- 1851

The Spring Creek Fellowship Church was filled with roses and wildflowers, provided by the deft hands of Corinne and Dolly. The small church was full to the brim with guests and the lovely singing of Violet Griffen and the sweet sound of the violin accompanied as the young couple were ready for the wedding to begin.

Her sweet voice sang out the song *Abide with Me* as Angela stood at the back of the church to walk toward the handsome man who waited for her at the front.

Abide with me; fast falls the eventide;
The darkness deepens; Lord with me abide.
When other helpers fail and comforts flee,
Help of the helpless, O abide with me.

Clive held Angela's arm and he walked her down the aisle. Her cream colored dress a sight to behold, with lace and small green silk flowers that were lovingly sewn over every inch. Her skirts billowed around her and the swish of the bell swayed with her steps. A veil of delicate lace covered her dark red curls, her cheeks blushed pink and her smile was bright as she joined her hand with Ted Greaves.

The words spoken by Pastor Pritchlan, blessed and encouraged all before the vows were spoken.

A promise to love and cherish, in sickness and health...

Tears flowed as the sweet girl said her words. The golden rings placed on each hand a promise for eternity.

The Greaves were settled in the front row, all dabbling at tears and were smiling brightly, even Amelia Greaves who had made the delicate veil that graced Angela's pretty head. The sweetness of the gesture had not been lost on both Angela and Ted, who felt the blessing in the act.

There may have been no fancy church bells, or stained glass windows, no society page announcements, or flowing champagne, but the simple beauty of two people in love joining together to face life as man and wife.

The crowd clapped and cheered as the announcement came and the sweet kiss was shared by Mr. and Mrs. Greaves.

The wedding party and guests gathered at the Harpole Ranch, music and dancing followed.

It pleased the crowd to tinkle their glasses and watch Angela blush as her husband kissed her throughout the evening to please the crowd.

The crowd settled down by dusk and they all watched happily as the newlyweds finally left the party to start their honeymoon together in their grand home, the finest house in Oregon City on the hill of the Greaves farm. Angela waved to her friends and clung to Ted's side as the made the short walk.

Her new life was finally beginning, it had taken so long and her heart felt near to bursting with happiness as she shared this experience with the man she loved so dearly. This was their true beginning, she felt God's blessing on her when she was carried across the threshold into her future.

Chapter 41

San Francisco – July 7
Megan Capron

The first few weeks Megan Capron had spent in the dirty and bustling city of San Francisco had surely been an education. It was truly nothing like any place she had ever been. The largest populace being men, uncouth, overly interested in alcohol, loose-moralled women and gold fever.

Her companion Stewart Ferrill had endeavored to protect her by finding the best hotel in town. A brick establishment outside of the raucous center of town.

Megan tried to enjoy her freedom, she truly did, but in most cases the only way to be certain of her safety was to remain locked up in the hotel. Stewart spent a week being gone most days, whenever he returned he would claim that he was talking with the dock master, or captains of vessels to assure them a safe and secure passage to Boston.

Megan got aggravated by Stewart's long absences, and made certain he felt her wrath. Stewart would lose his temper with her often. Megan would then plot and scheme about how to make it up to him.

Whenever Stewart would return Megan fully turned on her charm. Wearing her hair down in loose curls, the way he liked it and she would shower him with affection. A part of her realized that her parents would certainly be ashamed of the way she seduced the young man. But a part of her knew that she had already brought them shame when she ran away from Oregon territory. She wasn't certain that she could ever bring herself to contact her father again, knowing the stern lectures he would have for her.

Perhaps I will contact him once I am safely in Europe. Megan mused often.

The room she shared with Stewart was the best one in the hotel, they were promised but Megan had to ignore the shabbiness to remain docile. Stewart grew increasingly agitated about her complaining. It pricked at Megan's temper to have to bite her tongue. It had never been a strength of hers and having the ranch hand lecturing her had made her stomp her feet many times in frustration while he was away.

Megan was relieved when Stewart finally informed her that he had secured passage on a boat to Boston, with a promise of feather beds and luxurious meals. It would cost a pretty penny and Megan mourned the fact that it would take nearly half of her money to get to the east coast. She considered that she would borrow money from her Aunt when she arrived in Boston. Certainly her Aunt would treat her with a few hundred dollars to get her started.

Megan dug through her trunk and then handed over the money to Stewart, he had given her a sweet kiss before he left the next morning to purchase the boarding tickets. He came back triumphant, telling her to pack her trunks and satchels, they would be leaving the West in 2 days.

Megan was thrilled and they went to dine in a fine restaurant a block away that night, passing by saloons as they walked. Megan got whistles and a few crude comments as she walked along the wooden planks on the side of the street. Her burgundy gown was tasteful and should have declared her a lady, but it didn't seem to matter to the rough crowd that walked the city streets at night.

Stewart held her close and made her feel safe. The restaurant, named the Hampton House, was nicer than she had expected and had a small orchestra playing pleasant music as they dined on steak and potatoes. The crowd inside was a more gentile group of individuals, Megan and Stewart discussed that these men and a few women present must be part of the wealthy set in San Francisco.

The owner of the place came and greeted Megan and Stewart Ferrill at the table. Megan and Mr. Hampton got along well, chatting of nonsense and art, Megan complimented him sweetly on his establishment, declaring his place finer than any restaurant she had been in the rugged west. He had been charmed enough to bring her table some bubbling champagne. Megan giggled and flirted lightly with the owner. Stewart endured it, Megan gave him little winks, to assure him that flirting was just her way. Certainly he must know that about her. She amused herself by flirting, it never meant a thing.

Mr. Hampton lingered near their table the whole meal, and was delighted when Megan began to sing along softly when the orchestra played a tune that she knew. Her voice had always been a good one, and years of singing and piano lessons that had been forced on her over the years had made her a gifted vocalist. Mr. Hampton encouraged her to sing with a bolder voice and soon a few tables nearby joined in the song. The atmosphere had changed and everyone's mood was lifted. Stewart smiled at Megan with pride but Megan could tell that he was getting annoyed with the eager and flirtatious Mr. Hampton. Megan reached over to hold Stewart's hand a few times, to reassure him. She was not interested in any kind of romantic attachment with Stewart long-term, but neither was she interested in Mr. Hampton, though a mildly attractive man in his black suit with tails, but he was past forty and Megan only enjoyed the attention, not for any other reason, but that she could entice any man she wanted, or didn't want. Megan smiled as she sang and received stares from many tables. She was in her element.

Mr. Hampton gave her his card and invited them to come again before they left San Francisco. Stewart grumbled on the walk home, not appreciating the attention she received. Megan did her best to appease him.

The champagne had made Megan sleepy and she collapsed when they got back to their room at the hotel. She never woke up until it was mid-morning.

Megan sat up in her bed, it only took a moment to notice that her trunk was open, the green satin purse that had most of her money was on the table. Megan jumped up and ran to the purse and saw instantaneously that it was empty.

She panicked and shrieked as she saw that the trunk had been rifled through, a few of her dresses had been tossed to the floor. She found the book of poetry untouched on the bottom of the trunk and opened it nervously. She had several dollars in there and wondered if Stewart had taken that as well. She replayed the annoyed looks that Stewart had given her and Mr. Hampton the night before and called her self a fool.

She fluttered the pages and found eight dollars within its pages. They had only paid for two more days of the hotel and Megan searched the room for any kind of note, something that would explain that Stewart would be returning to her.

She found nothing.

Megan waited for a few hours, nervously tidying up the room, folding her dresses neatly. She dared not order room service, if this was truly all the money she had she knew better than to spend any.

By mid-afternoon Megan was certain of her fate. Stewart had left her in a jealous rage. A knock came to the door and startled Megan, not knowing what to expect.

A manager stood at the door, he had a thin mustache and his hair slicked back, a woman stood behind him.

"Your husband informed us this morning that your stay ends with us after this evening, I wanted to offer you our services. This maid can help you pack your trunks if you wish." The man said with a low voice.

Megan stared at him dumbly.

"Did Stewart say anything else?" Megan asked when she could. Her throat was tight with panic.

"No ma'am... He seemed to be in a hurry this morning. He was reimbursed for the unneeded night and he said he had a ferry to catch." The man said then gave her a concerned look.

Megan shook her head absently and dismissed the man.

If she went to the police then her father would certainly hear about it, a lady being robbed would make the papers. She had a momentary thought to send a telegram to her father, giving up her travels and going back to the safety of his home. It would be a simple matter she knew, they would scold and keep under their careful watch for a long while. He would be angry, her mother would cry fat tears and lock herself in her room for days to read her bible and pray for her wayward daughter. Megan laughed to herself, realizing that her mother was probably already doing that. She imagined that Corinne had contacted them the very morning that she had left.

"No, I will only contact my father as a last resort!" Megan said aloud to the empty room.

She sat on her bed and schemed, once she had an idea and quickly found her most appealing dress and rang for a maid to help her into her corset. She would pay a visit to Mr. Hampton.

Chapter 42

Willamette Valley

The summer past and the flowers bloomed, the purple lavender fragranced the air and the valley was on the eve of harvest when the riding scouts came.

The news spread quickly through town that the wagons would be coming soon.... More families to join their community, more wives and husbands, daughters and sons.

Angela and Ted rejoiced, when a letter arrived from the riders.

My dearest Angela,

The mountains have beckoned us forth and we are soon to be in your valley. The journey was long but knowing you were waiting on the other side eased my fears. You know I long held the desire to have children of my own and you were the first to give me the chance at mothering, it was as if my Lord saw how I did with you and gave me that next chance to take care of more. I can see through your letters the land and the mountains that surround you and wait impatiently to see it for myself.

The children have faired well for the journey, we all are a bit thinner with all the walking, which did me no harm.

They say its a few weeks more before we reach our new home and we sent this ahead to again thank you for your not so subtle suggestions that we come. I ache to see you and long to have days of baking and working side-by-side with you again.

In my heart you are the first daughter I adopted, and now with three adoptive siblings I come to you. Ready to share the blessing of the good Lord with you.

I pray you are well and that we see you soon.

Sincerely,

Mama Edith Sparks

Angela read through the letter again and thrilled with Ted by her side as they took the chance to walk down the hill and the short way to the land set aside for the Spark's cabin.

The cabin was finished, a pretty thing settled about a hundred feet away from Spring Creek. The back porch set up with chairs and a small table. Inside the fireplace was finished and the home neatly furnished with a few throw rugs and lanterns already in place for when they arrived. Ladies in town and throughout the valley had provided some sewn linens and a large trunk sat in the main bedroom, and the other bedrooms on the second story loft would give each child their own little room. The kitchen was spacious and had plenty of room for all the work that Edith Sparks loved, her canning and baking would be a blessing to others and her pantry would be full in no time.

Ted had even taken some time to break sod in the spot that was near the cabin for a good size garden. Angela felt at peace knowing that the place was ready. Mama and Papa Sparks were going to be here so very soon.

Dolly Bouchard

Dolly prepared the alembic pots for the coming harvest, the paid harvesters would be out in force and there would be a lot of work preparing the lavender for distillation. She had come back from her adventure with a new determination and she felt good at being at her work with Corinne, feeling more like a partner than just a visiting helper now that she was staying indefinitely.

The greenhouse addition had been completed by mid-august and Corinne and Dolly had spent the summer gathering plants and starters to add to their collecting of healing herbs. She spent her evenings at Chelsea Grant's home, with some family time with the children but more than an hour each night drawing plants and writing about what she knew. Each plant she drew she wrote out detailed descriptions of every leaf and petal and then any detail she knew or had learned about its properties. To some it may have seemed tedious but with every page she felt a sense of accomplishment.

She sent a letter off to Reggie Gardner when she had gotten over the disappointment of his leaving without coming to say goodbye, but she dealt with it as maturely as she could. That awkward moment on Angela's porch, now Angela and Ted's porch she corrected, had been intense and she felt that the attraction had been there. It had budded in her heart against her will and she would work hard to push it away.

If his calling was the sea and her calling was here then there was truly no future for them and she kept herself busy to ward off any unrealistic expectations she had of his ever returning.

Dolly was happy with her choices and only thought of her Shoshoni riding companions a few times over the summer months, glad that they hadn't returned to the valley to seek her out. She prayed that they had given up the search for her and had gone back home, she was certain that Bright Son would pass her message along to the Shoshoni chief. She was free.

Corinne Grant

Corinne held a hand over her swollen belly and walked along the edge of Spring Creek while she watched her husband work in front of her, he was checking his irrigation ditches for moisture and he was happy with what he saw. The plants were tall and the blooms were a rich purple. A few bees buzzed happily nearby as they were happy for the flower nectar they had provided. She felt the cool ground beneath her bare feet and she was so very happy.

She had received a letter from Mr. Capron and he was still searching for his daughter, but he had held no malice or blame for them having allowed her escape. She had always been a willful girl and he had thought that she could have easily done the same to them, had she been there. They kept in contact but Corinne wondered if the gal was long gone. Corinne hoped and prayed for the best for her wayward cousin, but sometimes that worry would rise within her, knowing a beautiful young lady on her own in the big world could be so very dangerous.

She rubbed her belly a little, pleased over the flutter of movement she felt now and again. She reveled in the thought of giving her Lucas a child, she knew it was for her too, but that strange inner part of her was so very pleased to give this shared gift to her husband. She had never fully known what a marriage was. She had thought as a child, she mused. A marriage in a young girl's mind is romance and sweet kisses and handholding. The reality was so very much bigger, sharing in the every day, the companionship, and the promise of a future. He wasn't demanding, and that made her realize in new ways all the time how much more that made her love him.

She looked forward to the months ahead, praying for a healthy child to hold. She felt at peace with her life and thanked God for it every day.

Angela Greaves

The wagons rolled into the Willamette Valley and the town rejoiced over having new members of their growing community. The weary travelers were met, as tradition by the edge of the mountain cutoff road, with food and a cheerful time of visiting.

Angela and Ted waited in the crowd to see if their 'family' had come and after watching twenty wagons pull around and park Angela recognized the tall and broad shouldered Henry Sparks waving an arm her way.

Angela squealed and squeezed her husband's arm in delight and pulled him forward and Ted laughed at her exuberance.

"They are here!" She said in a high voice.

She pulled Ted through the swarming crowd and broke free from her husband when she saw Edith and ran as well as she could for the long-awaited hug from Mama Sparks. There were tears and laughter and they swayed and hugged for a long minute.

Henry and Ted shook hands and Henry got his turn to give a bear hug to Angela before the introductions were made.

Edith was not as round as she had been at Fort Kearny and Angela vowed that she would make sure they were all fattened up in short order. She remembered coming over the long trail and how much she had eaten those first weeks home.

The eldest girl, a dark blond with large hazel eyes was introduced first.

"I would be so proud for you to meet Heidi."

"I am Angela Greaves, and this is my husband Ted." Angela announced and was pleased.

Henry gave a mild slug to Ted's arm and broad smiles were shared. Heidi said a polite hello and the smaller children were next.

"This is Peter and Fiona." Edith placed a hand on each of their heads. Both golden haired and so very near identical, Fiona's longer hair and dress made it easy to determine that she was the girl but their faces were a mirror of each other.

They shared some how-do-ya-dos and Angela shook each of their hands playfully.

"How old are all of you?" Angela asked, trying to ease them out of their shyness.

"I am ten, almost 11." Heidi said swiftly. She had a spark in her eyes and Angela was glad to see that she was finding her voice.

"We are both just turned 6." Peter spoke, seeming to be the speaker for the pair. Fiona nodded and looked to her brother. They shared a grin between them.

"You will both love the school that is a short walk up the road." Ted said to see them smile. "They start classes back up in a few weeks. You will fit right in."

The youngest smiled, seeming excited over the prospect of other children. Heidi nodded but remained quiet.

"Oh Angie. You look so very good!" Edith gushed and ran a hand over Angela's cheek.

They all walked together as Angela and Ted talked, sharing their wedding date and news about the cabin and then in turn asked them about their trip.

They joined the group and let the Sparks eat while they talked and talked. They were all hungry but also eager to be landed at their new home.

The children got a small chance to meet some of the neighbors when Chelsea and Russell Grant found them, then the Harpoles. The way of children was easy and there was a little playing and running that commenced shortly after more introductions.

After an hour the group was ready to depart and the Sparks piled into the covered wagon for the few more miles they would travel. The cabin more than met their expectations and everyone was so pleased.

The evening came and the meal around Angela's table was joyous. Henry stood before the meal and started a prayer.

"Lord, you have blessed my family beyond measure. We thank you for bringing us to this new land. We pray a blessing over every person here. Bring us your bounty and may our years be spent here in a constant reminder of your goodness."

Everyone said 'amen'.

The evening was spent peacefully as they all walked the land together.

The tired Sparks went home to their new cabin and sought some much needed rest. A new beginning for them all.

Wildflower Series

Book 1 – Finding Her Way
(previously released as Seeing the Elephant)

Book 2 – Angela's Hope

Book 3 – Daughter's of the Valley

Now released… Book 4 – The Watermill

Writing in Progress … Book 5 – Love In Full Bloom

Also by Leah Banicki

Runner Up – A Contemporary love story,
Set in the world of reality TV.

Also Coming Soon:

IMPARATOS Series:

Book 1 – Aurora

This is a young adult contemporary series, full of action and adventure.

Connect with me online:

https://www.facebook.com/Leah.Banicki.Novelist

Please share your thoughts with me. leahsvoice@me.com

The self-publishing world is very rewarding but has its marketing challenges. Please remember to spread the word about my books if you like them. By using word-of-mouth you

help to bless an author.
Like – Share - Leave a review

Thank you, Leah Banicki

Character List – Wildflowers Series

Corinne Grant - Married to Lucas Grant. Age 20. Started a business making medicinal oils from plants. Also has built a greenhouse for the cultivating of plants and herbs.

Lucas Grant - Graduate of Yale agricultural school, thrives on farming technology and making improvements in the agricultural field. Married to Corinne.

Chelsea Grant - Married to Russell Grant. Granddaughter of Clive Quackenbush. Mother of Brody and Sarah Grant.

Russell Grant - Lucas Grant's brother, owns a farm nearby. They help each other often on each other's land.

John & Marie Harpole - Corinne's father, first wife Lily (Corinne's mother) - deceased - 2nd wife **Marie Harpole** - Mother to Cooper and Abigail.

Megan Capron -17-year-old - daughter of Arnold Capron - granddaughter to Rose Capron. She enjoys painting and flirting.

Clive Quakenbush - Mountain man, fur trapper, Hudson Bay store owner, Government liaison for Indian Affairs, hunter and business man. First wife Christina – they had three children, Jedediah, Thomas and Greta. Second wife- Martha. He currently owns two fancy goods stores in Oregon Territory and a Hudson Bay store in San Francisco. He is also a business partner with Angela Fahey with a family legacy project.

Jedediah Quackenbush - (nickname JQ) son of Clive, works at Oregon City store.

Millicent Quackenbush - (nickname Millie) married to JQ. Works the counter in the store but is active in her community and church.

Dolly Bluebird Bouchard - (Indian name is Bluebird) half Indian, half white. Mother was Hopi and father was a French fur trapper. She was sent by her adoptive tribe to learn from Corinne about plants and medicines to bring back and teach the tribe. Her father's name was Joseph Bouchard.

Angela Fahey - Irish immigrant orphaned and sold into a workhouse at a young age with her brother. She became a maid in Corinne's Aunt's home and they were fast friends. She attempted to cross the Oregon Trail and was injured early on and had to recover before continuing her journey. She bought land outside of Oregon City and the boarding house in town. She is Corinne Grant's neighbor. She received an inheritance from her deceased parents after Corinne found a Boston lawyer.

Sean Fahey - Irish Immigrant who ran away from a Boston work orphanage. Older brother to Angela Fahey. Last know whereabouts, fur trapping along the Snake River in the company of Ol' Willie. He sent Angela away from San Francisco when she crossed the country to find him.

Thaddeus Greaves - (nicknamed Ted) – fiancé to Angela Fahey. They met in San Francisco, he traveled back to upstate New York and retrieved his family. He traveled back by boat with his family to the west and settled in Oregon City to reunite with Angela.

Amelia Greaves – Mother to Ted, widow. She is a skilled lace maker. She joined her son to get a fresh start and a guaranteed business. They live in a townhouse in Oregon City with a storefront in their home. She also has a daughter, Sophia.

Olivia Greaves – Sister to Amelia. She is also a skilled lace maker and has a yearning for adventure.

Warren Martin Jr. - Hired as a spare hand, does milking and odd jobs. Stays with Earl in his cabin during the week.

Earl Burgess – Works as the land manager for Angela Fahey. Also does maintenance for the Orchard House, the boarding house that Angela owns. Lost a hand in an accident years before, but is a hard worker with a lot of farm knowledge.

Henry & Edith Sparks - Henry is the Captain at Fort Kearney, they took Angela in after an unfortunate accident. Edith and Henry nursed her back to health. They adopted 3 orphan children from a wagon train passing through Fort Kearney. When Henry's post as Captain was completed they left the fort to travel west on the Oregon Trail. They will be living on Angela's land.

Galina Varushkin – age 14 – lives outside of Oregon City in a small cabin for her family. Not allowed to finish school she works at different homes throughout the week to earn money by doing laundry.

Slava Varushkin – Russian Immigrant -Father of Galina, Miloslava (age 10), Pavel (age 8), and Radimir (12 months). He was injured while working for a logging camp and left for the Gold Rush the year before, leaving his family starving and with no resources. He came back with nothing to find that his family had been given a cabin by the Spring Creek Church. He is currently working for Lucas Grant, clearing lumber for more crops.

Magdalena Varushkin – Polish immigrant. Married Slava when she was 16. Mother to all the Varushkin children.

Oregon City

Doctor Vincent Williams – Oregon City doctor. He works with Corinne and the apothecary to take care of the Oregon City citizens.

Persephone Willliams- the Doctor's wife and friend to Corinne. She helps with birthing and assists her husband in his duties.

Mr. Higgins - runs the local apothecary.

Gomer Hynes – Runs the Oregon gazette, a weekly newspaper.

Pastor Darrell Whittlan & wife Helen – run the Spring Creek Fellowship church outside of Oregon City on Spring Creek road. They adopted orphans and minister to the rural community.

Marshall Crispin - Schoolteacher outside of town.

Reynaldo Legales – Ranch Manager at Harpole Ranch. His father owns a ranch in California territory. Hard worker and right hand man for John Harpole

Amos Drays - local carpenter in town,

Mrs. Gemma Caplan- former owner of Oregon City boarding house, hired on as manager and head housekeeper.

Frieda Warhan- Manager for the Orchard House. She took over management duties when Angela bought the boarding house.

Sherriff Nigel Tudor - Sherriff of Oregon City. Acts as Judge, Sherriff and county law.

Governor John Pritchlan - resident of Oregon City, governor of Oregon Territory.

Jedidiah Prince - head of the town Council in Oregon City.

Effie Prince - wife of Jedediah prince. Head of the Christian women's group in town, headstrong and advocate for the poor - Mother of Sydney Prince.

Portland, Oregon Territory

Gabriel Quackenbush - Son of JQ and grandson of Clive, runs the Hudson Bay store in San Francisco, California territory, they moved to Portland when San Francisco became a dangerous boomtown.

Amber Quakenbush - Married to Gabriel, Irish immigrant came over as a child with her parents. Helps her husband run the fancy goods store in Portland. .

San Francisco, California Territory

Brian Murphy - Manager of Q & F Distillery, runs the distillery for the Irish whiskey recipe that Angela found in an old family diary.

Thank you so much for reading my book:

My Biography -

I am a writer, wife and mother. I live in SW lower Michigan near the banks of Brandywine Creek. I adore writing historical and contemporary stories, facing the challenges that life throws at you with characters that are relatable. I love finding humor in the ridiculous things that are in the everyday comings and goings of life. For me a good book is when you get to step into the character's shoes and join them on their journey. So climb aboard, let us share the adventure!

My writing buddy is my miniature poodle Mr. Darcy, who snuggles at my feet while I write until he must climb onto my chest for dancing or snuggles. My beagle Oliver is more concerned with protecting the yard from trespassers – squirrels and pesky robins.

I love hearing from my readers and try to answer every email personally.

I am always on Facebook and let my readers know about how the next books are coming along.

I have a slew of books in the works and plan on releasing 2 books in 2015. Keep your eyes peeled for news!

https://www.facebook.com/Leah.Banicki.Novelist

Please share your thoughts with me. leahsvoice@me.com

Website:
http://leahbanicki.wix.com/author

Printed in Great Britain
by Amazon